THE MAN WITH PSI

THE MAN WITH PSI

Alan Eagle

VANTAGE PRESS
New York

This is a work of fiction. Any similarity between the characters appearing herein and any real persons, living or dead, is purely coincidental.

Contents

Historical Note

More than a quarter century ago, a summit meeting in Moscow collapsed amid angry accusations between Richard Leonard, the president of the United States, and Vasily Sherkov, the general secretary of the Communist Party of the Union of Soviet Socialist Republics. The United States and the Soviet Union put their military forces on highest alert, and the world came to the brink of nuclear war.

Until the early 1990s, the bizarre CIA plot that precipitated the summit crisis remained shrouded at the highest levels of U.S. government security. However, on his death bed, Thomas Stratton, Richard Leonard's secretary of state, hinted to his friend, the famed Washington investigative reporter, Alan Eagle, that a super secret CIA covert espionage program called Project Psi had brought the world to the edge of the nuclear precipice.

Stratton died without revealing any details, but the hint was enough for Alan Eagle. He filed requests for U.S. government documents under the Freedom of Information Act and pursued court actions to force the CIA and the State Department to respond. Finally, in 1997, the Supreme Court ruled in Eagle's favor, and the dam of U.S. government secrecy surrounding the history of Project Psi burst. Alan Eagle interviewed most of the important living participants in Project Psi and painstakingly pieced together this tragic history of high-tech human spying gone wrong. Sadly, some of the central figures in Project Psi died in its debacle or still are being held somewhere in Russia.

THE MAN WITH PSI

PART I
THE OLD BUDDY

1

Pyramid Power

Jack Mason was having trouble concentrating on the slide being projected onto the small screen at the front of the dimly lit hotel conference room. The speaker was saying something about the correlation between visual stimuli presented to a cat and electrical signals detected by probes placed deep in its brain. Jack tried to pay attention, but his thoughts kept drifting away. His own talk, "Inferences Concerning the Likely Structure of Interconnections Behind the Retina of the Chimpanzee," apparently had been well received.

Several of his colleagues in the audience had asked germane questions, indicating, at least, that they had remained awake. Jack's thoughts drifted off again, but he was jolted back to reality by the polite riffle of applause that greeted the end of the cat paper and he realized from the perfunctory nature of the questioning that most of the audience was in a similar state of torpor. Subconsciously, he decided to sneak from the room as soon as the lights were lowered again.

Crossing the lobby, Jack quickly scanned the bulletin board containing messages for the conference attendees. Spying one with his name, he grabbed it and read it on the run while heading for his room.

If the meeting is dull, call Bob Green. OX-5-1379.

Jack's mind shot back to the last time he had seen Bob Green. The scene was the windswept deck of the aircraft carrier *Hancock* in the Sea of Japan somewhere off the coast of North Korea. Bob's fighter squadron was being rotated back to Japan,

3

and Jack had come to the flight deck to say good-bye. They clasped hands and shouted farewells over the roar of jet engines and the hiss of steam catapults. Jack watched as Bob lowered himself into the cockpit of the F-9F. The crew chief made a final check, gave the thumbs-up sign, and the plane hurtled forward through a cloud of steam toward the bow. It hesitated for a moment, gaining speed, and then banked to the left and climbed out of sight through the low overcast.

Jack entered his hotel room and fumbled through his pockets for the note with Bob's number. He dialed the telephone with strangely mixed feelings of expectancy and déjà vu, a premonition that scenes from the past were about to be replayed, but perhaps with a different ending.

When the ringing stopped, a female voice answered cryptically:

"Special Projects."

"This is Dr. Mason returning Mr. Green's call," Jack said coolly.

"Just a moment. I'll see if I can find him," chirped the reply.

At length, Jack was greeted with the unmistakable lilt of Bob Green's Irish brogue.

"Hi, old buddy, meeting's pretty dull, eh? How about a drink for old time's sake?"

"How are you doing, Bob?" Jack responded enthusiastically. "How the hell did you know I was at this conference?"

"You know me, old buddy," Green answered cheerfully, "I always know what's going on."

Jack's thoughts returned to the ship, and he smiled with remembered amusement. Bob did seem to have had an uncanny way of knowing who was doing what to whom and who was getting the five dollars.

"I'll meet you at the bar in the Jockey Club at about six o'clock," Bob continued jovially. "It's in the old Fairfax Hotel on Massachusetts Avenue. About three blocks from Dupont Circle."

The fleeting thought crossed Jack's mind that he would be missing the cocktail party before the official conference banquet. But, without a moment's hesitation, he found himself agreeing enthusiastically.

4

"Sure, Bob. I'll see you there at six. We sure have a lot of catching up to do."

"See you later, old buddy," Bob concluded matter-of-factly, and Jack felt that in some strange way their old friendship had already been renewed.

Jack had no trouble finding the Fairfax Hotel, but parking was another matter. He drove around the block several times and then finally squeezed his rented car into a tight spot between two VW's. When he first entered the bar, Green was nowhere in sight, so Jack took a seat and ordered a gin and tonic. No sooner had the bartender placed it before him than he heard Bob's voice over his shoulder.

"Still drinking the same stuff, I see. At least you'll never get malaria."

Jack turned with surprise and found Bob Green seated on the stool beside him.

"So, you're a pretty important professor these days," Bob continued. "Your own lab, and all that."

Jack marveled again at Bob's way of knowing what was going on, and his old friend offered some information of his own.

"Me, I'm still working for the government."

"Still in the navy?" Jack queried.

"No, another part of the government," Bob said and changed the subject.

The old friends reminisced about their Korean War adventures for more that an hour and through several rounds of drinks. After a while, despite growing intoxication, Jack was aware that Bob was steering the conversation around to his current research activities. Green enquired about the size of Jack's lab, the type of experiments they were conducting, and the principal results they had obtained. Nevertheless, Jack had the feeling that his questioning was perfunctory, an introduction to something more important to come. Suddenly, however, it was clear to Jack that Bob had gotten to the point.

"Do you academic guys ever get into anything really far-out? You know, ESP or psychokinesis or any of that stuff?"

Jack's immediate thought was to laugh. But he stopped himself for the sake of his old friend and their enjoyable evening of reminiscence. He decided to play it low key.

"Well, we don't do much of that at our lab. But there's a group at Duke University that was started by Rhine; they've done quite a lot of that kind of stuff."

Again Bob surprised Jack with his knowledge.

"Yeah, but you scientific types think they're lightweights, don't you?"

"Well, ah, let's say a lot of people don't think that their experiments are very well controlled," Jack responded, with scarcely concealed disdain.

"Well, anyhow," Bob continued cheerfully, "I'm talking about the *real* stuff. Like *pyramid power*."

"Pyramid power?"

"Yeah, pyramid power."

"What the hell is pyramid power?" Jack blurted out incredulously.

"This guy wrote a book, see," Bob replied enthusiastically, "showing all the things that can be done using the shape of a pyramid—the Great Pyramid. Seeds grow faster under one. Food doesn't spoil under one."

Jack shook his head in wonderment. Even half-drunk, he couldn't believe what he was hearing.

"Food doesn't spoil under one?"

"Right," Bob nodded affirmatively. "What this guy did was to make a bunch of models. A cube, a sphere, and a pyramid. He made them out of paper or plastic or something. And he put little bits of raw food, meat or fish, in each one. And the food that was in the cube or the sphere went bad, but in the pyramid, it stayed fresh. Maybe dried out a bit, but didn't go bad."

"And the pyramid did it?" Jack asked sardonically.

"Yeah," Bob responded seriously, "because it had the dimensions of the Great Pyramid."

Jack couldn't help himself.

"It all sounds like bullshit to me," he said emphatically.

"Yeah, I thought it would," Bob answered. "A hundred years ago, guys like you thought the airplane was bullshit. You scientists just don't know how to think about things you don't understand. See, the important thing is that this guy may have found a new kind of force, a force we could use."

6

We could use, thought Jack. *Who are "we?" And what could "we" use this force for?*

While Jack was musing, Bob continued enthusiastically, warming to his subject.

"The Russians have been looking at this stuff, too. They've held a bunch of symposiums. They want to use this force, too. But we're going to beat them to it!"

Jack snapped out of his reverie.

"Beat them to what? It sounds to me like you're trying to beat them to the loony bin!"

"Right," Bob responded with a smile. "It always sounds that way in the beginning. The important thing at the beginning is to get the right man. The right man to head the whole thing up. That makes it or breaks it."

"To head *what* whole thing up?" Jack asked, frowning.

"A project to develop this force before the Russians do," Bob answered matter-of-factly. "So we can use it on them before they use it on us."

"But how can you have a project," Jack responded and shook his head, "when you don't even know what the force *is?*"

"That's what makes it exciting," Bob responded enthusiastically. "We're probing the unknown!"

Jack felt like a drunken participant at the Mad Hatter's tea party. Nothing he said seemed to register on Bob, and nothing Bob said made any sense to him.

Suddenly, with an overwhelming feeling of relief, Jack thought of the conference banquet that was about to begin. He made an elaborate display of looking at his watch and then exclaimed:

"My God! I'm missing the banquet, and I'm supposed to make an after-dinner speech."

"Yeah," Bob replied, "I know. I thought I'd give you something good to talk about!"

Jack's instinct was to bolt from the table, but again, Bob anticipated his action. Placing his arm around Jack's shoulder, he began to talk in a serious tone.

"Look, old buddy, my agency is really serious about this thing. We want to spend some money to develop this force, and we need the right man and the right lab. And we, at least *I,*

7

think that you're him. So before you send me to the loony bin, give it a little thought. For old time's sake."

The two friends from the past stared at each other for a moment, secretly assessing their previous relationship, and then Bob continued.

"Do me a favor. Read up on this ESP stuff a bit, and then tell me what you think. And if you still think it's bullshit, I'll tell my boss just that. But at least give it a fair chance. Read a little and find out what these guys have been doing."

Bob's sudden seriousness and the reasonableness of his request caught Jack off guard.

"Well, it couldn't hurt me to do a little reading," he replied with a chuckle. "It might even be fun to see what these nuts have been up to."

"Okay," said Bob, with obvious pleasure. "I'll keep in touch. Now, you'd better get back to that banquet and start thinking about your speech."

The speech! thought Jack. *What am I going to tell them in the speech? I suppose I could tell them about pyramid power. At least that would keep them awake!*

2

Beyond the Senses

Several weeks after his reunion with Bob Green, Jack Mason stopped by the science library to glance through the most recent issues of several scientific journals. Finding no papers of particular interest, he was about to leave, when the thought crossed his mind to see if the card catalog listed any books on ESP. He was surprised to find only three entries. Apparently parapsychology was not a particularly respectable topic at MIT. On the shelf, Jack could find only one of the books, a well-worn copy of the classic by J. B. Rhine, *New Frontiers of the Mind.* He thumbed through it quickly, and then impulsively decided to take it out.

After lunch, Jack idly picked up the book and began to read. Much to his surprise, the opening chapters were more rational and less emotional than he had expected. At one point, Rhine summarized by saying:

> There is a common belief among all people that the reports of the recognized senses are not the only ones which the mind ever receives. Through all the ages of recorded history men have believed in the validity of intuitions, "hunches," mind reading, monitions or warnings of various sorts, and similar apparent manifestations of the mind's power to penetrate beyond the bounds of the mechanical and sensory world. Of course these beliefs have no place in the catalogues of scientific knowledge, and they are today quite widely supposed to be sheer superstition, error, or various forms of self-delusion.

Jack found himself unconsciously nodding in agreement with the last sentence. Nevertheless, he could not disagree with Rhine's stated goal:

9

The experiments described in this narrative of research in our laboratory at Duke University were undertaken with the express purpose of cornering the problem of whether anything enters the mind by a route other that the recognized senses.

Continuing his reading, Jack found that the principal tool of early ESP researchers was a pack of twenty-five cards. The deck contains cards bearing one of five different symbols: *star, plus, waves, circle,* and *square.* During the typical ESP test, the *experimenter* would look sequentially at each card while keeping it hidden from the *subject,* who would attempt to guess the symbol on the card. If the subject guessed correctly, he was said to have made a *hit.*

The goal of all avid experimenters was to find a subject who could make an exceptionally large number of hits during a *run* through the pack of twenty-five cards. Because a subject could achieve five hits during a run by dumb luck (or by guessing the same symbol for every card), experimenters sought subjects who could consistently score more than about ten hits per run, double the number expected from chance alone.

As Jack read further, Rhine described his excitement at finding his first high-scoring subject, a student called Linzmayer. Linzmayer's most memorable feat was a run in which he called correctly fifteen straight cards in succession and made a total of twenty-one correct calls out of a possible twenty-five.

Again Jack found himself shaking his head in disbelief. As Rhine states, the chance of such a feat occurring by accident, as a result of luck, is so remote as to be almost beyond comprehension. (By the operation of chance alone, twenty-one correct calls out of twenty-five ESP cards would be expected to occur once in 92,027,922,380 runs!)

Jack's immediate reaction was that Linzmayer must have cheated. He found that even Rhine entertained this possibility, stating that:

With all the skepticism I can muster, though, I still do not see how any sensory cue could have revealed to Linzmayer the symbols of those 21 cards he called correctly.

Jack's reading of *New Frontiers of the Mind* was interrupted by one of his post-docs entering the office. Jack looked up with a puzzled expression and queried his assistant.

"Hey, Barney, do you think there's anything to this ESP stuff?"

"What ESP stuff?" Barney O'Neil answered quizzically.

"I found this book in the library," Jack said, holding it up, "by that guy Rhine at Duke."

"Oh?" said Barney, still perplexed. But then he remembered something and continued with a broad smile. "I knew this girl once who could call long strings of cards out of the deck correctly. But I think she cheated. She couldn't do it if you shuffled the deck."

Jack returned Barney's smile momentarily, but then continued.

"Well, suppose I was concentrating really hard on a card. Some signals would be going through my brain representing the symbol on the card, wouldn't they?"

"Yeah, I suppose so," Barney grunted.

"Now, suppose you were with me and you concentrated really hard on trying to perceive the symbol. Maybe your brain could pick up the signals from my brain?"

"Uh-huh!" laughed Barney. "What have you been reading, Jack? *MAD Magazine!*"

Several evenings later, Jack was at the public library, when the thought of Rhine and Linzmayer crossed his mind. Impulsively, he checked the card catalog and was surprised to find a large number of listings under ESP. Apparently, the residents of Lexington, Massachusetts, were far more interested in the occult than his colleagues at MIT. Most of the books he took from the shelf recounted the amazing capabilities of seers, mystics, and mediums. To Jack, the stories were amusing, but almost certainly apocryphal. Finally, a title caught his eye that seemed to promise what he was looking for. *ESP, A Scientific Evaluation,* it proclaimed. Jack felt certain that the author would debunk ESP and pronounce it a fraud, and he was not disappointed.

The author, Professor Hansel of the University of Wales, spent several years investigating outstanding examples of claims for various forms of extrasensory perception. They included:

Telepathy, a person's awareness of another's thought without there being any communication through sensory channels.

Clairvoyance, knowledge acquired of an object or an event without the use of the senses.

Precognition, knowledge a person may have of another person's future thoughts (precognitive telepathy) or of future events (precognitive clairvoyance).

Psychokinesis, a person's ability to influence a physical object or an event, such as the fall of a die, by thinking about it.

What Professor Hansel found ranged from rather clear evidence of cheating and collusion to poorly planned, loosely controlled, and undocumented experiments. An outstanding example of apparent fraud was the case of the telepathic Welsh schoolboys. A well-known British ESP researcher, one S. G. Soal, reported in a book called *The Mind Readers* how two Welsh schoolboys, Glyn and Ieuan, exhibited remarkable telepathic powers in return for financial rewards their families direly needed—fifteen pounds thirteen shillings each after Soal's initial visit. Upon investigation, Hansel found that the boys had been repeatedly caught making signals to each other by such obvious means as kicking under the table. Furthermore, even in the experiments in which the boys were not actually caught cheating, Hansel concluded that the conditions were such that cheating would not have been difficult.

With regard to the experiments conducted in Rhine's laboratory at Duke University, Jack found that Professor Hansel's conclusions were not so open and shut. Hansel had visited the laboratory as Rhine's guest and had attempted to reconstruct the circumstances surrounding the most famous series of positive ESP tests conducted there—the so-called Pearce-Pratt and the Pratt-Woodruff experiments.

Hubert E. Pearce was a Duke University divinity student who exhibited remarkable powers of long-distance telepathy

12

during a period in late 1933 and early 1934. The experimenter, a graduate student by the name of Pratt, would sit in his research room on the top floor of the physics building, while Pearce would sit in a cubicle in the stacks of the general library, a distance of about a hundred yards from Pratt. At a prearranged time, Pratt would take the top card from a face-down, shuffled pack of ESP cards and place it, still face down, on a book in the center of his table. After one minute, he would transfer the card to the other side of the table and replace it on the book with the second card in the pack. Thus, after a period of twenty-five minutes, each card in the pack would have been isolated on the book in the center of the table for a period of one minute. While each card was resting on the book, Pearce, in his cubicle in the library, supposedly wrote down on a score sheet his perception of the symbol printed on the card.

At this point in his reading, Jack was already deeply puzzled. Since Pratt always handled the cards face down, even when he placed them on the book in the center of the table, the symbol on each card was *unknown to him* as well as to Pearce. Thus, to believe that the positive results of the experiment constituted a demonstration of ESP, one would have to believe not simply that Pearce was able to read Pratt's mind at a distance of one hundred yards, but more incredibly, that Pearce was able to *perceive the symbol* on each card at this distance.

Jack shook his head in disbelief, but he continued reading.

Pearce's performance was erratic, but on many occasions he scored as high as twelve or thirteen hits out of twenty-five cards. The likelihood that chance alone caused this repeated excellent performance is sufficiently remote that Jack dismissed it as an explanation. Either clairvoyance or fraud must have been involved. (By chance alone, twelve hits would be expected once in every 854 runs, and thirteen hits once in every 3,416.) On other occasions, Pearce's performance was much more normal, with the numbers of hits he obtained during runs ranging above and below the score of five expected from pure chance.

Although Professor Hansel could not establish positively that trickery was involved in the runs in which Pearce obtained exceptionally high scores, he was able to show that deception was certainly possible. There was ample time for Pearce to have left the library before the scheduled time for the experiment to have commenced, and to have taken up a position in the corridor outside Pratt's room, from which vantage point he might have been able to view the symbols on some of the cards as Pratt transferred them to and from the book. Then Pearce could have returned to the library to write down his telepathic perceptions aided by his visual observations.

Jack closed Hansel's book and his mind returned to the puzzling circumstance that the symbols on the cards supposedly were seen by neither Pearce nor Pratt. Mind reading, maybe, he mused, but *card* reading at one hundred yards is crazy.

Jack stared vacantly at the office wall and then smiled furtively as a silly, irrational thought crossed his normally staid scientific mind—it might be fun to try to do a calculation about mind reading. . . . *Now, let's see,* he mused. *The currents in the brain set up an electromagnetic field and* —

But Jack's momentary flight of fancy was interrupted by his secretary.

"Time for class, Professor Mason."

3

The Egg Heads

Jack's curiosity about ESP persisted. He found himself drawn to reading bits and pieces of various books on the subject. Most of them he could not finish, because the tales they told were beyond belief to his orderly, scientific mind. The authors reported in emotional terms the abilities of gifted individuals to see the future, to discern thoughts at great distances, or to communicate with the dead.

Throughout this melange of occult happenings, one idea persisted: the belief that the powers these unique people possessed were the result of a strange force, the psi field. What the psi field is, its believers did not report, but that it is not one of the normal senses, they unanimously agreed. Most astounding to Jack, the psi field was believed to act over great distances, thousands of miles, almost as easily as within a room.

Despite his skepticism, Jack found the idea of the strange psi field impossible to put out of his mind. Whenever he daydreamed, at lunch or in the car or in bed, there it was, demanding to be understood and explained. What could it be? Electromagnetism? Gravity? Or perhaps, most fancifully of all, the quantum-mechanical wave function, which ironically bears the same designation, the Greek letter psi.

The mysterious psi field dominated Jack's waking and sleeping thoughts. The claims for its strange powers boggled his mind. Could it be real? Or was it just the summation of the irrational hopes and fears of its believers? The conundrum persisted, distracting his thoughts and disrupting his routine. So maddening it became that, finally, he vowed to exorcise this devil from his thoughts by the scientific method; he would analyze the dragon and thereby hope to slay it.

15

Jack began his investigation by thinking about ways for two minds to communicate over short distances—within the same room. Rather quickly, he decided that gravity forces could not possibly be responsible for such communication; they are simply too weak. Likewise, despite being a namesake of the psi field, the quantum-mechanical wave function acts over such microscopic distances, within atoms and molecules, that Jack could not conceive of it being responsible for the strange psi force.

Could it be sound? Jack thought about this possibility. Perhaps some part of the body, like the eardrums, vibrates microscopically in response to intense thoughts. The sound waves produced by these tiny motions might be perceived by a second person, not as sounds, but as some mysterious communication by the psi field.

After a while, Jack came to two conclusions concerning the possibility that sound waves were responsible for the psi field. He thought that experiments would be necessary to determine whether or not some organ, such as the eardrums, did in fact vibrate in response to intense thoughts. But more importantly, he concluded that sound waves could not possibly be responsible for ESP occurrences over distances of hundreds of yards, feats that were commonly reported. After traveling such distances, the microscopic, thought-produced sounds would be so greatly diminished that human ears could not possibly detect them in the presence of the normal background noise present in even the quietest rooms.

In the end, Jack was left with electromagnetic waves as the only known physical phenomenon that could possibly be responsible for the psi force. Electromagnetic waves, those ubiquitous but unseen carriers of so many essentials of our daily lives: radio, television, electrical power, and long-distance telephone calls. Perhaps electromagnetic waves could explain the psi force.

The possible connection between electromagnetic waves and the mysterious psi field incubated in Jack's brain. He poked it and turned it over and viewed it from different angles. He didn't really *do* anything about it, but neither would it go away.

Finally, while sitting in his office one afternoon and without really knowing why, he doodled a sketch on the pad in front of him. Two eggs for heads near the left- and right-hand margins, and between them the empty white space over which the electro-magnetic field would have to carry psi signals.

Jack smiled at the silly cartoon, but the thoughts persisted.

Now, let's see, he mused. *We measure signals as large as microvolts on wires placed in the brains of animals. And suppose that voltage existed over a distance as large as a millimeter. That would be an electric field of a thousand microvolts per meter. And suppose the other head was a meter away and the field was a dipole that goes down like the cube of distance. That would make the field at the other head a micro-microvolt per meter.*

Jack stared intently at the pad, unaware that Barney O'Neil had entered the outer office.

"Hey, Jack!" Barney shouted. "Time for the seminar."

Jack's musings were interrupted. He stared vacantly up from his desk at Barney's smiling face peering through the open door to his office.

"Okay, Barney, thanks. I'll be right there."

Jack picked up the pad with the cartoon on it and shuffled off down the hall toward the conference room, staring at the egg heads as he went. He took a seat in the back with several other professors, but his thoughts were on the psi field. The room soon filled with graduate students, and, finally, Barney began to speak.

"Uh, we're here this afternoon to, uh, hear about the stuff that Sam Klein has been doing with the cat. You know, trying to correlate the signals he gets from the optic tectum with different stimulations of the visual field. You know, like lines or black spots."

Barney shuffled to the back of the room and took a seat next to Jack. Sam Klein got up a little hesitantly and started drawing a sketch on the board of a cat, or at least of its eyes and optic nerves and brain. But Jack found himself still staring at the pad with the two eggs. He nudged Barney, sliding the pad over so that O'Neil could see it.

"Do you think the brain could sense a micro-microvolt per meter?" Jack whispered.

Barney stared at him and then at the ovals on the pad and shook his head slowly from side to side with a perplexed look on his face.

17

"I mean," Jack persisted, "suppose one guy thought really hard, and that produced a signal of a microvolt somewhere in his brain. Then the other guy might feel a micro-microvolt per meter, if he was a meter away."

Barney smiled, beginning to get a glimmer of what Jack was talking about.

"You're still worried about that ESP thing, aren't you?" he whispered.

"Yeah," Jack nodded.

By this time, Sam Klein had started to speak, and Jack felt it his duty to pay attention. Partly because he was interested in cat vision, and partly because Sam's experiments were one of the projects that he would have to justify next week in a meeting with the National Science Foundation.

Several days later, Barney's cherubic face appeared in Jack's doorway.

"Hey, Jack, I did some calculations on that ESP thing."

Jack looked up in surprise, and then a broad smile crossed his face.

"I get a micro-micro-microvolt," O'Neil continued, "and that's pretty goddamned small!"

"You must have had a smaller signal or a smaller part of the brain or a bigger distance between the heads or something?" Jack responded defensively.

"Yeah," Barney agreed. "I kept your distance of one meter between the heads, but I took a bunch of numbers out of our experiments for signal strengths and the distances in the brain over which they seemed to exist."

Jack's smile disappeared, and he began to argue.

"Yeah, but those measurements were for animals."

Barney nodded his concurrence.

"But the literature seems to say it's about the same for humans."

Jack frowned.

"Maybe we should put the heads closer together," he offered and then, suddenly, caught himself.

He *wanted* the calculation to yield a positive result. A detectable signal. A plausible explanation of the mysterious psi field.

Had he too become a true believer?

18

4

"Garadasrowlscldker"

The flight from Boston to Washington had been uneventful, and Jack Mason now stood at the front of a small conference room in the National Science Foundation building on Constitution Avenue, addressing a tweedy committee of his scientific peers.

"And so, gentlemen, I believe that the programs I have described to you this morning, and particularly the new results that have been obtained, fully justify your recommendation that the National Science Foundation continue to fund the Laborabtory for Perceptual Research at the level of six hundred thousand dollars for the fiscal year beginning next October."

Jack glanced quickly around the table at the members of the panel. He hoped to discern in their facial expressions some clue to their reaction to his description of the laboratory's activities of the preceding year. Although all of the committee members were his technical colleagues, and some were personal friends, one could never be certain what their recommendation would be or how enthusiastically their report would be worded.

"And now, gentlemen, I would be pleased to try to answer any questions that you may have concerning the scientific results that have been obtained in the laboratory, the details of the programs we propose for the coming year, or the breakdown of the budget we have requested."

Jack hoped that friendly questions would allow him to expound on favorable aspects of his laboratory's proposal. Unfortunately, however, his supporters nodded their heads in agreement and seemed satisfied, while Professor Krauss of Yale, with whom he had never been on particularly good terms, knitted his brow and seemed perplexed.

"Professor Mason," Krauss began in an accusing tone, "you have requested seventy-five thousand dollars for continued experimental research on the correlation between signals measured in the optic tectum of a cat and visual stimuli presented to it."

"Yes," Jack responded, trying to maintain a smile. But his mind raced ahead. Krauss had already found the weakest part of the program, and Jack struggled to anticipate the line his questioning would take.

"Seventy-five thousand dollars is a lot of money, Professor Mason, isn't it?"

"Yes," said Jack again, with a slight, but noticeable, hesitation.

"You must be planning to do some fundamental new experiments," Krauss continued, his voice seeming to Jack overly pleasant to hide his real intention. "Would you tell us what these original new experiments are to be?"

The remaining smile left Jack's face, and he struggled to outline a response in his mind. His thoughts raced back over what he had written in the proposal to NSF so many months ago and the talk that Sam Klein had given last week. After hesitating for a moment, Jack stepped to the blackboard and nervously began talking and writing, trying to describe enthusiastically the major experiment that was at the heart of the cat-perception program. During this exposition, his friends again smiled, but Krauss's look of perplexity slowly changed to a thin smirk. Jack knew that the old bastard had something up his sleeve, but he couldn't imagine what it could be.

When at last Jack wound down and stood exhausted at the blackboard, Krauss ceremonially pushed back his chair and stood at his place at the table. All eyes turned toward him as he opened his briefcase and handed out copies of a scientific paper to the members of the panel and, as a condescending afterthought, to Jack.

Jack had read only far enough to notice that the reprint was from the obscure *Indian Journal of Perceptual Research,* when Krauss started to speak again aggressively.

"Gentlemen, I believe you will find that the paper I have laid before you describes a set of experiments far more definitive than those proposed by Professor Mason. In addition, you will find that it provides a very complete set of *results*."

Krauss smiled triumphantly and slowly surveyed the room. The other panel members stared back at him, their mouths slightly open, and Jack frantically tried to read the paper. He skimmed the introduction, which was full of pompous generalities, and searched anxiously for the purported comprehensive results.

But Krauss continued his attack before his opponent could recover from the shock.

"Gentlemen, I hardly see how we can recommend to the foundation that it expend seventy-five thousand dollars to allow Professor Mason the luxury of duplicating previously published results. It would seem to me irresponsible of us not to reject this part of Professor Mason's proposal."

The color drained from Jack's face, but before Krauss could press home his advantage, the chairman broke in.

"Gentlemen! I believe we should adjourn this meeting for at least a week to give Professor Mason a chance to assess the impact of this new evidence on his proposal. Is that acceptable to the members?"

All nodded yes with the exception of Krauss. The others stared at him hostilely. Still he did not acquiesce and finally one of the older panel members spoke.

"Come now, Henry, you certainly have to give Mason a chance to read the paper you've presented to us."

Krauss looked slowly around the table and felt the silent condemnation. At last, hopelessly outnumbered, he sat down without a word.

All the while, Jack had continued reading the paper frantically. But still he had not been able to find the comprehensive results that Krauss was claiming it contained. He began to suspect that Krauss was exaggerating the paper's significance as part of a tactic to cut Jack's budget and to boost his own, when Steve Johnson, a friend from graduate-school days, approached him.

"Take it easy, Jack. I don't think there's much to Krauss's paper."

21

"I haven't found any great results yet," Jack said emotionally, "but I can't believe Krauss would try this stunt if there was nothing in the paper at all."

"We've all got time to read it now," Steve continued reassuringly. "Let's call it quits for today."

When Jack returned to the hotel, he went directly to his room and began to study the article from the *Indian Journal of Perceptual Research*. The authors had in fact performed a number of experiments in which the signals from the optic tectum of a cat had been observed. However, the method of implanting the probes was crude in comparison with the techniques employed in Jack's laboratory. As a result, the signals measured by the Indian observers undoubtedly came from a combination of several nerve fibers. This made interpretation of the results in terms of visual stimuli difficult, if not impossible. In contrast, experiments performed in Jack's laboratory isolated single nerve fibers, permitting deductions to be made concerning the interconnections of nerve fibers behind the retina.

Jack breathed an audible sigh of relief. He felt sure that the members of the committee would conclude that the work described in his proposal was far more detailed and systematic than that described in the paper and not preempted by the Indian results. A smile returned to Jack's face and his anxiety quickly dissipated. He put down the paper and began to think about having a drink and some dinner. He shed his clothes on the bed and was about to head for the shower, when the phone rang noisily.

Jack reached for the receiver and was greeted by the cheerful voice of Bob Green.

"Hi, old buddy! How about slumming at the British Embassy?"

"What do you mean?" Jack responded with surprise.

"I've got a friend over there," Bob continued. "And they're having a reception. For the minister of trade or something. And we're invited."

"What do you mean, *we're* invited?" Jack replied skeptically.

"Just what I said," Bob responded jovially. "My friend invited us. I've even got the engraved invitations. There'll be lots of good food and plenty of champagne. I'll come by your hotel in about an hour."

After his encounter with Krauss, Jack welcomed the chance to relax with his old friend and accepted without hesitation.

"Okay, Bob. Thanks a lot. I'll see you later."

Jack hung up and headed for the shower.

The rhythmical knocking on the door to Jack's hotel room could only be announcing Bob Green. Jack rose from a chair by the window and shouted toward the closed door to the hall.

"Come on in, Bob!"

"The door's locked," shouted a muffled voice from outside.

"Be right there," Jack responded with a smile.

Finally admitted, Bob was instantly impatient to be moving again.

"Let's get going, old buddy, I've got the doorman watching my car."

Bob hustled Jack from the room and down the hall to the elevator. There, he nervously punched the down button every thirty seconds or so until the car finally appeared. When the doors opened on the ground floor, Bob fairly burst into the lobby. With a broad grin, he led the way through the street door of the hotel, tipped the gaudily uniformed doorman, and jogged toward a shiny red sports car at the curb.

"What is it?" Jack queried, eyeing the car with obvious interest.

"A Fiat Spyder," Bob chirped proudly.

They jumped in, and Green accelerated the open car up Massachusetts Avenue toward Embassy Row. The wind in their faces and the roar of the engine made conversation impossible, but Bob seemed on top of the world and his cheerfulness dispelled Jack's last thoughts of Krauss. At length, Bob wheeled the car through the gates of the embassy courtyard and shouted over the muffled grumbling of the engine to the uniformed attendant.

"We're guests of Mr. Worthington! My name is Green! He said you'd have a space for us."

"Over there, sir, against the outside wall," said the attendant, pointing.

With a roar and a screech, the car was parked and Bob jumped out and headed across the cobblestone courtyard toward the entrance with Jack hustling along behind. At the door, Bob flashed the engraved invitations and repeated jauntily to a formally attired butler:

"Guests of Mr. Worthington. Professor Mason and Mr. Green."

The butler took the cards and bowed slightly.

It was Jack's first visit to an embassy. He gawked with a tourist's curiosity at the ornate surroundings and clusters of stylishly dressed Washingtonians. But Bob led the way with an old hand's self-assurance. As they crossed the large, marble-floored entry hall, he turned and whispered to Jack.

"I want you to meet Bill Worthington. He's really *Commander* Worthington, but we don't mention that in public. He's in the same business I am."

Approaching a group of people clustered around a waiter with a tray of glasses of champagne, Bob spied his colleague.

"Bill," he announced, tapping a tall, thin, wavy-haired man on the shoulder, "I'd like you to meet Professor Mason; Jack, this is Bill Worthington."

"A distinct pleasure to meet you, Professor," Worthington responded with a warm smile. "Bob has told me a lot about you. Says he's even got you interested in ESP."

Aha, Jack thought, *that's what Bob is up to.*

"Yes, that's right," he responded noncommitally.

When the initial conversation with the mustached commander ended, Bob and Jack wandered leisurely through the crowded embassy reception rooms, eating from several lavishly set buffets and consuming numerous glasses of champagne proffered by ubiquitous tail-coated waiters. From time to time, Bill Worthington reappeared and generously introduced them to one or another of their fellow guests. Some of them were apparently other embassy staff members, but Jack got no clear picture of what any of them really did. *Perhaps,* he began to think, *they are all in Bob Green's business. Whatever that really is?*

After several hours of overindulgence, Jack's head was beginning to swim, and his vacant grin revealed his condition.

24

So when Bob suggested that they adjourn for some air, Jack readily agreed.

Green led the way to the terrace and, once outside, continued down the steps into the garden. Jack was sure that Bob was seeking privacy for their conversation, but he could not focus his woolly brain on surmising Green's purpose.

"You told Worthington that you've been doing something about the ESP thing," Bob began with obvious interest. "What have you found out?"

For a fleeting moment, Jack considered toying with Bob. His desire to get Jack involved in ESP was so obvious that leading him on would have been easy. But the evening was pleasant and the champagne disarming, and Jack couldn't bring himself to pull his old friend's leg.

"I've done quite a bit of reading and even made a few calculations."

"You have!" Bob's whole face brightened. "You work fast, old buddy!"

Jack smiled at Bob's childlike enthusiasm and responded sardonically.

"The stuff I read was mostly bunk. You know, the little old lady in London who could tell what her niece in Peoria was thinking. And even the supposedly scientific stuff isn't very well done."

"What's wrong with it?" Bob interjected with a frown.

"Well, take the early Duke stuff," Jack responded, the professor in him warming to the subject. "When an Englishman who is a serious scientist looked into it, he found considerable circumstantial evidence that people might have been cheating."

Bob nodded knowingly.

"You mean, they really wanted the experiment to go well," he said with a smile, "so they gave the results a little nudge. We call that the can-do spirit in my business."

"Right!" said Jack sarcastically and continued.

"The worst case was this fellow Soal and the Welsh schoolboys."

"*Welsh schoolboys?*" Bob responded quizzically.

"Yeah," Jack answered, shaking his head in the affirmative. "Soal wanted good results, so he paid them for good results.

Their families needed the money, so they cheated, and everybody was happy."

Bob nodded dolefully.

"But weren't some of the experiments more scientific than that?"

"Yeah," Jack agreed, "Rhine and others tried to control cheating, but there are other problems, too. For example, ESP researchers tend to report only the *positive* results. And if you do that, you can prove *anything*."

Bob nodded, but Jack doubted that he understood.

"Now, let's say that you and I go back to my hotel room," Jack continued, "and we stay up all night making runs with ESP cards. The chances are fair that we would get a run with ten or more hits, double the average value of five."

Bob's smile returned instantly, but Jack frowned and continued.

"And tomorrow morning, the one of us who was looking at the cards could call himself an *experimenter* and write a paper reporting that the *other one,* the one who got the ten hits, has remarkable telepathic powers."

"Gee," Bob gasped. "Do you really think we could do it?"

Jack smiled, his hypothesis concerning Bob's gullibility confirmed.

"Sure we could, if we tried enough times. And it wouldn't prove a damn thing. All it would confirm is that events of low probability do occur—if you wait long enough."

Bob looked disappointed, but Jack persisted.

"There's another problem with a lot of the experiments reported in the parapsychology literature. People start out to test one thing, say telepathy. But when they don't get a positive result, they analyze the data for *something else.* Perhaps differences in telepathic ability according to the sex of the experimenter and the clairvoyant."

"What's wrong with that," said Bob with a chuckle.

"Nothing," Jack responded sarcastically, "if you designed the experiment to test for that conclusion in the beginning. The trouble is, if you do the experiment *first,* and then *afterwards,* keep changing the conclusion that you're trying to establish, you'll always find some conclusion that seems to fit."

Bob appeared perplexed, and Jack decided to give him an example.

"I could give you a bunch of numbers out of a random number table, and if you tried enough different possible explanations of the pattern of the digits, you'd find one that fit. But the next set of numbers I gave you wouldn't fit that pattern at all. So you'd have to change your conclusion about the pattern."

Bob still didn't understand, but he got the message.

"So you think they're all a bunch of frauds?" he said dejectedly.

"Frauds is a strong word," Jack replied seriously. "I think many of them, like the people at Duke, are honest and serious. The trouble is that they believe so strongly in ESP that they can find a parapsychological explanation for almost any experimental result. If I were looking at the same data, I would find some other explanation, because I don't believe in ESP. I'm prejudiced too, and it's hard to be certain which of us is right."

"So it's not a dead issue?" Bob offered, cheering up a little.

"No," said Jack, smiling. "Not dead, but certainly moribund! I made a few calculations."

Bob's face brightened visibly and Jack continued.

"If two people had their heads very close together and one of them concentrated on a simple thought very intensely, it's just conceivable that his brain might produce an electrical signal that could be sensed by the other person's brain."

"It is!" Bob's normally ebulent mood returned completely.

"Well, it *might* be," Jack continued, trying to inject a note of caution. "At least it should be possible to do some scientific experiments to see if—"

"When do we start!"

Bob was ecstatic, his mind racing ahead to future possibilities. But Jack continued unemotionally.

"I think you could build this double chair. With the people seated back to back, but with their heads overlapping side to side. That way, their heads would be as close together as possible. But you could put a lot of padding between their bodies. So that they couldn't communicate by sights or sounds or motions or any other normal way. Only by electromagnetic waves, electrical signals between their brains."

"Wow!" Bob exclaimed. "How much would it cost? And when could you start?"

When could I start? thought Jack. *When could I start?*

He looked up and saw that Bob's eyes had glazed over with a faraway look; his thoughts were clearly elsewhere. A strange feeling overcame Jack. That feeling that occurs only a few times during one's life. The feeling that one is at a turning point, where he must choose between two radically different paths for the years to come. The old, known, boring path, or something new and dangerous and exciting.

Bob returned to the present, bubbling over with enthusiasm.

"This will revolutionize my business. In the past, we used spies, and now we rely mostly on satellites. The man and the excitement have pretty much gone out of the game. But your discovery will bring them back. We'll have the ultimate human collection system—the man with psi."

The man with psi? thought Jack.

Suddenly, it all became very clear to him. The business Bob was in. The reason for his interest in ESP. And the reason he had revived their friendship. The turning-point feeling came back. In the pit of his stomach. Suddenly, he was afraid.

But Bob was jubilant.

"Think what this means," he whispered. "When the president goes to a summit meeting in Moscow or Peking, our man will be there—the man with psi. And *we* might even be there, too. It's fantastic! Why, I can even imagine—"

'Hold it, Bob!" Jack injected. "You're dreaming! All I said was that somebody could do an experiment. To see if there is a possibility. When two people's heads are extremely close together. . . . And all of a sudden, you're dreaming about summits."

"Right!" Bob enthused. "With the president and the secretary of state asking our man—the man with psi—what is in the minds of their adversaries. Are they bluffing? Or are they scared? Or do they really want peace? Or—"

"Bob! Slow down!" Jack almost shouted. "You're losing your mind! This is a bad dream."

The sudden turn of events was extremely disturbing to Jack. The knot in his stomach tightened. He felt suddenly chilled, though the evening was mild. He tried to back up the discussion. Back to reality.

"Look, Bob, this isn't some kind of spy game. It's a scientific experiment. A very difficult one. And very unlikely to succeed. It would have to be done slowly and carefully by good people. And in the end, if they were successful, all you'd know was that there was a *possibility*."

"Right!" Bob injected. "But think of the possibilities! In negotiations, we would be invincible. No one could bluff us. No one could lie to us. And if they were weak or afraid, we'd know it. And could take advantage of it. It would bring in a new era, an era of peace, engineered by America."

Pax Americana shot through Jack's mind, with all its negative connotations. But he despaired of trying to reverse the conversation. Instead, he decided to try to change the subject.

"Let's go inside and get something to eat. I've had too much to drink on an empty stomach."

"Okay," said Bob, and with a jubilant smile still on his face, he placed his arm around Jack's shoulders as they strolled through the embassy grounds. Jack felt strangely like a nervous football player about to receive a reassuring pep talk from his coach.

Jack was in the Admirals Club at National Airport waiting for the appointed time to call Professor Hardy. He had had a drink and a cracker and was aimlessly scanning the evening *Star*. The news didn't make much of an impression on him; he was just nervously killing time.

It had been a long day. He had gotten up at 6 A.M. to continue studying the paper from the *Indian Journal of Perceptual Research*. By 8:30, he had concluded that it was trash. He had been infuriated by the ploy that Krauss had pulled on him and the NSF committee. And, as a result of phoning several of the panel members at their hotels, he had succeeded in getting the chairman to reconvene their deliberations at 10:30.

Krauss had not shown up for the meeting, apparently fearing that his trickery had been exposed. However, he had phoned the chairman during the lunch break to make a rambling, impassioned plea for reductions in Jack's budget. The discussions had continued into the afternoon, and at about three o'clock, the panel had asked Jack to leave the room, so that they could deliberate and write their recommendations. The chairman had told Jack to call him at 5:30 or 6:00 to learn the outcome.

Jack nervously dialed the number of Ralph Hardy's hotel, and, when the switchboard got a response at his room, Jack began tentatively.

"Professor Hardy? This is Jack Mason. How did things come out?"

"Okay, Jack," the kindly voice responded. "Everything is okay. Krauss called me a couple of times, but in the end, he didn't even show up. So we approved your program—unanimously—with one member absent. You've got nothing to worry about, Jack. We think it's a good program. Krauss is just sore because he hasn't done anything very original lately and you have. So you're the target."

"Thanks a lot, Ralph," Jack said with great relief. "You've certainly been very fair and considerate."

"You deserve it, Jack," Hardy answered sincerely. "You're doing good work. See you at the next conference."

"Thanks again," Jack replied and hung up.

He sat back in his chair and closed his eyes. His tired brain began reliving the hectic events of the day.

Jack was roused from his dream-filled sleep by the feeling of someone shaking him and the sound of a soothing voice in his ear.

"Your plane will be boarding in a few minutes, Professor Mason," the hostess said softly. "You had better head for the gate pretty soon."

"Thanks," Jack responded groggily and began to gather up his papers.

The plane was full, but Jack had managed to get a window seat in the front part of coach. As many times as he had flown in and out of Washington, he never tired of looking at the city below on takeoff or landing. His gaze traversed the Mall to the Capitol in the distance, past the Lincoln and Jefferson memorials and the Washington Monument in the foreground and the White House nestled among the buildings on the left.

"Would you care to purchase a cocktail, sir?" chirped the stewardess.

Jack turned from the window and handed her three dollar bills distractedly.

"Two Jack Daniel's on the rocks, please."

He downed the whiskey more quickly than usual, and then eased his seat back to take a nap.

Jack was being led down a long, dark hall in a strange building by Bob Green.

"Come on, Jack. Let's get down there," the dream voice of Bob Green demanded. "He's ready to be debriefed."

They entered a room where a man was lying on a medical table and was being ministered to by a cluster of white-coated attendants. A person who appeared to be a doctor looked at the pupils of the supine figure's eyes, checked his pulse and respiration, and then said unemotionally:

"He's ready any time now. You can start questioning him."

A man with a clipboard moved to the head of the table and began conversing with the reclining figure.

"How do you feel, Alton?"

"Okay, I guess," the supine form answered groggily.

"All right," his interrogator continued, "let's start from the top. The president made his opening remarks about being here in search of world order and of his desire to see a generation of peace for Russian and American families. Now, while the President was speaking, did you get any thoughts from the general secretary?"

"Just . . . gar ad as rowl scld ker," the reclining man mumbled slowly.

"What?" responded the man with the clipboard incredulously.

"*Garadasrowlscldker*," the supine figure repeated more clearly.

"What the hell is *garadasrowlscldker*?" said the man with the clipboard accusingly. "Is it Russian?"

"I don't know," the prostrate form responded meekly.

"Get the translator!" a voice from the shadows commanded authoritatively.

"Yes, sir," replied another indistinguishable person rushing from the room.

The shadowy figure returned shortly with a person who Jack thought must be the translator, and the questioning was resumed. But the answer was the same.

"Garadasrowlscldker."

"Fluval!" demanded the authoritative voice. "What does that mean?"

"I don't know, sir," the translator responded meekly.

"Is it Russian?"

"I don't think so, sir."

"The president," the authoritative voice continued slowly, "will insist upon knowing what it means."

The mysterious speaker emerged from the shadows, stared at them intently, and then left the room.

"What does it mean?" the man with the clipboard said to the translator imploringly.

"Got me," the latter responded dumbly.

"Maybe Mason can help us," the man with the clipboard continued.

"That's a good idea," agreed the translator.

All eyes in the room turned toward Jack. He felt them boring in. They were all staring at him.

"Tell us what it means," they all echoed.

Panic overtook Jack. He scanned the room for a way out, but it had no doors. The white-coated figures all continued to stare directly at him, and he was terrified.

There was a loud thump and a jolt as the landing gear were lowered and locked into position. Jack was suddenly wide awake. In place of the room without doors, the lights of Boston twinkled below through his window.

His body was covered with a cold sweat and dampness. The memory of the dream was so vivid that he could recall the dialogue word for word.

What does garadasrowlscldker mean? he thought desperately. *What in God's name does it mean?*

PART II
POTOMAC FEVER

5

Washington Calling

More than a week had passed since the evening that Jack had spent with Bob Green at the British Embassy, and the strange dream during the plane trip back to Boston had faded from his thoughts. But when he returned to the office after giving a lecture, his secretary greeted him in a state of excitement.

"Some strange people from Washington called you. Their secretary said, 'This is Washington calling. May we please speak to Professor Mason?' What kind of a way to call someone is that?" she asked rhetorically and then continued before Jack could respond. "I said, 'Professor Mason is out of the office. May I tell him who called?' And they just said, 'Tell him that Washington called. We will place the call again.' Now, that's a strange message if I ever heard one," she concluded emphatically.

"It must just be some nuts trying to sell something," Jack said, trying to be funny, and continued into his office.

"Bob Green," he said to himself. "It must be Bob Green. But Bob would leave a number. He has before. Perhaps it's someone else in his business, he concluded, shaking his head."

Jack's thoughts drifted back to the discussion with Bob in the garden of the British Embassy and to the nightmare he later experienced on the airplane. He again shook his head slowly from side to side, trying to dispell the disturbing memories. *That was certainly a bad omen,* he thought. *And now Bob's trying to involve me in a crazy scheme to read men's minds. To read the minds of heads of state. It's insane. It's really all insane.*

Jack was becoming increasingly disturbed. His emotions grew, and his thoughts rambled.

All I told him was that somebody could do an experiment. A scientific experiment. To see if there is a possibility. And now he wants to read men's minds. In Moscow. It's nutty. He's nutty. And if I get involved, I'll be nutty, too.

"Professor Mason! Are you all right?"

His secretary stood in the doorway, looking concerned as Jack mumbled to himself behind his desk.

"They're crazy!" he blurted out.

"Who's crazy?" the secretary responded, looking even more perplexed.

"Those guys in Washington."

"*What* guys in Washington? The ones who called?"

"I don't know. Probably," said Jack, partially regaining his composure.

He stared at her for a moment and then decided to change the subject. The whole business was too complicated and too crazy to try to explain.

"I'm okay, Marcia. I just need a little fresh air."

Jack got up from behind his desk, smiled at his secretary reassuringly, and headed off down the hall.

Washington continued to call. Twice the following day and once more the next morning. Jack was sitting at his desk, trying to make some calculations, when they called again.

"It's them again!" Marcia's voice suddenly burst into the room through the open door. She clearly was agitated.

"What the hell, I'll take it!" Jack shouted back, determined to deal with the nuisance. He picked up the receiver and began aggressively.

"Mason speaking!"

"Professor Mason? This is Frank Alvisi," the mysterious caller said calmly. "I work for the government, and we need your help."

"Help with *what*?" Jack growled.

"It's a scientific problem," Alvisi continued soothingly. "Right up your alley. You're in perceptual research, aren't you?"

"Right!" Jack responded brusquely. "What's the problem?"

"It's quite sensitive, Professor, and *very* important. I'd like to get together with you to discuss it. How about—"

"Let's discuss it *now*!" Jack broke in crossly.

36

"I'd rather not do it on the phone," Alvisi responded unemotionally. "How about getting together the next time you're in Washington?"

"What for?" said Jack, his annoyance growing.

"It's quite a complicated problem, Professor Mason, and extremely sensitive. And I want to discuss it all with you in detail. This thing has very high level backing, and we need the best advice we can get. And everyone tells us that you're the man we should turn to."

The combination of Alvisi's flattery and Jack's curiosity had a calming effect. Jack's temptation to hang up disappeared and he became more conciliatory.

"Well, ah, it'll be a week or so before I'm in Washington again."

"The week of the twenty-eighth? That would be fine. What day do you have in mind?"

Jack felt trapped. To get out of it now, he would have to lie. Anyhow, his curiosity had gotten the better of him.

"I have to be at NSF on the morning of the twenty-ninth. I guess I could see you in the afternoon. Where are you located?" "And for that matter, who are you?" Jack said to himself.

"The afternoon of the twenty-ninth would be fine," Alvisi responded enthusiastically. "We're not far from NSF. On the corner of Nineteenth and M. It's a big office building. Come up to the tenth floor and ask for me. What time is convenient for you?"

"I can be there by two without any trouble," Jack responded easily.

"Fine!" Alvisi enthused. "I'll see you then. And *thank you*, Professor Mason. You're doing something very important for the country, and we appreciate it."

Appreciate what? Jack thought, frowning.

"Okay, Mr. Alvisi, I'll see you on the twenty-ninth. Good-bye."

"Good-bye, Professor Mason. And thanks again."

"What the hell have I done?" Jack asked himself. "Who the hell is this guy? And what does he want to talk about? It must be the ESP business. And Green must be behind it. That's it. I'll get ahold of Green and get to the bottom of this."

37

Jack rummaged through the top drawer of his desk and came up with the scrap of paper on which was written the message that Bob Green had left at his hotel back in May. He got up from behind the desk, walked to the outer office, and handed the note to his secretary.

"Marcia, will you try to get this fellow, Bob Green, at this number in Washington."

"What area code is it?" she asked, with a small frown. "Do you know?"

"Two-oh-two, I think," Jack replied and returned to his office.

In a few moments, Marcia's cheerful voice drifted in through the doorway.

"I got his office, but he's out right now. He'll call you back."

By the time Bob Green returned the call, Jack had had time to do some thinking. He would act dumb and try to get as much information out of Bob as possible. But without sounding too interested.

"Hi, old buddy," Green began jovially. "What can I do for you?"

"Say, Bob," Jack answered, trying to be casual, "I got this call from a fellow called Frank Alvisi. Said he worked for the government. I thought you might have some idea who he is."

"So he called you already," Green replied enthusiastically. "Things are really moving right along. That's great!"

"What's great?" Jack responded emotionally.

"That they're moving so fast," Bob continued, as if the answer was obvious. "To get things going. And get you on board."

"On board what?" Jack injected aggressively. "It's that damn ESP business, isn't it? You've been pursuing that crazy conversation we had. Haven't you?"

"Well, ah, old buddy," Green backtracked, "we can't exactly discuss it on the phone. But you're, ah, on the right track, let's say. I'll see you at Alvisi's place on the twenty-ninth, and we'll discuss the whole thing in detail."

Jack exploded.

"You know all about it, don't you! Alvisi's phone call. And my agreeing to a meeting on the twenty-ninth. You guys are manipulating me. Aren't you?"

"Take it easy, old buddy," Bob responded with obvious concern. "This thing is very important for the country. We all have to do our bit, and you're the key man. You're the guy who knows how to do it. Why, without you—"

"Knows how to do what?" Jack injected. "All I told you was that somebody could do an experiment. And you ran off and told God-knows-who that we could read men's minds!"

"Calm down, old buddy, calm down!" Green replied excitedly. "I told them just what you said. And they're still very interested—at the highest levels of my organization. But we can't discuss it any more on the phone. We'll talk it all over at Alvisi's, and you'll see that it's a sensible program. And if you don't like it, you can change it. You're the key man. We're relying on you. Now just keep the faith."

Jack's plan to gather information surreptitiously had disintegrated. He felt like an unwitting participant in Alice's tea party, and, clearly, Bob did not intend to enlighten him.

6

Project Psi

Jack's morning at the National Science Foundation was uneventful. As Professor Hardy had privately assured him, Jack was told that his laboratory's plan and budget for the coming fiscal year had been approved. He politely feigned surprise and pleasure when the grant administrator guardedly revealed to him several complimentary phrases from the peer panel's report. And after they concluded the final details of the grant, Jack invited the administrator for a quick sandwich lunch at a local delicatessen.

The day's academic business over, Jack's thoughts turned to the coming afternoon meeting with the mysterious Frank Alvisi. The weather was remarkably pleasant for late August in Washington, and Jack had time to spare, so he decided to walk to Nineteenth and M. He tried, without success, to remember what sort of building was on the corner, as he walked along. Finally, he concluded that it must be unremarkable. Probably one of those steel and glass nonentities that were gradually replacing the city's older architecture. The perfect place, he supposed, for people like Alvisi to hide.

Jack's suspicion was correct. Like its nondescript facade, the lobby of the building at Nineteenth and M revealed little about its occupants. Jack scanned the building directory mounted on the wall between the elevators and found the appropriate entry.

"United States Government, Floors 8, 9, and 10," it proclaimed uninformatively.

When he stepped off the elevator on the tenth floor, Jack was confronted by a uniformed guard and a receptionist seated behind a high-topped counter.

"May I help you, sir?" she enquired.

"I'm Professor Mason," Jack said. "I'm here to see Mr. Alvisi. He's expecting me at two o'clock."

"Fine," said the receptionist. "Would you please sign our visitors' register."

She swiveled a strange-looking metal box with a crank handle on the side around to face Jack. It looked like the receipt machines used in old-fashioned hardware stores. It contained a visitor registration form requesting his name, home address, and signature. The receptionist had already filled in Frank Alvisi as the person visited. Jack signed with a flourish, and the receptionist swiveled the box around again, turned the crank, and handed him a copy of the form along with a plain white badge marked "visitor."

After a few minutes of waiting, during which he was totally ignored by the obviously bored guard and receptionist, a secretary appeared and escorted Jack to a conference room. It was dominated by a large, mahogany table, around which were arranged a number of chairs upholstered in leather with brass hobnails. From past experience with government offices, Jack judged the owner of the conference room to be fairly high up the bureaucratic ladder. *Probably a GS–16,* he thought, *and maybe a 17.*

"May I bring you a cup of coffee, Professor Mason?" the secretary enquired solicitously.

"Ah, fine," Jack responded automatically. "Just black, thank you."

After the secretary retired again, Jack sat sipping his coffee and studying the photographs that adorned the walls of the room. They were striking scenes from the Far East: Buddhist temples, a snow-capped Mount Fuji, a giant pair of Sumo wrestlers, an aerial view of the Great Wall, and other equally dramatic scenes he could not identify. At length, his mental travelogue was broken by the voice of Bob Green.

"Hi, old buddy. I see you made it all right."

Jack turned toward the sound and smiled with relief to see his old friend.

"Hi, Bob. How are you?"

"Just fine, old buddy. And really glad you're here. You don't know how important this thing is. Or how many big people are interested. It's really exciting to have a project that people really care about, for a change."

Jack nodded perfunctorily, but then continued the conversation with an edge on his voice.

"Okay, Bob, let's cut out the mystery. What's going on? What have you told people? I think this thing is getting out of hand."

"Just wait a bit, old buddy," Green responded with a concerned smile. "Frank will be here in a minute, and then we can talk the whole thing over. After we get you signed up."

"Signed up for what?" Jack responded with growing irritation.

"It's just a formality, old buddy," Bob tried to reassure him. "Nothing to worry about."

Their increasingly tense conversation was interrupted when a tall, thin man with a small, black mustache entered the room silently. Bob Green rose to make the introductions, and Jack knew that this must be the mysterious caller from Washington.

"Frank, I'd like you to meet Professor Jack Mason. Jack, this is Frank Alvisi."

Jack shook Alvisi's outstretched hand warily, and the latter motioned for them to be seated again at the conference table.

"Would you like some more coffee, Professor?" Alvisi offered, trying to break the ice.

"No, thank you. No more for me," Jack replied impatiently. "I'd just as soon get down to business. I'd like to find out what you guys are up to."

Bob Green grinned at Frank Alvisi. That little surreptitious grin of a child who has a surprise in store for its parents. Alvisi returned the grin, but so fleetingly that Jack only caught it because he was studying his mysterious host intently.

"Look!" Jack exploded. "Enough is enough! What the *hell* are you guys up to?"

"Hold on for a few minutes more, Professor Mason," Frank Alvisi said reassuringly. "We just have a couple of administrative things to get over with, and then we'll discuss the whole thing."

He opened a folder in front of him on the table, handed a sheet of paper to Jack, and continued matter-of-factly.

"This is a little security oath we'd like you to sign. Just a formality, you understand. It simply says that you won't discuss the project with unauthorized people."

Jack was taken by surprise. Even before he started to read the piece of paper, his brow knitted quizzically. Alvisi spotted this obvious sign of discomfort and again tried to put Jack at ease.

"It's okay, Professor Mason. Really it is. We sign these things all the time. Dozens of them. It's just a formality."

Bob Green eagerly signaled his agreement by nodding his head up and down exaggeratedly, and Jack began to read.

CONFIDENTIAL—PSI

Security Oath

I, the undersigned, hereby acknowledge that I understand that Project Psi is of the highest importance to the United States and that revelation of information concerning the project to unauthorized persons may cause grave damage to the national interest. I solemnly swear that I will not discuss, convey, or otherwise transfer information concerning Project Psi to any individual, group, or organization not officially authorized to receive such material. I understand that there may be administrative sanctions and/or criminal penalties for failure to abide by this oath.

Witness	Name:	John W. Mason
Date: 29 August 1967	SSN:	070-41-9165

CONFIDENTIAL—PSI

Jack shook his head, his brow deeply furrowed. His thoughts shot back to his college reading of Kafka's novels. He dimly remembered scenes of a person requesting information at an endless sequence of government offices. The character was told to fill out numerous forms and to submit them through narrow windows to faceless clerks. But he never received any replies.

"I'm sorry," Jack said firmly. "This has gone far enough. I'm not going to sign this thing, or anything else, until you tell me what's going on."

Green and Alvisi glanced at each other furtively, but their smiles were gone.

"Now, take it easy, old buddy," said Bob, trying to calm him down. "It's nothing to get upset about. Just the way we do things around Washington. Why, I bet I've signed a hundred of these things. Maybe more. They don't—"

"I know it must seem strange to you, Professor Mason," Frank Alvisi interjected in a measured tone, "particularly for the first time. But try to see our side of it for a moment. We have a lot of projects that, particularly in their formative stages, we don't want everyone in the world knowing about. And yet we have to get good advice from people like yourself at various universities and companies. Now, if we discuss these projects with people like that, we need some assurances. You know, that they won't just go and tell the *New York Times* or the *Washington Post*," he ended with a chuckle.

Jack began to feel a little more in control of the situation. He was actually beginning to see the funny side of it.

"I think you've got it backwards," he said half jokingly. "*I'm* the one that should have gotten *you guys* to sign an oath. An oath that says that you won't misuse the scientific information I give you. That you won't distort some brainstorming about a possible scientific experiment into a crazy spy project. Now, what do you say to that?"

Frank Alvisi glanced cautiously at Bob Green, and the latter answered with a furtive smile. Reassured, Alvisi responded with a broad grin, and he and Bob both began to chuckle. And when Jack joined in, they knew the confrontation was over.

"Fair enough, Professor Mason," Alvisi said. "That will be a good guideline for the project. You write it down and I'll get my secretary to type it up. Now, how about just signing the oath so that we can get on to the technical discussion?"

Jack suddenly realized that his desire to be clever, his sudden urge to turn the tables on them intellectually, had gotten them off the hook. He couldn't very well refuse to sign now. After all, they had accepted his suggestion, with its implied criticism. Reluctantly, he took out his pen, signed with a flourish, and returned the paper to Alvisi.

Much to Jack's surprise, the latter traded the signed oath for a second sheet of paper. Jack began to read it in silence, while Alvisi and Green looked on apprehensively.

TOP SECRET—PSI

Project Psi Indoctrination

Project Psi is an activity of the highest potential importance to the United States. It encompasses the research, development, and planning necessary to find, train, and utilize individuals who possess the ability to read other men's minds through reception of the psi field. The ultimate objective of the project is to make available to the highest level leaders of the United States one or more of these men with psi to be used to gather information concerning the intentions of adversaries during international summit negotiations. The successful completion of Project Psi will result in a breakthrough toward the objective of the United States in world diplomacy—a just, honorable, and secure peace.

The accomplishment of the project's objectives will require the dedicated cooperation of technical, administrative, and operational personnel both within and outside the government. Secrecy is essential in the conduct of the project. Were the psi weapon to fall into the hands of an adversary, the achievement of world peace could be denied and the security of the United States threatened. Those devoting their efforts to the project can be assured that they are making significant contributions both to America's strength and to the ultimate goal of world peace.

Witness	Name:	John W. Mason
Date: 29 August 1967	SSN:	070-41-9165

TOP SECRET—PSI

When Jack finished reading, he looked up at Alvisi and Green with a bemused smile on his face.

"Look, guys, I thought you just agreed to take an oath to act rationally about this whole thing. And now I find out that you've got this whole crazy project ginned up. If you're not careful, somebody will take this thing seriously. And then you'll really be in trouble."

Frank Alvisi put on his best sober-government-official look.

"I assure you, Professor Mason, that Project Psi is taken very seriously at the highest levels of the government. I believe that I can tell you, in the strictest confidence, that we have reason to believe that the secretary of state already has discussed the matter with the president."

The secretary of state, the president, thought Jack. *What have these lunatics done?*

But Alvisi continued unemotionally.

"As you know, Professor Mason, the president and the secretary of state have devoted themselves to the search for world peace. And my understanding is that they believe that personal summit diplomacy is the way to achieve this goal. Now just conceive, for a moment, the incalculable advantage they would possess in these negotiations were they aided by a man with psi. A man who could reveal to them the most intimate thoughts of their adversaries. They would be—"

"Wait a second! Wait a second!" Jack broke in. "Your goal might be laudable, but we don't know how to do it. There is no such thing as a man with psi. It's just cocktail conversation. Just bullshit! All I told Bob was that somebody could do an experiment. A scientific experiment. To see if there was a possibility that for very short distances—"

"We agree," said Bob, breaking in. "That's what we want you to do. A scientific experiment. To see if there is a possibility. That's where we want to start. And that's why we need you."

Need me? thought Jack. *There must be lots of nuts running around Washington that would be better suited to this project than me.* Finally his thoughts erupted.

"What do you need me for? You guys have this whole thing figured out. Why, I bet you've even got a budget and a manning

46

chart, and you're worrying about cover stories and all that kind of garbage."

Bob and Frank looked at each other with childish smirks again, and Jack knew that his fears were correct. He reacted emotionally.

"Look, let's just forget that we ever talked about ESP! I'll go back to my lab, to my dull research on perception in monkeys, and you guys can go do something exciting—like peeking in embassy windows or following people or whatever gives you kicks. But not me. I'm just a straightforward scientist, running a lab and trying to do some experiments about simple things like cats and monkeys."

By now, all traces of humor had disappeared from the faces of Alvisi and Green, and they stared at Jack with looks of growing concern. But he was wound up and continued vehemently.

"If you guys need a nut, a nut scientist, there are a lot of them around. Just go to any parapsychology lab. They'd love a project like this. You'd have them fighting to join. Here, I'll make you a list," he concluded emotionally, grabbing a pad from the conference table. "And all you'll have to do is call them."

"Yeah, we understand," said Bob dejectedly, "nuts are a dime a dozen, and enthusiastic. But we don't wants nuts. We want good scientists. Because we want the project to succeed. And you're the best. So we want you."

"Want me for what?" Jack responded hostilely.

"To head the project," Bob said firmly.

The room was silent. *To head the project* echoed in Jack's brain. *Head of Project Screwball,* he thought. *How would that look on my résumé?*

Still no one spoke. Finally, Frank Alvisi tried to break the tension by appealing to Jack's ego.

"Try thinking about it this way, Professor Mason. Studying chimpanzees may be a perfectly respectable career for an ordinary scientist. But for an exceptional man, like you, there are better things. Still scientific things, but things that affect the nation and the world. You'll still be heading a group of scientists, but the objective will be more important. Something you will all feel proud to be accomplishing. Because you'll be helping the nation and the world. You'll be helping to build a generation of peace."

Jack felt the strange logic getting to him. Could he really contend that chimpanzees were more important than world peace? What he wanted to say was that he knew how to handle cats and monkeys. They were simple and impersonal, but their visual perception was scientifically interesting. But how could he compare that to secretaries of state and presidents and summit meetings and world peace. Monkey vision sounded trivial in comparison.

Seeing that his approach was working, Frank Alvisi interrupted Jack's thoughts in a parental tone.

"I think you have a clear choice, Professor Mason. On the one hand, you can continue with your present, well-respected research. You are sure to be remembered in scientific circles as one of the pioneers in primate vision. On the other hand, you can take on this project and broaden your scope to something with national and world significance. You'd be taking a chance, of course. The project might not be successful. Or some of your scientific colleagues might find out about it and ridicule or ostracize you for being involved. Those are the risks you'd have to take."

What was Jack supposed to say to that? That he doubted his own ability to make the project succeed? Or that he was afraid to take a chance? To try something new? That he liked the rut he was in? All these thoughts and more flashed through his mind as the three men sat in silence.

After a calculated interval, Frank Alvisi continued, subtly letting Jack defer announcement of the inevitable choice.

"Well, Professor Mason, there's no need for a hasty decision. Right now, what we'd like to get from you is some technical advice on how we should start. Bob tells me that you have an idea for an experiment in which two people's heads would be placed as close together as possible. I'd like to hear a little more about your idea."

Jack was visibly relieved that they were not pressing him for an immediate decision. He found himself anxious to launch into a description of the experiment, if only to prevent the conversation from returning to the previous subject.

"Well," he began, with much of his professorial confidence returned, "after some thought, I concluded that the only physical phenomenon that could be responsible for mental telepathy is the electromagnetic field."

Bob Green nodded enthusiastically as if he understood, although Jack was certain that he hadn't the slightest idea what an electromagnetic field was.

"The idea is," Jack continued, "that if a person concentrates very intensely on a particular thought, the concentration produces electrical signals in his brain that contain information about the thought. Now, if a second person's head is very close to that of the first person, the second person's brain might sense the electromagnetic field produced by the electrical signals in the first person's brain. In that way, the information concerning the thought might be transmitted between the two brains."

"That's very interesting," said Alvisi thoughtfully, and Bob Green chimed in.

"Didn't I tell you he had a simple way of explaining it? He's a genius, my old buddy."

"This experiment, Professor Mason," Alvisi continued, like a conscientious graduate student, "exactly how would it be conducted?"

"I'm not really sure yet," Jack replied, a little more relaxed. "The concept I had was to build a special chair for two people. Sort of like two astronaut couches back to back. But with the two people's heads positioned side by side, as close together as possible. The idea is to have their brains close together, but to shield them completely from signaling to each other by normal means. By sounds, or thumps, or hand signals, or whatever. If you really wanted to do it right, the two couches could be in individual, soundproof rooms, with a few layers of fiberglass, or even a vacuum, separating the two heads. The electromagnetic waves would go right through the fiberglass and the vacuum, but any sounds or vibrations or whatever wouldn't."

"This gets more interesting all the time," said Alvisi sincerely. "Suppose we had it all built, the two soundproof rooms and the chair for the two people. What would we do then?"

"I'm not quite sure about that either," said Jack, warming to the subject like the old racehorse of a lecturer that he was at

49

heart. "But the way I think I'd start would be to test quite a few different people. Some people may have more natural ability to transmit or receive psi signals; at least that's what the ESP researchers say."

"Okay," said Alvisi. "Suppose we had a bunch of volunteers. How would you test them?"

"Well," said Jack, now fully involved, "the most difficult thing would probably be to distinguish between people who had some real telepathic ability and people who were cheating. You'd have to have the person who was trying to transmit his thoughts concentrate on a idea that was very simple and could be chosen at random, without the knowledge of either of the people."

Bob and Frank nodded like enthusiastic students and Jack continued his lecture.

"You might have a screen display one of the digits from zero to nine to the person who was trying to transmit his thoughts. Then you would ask him to concentrate on the number intensely for a period of time, say a minute. And during that same minute, the person in the other room, the one who was trying to receive the thought, would press a button to indicate which number he perceived was being thought about. Now, if you tried that experiment over thousands and thousand of times, you probably could tell statistically whether or not the two people demonstrated any ability for telepathic communication."

"How would you tell?" said Alvisi, continuing to lead the witness.

By now, Jack was expounding as if to a hall full of eager freshmen.

"The idea would be to have the computer select the digits displayed on the screen exactly at random. That way, over thousands and thousand of trials, each digit from zero to nine would be displayed exactly ten percent of the time. And if the person that was trying to receive the thoughts was just guessing, the best he could do would be to be right ten percent of the time."

"How could he even do that well," said Bob, asking the obvious question.

"It would be hard to avoid it," Jack responded with professorial condescension. "One way he could do it is by guessing the same digit all the time."

"Is that as good as he could do—ten percent, I mean—by guessing?" Alvisi injected seriously.

"Right," said Jack, nodding in the affirmative. "If the computer picked the numbers properly, the best he could do is ten percent by guessing. No matter how he guessed; no matter what rule he used. Guessing at random, or always guessing the same number, or whatever. The best he could do would be ten percent if he had no telepathic ability. Thus, if you found two people who consistently scored above ten percent in thousands and thousands of trials, you would have to conclude that they were demonstrating some telepathic ability."

"Isn't that great!" Bob Green enthused. "It's so simple that even I can understand it. All we have to do is test enough volunteers and we're bound to find some with a lot of telepathic ability. Why, the sooner we get started, the sooner—"

"Suppose they all get ten percent," Jack interjected facetiously. "What'll you do then, Bob?"

"Me?" Green responded instantly. "I'll just round up more volunteers. It'll be up to you to find the ones with the ability. Or to teach it to them, or something."

Teach it to them, thought Jack. *Teach someone to have his brain transmit or receive electromagnetic signals?*

Suddenly his thoughts flashed back to the dream on the airplane. To the room without doors in the embassy in Moscow. To the man on the examining table mumbling *garadasrowlscldker*. And, most disturbing of all, to the image of everyone in the room staring at him and saying, "What does it mean, Professor Mason? What does it mean?"

Jack felt the cold sweat and the terror of the nightmare returning. What was he getting involved in? What *was* he involved in? Were they crazy? Or was *he* crazy? Was he losing his mind? He stared off into space with a detached look.

Gradually the smiles disappeared from the faces of Alvisi and Green, and when Bob spoke again, the jovial tone had left his voice.

"Are you okay, old buddy?"

"Ah, yeah, I'm okay," Jack said, trying to sound reassuring. "Just a bad dream I had."

"Well, Professor Mason, you've certainly been a tremendous help to us already," said Alvisi, clearly trying to relieve the tension. "Perhaps we shouldn't take any more of your time today. We'll keep in touch with you. And we hope that you can give us a decision within a few weeks. If you have any further questions about the project, just call me or Bob anytime. Of course, we can't talk about the details on the phone. But we'll be glad to meet with you again at your convenience."

Much to Jack's relief, Frank Alvisi stood up, indicating that the seance was ended. Bob Green began to smile again and injected casually:

"Where are you headed for, old buddy?"

Jack glanced at his watch and responded honestly.

"Well, I don't have a plane until six thirty. I guess I've got some time to kill."

Bob smiled broadly.

"I've got some time too. Why don't I give you a lift to the airport? And we can stop off for a drink on the way."

"Okay. Sounds good to me," Jack replied. "I think I need one."

After taking leave of Frank Alvisi, Jack and Bob used the elevator to reach the parking garage in the basement of the building. Bob led the way to his Fiat Spyder and they soon emerged from the gloom into the welcome sunlight. With a roar and a screech, Bob turned left on Nineteenth and left again on M and headed toward Georgetown. Jack breathed deeply and soaked up the sanity of the warm August afternoon. And, remarkably quickly, thoughts of Frank Alvisi and Project Psi faded from his consciousness.

"Let's hit the penthouse lounge at the Key Bridge Marriott," Bob shouted over the roar of the engine. "The view's good, the drinks are large, and the place will be deserted this time of the afternoon."

Jack was distractedly watching the modish Georgetown scene flash by and nodded his agreement casually.

"Sounds okay to me."

Bob took the turn onto Key Bridge with a long squeal and accelerated with a roar to sixty miles per hour, before frantically braking on the Rosslyn side. He was obviously enjoying himself. Jack was forced to reach for the grab bar as they swung into the Marriott parking lot. Bob reacted with genuine pride.

"Those Pirelli radials really hold the road, don't they?"

The lounge was virtually empty as Bob had predicted. He smiled at the buxom, short-skirted hostess and headed for one of the round leather booths overlooking the Potomac. As they settled in, Bob waved his arm expansively and enthused:

"Look at that city. The Watergate, the Capitol, and, if you look carefully, you can just see the top of the White House."

Jack had to admit that the view was impressive. His eye followed down the Potomac. The cathedral at Georgetown University. The Watergate. The Kennedy Center. The Lincoln and Jefferson Memorials and the Washington Monument. Even the tablets on Roosevelt Island, which he had never seen before, were visible in the foreground.

"Gentlemen?" said the waitress, disrupting their musings.

"Two Bloody Marys," Bob replied without consulting Jack. And then he explained. "They're the specialty of the house. Really large. With a whole stalk of celery and a scallion."

Jack tried idly to visualize this gargantuan Bloody Mary, while continuing to appreciate the view. And Bob began again, this time more reflectively.

"You know, old buddy, the project we were just discussing may sound crazy to you. But out there, in some of those office buildings, people are cooking up schemes that would make our thing look sane and simple in comparison. Why, I remember a senator from the Midwest somewhere. He wanted to corner the world supply of rain by seeding the clouds. That way, we'd have all the food, and the other countries would have to come to us. Now *he* was really a nut."

Jack's mind drifted to the image of a portly senator in a wide-brimmed hat intently watching an Indian rain dance.

"Seriously, old buddy," Bob continued, "I think you've got to put this thing into perspective. For you, a university guy, it sounds crazy. But for me, who's been around Washington, around the intelligence community, it's par for the course. In fact, way above par. This thing has real potential. You've admitted yourself that you can at least conceive of a technical basis for it. And a scientific experiment to start with. And I think you'll have to agree that our vision of the way to use it could have tremendous impact. So, all in all, it sounds pretty good."

Jack mentally substituted *crazy* for *pretty good* in Bob's last sentence. And then he repeated slowly to himself, *It's all crazy. The whole thing is crazy.*

"I think the big thing for you, old buddy," Bob Green said, oblivious of Jack's thoughts, "is to decide if you want to break out, get out of the rut, try something new—something that could be really important."

Bob's words struck home. Jack found himself thinking: *Cats and chimpanzees, they aren't really very important.* He groped for a way to respond.

"You may be right. But think of it this way. What about my lab? And my students? And my reputation?"

For once, Bob saw the opportunity to respond in a logical, fatherly way.

"Well, let's take them one at a time. Your lab would certainly continue to function, even if you spent some of your time in Washington."

Jack had to admit that Bob was probably right. He was important around the lab, he thought, but not indispensable.

"As far as your students are concerned," Bob continued, "aren't there some younger professors who could supervise their work?"

Again, Jack had to agree that there was some truth to what Bob was saying. There was Al Lewis, the young assistant professor who worked with Jack on the chimpanzees. And Dr. Thorberg, from Mass. General, who did the surgery. And as far as most of the younger graduate students were concerned, Barney looked after them pretty well right now. Barney really supervised all the cat-vision stuff, like Sam Klein's work. *In fact,* Jack thought, *the only time I really get involved is when it's time to get our grant renewed at NSF.*

"Now, as far as your reputation is concerned," said Bob, with a chuckle, "I guess it depends on what you believe people think of you now. And how much it matters to you."

Jack had to smile, too. What the hell did it matter what people thought of you? As long as you thought well of yourself.

"Seriously, though," Bob continued, "since this thing is going to be run undercover, no one's going to hear much about it. Particularly, if it isn't successful. And if it is successful, you'll be a hero. Not just to spooks like me, but to scientists all over the world. Why, I'll bet that it will be called the greatest discovery of the latter half of the twentieth century."

Jack smiled at Bob's enthusiasm and naiveté. But he could not reject the idea that successfully demonstrating mental telepathy would be a scientific breakthrough. For an instant, the image flashed into his mind of himself in formal attire delivering his Nobel-prize acceptance speech. He felt strangely comfortable and warm all over. *It must be the king-sized Bloody Marys,* he thought, with a smile.

7

Hooked

Sue and Jack Mason lingered at the table after dinner. The children had been excused and had gone off to the family room to watch TV. Jack sipped his coffee pensively and searched for a way to discuss Project Psi with his wife.

"I have an offer to work part time with some people in Washington," he finally ventured.

"Oh?" she responded, instantly feeling threatened. "Doing what?"

"Helping them start a new project. Sort of related to the work my lab does."

"Helping who?"

"Well, ah, do you remember that fellow Green that I told you about? The guy I met during the Korean War. The pilot."

"The one who minded everyone else's business on the ship?" Sue said, with a frown.

Jack smiled and nodded in the affirmative.

"Yeah, that's the guy. Bob Green. He always knew what was going on. Who was cheating on the football pool. And who got scared and dropped his bombs in the water instead of on the target."

"Why would you want to get involved with a nut like that?" she said, with surprising vehemence.

"Well, he's working for the government now," Jack continued, trying to explain. "And they want to start a new project. They think that I'm the guy to tell them how to get it going."

"How can it make any sense with a guy like Green involved?" she persisted.

"He's not in charge or anything," Jack replied defensively. "He just got the idea for the project from some things I told him about ESP."

"ESP," Sue responded, more positively. She had long had an interest in things like astrology and handwriting analysis, but Jack had always said that they were bunk.

"I thought there was nothing to that stuff?" she continued.

"I think that's right," Jack said. "But Bob kept after me. With things like pyramid power. So I started to do some reading."

"Pyramid power?" Sue repeated, her curiosity aroused.

"Yeah," Jack replied, nodding in the affirmative. "There's this guy who believes that things the shape of the Great Pyramid have extraordinary powers. He wrote a book, and Bob read it."

For the first time in quite a while, Sue Mason found their after-dinner conversation actually interesting.

"The Great Pyramid?" she asked. "In Egypt? How does it work?"

"I don't think it works at all," Jack said with a smile. "But, in his book, this guy recounts all the wonderful things that pyramid power can do."

"Like what?" she enquired.

"Well, you know those little paper cones that people put over seedlings in the garden?" Jack asked.

"Yes," she nodded.

"This guy says that if you make them the shape of the Great Pyramid, with a square base instead of a round one, the seeds grow faster."

"They do?" Sue said quizzically, her smile broadening.

"That's what he says," Jack confirmed.

"But *you* don't believe it?"

"No, I don't," Jack replied firmly.

Sue nodded her understanding of her husband's scientific stodginess and then began to chuckle.

"Well, we could try it next spring. That's the scientific method, isn't it?"

Jack smiled back at her broadly.

"I guess so," he responded.

"But Green doesn't work for the Department of Agriculture, does he?" Sue continued, half seriously.

"No," said Jack, laughing out loud. "He just likes to read about all sorts of occult stuff. The thing he got me interested in is ESP. You know, people who can predict what's going to happen or can make objects jump off the table or can tell you the order of the cards in a deck."

"I read a novel like that once," Sue said, with genuine interest. "About this woman who kept having premonitions that people were going to die. And they did."

"Yes," Jack responded, nodding his head in agreement. "There are a lot of stories like that around. And not just in novels. But also in supposedly factual accounts. I looked at a few of them in the library and—"

"So what does Green want *you* to do?" Sue injected, frowning again.

"He's interested in telepathy," Jack answered. "The possibility that signals might be communicated between people's minds."

"They might be?" she said, incredulously. "You believe that?"

"I'm not sure," Jack replied, a little defensively. "When I started reading, I thought it was all bunk. And the more I read, the more convinced I became that I was right."

"What changed your mind?"

"Well, I decided to do some calculations."

"Oh!" she said, with a smile.

"Yeah," Jack continued. "I did some, and so did Barney. The numbers came out very small. But maybe not *impossibly* small, if the two people's heads are close enough together."

"So, you believe it could happen?" Sue said, with widening eyes.

"I'm not sure," Jack answered honestly. And then he continued with emphasis that surprised even him. "But I think an experiment should be done. A scientific experiment."

"And that's what Green is interested in?" she asked, slightly perplexed.

"Yes, that's right," Jack answered, without offering an explanation.

"It sounds fascinating," Sue concluded, sincerely.

Jack smiled. Perhaps the idea wasn't so crazy after all.

The next evening, as Jack and Sue were driving home from the theater, the conversation again turned to Bob Green. Sue's curiosity had been aroused.

"This guy, Green," she asked, without preliminaries. "Who does he work for?"

Jack was taken by surprise, and he didn't know how to answer.

"Well, er, I'm not quite sure," he demurred. "I think he has something to do with intelligence."

"Intelligence?" Sue said with a frown. "You mean spies?"

"Oh, no. Not spies," Jack replied defensively. "He's some kind of analyst or administrator or something."

"It sounds fishy to me," she continued, firmly. "What does a guy like that want with someone like you?"

"Well," said Jack hesitantly, "I told him about the calculations that Barney and I did. And about the possibility for an experiment. And he got very excited."

"Excited?" she repeated. "About what?"

"Well, er, ah, I'm not supposed to talk about it," Jack answered with obvious embarrassment. "But basically, he thinks that if the experiment were successful, it could lead to a method of gathering intelligence."

"Sort of superspies?" she said with a smile.

Jack had to smile, too.

"Yeah, that's the idea."

"Well, I knew it would be crazy with that guy Green involved," Sue replied emphatically. "Why, I can see it now. He's probably thinking about an army of these guys. Wandering around all over the world reading people's minds."

"Not an army," Jack injected, "just a few in the right places."

"Right places?" she repeated, with a frown.

"Yes," Jack affirmed and then, without really thinking about it, spilled the beans. "Like summit meetings and that sort of thing."

"Summit meetings! Sue exclaimed, the whole thing suddenly clear to her. "I knew it was crazy. Why the next thing you know he'll want to have one of these people, a woman I guess, in the premier's bedroom."

They both laughed out loud.

"This is the best story I've heard in a long time," Sue continued, her aggressiveness gone now that she knew the secret. "You're finally beginning to meet some interesting people in Washington. Not just those stodgy old scientists."

"Yeah," Jack agreed with a smile. "The trouble is that Green is serious. And he's convinced a lot of other people to take the thing seriously, too."

"Serious?" Sue repeated incredulously, her smile disappearing.

"Yes, that's right," Jack nodded. "They're serious. About the project and about trying to get me to head it up."

"Well, they're nuts," she said, firmly. "And you're crazy to listen to them. Why do you have anything to do with these people?"

That's a good question, Jack thought. *Why do I have anything to do with them?*

"Well, I'm really not sure why. It all started accidentally in the beginning. At least I think it did."

Sue frowned her disbelief, and Jack continued, trying to explain his predicament to both of them.

"Green left a message at my hotel when I was at that conference in Washington back in May. And you know how it is, an old friend shows up and wants to get together. Well, from then on, it just grew. He got me interested in reading about ESP. And then Barney and I made the calculations. And then I thought of the experiment and told Green about it."

Sue nodded her understanding, but said nothing. Jack sat pensively for a moment too, but then exclaimed with sudden vehemence.

"That was my mistake! I knew he was a nut. I never should have told him about the experiment. And now—"

"And now, you're hooked," she injected, with a trace of sarcasm.

Hooked, thought Jack. *Like an addict? Hooked on what? Curiosity? Power? A chance to get out of the rut?*

"Not exactly hooked," he replied, searching for an intellectual way out, "but I guess it's fair to say that I'm involved."

"Hooked! Involved! What's the difference?" Sue responded emphatically. "They both add up to the same thing. These nuts

60

have you believing in their scheme. And the biggest joke of all is that they've got you convinced that you thought of it yourself. That it's *your* idea!"

A sudden chill ran through Jack's body. Could she be right? Was Green conning him? Was it conceivable that Green knew about the experiment, or something like it, all the time? And the use. The man with psi. Was that Green's plan all along?

Jack stared blank-faced at the road in front of the car and continued to ponder his dilemma silently.

Had he been fooled? Could he admit that he had been fooled? He was still wrestling with these questions when Sue resumed the conversation softly.

"I don't know, Jack, it seems simple to me. These guys are nuts, and you should stay away from them. All this stuff they've probably been giving you about the strength of the nation and the quest for world peace, it's all bullshit. They just want to make you feel important, so you'll do what they want."

Jack was still silent.

How did Sue know the kind of arguments that Alvisi and Green had been using on him? It was almost as if she had read his mind.

Seeing that she was on the right track, Sue delivered the coup de grâce.

"Why, if you really want to do something for the good of the nation—the taxpayers—write to your congressman or to the *Washington Post*. All you have to do is tell them what these nuts are up to, and you'll be a hero all right, at least to people like me."

8

The President Believes?

As Jack drove down Memorial Drive toward the Institute the next morning, the conversation with Sue the previous evening played over and over in his mind. When he thought about it logically, Sue's contention that Green had conned him seemed convincing. It was hard to believe that the events of the last few months had occurred spontaneously. Believing that, he thought, with a smile, would be like believing that someone who claims the powers of psychokinesis can really manipulate objects at a distance.

Jack mentally reviewed the sequence of events that had led to his involvement in Project Psi. Certainly Green had initiated their original meeting by leaving the note at Jack's hotel. And Green had raised the subject of ESP. And told him about pyramid power. And pressed him to do some reading. But how could Green have been sure where it would lead him? After all, he had rejected everything he had read. At least almost everything. And it finally came down to mental telepathy over very short distances being the only ESP phenomenon that might have a chance of really existing. How could Green have known where he would end up? *If he knew that,* Jack thought, shaking his head, *he must have the power to see or influence the future course of events. Some strange mixture of clairvoyance and psychokinesis.*

When Jack returned to his office after giving a lecture at about 10:30, his secretary greeted him cheerily with an announcement:

"Those guys in Washington called you again, Professor Mason. It's a new one this time. A Mr. MacFarland. He wasn't as mysterious as the others; the secretary left his name and telephone number."

MacFarland, MacFarland, Jack repeated as he went into his office. He thought he had heard the name somewhere before. From Bob Green? Or maybe he had read it in the paper. In one of those *Washington Post* stories about the intelligence community.

"Did they say what he wanted, Marcia?" Jack called back through the open door.

"No, just asked that you return the call."

Jack decided that MacFarland must be some kind of wheel in the intelligence apparatus. Apparently Frank Alvisi was trying to put the pressure on by getting the boss to give him a call. Jack decided to wait them out for a while.

A couple of hours later, when Jack got back from lunch, Marcia jumped up from behind her desk and began excitedly.

"Professor Mason! Professor Mason! It's very important that you call Mr. MacFarland back this afternoon. He has to go to the White House tomorrow!"

"The White House!" Jack repeated with surprise. *This little joke of theirs is getting out of hand,* he said to himself.

"Slow down, Marcia, slow down! Exactly what did he say?"

"It was his secretary. I got it all down," she continued breathlessly, reaching for her stenographer's notebook.

" 'It is very important that Mr. MacFarland speak with Professor Mason this afternoon. Mr. MacFarland has to meet with General Ryan at the White House tomorrow morning, and he needs Professor Mason's advice on one of the subjects they will discuss. Mr. MacFarland will be in his office until at least six o'clock this evening. Please urge Professor Mason to call him as soon as possible.' "

Boy, Jack thought, *they don't fool around. How can you refuse to return a call like that.*

"I guess we'd better call him back," he said, with a smile.

Marcia was already dialing, and Jack went into his office and picked up the extension.

"Professor Mason?" said an official-sounding secretary. "Just a moment for Mr. MacFarland."

Jack nodded, but did not reply.

"Professor Mason, this is Bryan MacFarland. Thanks a lot for returning my call. I need your help with a problem."

"A problem?" Jack said innocently. "What problem?"

"The thing you've been discussing with Alvisi," MacFarland responded, coming right to the point. "We think your idea is really great. Even Sam Ryan's interested."

My God, thought Jack, *they've got the president's chief of staff convinced. This thing is spreading like wildfire. And the fact that it's bullshit doesn't matter.*

As Jack groped for a response, Brian MacFarland continued the pep talk.

"As you know, we're very anxious to get you to head this thing up. Everyone tells us you're the best man for the job. Tomorrow morning I've got to give Sam Ryan a rundown on our progress to date. And I would very much like to tell him that we have you signed up."

"Wait a second, Mr. MacFarland," Jack injected a little nervously. "You're going too fast. Signed up for *what*? To do *what*?"

"Okay, Professor," Brian MacFarland responded jovially. "I realize this thing's moving kind of fast for you. But, unfortunately, that's the way things go in Washington. You've got to strike while the iron is hot. While people at the top are interested. And what we'd like out of you right now goes something like this. The way we see it, the experiment you have suggested is crucial. If it's successful, we go ahead. If not, this was just another hot idea that didn't pan out. So, in the beginning, what we want you to do is plan the experiment. And tell us how to carry it out."

Well, thought Jack, *at least this guy is smart enough to consider the possibility that the experiment might not work. I guess the guys at the top are a little brighter than the ones down below.*

"Look, Mr. MacFarland, I understand, I think, the kind of pressure you're under. But it's a big decision for me, too. Whether or not to get involved in something like this."

"I understand, Professor," Brian MacFarland responded. And then he continued in a disarmingly persuasive way. "Try thinking about it like this. You've been conducting basic research for a number of years now under government sponsorship, through NSF and the like. Now there's a chance to take the base that you've built and apply it to something that's really important for the nation. You read the papers. You know how

64

important world peace is to the president. Now, if this project, your idea, could contribute to the president's quest for world peace, you would have made an invaluable contribution."

Jack felt overwhelmed. The words were so grand, particularly in comparison with the idea. And he seemed to be the only one who was out of step. Green believes, Alvisi believes, MacFarland believes, and even Sam Ryan believes. *God knows,* Jack thought, *maybe the president believes.* Who was he to tell them they were all crazy? Maybe he was just too timid. Didn't have enough faith in his own idea. He fumbled for a reply.

"It certainly sounds important, the way you put it, Mr. MacFarland. My problem is that I'm not sure that it will work."

"Don't let that bother you, Professor," MacFarland replied matter-of-factly. "Neither are we. The important thing is to try. To see if it works. Because, if it does, we've gained a tremendous new tool. And if it doesn't, all we've lost is a little time and money. So don't let the possibility that it won't work bother you. Why, if anyone should worry about that, it's me. I'm paying the bills!"

Jack felt trapped. How could he refuse a request to serve his country with no strings attached? Especially when the experiment would be scientifically interesting.

"Well, ah, okay, Mr. MacFarland. Suppose we leave it like this. I'm willing to serve as a scientific advisor to the project. But I'd prefer that you didn't tell anyone that I've agreed to head it up, at least not yet."

"Excellent, Professor Mason! Excellent!" Brian MacFarland concluded, with genuine enthusiasm. "You're just the kind of responsible scientist I was told you were. Why, if everyone in the academic community was as patriotic and easy to work with as you are, I'd have a lot fewer problems. Maybe it's because you're an ex-navy man. I am myself, you know. Well, anyhow, thanks again. We'll be keeping in touch with you."

Ex-navy man, Jack thought. *How did he know that? Could Green have told him? Not likely. I'll bet Green's never spoken to him. They must have been looking into my background. So Sue's right. They are manipulating me. As part of some grand scheme.*

After stewing about it for more than a week, Jack decided to try discussing the possibility of his becoming involved in a

Washington project with some of the people around the lab and the Institute. Perhaps, being academic types, they would reinforce his gut feeling that it was dangerous. He decided to start with Barney O'Neil because he would be the easiest. They had discussed ESP several times while Jack was reading the literature, and, of course, they had made the calculations that led to the experiment. Also, his discussions with Barney had started before Jack signed the security oath. So perhaps that was better with respect to the "administrative sanctions" and "criminal penalties"—whatever the hell they were—for revealing Project Psi information to unauthorized people.

Jack found Barney in one of the labs with Sam Klein. They were discussing a new dissection technique with Olaf Thorberg, the surgeon who was assisting them with the cat-vision experiments. The goal of the procedure was to isolate specific fibers within the optic tectum. This had to be done reliably and routinely, if accurate conclusions were to be drawn concerning the nerve interconnections behind the retina.

Jack listened politely for a while and then, at a lull in the conversation, spoke quietly to O'Neil.

"Say, Barney, can I see you in my office sometime this afternoon?"

"Sure," O'Neil responded with a puzzled expression. "What can I do for you?"

"Let's talk about it later," Jack said mysteriously and slipped from the room.

Barney looked at him strangely for a moment and then enthusiastically returned to the discussion of dissection of the cat's optic tectum.

Later on that afternoon, Barney O'Neil's cherubic face appeared in the doorway of Jack's office.

"What's the mystery? Did somebody cut our budget?"

"Come on in, Barney," Jack responded with a smile, "and close the door."

The perplexed look returned to Barney's face.

"What's the trouble, Jack?"

"No trouble," Jack assured him, smiling again. "I'd just like to talk something over with you and get your advice."

Barney brightened up. He liked being asked for his advice, particularly by Jack.

"You know me, full of free advice. And every bit of it worth what you pay for it."

"Seriously, Barney," Jack continued, "I'd like you to keep this conversation in confidence. Not discuss it with anyone."

Barney became sober again, at least as much as an open-faced, good-natured Irishman could.

"Sure, Jack. Serious. And confidential. What's the problem? Shoot!"

"Well," Jack began tentatively, "do you remember those calculations we did about the electromagnetic field as a possible basis for mental telepathy?"

Barney brightened up again.

"Yeah, vaguely. You got a micro-microvolt, and I got a micro-micro-microvolt. And we both laughed and agreed that the signal was certainly pretty goddamned small."

"Right," Jack agreed, smiling too. "But remember the idea for the experiment with the two heads close together?"

"Oh, yeah," Barney nodded. "You started out with those two heads that looked like eggs on either side of your pad at Sam Klein's seminar. And I kidded you about eggheads. And then later, you showed me a drawing of this funny chair. With two people seated back to back, but with their heads next to each other, side to side. And you said—"

"Right," Jack confirmed. "That's the experiment. The trouble is that people are taking it seriously."

"People?" Barney frowned. "Who?"

"Well, I can't go into details," Jack evaded, "but it's some people in Washington."

"NSF?" Barney persisted.

"No," Jack responded, shaking his head. "Some other people in the government."

Barney's brow wrinkled.

"Why are they taking it seriously? Did you convince them?"

Jack smiled sardonically.

"No, it was the other way around. They're the ones who are hot to do the experiment."

"Why?" Barney asked incredulously. "It hasn't got a snowball's chance in hell of working. Why, I'll bet that in a hour, I could write down half a dozen sources of electrical noise that are much larger than the biggest signal you could expect."

Finally Jack's face brightened, too.

"Do you think you could? That would be a big help. In fact, if you could take a little time and do a few calculations to support your assertions, that would be even better."

"Sure," said Barney, with a smile. "It'll be kind of fun. I'll redo the signal calculation too, including the quasi-static magnetic field. For two brains as close together as possible."

"Great!" Jack responded. "Thank's a lot, Barney. You've been a big help already."

Barney's cherubic look returned. He ambled out of Jack's office in his normal good-natured way and then stopped at Marcia's desk for a parting shot.

"You know me, Jack. Anything to keep the boss out of trouble."

Jack had never liked going to department meetings very much, and this one was likely to be worse than most. The department head, Peter Fry, was seated docilely at a table at the front of the seminar room. About half the professors in the electrical engineering department and a goodly smattering of instructors and teaching assistants sat randomly around the room facing generally in Fry's direction. Jack sat in the back near the door so as to be able to beat a polite retreat when the pettiness of the discussion and the boredom of its length became intolerable.

Fry had been third choice as department head. Two strong groups had desired control, and each had put forward a strong partisan as its candidate. But in the end, neither group was willing to let the other take over and, in the inevitable way of universities, a compromise was sought.

Peter Fry had emerged as acceptable to both groups. He bore no strong allegiance to either, had no clear concept of a direction for the department, and generally avoided serious problems or difficult decisions. His stewardship was rather like that of a fool king pretending to rule a group of strong-willed dukes. As long as he did not oppose any of their pet schemes, they all would dutifully praise his fine new suits of clothes. And, when two of them became locked in conflict, he would retire from the field to await news of the outcome, brought in whispered tones by the minor barons and pages of the department.

At the moment, the discussion concerned the department's core curriculum, that minimum set of courses that an undergraduate student had to take to receive a degree in electrical engineering. A young, eager assistant professor had just finished an impassioned presentation to the effect that his new course should be made part of the core curriculum.

Jack smiled to himself during the presentation and watched the facial expressions of the older professors present whose courses were already part of the core curriculum. What they knew, but the young professor had not yet perceived, was that one of *their* courses would have to be dropped from the core curriculum were his to be added. Furtive glances and knowing smiles sealed the alliance. One by one, seemingly spontaneously, they probed the young man's position for weakness.

Jack was mildly amused watching the uneven battle unfold. The experienced hands quickly had their outnumbered colleague on the defensive. Yes, he had to admit, parts of his course were included in existing core curriculum subjects. No, his new book would not be ready for the fall semester. Soon the clang of battle axes was heard, and all that remained to be anticipated was the final moan of the vanquished. Jack was disgusted by their performance and by his own silent acquiescence.

With the day's victim dispatched, the meeting began to break up. It had been so long since Jack had stayed to the end of one of these affairs that it suddenly occurred to him that it might be an opportune time to talk to Peter Fry, to plant the seed that he might be spending some time in Washington. Not that Fry's personal reaction mattered much. But he was sure to tell the dukes, and their responses were of considerable concern. Would they try to dismember Jack's lab in his absence? Or would they simply regard his temporary withdrawal from the lists as lessening the risks in their own situations?

Jack moved to the front of the room where Peter Fry sat disconsolately, head in hands, ashamed of his colleagues behavior and his own lack of leadership.

"Peter," Jack quietly said, "have you got a minute?"

Fry looked up and was obviously surprised to see that it was Jack. He almost smiled.

"Sure, Jack, pull up a chair."

Jack was uncertain how to begin.

"I have a new opportunity that I'd like to discuss with you."

The color drained from Peter Fry's face.

"You're leaving us?"

Jack smiled to himself and hastened to repair the damage.

"Oh, no. Nothing like that. It's just a chance for some additional responsibility. A project in Washington."

Fry perked up noticeably.

"Washington," he repeated and immediately thought of the department's dwindling research budget. "Washington! That's very good. Are you being made head of a panel or something?"

"Not exactly," Jack replied, disingenuously. "They're asking me to help them get a new project started. A project in perceptual research. They seem to think that I have a good reputation."

"You do. You certainly do," Fry agreed. "And I'm glad to see that those bureaucrats in Washington have finally come to realize what I've know all along."

"Well, thank you, Peter," Jack replied, continuing the charade. "It's good to know that you have such confidence in me."

"Now, this project?" Fry persisted, almost eagerly. "How big will it be? And what part will your lab play in it?"

The question caught Jack off guard. What part would his lab play in Project Psi? He hadn't thought of it playing any part at all. But perhaps Fry had made a good suggestion. A way for Jack to have his cake and eat it, too.

"Well, I'm not sure," he offered, not untruthfully. "We haven't gotten that far yet. Things are just in the planning stage."

Peter Fry was actually smiling now.

"You're in on the planning phase, eh? That's good. Excellent! You can work the lab's participation right into the project plan."

"That's a clever idea," Jack said. "I hadn't thought about it that way."

"Well, you should, you certainly should. And keep me informed, Jack. Please, keep me informed. And if you need any help, don't hesitate to call on me."

70

"Oh, I won't." Jack said, trying not to smile. "You've been a lot of help already."

Jack turned to leave, but Peter Fry added a telling final remark.

"Thanks, Jack. Thanks a lot. You've really made my day."

9

Hoagie Machinists

About a week after his conversation with Peter Fry, Jack was working in his office when he received another call from Frank Alvisi. When Jack picked up the receiver, Alvisi got right to the point.

"Professor Mason? Frank Alvisi. I thought you'd like to know that we got an initial budget approved for the project. Five million. Pretty good, if I do say so myself."

To Jack, who had never had a grant larger than $600,000, five million sounded pretty good indeed. He immediately thought that Peter Fry would think so, too.

"You certainly work fast, Frank," Jack responded, trying to sound nonchalant.

"Yeah," Alvisi replied, "you know the saying, got to strike while the iron is hot. Now, what I want to talk to you about is this. We've got to get started fast, now that we've got the money. Because if we don't get going, somebody will have second thoughts about giving us this much. So what we want to do is to have a planning meeting as soon as possible. You and Bob and me and maybe MacFarland. But you're the most important person. We've got to have you there. When can you make it?"

Jack fumbled for a response, still unsure of how involved he really wanted to be.

"Well, er, I haven't any plans to be in Washington in the near future."

"How about next week?" Alvisi persisted. "We've got to get moving. We'll pick up the tab, of course."

"Next week?" Jack replied, defensively. "Well, I, ah, teach on Monday, Wednesday, and Friday. How about Tuesday?"

"Fine," Alvisi concluded, forcefully. "Tuesday it is. How about first thing? Say, nine-thirty?"

Jack felt trapped again. When the conversation started, he had intended to beg off. But now he found himself agreeing.

"Okay, first thing Tuesday. At your office?"

"No, we've been getting a head start on a new place, and I think you should see it," Alvisi responded. "Let me tell you how to get there."

"Uh, okay," Jack grunted, putting down the receiver and reaching for a pad and a pencil. "Okay, go ahead."

"The best thing for you to do is to rent a car at National," Alvisi began. "When you leave the airport, take 95 South to the Beltway. Then go north on the Beltway for three exits and get off on Gallows Road heading in toward Washington."

Jack frantically sketched a map on the pad in front of him, while Alvisi continued his rapid-fire description.

"You'll see a shopping center and a bunch of office buildings on the right. There's a new, fairly tall building in the back—glass with white fake stone—that's the one we're in. Take the elevator up to the sixth floor, and we'll meet you there."

"Okay," said Jack, unwilling to admit his confusion. "I'll see you next Tuesday."

"Okay, Professor Mason," Frank Alvisi ended the conversation jovially. "Thanks a lot. You're sure an easy guy to work with."

Only later, when he went to record the appointment with Alvisi on the calendar in his briefcase, did Jack realize that next Tuesday was the thirty-first of October—Halloween.

That afternoon, Jack could not resist calling Peter Fry and telling him about the planning meeting and the five-million-dollar budget. As he expected, Fry was quite impressed.

"You certainly work fast, Jack," he said, with wonderment. But then, unexpectedly, he threw a curve. "How much of the five million are you going to try to get for your lab?"

"Ah, I'm really not sure," Jack said, not untruthfully. "How much do you think I should ask for?"

"Well," Fry responded, "if they think you're the key man, they should be willing to give you more than half. If I were you, I'd ask for three and see what they say."

"Good idea," Jack politely agreed. "You sure know how to handle these administrative things, Peter."

"Well, I've got to be good for something around here," Fry said, with a half-hearted chuckle. "And I guess that's it."

"Okay, Peter," Jack concluded. "Thanks again for the advice. Good-bye."

Jack felt rather sheepish for having let Fry deceive himself. *But,* he thought, *I've got to do something to protect my lab and my people while I'm fooling around with this thing in Washington. And letting Fry dream about three million dollars ought to help.*

Jack found the office building described by Frank Alvisi with less trouble than he had expected. It clearly was brand new, and men were still working on the parking lot and part of the lobby. The only clue to the presence of Project Psi was a cryptic listing in the building directory, "U.S. Government, Floors 6–9."

Jack shook his head. *They sure don't fool around,* he thought. *Four floors in a brand new office building. That's the government, I guess. They don't know what they're doing, but they've got the office space.*

When he got off the elevator on the sixth floor, Jack was confronted by an armed guard and a young woman seated behind a battered steel desk.

"I'm Professor Mason," Jack announced defensively. "I'm here to see Mr. Alvisi."

"Oh, yes, Professor Mason," the receptionist responded, clearly impressed. "We've been expecting you."

She opened one of the squeaky desk drawers, reached inside, and, to Jack's surprise, produced a badge with his name and picture on it. Holding it up for his inspection, she asked solicitously:

"How do you like it?"

Jack did a double take. Where had they gotten his picture? It looked sort of like his last passport photo, or perhaps the picture he had sent in with the registration form for the Third International Conference on Perceptual Research.

"Oh, it's fine," he answered weakly. "Just fine."

"If you'll sign this receipt," she continued, "you can keep it. That way you can come and go whenever you please. Just wear it whenever you're in the facility. But when you go outside, keep it out of sight."

Jack nodded as if the instructions were old hat, but his perplexed look revealed otherwise. He took the pen she was proferring and signed the receipt, and then self-consciously fumbled with the badge, at last managing to clip it to the pocket of his tweed jacket.

"I'll give Mr. Green a call, and he'll come out and get you," the receptionist concluded. "We're still kind of shorthanded."

Moments later, Bob Green entered the sixth-floor lobby through the closed door behind the guard.

"Hi, old buddy," he greeted Jack cheerfully. "I see that Susie's gotten you all fixed up."

"Hi, Bob," Jack responded with a smile, glad to see a face he recognized.

"Come on, old buddy," Green jovially continued. "I'll give you the fifty-cent tour before we get down to business."

The guard reopened the door, which sported an impressive-looking combination lock, and admitted them to the interior. To Jack's considerable surprise, it appeared to be largely unfinished. Lighting fixtures hung from the ceiling, and air-conditioning ducts were exposed. Here and there the studs were up for interior walls, and in a few places the framing had begun to be covered with Sheetrock.

"It doesn't look like much right now," Bob offered, by way of explanation. "We've only been in here about a month."

"What's all the space for?" Jack finally blurted out.

"Well, let me give you a rundown," Green responded nonchalantly. "The sixth floor, the one we're on right now, will have the general administrative offices and the preliminary subject screening areas. This floor will be the place where we deal with the public, so to speak. No nonproject personnel will be allowed above this floor. If they try to go to a higher floor," he concluded with a chuckle, "the elevator will just stop at six anyway."

Jack envisioned a carload of perplexed passengers being shanghaied by the robot elevator, while Green enthusiastically continued his description.

"The seventh floor, the one directly above, will be our real lab space. You know, electronic assembly and testing areas, a small machine shop, and things like photography and chemistry labs if we need them."

"What do you need all those fabrication facilities for?" Jack said, shaking his head. "Why not just get a bunch of job shops to build the stuff you need?"

Bob Green grinned broadly.

"Come on, old buddy. How long do you think it would take the Russians to figure out what we're doing if we went down and ordered a bunch of those funny two-person chairs of yours?"

Jack smiled too, acknowledging his own naiveté, and Bob continued, pointing upward through the ceiling.

"The eighth floor will be mostly staff offices and advanced testing areas. Each of the professionals, PhDs, MDs, et cetera, will have his own office. And they'll be arranged in groups of three or four sharing a secretary. Then we thought we'd need some space for advanced testing, perhaps psychological interviews or drug effects evaluations or things like that. That's one of the areas where we'd like to get some advice from you. Some thoughts on how much space we should set aside for various activities."

"Look, Bob, don't you think you're overdoing it a bit?" Jack said, frowning. "All this space, when the first experiment may be a complete flop."

"That's the way the game is played, old buddy," Green replied wryly. "If we ask for the space on the come, before the first experiment, while the outcome is still in doubt, they'll give it to us. Almost any amount we want. Because they don't know how much we need and neither do we. But if we wait until after the first experiment, particularly if it isn't so successful, they'll nickel-and-dime us to death. You know, they'll say, 'Now let's see, you did the first experiment in a thousand square feet, so you can't need more than five thousand square feet for the second round.' So the way to avoid all that is to get all you can in the beginning. Before anybody really knows what it takes."

Jack found himself frowning and shaking his head at the same time. But Bob only smiled at his reaction and continued the description with undiminished enthusiasm.

"The best is yet to come. The ninth floor. That's where we'll deal with the customer. You know, agency heads and cabinet officers and White House assistants. It's important in dealing with those guys to give the right impression. If your conference room is crummy, they'll assume that the project is crummy, too. We'll have a fully certified, secure conference room. With a table that seats twenty and additional chairs for twenty more. And all the standard projection systems for visual aids: viewgraphs, movies, slides, and an opaque projector. And a complete sound system, with a recording capability, just in case."

Jack had given up. He just stood, shaking his head and listening to his old friend in open-mouthed disbelief.

"And your office suite will be up there too, of course. You'll have a corner office with plenty of windows. And then, across the hall, a small secure conference room for staff meetings and sensitive discussions. And you'll have a private secretary, with her own office."

Jack finally had to speak up. He felt like Alice being given a prospective tour of Wonderland.

"Look, Bob, can't we back up for a minute and talk about some simple, technical things? Like what the first experiment might look like. And what kind of people ought to be involved in doing it."

"Right," Bob responded, sensing Jack's discomfort. "Good idea, old buddy. That's what we really got you down here for today, anyhow. I guess I went a little overboard with the description. But I'm sort of proud of the place. Come on, we've got a small conference room fixed up enough that we can use it. Frank's down there with one of our administrative assistants—a personnel type. We've got some paperwork we'd like you to look over."

Bob headed off down what was apparently to become a hallway and Jack followed, his gaze aimlessly searching the maze of wires and ducts for some clue to reality.

At the end of the corridor-to-be, they came to an area where most of the interior walls had been erected. After passing through several normal doors, they reached one that displayed a large combination lock. Bob reached his hand into a small metal box on the wall and pushed a series of buttons in a certain sequence. The cypher lock responded to the correct combination electronically, and the bolt barring the door snapped open. Bob grasped the knob with his right hand and opened the door wide, gesturing expansively with his left for Jack to step inside.

Frank Alvisi and a younger man in shirt-sleeves were seated at a makeshift conference table strewn with papers, folders, and blueprints. Alvisi smiled and rose to shake Jack's hand.

"Hi, Professor Mason. It's good to see you. You'll have to excuse the mess we're in."

"I gave Jack the fifty-cent tour," Bob Green injected. "And now he's anxious to get down to business."

"Professor Mason, I'd like you to meet Bill Wilson," Alvisi continued. "Bill's trying to help us get our staffing request straightened out. That's one of the first things we'd like to talk over with you."

The man in shirt sleeves rose and extended his hand to Jack.

"Pleased to meet you, Professor Mason. Frank and Bob have told me a lot about you. All good."

"Nice to meet you too, Bill," Jack replied. "Flattery will get you everywhere."

"Well, that's the way you get along when you're an administrative assistant," Wilson said with a chuckle.

The others joined the general laughter, and they all sat down around the table.

"Bill, show Professor Mason the staff authorization request," Frank Alvisi began.

Wilson searched among the papers in front of him and finally slid one across the table to Jack, who picked up the sheet and began reading.

Special Project 8127

31 October 1967

To: Director of Special Projects
Subject: Initial Project 8127 Personnel Requirements

In order to accomplish established objectives and within its approved budget, Project 8127 hereby requests authority to hire the following professional personnel beginning immediately.

1. Three (3) clinical psychologists (PhD)
2. One (1) internist (MD)
3. One (1) neurophysiologist (MD)
4. Two (2) physicists (PhD)
5. Three (3) electrical engineers (PhD)
6. Five (5) electrical engineers (MS/BS)
7. Two (2) statisticians (PhD)
8. Four (4) statistical analysts (BS)
9. Two (2) computer scientists (PhD)
10. Four (4) senior computer programmers (BS)

Additional personnel requirements will be forwarded for approval as the need is determined.

John W. Mason
Technical Director

Jack stopped reading abruptly when he saw the signature block. When he looked up, he found Green and Alvisi staring at him apprehensively.

"Where did all these numbers of people come from?" Jack enquired sarcastically. "Out of thin air?"

A barely perceptible smile came over Bob Green's face. He knew they had won. Jack had chosen to question the details of the staffing requirements rather than the fundamental issue of whether or not he would lead the project.

"Right," Bob responded agreeably. "It's just a bogey to be shot at. Frank and I gave Bill some numbers, the best we could, and he put together a draft memo. What we'd like you to do is mark it up or change the numbers any way you want."

"I'm not sure I know how to," Jack answered, still a little annoyed. "I don't understand where the numbers or the kinds of people came from in the first place."

"Well, ah, that's a good question," Bob conceded, a little embarrassed. "I just tried to think about what this place would be like six months from now. What kind of people we'd need on the staff. I thought we'd have a bunch of volunteers from around the intelligence community coming in for initial screening—in several pairs of your two-person chairs—kind of like a queer barber shop."

"Or a barber shop for queers," Frank Alvisi injected.

They all laughed, and the tension was relieved. Even within the intelligence community, the notoriety received by a few homosexuals who had defected was the source of gallows humor.

"And then I thought we'd have a few people, the ones who showed some psi ability, undergoing some kind of advanced testing," Bob Green continued more confidently. "I didn't know what the testing would be, but I figured you would. In addition, I thought we'd need enough guys to design the electrical and mechanical equipment. And to run the computer and analyze the data. So I just estimated what I thought it would take. How many of each kind of person. Bill's got another memo on nonprofessional personnel: machinists, technicians, computer operators—"

"The numbers sure look high to me," Jack interjected, shaking his head.

"Remember, Professor, the project will have to do almost everything internally," Alvisi responded. "You can't maintain security in a thing like this if you send out for much of anything. Even sandwiches," he added with a chuckle.

Bob Green and Bill Wilson smiled broadly, encouraging Frank to continue with the story.

"Why, I remember the time when a guy from the Soviet embassy was keeping track of the numbers of different kinds of sandwiches that went into one of our buildings downtown from a takeout place across the street," Alvisi recounted, beginning the tale.

Jack joined in the general laughter, and, with this further encouragement, Frank continued.

"Apparently the KBG guy thought he had found some correlation between the kind of job that someone does and the sandwich he orders."

More general laughter ensued.

"I forget the details," Alvisi said with a smile, "but it happened something like this. I think one of our guys overheard him in a phone booth, or something. Scientists liked roast beef or ham and Swiss. But medical doctors always wanted lean meat. You know, like lean corned beef. I guess they were worried about cholesterol. Secretaries were always on a diet. They went for cottage cheese. Or tuna salad on lettuce. But the working troops, they were the ones who really knew how to eat. The computer operators and the electronic technicians went for pizza, with everything. You know, pepperoni, onions, mushrooms, peppers, olive oil—the works!"

Jack and Bob began to guffaw almost uncontrollably. And even Frank Alvisi had difficulty continuing with the story.

"So this Russian thought he had our staffing all figured out. Just from the sandwiches. So many hoagie machinists, so many lean-meat doctors, so many cottage-cheese secretaries, ha, ha, ha—"

"Well, you've got to admit the guy had imagination," said Bob Green, who was the first to recover. "Let's get a cup of coffee and then get down to business."

With that, Green stood and led the way to a coffee pot on the floor in the corner of the room.

In a few minutes, when they sat down again, their demeanor was more serious and Frank Alvisi took charge of the meeting.

"Look, Professor Mason, as far as the staffing memo is concerned, why don't we handle it this way. You take a sanitized copy with you. We'll just cut off a few things, like the classification and the project number. Then you rewrite it any way you want and send it back to me at this address by registered mail. Just write it out longhand; don't get your secretary to type it, or anything like that."

Alvisi produced a plain, white three-by-five-inch card from his shirt pocket and handed it to Jack. On it was typed:

R. C. Thornberry, Jr.
P.O. Box 149
Fairfax Station, Virginia 22039

"Who's Thornberry?" asked Jack, with a puzzled expression.

"Oh, he's the assistant security officer," Alvisi responded. "He lives out that way. It's just a mail drop. To make it a little harder to trace stuff back here. We'll change it every once in a while. Otherwise some other guy from the embassy might try counting the letters or copying down the return addresses or something."

"Okay," said Jack noncommittally. "When do you need it?"

"The sooner the better," Alvisi replied. "You know how long it takes to get people on board. And the way the space is shaping up, people are going to be the pacing item. But we'd rather have you do it right than fast. The staff is clearly going to be the most important thing in this project, so give it as much thought as you want. We don't want to end up without some specialists that we desperately need at a critical moment. Why, if that happened, and we had to go out find a guy, and get him cleared, and get him on board, and—" Alvisi shook his head dolefully. "A thing like that could set the whole effort back weeks or even months."

Strangely, Jack felt a little better. At least they seemed to want him to be in on the critical decisions.

"Bill, let's get out a set of those blueprints and go over them with Professor Mason," Alvisi continued.

Wilson grabbed a large roll of paper from the far end of the table, swept aside some of the debris and spread the blueprints out, facing Bob and Jack.

"We've got the interior pretty well laid out, Professor Mason," Wilson began, "but I have a bunch of specific questions that I'd like to go over with you."

"Okay," said Jack, with increasing confidence. "Shoot."

"Well, let's start here on the sixth floor," Wilson continued. "I think we've gotten the administrative offices laid out pretty well. You know, security, mailroom, personnel, that kind of stuff.

But, the thing we don't have a handle on is how much space we'll need for preliminary screening of volunteers. As I understand it, we are going to need two adjacent, soundproof rooms, with one of your two-person chairs installed in the common wall, to test each pair of subjects. Is that right?"

Jack wasn't really sure what to say.

"Well, I guess it's as near to being correct as I know how to tell you right now. After we get going, we might decide to do some other kinds of tests, too. But the two-person chair is the only good idea that I have right now for getting started."

"Okay, that's fine," said Frank Alvisi. "We think it's a great idea."

Jack felt even better. He was almost beginning to enjoy making decisions that would shape the direction of the project.

"Now, how many two-person chairs and pairs of rooms do you think we'll need?" Bill Wilson enquired.

"That's a good question," said Jack. "If I knew the answer to that, I'd almost be able to tell you if the project is going to be successful."

"Well, ha, ha, let's just assume that it's going to be," Bob Green injected. "At least for planning purposes."

"The problem is as follows," Jack said. "If a pair of volunteers has a lot of telepathic ability—if the person trying to receive the thoughts guesses far more than ten percent of the digits correctly—then we won't have to test the pair very long before we're confident that they should be selected. But suppose that very few, or none, of the pairs of volunteers score higher than, say, fifteen percent on any of the runs. Then we'd have to test a pair for quite a while before we could be sure that they should be selected. To be sure that the fifteen percent wasn't just chance or cheating or a computer problem or something else."

"Let's assume that we have to test each pair for quite a while," Frank Alvisi injected, "just to be on the safe side. Now, how many pairs of volunteers do you think we might have to test before we find some good ones?"

"Well," said Jack with a chuckle, "that's the sixty-four-dollar question. From my reading of the ESP literature, I wouldn't be surprised if we tested everyone in Washington and didn't find a soul with any telepathic ability."

They all laughed again, but then Alvisi continued seriously.

"What you're telling us is that we ought to have as many chairs as possible. What does that mean? Five? Ten? Twenty? One hundred?"

Jack tried to be serious too, but the vision of a hundred queer-looking barber chairs lined up on either side of an almost endless wall brought a smile to his lips.

"I honestly don't know. If everything else is random, the more chairs you have, the faster you'll find acceptable pairs. You know, if five chairs find one pair per month, ten chairs will find two pairs per month, and so on."

"There must be some practical limit," said Alvisi, with concern. "What do you think it is?"

"I'm not sure about the maximum," said Jack thinking out loud. "But five might be a minumum. If we have fewer than that, we might all grow old before we find anyone."

"Okay," Alvisi agreed. "Five's the minimum. Now, what's your best guess about the maximum? What limits it, practically?"

"Ideally, as I said," Jack continued, "the more chairs the better. But, if I had to take a wild-assed guess, I'd say that by the time you got to ten, or certainly to twenty, the supervision would get out of control. You'd begin to get false alarms—pairs of volunteers that you thought had telepathic ability, but who really didn't. The mistakes would come about because people would get careless in administering the tests. And you might even get collusion between subjects and test technicians. Policing the whole thing would be very difficult. So, my guess is that ten is about the most we'd want to start with."

"That's a big help," said Frank Alvisi, with obvious relief. "You're saying a minimum of five and a maximum of about ten."

"Right," Jack agreed, a little more confidently. "And there's another point you might want to think about. We're probably going to modify the testing procedures as we go along. For example, suppose that we find a person who appears to be very good at transmitting his thoughts. Then we might want to use him in all the screening tests. Now, it isn't very likely that we'd find very many people like that, maybe just one or possibly two. So that limited number of excellent thought-transmitters might limit the number of chairs we could operate."

"That's a factor I hadn't thought about," Alvisi said, making a note on the pad before him. "Suppose we try something like this. We'll leave space on the plans for ten pairs of screening rooms. But in the beginning, we'll only finish off five of them and hold off on the rest until you see what the results look like from screening the first group of volunteers."

There was general nodded agreement with Alvisi's decision. Bill Wilson checked the item off his list and went on to the next question.

"Another big problem is the computer, Professor Mason. What kind should we get? And how much space will it need? And what kind of special arrangements will we have to make for it? Like a raised floor and air conditioning and special electrical power and that kind of stuff?"

By now, Jack was truly enjoying his role, and he responded professorially.

"Basically, there are three functions that the computer will be called upon to perform. First, it will be used to control the screening tests—to generate the random digits that are displayed to the people who are trying to transmit their thoughts and to record the perceptions of the people in the other sides of the two-person chairs. The second thing we will use it for is to statistically analyze the guesses of the people who are trying to receive the thoughts. The results of these computations will show whether or not any of the individuals or any of the pairs has real telepathic ability.

"And finally, the computer will be used for general scientific calculations. For example, refinement of the estimates that Barney O'Neil and I made of the electrical signals that might be perceived in a second person's brain due to intense mental concentration by a person trying to transmit his thoughts."

Bob Green and Bill Wilson stared at him like new sophomores in the front row of their first lecture by a Nobel laureate. Jack basked in the adulation, but Frank Alvisi was anxious to get to the bottom line.

"That sounds quite complicated, Professor. Do we need a very large computer to do it?"

"No, I don't think so," Jack said, shaking his head. "The important thing is to get a computer that is designed to do several kinds of work at the same time. People in the computer business call it time sharing."

"Why do we need that?" Bill Wilson asked, with the kind of eager naiveté that every professor loves.

"Let's think about what will be going on during a typical day," Jack replied. "There will be ten volunteers seated in the five two-person chairs. And the computer will have to display a new random digit every ten seconds or so to each of the five people who is trying to transmit his thoughts. But at about the same time, the computer will have to record the guesses made by each of the five people who are trying to receive the thoughts. Again, once every ten seconds or so. And on top of all that, some of the staff members are going to want the computer to do analysis for them. One of the staticians may want to run a program to tabulate the results of the previous day's testing. One of the physicists may want to calculate a complicated electric field pattern. And so on. The important point is that lots of different people are going to want the computer to do lots of different things at the same time. And that's why we're going to need a computer that is especially designed for time sharing."

Jack gave the confident little smile of a lecturer who thinks he has successfully gotten the point across. Even Frank Alvisi seemed interested, but he still wanted to get down to the specifics.

"Okay, I'm beginning to understand what it has to do. Now, who makes machines that can operate that way?"

"Well, I think the new PDP-Eleven might do the job," Jack offered.

Alvisi looked pleased, and Bill Wilson wrote down "PDP-11" on his pad and then asked:

"Who makes it? And when can we get one?"

"DEC makes it," Jack replied. "Digital Equipment Corporation. They're out past Route 128 now, west of Boston somewhere. As far as delivery is concerned, I'm not sure. I think it's a brand new machine."

"Okay," said Frank Alvisi. "Suppose we can get a PDP-Eleven. What do we have to get to go with it?"

"Well, let's see," said Jack. "We'll certainly need one or two real-time data buffers to form the interface between the testing chairs and the computer. And we'll need some time-sharing terminals for the staff. You know, those things that look like TV sets with typewriter keyboards attached. We'll probably need quite a few of them. And then, of course—"

"This is getting kind of complicated for us high-school graduates," Alvisi interjected. "Could you write a memo saying what we need and send it to me? By registered mail, of course."

"Sure," Jack agreed, wondering about the registered mail. "We've got some information on the Eleven around my lab. And there are some good time-sharing people in the department that I can talk to."

"Be careful!" Alvisi said with a frown. "It doesn't take many careless words before a smart guy can piece together what's going on."

"Don't worry, I'll be careful," said Jack, trying to be convincing, but his thoughts turned to the conversation that he had already had with Barney. Had he let the cat out of the bag? After all, Barney had helped him make the original calculations. Anyhow, Barney might be a good person to have on the project staff.

Jack's concern was interrupted by the cheerful voice of Bob Green.

"Is anyone else getting hungry? It's almost one o'clock. Most of the crowd has probably cleared out of the Holiday Inn dining room by now."

"Good idea," said Bill Wilson, and Jack nodded his agreement.

"Let's try not to take too long," Wilson continued. "I still have quite a few questions on my list for Professor Mason."

They all smiled at Wilson's remark and all but Alvisi rose to leave.

"Not going to join us, Frank?" Bob enquired.

"No, maybe I'll take a rain check," Alvisi responded. "Stomach's been bothering me."

"Nothing serious, I hope?" Bob asked with a frown.

"No," Frank replied. "Just working too hard on this project."

After the others had left, Frank Alvisi went to the telephone that was sitting on the floor in the corner of the conference room and dialed one of Brian MacFarland's unlisted telephone numbers. When the secretary had gotten his boss, Alvisi delivered a cryptic message of success.

"Brian?"

"Yes."

"The professor is visiting us. He's being very cooperative. I think you can tell people that we've got him on board."

"Excellent! Your timing is perfect. Thank you, Frank."

Brian MacFarland pressed an intercom button, and a light began to flash on a similar console on a credenza behind the desk of Stuart Bennington, the Director of Central Intelligence. Bennington was conferring with some aides at the large mahogany table in the center of his office, when he noticed the light. Its position on the console indicated that the caller could only be his deputy, Brian MacFarland. Bennington excused himself from the conference table and stepped behind his desk to take the call.

"Yes, Brian?"

"Good news, Stuart. About Project Psi. Can you talk?"

Stuart Bennington glanced at the aides at the table, mentally assessing their discreetness, and then responded simply:

"Yes."

"Professor Mason is visiting the new facility today," MacFarland began. "Alvisi is going over the staff requirements and the interior space layout and things like that with him. Frank just called and told me that Mason is being very cooperative. He seems to be getting into the swing of the project. Frank even implied that he has agreed to be the technical director. I thought you'd like to hear the news right away because of the way that Ryan has been on your back about it."

"Yes, I'm glad you called," Stuart Bennington agreed. "The general has been asking me how the project is coming along at least once a week. And all I've been able to tell him is that we've started building a facility and that we're talking to the professor. And, of course, he wants more that that—some real progress. But I think your news should calm him down. My guess is that he's told the boss about it. And now he's out on a limb unless

88

we come through. So when we do, let's be sure to remind him that he owes us one. A big one. Thanks again, Brian."

The Director of Central Intelligence glanced at his watch, sat down behind his desk, and addressed the staff people at the table.

"Gentlemen, will you excuse me for a little while, please?"

The aides hurriedly picked up their papers and soon left the room. Bennington gave them time to leave his outer office, and then picked up the telephone and pushed the intercom button for his secretary.

"Elizabeth, will you please get General Ryan at the White House on a secure line."

Stuart Bennington waited in silence with his head in his hands, thinking of what he was about to say. His words, however carefully chosen, would probably imply to the president's closest aide that the ultimate tool for successful summit negotiations might shortly be placed at the chief executive's disposal. How cautious should he be in speaking to Ryan? If he was too cautious, Ryan might conclude that he was not pushing the project hard enough. Worse than that, if Ryan was out on a limb, he might seize the opportunity to put Bennington out there instead. So he had to be positive, especially when he had good news to report. But what if Ryan made too much of the good news? Got the idea that all the difficulties could easily be surmounted and gave that impression to the president. Then they'd both be out on a limb.

These thoughts and more continued circling in Bennington's brain as a light began to flash on his telephone console. He snapped back to reality and picked up the receiver.

"Your call to General Ryan is ready on line three, Mr. Bennington. He will be on momentarily."

The Director of Central Intelligence pushed the button marked "Secure #3" and lifted the handset of a gray telephone.

"Bennington speaking."

"Good afternoon, Mr. Bennington," a secretary's voice replied. "Just a moment for General Ryan."

"Stuart!" Sam Ryan boomed. "What can I do for you?"

"It's about Project Psi," Bennington began cautiously. "We've begun to make some real progress."

"I'm damn glad to hear that," the general responded crustily. "The Old Man is going to ask me about it one of these days, and I want to have a good answer. So, what's happening?"

"Well, do you remember my telling you about Professor Mason?" Bennington inquired in return.

"Of course I do," Ryan responded impatiently. "He's the guy from MIT who's going to head up the project. Have you got him signed up yet?"

"He's visiting the new facility today," Stuart Bennington continued, "and going over the staffing plan and the interior layout."

"That's all fine," the general shot back, "but did you get him signed up?"

"Well, just about," Bennington equivocated.

"Just about!" Sam Ryan exploded. "What the hell does that mean?"

"Well, er, ah, our man says that we've got him hooked," Bennington said, a little shaken. "But he hasn't formally agreed yet."

"Look, Bennington," the general shouted, "what the hell are you running there? A fishing expedition or an intelligence agency? Now, you get your dead ass out of that plush chair in that soundproof office and get this project moving. Do you understand me?"

Stuart Bennington was getting an awful headache. The conversation was going the way he had feared it might, and he saw no way to change its direction. Reasoning was not one of Sam Ryan's strong suits.

"Wait a second, Sam, the project is going pretty well," Bennington offered, his own voice raised above its normal well-modulated level. "Mason has given us the idea for the basic experiment. And we're building a facility. And Mason is working with us. And—"

"Don't give me that 'pretty well' and 'working with us' shit, Bennington," Sam Ryan continued loudly. "The Old Man knows all about Mason. He's read the write-up on him in *Who's Who*. And he thinks we've found the right man to head the project. Now, unless you want me to tell him that the DCI can't get one lousy college professor to do his duty for his country, you had better get your ass over to wherever Mason is and talk to him."

"Look, Sam," Stuart Bennington responded, his anger building, "there's no need to get vulgar just because you're out on a limb. We've got Mason hooked. It will just take us a few weeks to reel him in. But he won't get away. We're used to dealing with these academic types. You have to do it slowly and flatter their egos. So just keep your shirt on and you'll be able to hang the fish on your office wall."

"Okay, Stuart," Ryan answered more normally. "Sorry I blew up. But you know that fancy words aren't much good around here if you haven't got the job done. The Old Man doesn't like to hear excuses. So please stay on top of this thing. And thanks for calling."

"Okay, Sam," Bennington answered in his usual Ivy League tone. "I'll give it my personal attention. And I'll call you as soon as there are any substantial developments."

Stuart Bennington pushed the green button that disconnected the telephones entirely. His brain instantly repressed Sam Ryan's vulgarity, and his gaze slowly circled the tastefully decorated office. One wall displayed a series of lithographs of early defenders and challengers for the *America*'s Cup. Grand old sailing yachts with dozens of paid crew members to do the bidding of nattily attired owners. Names like Cornelius Vanderbilt and Sir Thomas Lipton. But Sam Ryan's remark about one lousy college professor doing his duty for his country returned to Bennington's thoughts. He had been a college professor once himself, of political science at Yale. And now he was the Director of Central Intelligence. Was that doing his duty for his country?

His gaze continued to the other wall and its display of ancient Chinese art, leaving the fundamental question unanswered.

PART III
THE PRESIDENT'S DECISION

10

The Kickoff

As the trees shed their last golden leaves and Indian summer gave way to the cold, clear days of November, Jack found Project Psi absorbing more and more of his time. Bob Green called him almost every day with a list of questions. Some were mundane, like the color of the carpet to be installed in Jack's private conference room. Others were matters of technical detail, such as the number of disk drives to be ordered with the PDP-11 computer. And a few were of fundamental importance to the success of the effort.

Jack was most concerned about recruiting the proper people to the senior staff. They would set the tone and style of the project. His goal was to get the right mixture of sound professional training, enthusiasm, and desire for success. If the balance tipped too far in the direction of academic excellence, the experiments might be so conservatively planned and carefully executed that progress would be excruciatingly slow. On the other hand, if enthusiasm overwhelmed clear thinking and critical judgment, the project would lurch, like a Saturday-night drunk, up one blind alley after another. At the start, Jack felt that the balance should tip toward professionalism. They were, after all, embarking on a fundamental research project in an area that had previously been dominated by workers ranging from mystics through charlatans to scientific incompetents.

Jack's initial recruiting effort had been to convince Barney O'Neil to join Project Psi. It hadn't taken much pursuasion. "Sounds a lot more exciting than cats and monkeys," Barney had concluded.

O'Neil had been one of Jack's finest graduate students. Although not a flashy genius, he possessed both theoretical and experimental ability and was endowed with common sense and good judgment far beyond his years. Furthermore, his even temper and Irish humor would help to see all of them through the stressful days that were certain to come.

Barney had plunged into his new career as Jack's deputy in Project Psi with characteristic enthusiasm. He had already worked up a preliminary design for the two-person chair and the associated electrically screened and soundproofed rooms. In addition, he was handling many of Bob Green's day-to-day inquiries, much to Jack's relief.

By early February, the gestating embryo of Project Psi was beginning to assume a recognizable form. Much to his satisfaction, Jack had been able to attract several high-caliber people to senior staff positions. Nevertheless, he was seriously concerned about how they would perform when brought together to venture into the unknown world of mental telepathy under the stress of the Washington pressure cooker. He would have to try to insulate them from the searing steam of the Sam Ryans, while letting them feel the urgency and exhilaration of working on a project that had presidential attention. Some of the key people Jack had known long or well, and he thought they could stand the heat and take the ego trip in stride.

About others, he could not be certain. Their résumés and references were excellent, and their behavior during his discussions with them had been professional and well balanced. Nevertheless, he would not be sure until they were tested under fire. How would they react at three A.M. with the latest experiment a failure and the president's chief of staff on the phone?

Jack's thoughts drifted to one of the people who might cause trouble under stress. Professor Hermann Anton Stark, a brilliant young behavioral psychologist from Harvard. Jack smiled to himself. How could it be, he mused, that a man whose avowed aim was to understand human motivations was so oblivious to his own striving for power?

When Jack had first approached Stark about joining an ESP research project, the eccentric genius had shown little interest and had broken several luncheon engagements. Jack had finally had to seek him out in his basement lair for a face-to-face discussion.

Jack had found Stark hunched over a small desk in a corner of his laboratory. The room was used primarily to house the rats that were the subjects of Stark's famous experiments on stress induced by overcrowding. The air was filled with a strange cacophony of rodent sounds: squeaking cries, the crunch of teeth on extruded food pellets, and the eerie scratching of claws on the wire mesh cages.

Stark seemed surprised to see his visitor and motioned for Jack to sit down on a chair stacked with laboratory notebooks. Stark's desk was a disaster area. It was strewn with the tools of his trade: open books, disordered piles of papers, assorted pens and pencils, empty plastic coffee cups, pieces of laboratory glassware, and a half-eaten sandwich.

Stark hardly listened while Jack described the ESP research project in terms intended to be scientifically interesting, but with the ultimate objective disguised. Occasionally, Stark interrupted to protest his busyness or to describe some aspect of the latest scientific paper he was writing. Jack became quite frustrated, and was about to end the interview and write Stark off. But, in one final act of desperation, he decided to hint that the White House was interested in the project.

Miraculously, Stark's behavior changed almost immediately. He began to listen attentively and to probe Jack with questions designed to ferret out the ultimate goal of the project. Their wide-ranging discussion finally turned to the obvious advantages that telepathic ability would give an espionage agent. Fortunately, Stark did not stumble upon the idea of using men with psi in summit diplomacy, and of course Jack did not reveal it. Nevertheless, the thought of intelligence agents collecting information through telepathic powers was enough to whet Stark's appetite. Late in the afternoon, the interview finally ended at the coffee machine down the hall from Stark's laboratory, with the young professor pressing to know what position he would hold in the project's management structure.

Abruptly, Jack's thoughts turned to a more pleasant subject: Phyllis Jackson. A beautiful woman who had been his wife's roommate in college; she was now a clinical physiologist at Cambridge City Hospital, specializing in the effects of drugs on mental and physical behavior. Phyllis would certainly be a welcome counterpoint to the intense competitiveness and childish reactions of men like Stark. She always seemed poised and self-assured, and yet conveyed a genuine interest in other people's ideas and activities.

Phyllis had served her medical residency in a methadone clinic in a large New York City hospital. She told Jack and Sue many stories of harrowing experiences in dealing with the frantic, and sometimes violent, behavior of addicts. Jack shook his head in admiration. How could a woman who was so gentle and unaggressive cope so successfully with such stressful and potentially dangerous situations? In addition to her charm, Phyllis must have tremendous inner strength and sense of purpose. Jack was secretly counting on her to help him and the project through the crises that were certain to occur.

There was another advantage to having Phyllis associated with the project. She and Sue were still good friends, and his wife's objections to Jack's involvement in Project Psi had diminished considerably since Phyllis had joined the effort. Somehow, Phyllis had been able to talk to Sue about the reasons for becoming involved in such a risky and clandestine enterprise in a convincing or, at least, pacifying way. Perhaps Sue subconsciously felt that she too was participating, through Phyllis.

Jack's thoughts were interrupted by his secretary's voice drifting in through the open doorway.

"It's Mr. Green, Professor Mason."

Jack snapped out of his reverie and stared vacantly for a moment. Finally, he reached for the phone and answered it distractedly.

"Mason speaking."

"Hi, old buddy. This is your Washington quizmaster calling. Today, the sixty-four-thousand-dollar question is: When are we going to have the kickoff meeting?"

"Well, I, er, thought you'd be pushing me about that pretty soon," Jack responded defensively. "I guess we're just about ready. I've got commitments from most of the key people. I talked to Rosenfeld, the computer type, yesterday. He's made up his mind to join us, but he's got to convince his wife to move to Washington. He'll probably commute for a while, like some of the rest of us. That leaves only the head of the theoretical group open. I'm still trying to get the man I told you about. Walter Patton. He's a physicist here at the Institute. Very good at electromagnetic theory. Just the kind of guy we need. And he's got some good post-docs. He could probably bring one or two along, like I'm doing with Barney. So, all in all, I think we should be ready by the end of the month. And maybe some of the snow will be gone by then, too. It's been a pain in the ass getting to the airport since that big storm back in the middle of January."

"You got snow up there in bean town, old buddy?" Green replied facetiously. "Maybe you should think about moving to Washington. It's almost spring down here. Why, I was thinking of playing golf one of these weekends soon."

"Uh-huh," Jack responded good-naturedly, "I'll remind you how nice it is in Washington next August."

"Touché, old buddy," Bob conceded. "Now, about the kickoff meeting. Why don't you call the key people and try to get them all down here some time during the week of the twenty-sixth. Any day is all right with us. Just give me a few days' notice so that I can warn people around here."

"Okay, Bob," Jack agreed with some trepidation. "I'll try for the middle of the week. The twenty-seventh, twenty-eighth, or twenty-ninth. I'll give you a call as soon as I have them all lined up."

"Okay," Bob concluded and then changed the subject. "Now, let me go down the list and tell you where we stand with the paperwork on each of them. Everything's done on Barney O'Neil. I gave him his permanent badge the last time he was down here. Dr. Jackson is okay, too. All we have to do is take her picture when she comes to the kickoff meeting. Same with Professor Stark. Mr. Anderson has filled out the security questionnaire, but they haven't finished his background investigation. I'll make sure that it's done before the meeting. I don't have anything on Rosenfeld or Patton yet, so if you want to have them at the meeting, we're going to have to move fast. You had better get after them to get their questionnaires in right away."

Jack nodded to himself, scribbling frantically on a pad, and Bob signaled jovially that the day's interrogation was over.

"Well, old buddy, I've taken up enough of your time today with this security bullshit. See you at the kickoff meeting."

A strange uneasiness came over Jack.

"Right, Bob, see you at the meeting," he answered distractedly.

When the day of the Project Psi kickoff meeting arrived, Jack Mason felt like an untested high-school quarterback about to play his first game. He and Barney O'Neil had flown to Washington from Boston the night before so as to be at the project facility well ahead of the others who would attend the meeting. The two old friends were now seated alone at the large table that dominated the recently completed conference room. They noticed several microphones arranged along its length, apparently indicative of Bob Green's intention to record the proceedings.

"I guess Bob must think that someone is going to say something worth remembering," Barney said with a smile.

"Yeah," Jack responded. "He must think we know what we're doing."

At that very moment, as if on cue, Bob Green himself arrived, wearing his usual cheerful expression and carrying a large pot of coffee.

"How's the brain trust? Try a little of this black stuff to get the old gray matter moving."

Green placed the pot on a small stand in the corner of the room, and the three men filled their cups and then reseated themselves at the conference table. Jack took the place of authority at the head, and Bob and Barney arranged themselves on either side next to him. Once he was ensconced, Bob opened a folder and slid a copy of the agenda across the table to Jack. The latter pulled the sheet of paper toward him and began to scan its contents.

Project Psi Kickoff Meeting

Agenda

Morning

- Welcome—Prof. Mason (5 min.)
- Administrative Matters—Mr. Green (10 min.)
- Introduction and Objectives—Prof. Mason (15 min.)
- Preliminary Calculations of Electromagnetic Coupling
  —Dr. O'Neil (45 min.)
- Psychological Aspects in Screening of Human Subjects
  —Dr. Jackson (45 min.)

Working Lunch

Afternoon

- Effects of Stress in Human Experiments
  —Prof. Stark (45 min.)
- High-Confidence Statistical Screening
  —Dr. Franklin (45 min.)
- Discussion and Formulation of Plans—All (90 min.)

TOP SECRET—PSI

Jack finished proofreading the agenda and wondered idly if Bob would give them beer with the sandwiches at lunch; he thought they would need it by then.

The private meeting of the three old friends was ended abruptly by the arrival of Hermann Anton Stark.

"Well, *Mason*," he greeted Jack loudly, "are you going to tell us how to accomplish this impossible task?"

"Not me, Anton," Jack responded, with a smile, "but I was hoping that you would tell us that it's only a small step from what you've been doing with rats."

"The nice thing about rats," Stark countered aggressively, "is that they don't talk back. Or write scientific papers."

Barney O'Neil smiled broadly at what he hoped was a Teutonic attempt at humor; Jack ignored the thrust entirely.

"Good morning, Anton, it's good to see you," he said heartily.

Anton Stark surveyed the conference table, looking for a seat from which to exert the greatest possible influence. The two places next to Jack being taken, he contented himself with sitting next to Bob Green.

During the next fifteen minutes, the conference room slowly filled to capacity. Phyllis Jackson took the seat next to Anton Stark and immediately began to charm the savage beast. Ken Anderson sat next to Barney O'Neil and insisted on showing him some calculations he had made last night. Anderson thought that his last-minute results were an essential addition to the talk that Barney was about to give, but O'Neil was not so sure. Gradually, the seats at the far end of the conference table and along the walls of the room began to fill with junior staff members. Finally, when Frank Alvisi entered the room and took the seat at the foot of the table, Jack concluded that they might as well begin. He rose and the private conversations slowly died away.

"Well, here we are," Jack began, with a broad smile and the most confident voice he could muster. "Embarking on what for a lot of us is the most adventurous thing we've done professionally for years. I know that you all have doubts—so do I. But I don't think that the task is impossible. And I do know that the team is the best that I have ever had the privilege of being a member of."

Jack surveyed the suddenly serious faces around the room and then made a conscious effort to continue enthusiastically.

"If we succeed, the payoff will be incalculable. Both from the standpoint of scientific knowledge, and because of the advantage it will give the United States in the world arena. None of us can foresee what the outcome will be. And all that I can promise you is a lot of hard work, a little private praise, and no public recognition."

Jack looked around the room again, unaccustomed to the role of the coach delivering the pep talk. He needed it himself at least as much as the others.

"Welcome to Project Psi," he concluded, with a broad smile and arms extended.

After Jack sat down, Bob Green took the floor and began to go fairly quickly through a list of administrative matters—who still needed to get his picture taken, why it was dumb to wear your badge when you went out to lunch, where you could lock up classified material, and that sort of stuff. In spite of his brevity, there was a general rustling of disinterest around the room and several side conversations sprang up. Ken Anderson and Barney O'Neil became engaged in an animated, whispered discussion. From what Jack could catch, Ken thought that his new results were of fundamental importance, while Barney was not sure that he understood or trusted them enough to include the implications in his talk.

Mercifully for the audience, Bob finished and Jack was again on stage. This time to tell them what they had all come to hear: Where was this crazy project really going?

Jack rose slowly from his chair, and the room fell silent. He placed a viewgraph on the projector and motioned to Bob to dim the lights.

TOP SECRET—PSI

Project Psi

Initial Objective

TO CONDUCT A DEFINITIVE, CAREFULLY-CONTROLLED, WELL-DOCUMENTED, SCIENTIFIC EXPERIMENT TO DETERMINE WHETHER OR NOT THOUGHTS CAN BE TRANSMITTED AND RECEIVED OVER SHORT DISTANCES BY HUMAN BRAINS THROUGH THE ELECTROMAGNETIC FIELD WITHOUT THE ASSISTANCE OF THE NORMAL SENSES

TOP SECRET—PSI

Jack allowed them time to read the projected text and then began in a measured tone.

"As far as I am concerned, this is the only objective of the project at the present time. Unless and until we accomplish this task, by determining beyond a shadow of a doubt whether or not mental telepathy is possible under the most favorable conditions, it is both meaningless and counterproductive to speculate about more grandiose objectives."

Having thrown down the gauntlet, Jack stared the length of the room at Frank Alvisi, clearly challenging him to respond. Slowly people shifted in their seats until finally all eyes were turned toward the far end of the table, and Alvisi realized that they were demanding a response.

"I don't think that Professor Mason could have stated our initial objective better," the CIA man began with apparent sincerity. "Or assembled a finer team to accomplish it. I want to assure you all, on behalf of the top management of the Agency, that you will have absolute freedom in setting the scientific direction of the project and the highest priority support in accomplishing its objectives."

Alvisi folded his hands and smiled benignly back at the staring eyes. Slowly, the faces began to smile back.

Having elicited the public assurances he wanted, Jack decided to respond graciously.

"Thank you, Frank. I think that is just the kind of commitment that we all are looking for from the government. Most of the people in this room have made a decision to devote several years of their very productive careers to this project, and it's important to them to know that the scientific aspects will be handled in the most professional manner possible."

"You have my assurances," Alvisi responded seriously. "You people are the scientists—the best in the country. And we want the project to go the way you say it should. Because we want it to succeed."

"Well, that's all I had by way of an introduction," Jack concluded, after allowing a moment of silence. "Let's get on to the technical meat."

He placed the agenda viewgraph back on the projector and motioned to Barney O'Neil.

"Barney, you're up."

O'Neil swept together a pile of viewgraphs in front of him on the table, rose at his place, and began speaking in a relaxed manner.

"I'm going to describe a refined set of calculations that Jack Mason, Ken Rosenfeld, and I have done of the electromagnetic coupling that might exist between two human brains that are close together."

Barney replaced the agenda with his first viewgraph on the projector and motioned to Bob Green to dim the lights.

TOP SECRET—PSI

Thought Transfer between Human Brains

Basic Assumptions

Signal Source: Time varying currents in brain of
person transmitting thoughts
Coupling Mechanism: Quasi-static magnetic field
Detected Signal: Currents induced in brain of
person receiving thoughts

TOP SECRET—PSI

After hastily reading the words on the screen, Anton Stark could remain silent no longer.

"Why have you calculated only the magnetic field?" he began aggressively. "Have you proven that electric-field effects are unimportant?"

Barney O'Neil smiled good-naturedly, knowing that he was in for a long forty-five-minute talk. Two hours later, he was proven correct.

Jack had warned each of the speakers ahead of time to be particularly tolerant of questions and debate at this initial meeting. He felt that it was particularly important for the senior staff members to get to know one another at the outset and to develop an understanding of each other's style of working and communicating.

Barney had taken Stark's questioning with considerable grace and some of the suggestions were actually helpful. And Stark's own presentation had not escaped the skeptical probing of his colleagues. It seemed to Jackson, on psychological grounds, that he drew much too close a parallel between extremely simplified screening and training experiments with rats and what might be possible with human subjects. Although she did not say so, Phyllis also felt that Stark had recently spent too much time with rats and too little with people and had begun to lose sight of the distinctions between them.

At the outset, Bob Green had bravely planned the meeting to conclude at 1600, although Jack knew that it would take much longer. Shortly after six, when exhaustion and thoughts of dinner had begun to dissipate the passion of the debate, Jack rose and went to the blackboard. When the discussion quieted down, and their attention was more or less focussed on him, Jack suggested to the weary combatants that they try to list the major approaches their research initially would take. Three major thrusts were fairly quickly agreed upon—*Transmitter / Receiver Screening, Stimulus / Brain-Wave Screening,* and *Theoretical Investigations.*

However, filling in the details proved to be far more difficult and time consuming. Not only were they breaking new scientific ground, but each idea that was accepted or rejected carried with it the ego and aspirations of one or more of the strong-willed participants.

By seven-thirty, they had filled all the available blackboards with the major elements of the test that would screen volunteers for natural ability to transmit or receive thoughts.

A pair of test subjects will be enclosed in adjoining soundproofed and electromagnetically screened rooms. Each person will recline on a specially modified astronaut flight couch, with their bodies extending in opposite directions along the intervening wall. Their heads will be positioned exactly opposite each other, separated only by a thin layer of vacuum between two sheets of opaque glass. The dark glass will prevent the test subjects from communicating through visual cues, while the vacuum will stop acoustical and mechanical signals. However, the glass-and-vacuum sandwich will present no resistance to the free transmission of electromagnetic signals between the brains of the two volunteers.

As a further precaution against attempts by the people being tested to signal each other by sounds or thumps, microphones will be mounted on either side of the wall separating them and motion sensors will be installed in each of the astronaut couches. Comparison of the signals from these cheating detectors with the visual stimuli presented to the person who is trying to transmit his thoughts and with the responses of the person who is trying to receive the thoughts will provide a confident and routine method for discovering collusion between the volunteers. In addition, each of the astronaut couches will be totally soundproofed and screened from the rest of the room to preclude distraction or coaching of the test subjects by the experimenters and to prevent stray sounds or electromagnetic signals from entering the space through which the two people's brains are attempting to communicate.

The person who is trying to transmit his thoughts will recline in total darkness within his soundproofed cocoon. At intervals of twenty seconds, one of the digits from zero to nine will appear on a screen before his eyes. The display will be carefully designed to be clearly visible, yet not so large or bright as to frighten the volunteer in the darkness.

Each number will appear on the screen before the person trying to transmit his thoughts for a period of ten seconds. During this time, the volunteer will be asked to concentrate all his thoughts on the number. Between each pair of numbers, the screen will be dark for ten seconds to allow the subject to rest and to provide a control period during which he is receiving no visual stimulus.

The design of the couch for the person who is trying to receive the thoughts will be somewhat different. One of his hands will be supported on a special arm rest with his fingers positioned comfortably over a set of lighted buttons labeled with the digits from zero to nine. On a screen before his eyes, two additional lights, one green and one red, will invade his world of darkness.

During the ten seconds when a number is being presented to the eyes of the person who is trying to transmit his thoughts, the green light will be on in the cocoon of the person who is trying to receive the thoughts. He will then know that the other volunteer is concentrating on a number and that he has ten seconds in which to push the button corresponding to the digit he perceives is being transmitted. At the end of the ten seconds, the green light will go out and the red light will come on, indicating to the volunteer who is trying to receive the thoughts that he can rest too and that any button he pushes will not be counted in his test score.

A screening test run will consist of attempts by a pair of volunteers to transmit and receive one hundred numbers selected at random by the computer and will take a little more than half an hour to complete. Following each run, the two people being tested will be given the remainder of each hour off to relax outside their cocoons.

Each volunteer will initially be tested for two days. On one day, he will make five runs in which he attempts to transmit his thoughts; on the second day, he will make five runs trying to receive the thoughts of another volunteer. In each test run, every person will have a new partner, because individual differences in brain signals may make it easier for certain people to receive the thoughts of certain other people, a recurring suggestion in tales of the occult.

The computer will be used to identify volunteers whose performance in either transmitting or receiving thoughts is significantly better than that predicted by the laws of chance. A person who simply guesses would be expected to get an average of ten correct digits in each run of one hundred numbers. A modestly better score of fifteen proper answers would be expected about three times in every hundred runs simply as a matter of chance. However, a score of twenty correct would occur very infrequently (once in about 854 runs) if only chance were operating and not some other phenomenon, presumably either mental telepathy or cheating. And a score of twenty-five or greater would be a truly rare chance event, occurring only once in about 76,495 runs.

Thus, a score this high would almost certainly mark the individuals who achieved it as either perceptive psychics or clever scoundrels. Each night, the computer will process the results of the day's testing so that summary reports identifying volunteers who appear to have psychic ability will be available at the daily staff meeting the next morning.

There was heated discussion concerning the level of performance a volunteer would be required to achieve during the initial two days of screening in order to be retained for further testing. Some people argued for setting the standard high so that they would not be fooled by chance occurrences of good performance. However, others countered persuasively that setting the standard too high might lead to the retention of few, if any, of the subjects. Barney O'Neil summed up the situation succinctly.

"We don't want to put ourselves out of business in the first week."

In the end, on a trial basis, they agreed to retain any volunteer whose performance would occur by chance less than five percent of the time.

By now, the conference area looked and smelled like the infamous smoke-filled back room of political conventions. The table was strewn with numerous empty styrofoam coffee cups, a few remaining paper plates with half-eaten sandwiches, and a myriad of papers, notes, reports, viewgraphs, and computer plots and printouts. The smell was a mixture of the pungent odor of a delicatessen, the sweaty stench of a locker room, and the stale, acrid pall of the smoking section on an Eastern shuttle.

By eight o'clock, more than half of the original attendees had already left for one reason or another, and the survivors were more than willing to accept Jack's suggestion that they reconvene in the morning to fill in the details of the other two major efforts and to review the results of the entire meeting. Bob Green and one of the security officers collected the notes and papers, and tried to place them in appropriate manila envelopes, each marked with the name of a participant, for overnight storage in one of the many safes. Unidentifiable scribblings were unceremoniously dumped into an envelope marked "Miscellaneous" to await uncertain rescue by their authors in the morning.

Jack returned to his office and aimlessly began to shuffle the papers on his desk in preparation for leaving. He was soon joined by Bob Green, who was in high spirits despite the late hour and the tiring day.

"Well, old buddy, I think we're off the ground. Not much airspeed yet, but the thrust feels good, and we'll start gaining altitude soon."

Jack's mind flashed back to the windswept aircraft carrier deck, and he visualized Bob's F-9F disappearing into the low overcast. *If Bob hadn't made it that night,* he thought, *we all wouldn't be here today. What crazy twists and turns life takes. Bob might be at the bottom of the Yellow Sea and I might be back in my comfortable laboratory, worrying about the optic tectum of the chimpanzee.*

"Come on, old buddy, let's get out of here," the Bob Green of the present interjected. "Get your stuff locked up, and we'll get a drink and something to eat. I've found a good pizza place that's open till midnight."

Next morning, with clearer heads and a smaller group, they were able to fill in the details of the other two major efforts fairly rapidly. The second kind of test, which they had called "Stimulus/Brain-Wave Screening" the night before, will be conducted in a manner similar to the tests in which volunteers try to transmit and receive digits, but with several important differences. Instead of asking a second person to attempt to perceive the numbers being displayed to a volunteer who is trying to transmit his thoughts, sensitive electrical sensors will monitor the single test subject's brain waves in an attempt to determine if the signals in his brain reflect in any way the digit that is being shown to his eyes.

At last the discussion turned to the final major effort listed on the blackboard the previous evening: "Theoretical Investigations." They agreed that the thrust of this work will be an attempt to provide a physically sound theoretical basis for the transmission of signals between two closely separated brains via the electromagnetic field. As a first step, the theoreticians will refine the calculations begun by Jack when he drew the two egg heads on his pad before attending Sam Klein's seminar.

The last throes of the meeting occurred in Jack's office late that afternoon. Only the truly committed remained: Jack and Bob and Barney and Phyllis and, perhaps not surprisingly, Hermann Anton Stark. Strangely, the prevailing mood was one of optimism despite their ready acknowledgement that no one among them was confident that any of the experimental tests or theoretical calculations necessarily would lead to positive results.

While secretaries frantically typed the proceedings of the meeting, the final weary warriors bantered with the easy over-confidence that comes from shared struggle. At last, Anton Stark rose to leave and, in a parting soliloquy, summed up their feelings with Teutonic exactitude.

"Colleagues! We are about to embark upon an expedition of historic significance. An adventure to the inextricably intertwined frontiers of science and espionage. If we succeed, presidential citations and eventually the Nobel prize will be ours. If we fail, our ignominious record will be that of scientific charlatans and geopolitical neophytes."

11

Brain-to-Brain Communication

It was early on a Monday morning at the end of July of 1969, and Jack Mason sat alone in his office thinking about where Project Psi had been and where it was going. A hectic year had passed since the screening of volunteers for telepathic ability had begun. Almost 500 people had been tested for a two-day period, one day as a transmitter of thoughts and another as a receiver. The number of two-person chairs, isolated in adjacent soundproofed, screened rooms, had been expanded from the initial five to a current complement of ten. This growth in testing facilities had been necessitated both by the desire to screen more volunteers for ability to transmit or receive thoughts and by the need to further examine people whose brain waves showed patterns that could be related to the number displayed to their eyes.

They had made remarkable progress in a relatively short time, and, early in June, Jack had decided that they should pause and take stock. Accordingly, he ordered that all screening of volunteers be suspended and that the staff spend a month analyzing the data that had been collected and writing up summaries of the results and implications. This effort was about to culminate in a week-long internal seminar and the publication of a massive, highly classified report.

Jack's thoughts returned to the present, and he picked up the agenda for the week's activities. He read it once again, for what must have been the fifth time, and reflected on possibilities for last-minute changes that might improve the group's communication and productivity.

The week would be crucial. If the seminar was good, the report would be good, and those above him would be pleased—right up to the president, Jack hoped. He reflected upon the people through whom the report would have to pass if it was to reach the president:

Brian MacFarland, a spy who had come in from the cold. A bluff, hearty, friendly man who was practical and liked concrete, usable results. Brian probably appreciated better than anyone else the operational possibilities for using a man with psi. And he knew about the risks, too. He had lost a lot of agents in his time. Most quietly, without a trace. But some more violently: a car reduced to charred pieces of twisted scrap by a blast of plastic explosive or a body torn apart by the crossfire from a pair of Uzi machine guns.

Stuart Bennington, the Director of Central Intelligence, from a Boston Brahmin family by way of Yale, a blue-water sailor by avocation and an intelligence administrator by profession. What Stuart knew about spies, he had gotten from Howard Hunt's novels or their highly classified equivalents. But when it came to politics, Stuart was a master. He knew what the bosses wanted, who they really were, and whether they were on the way up or down. While Stuart worked for the president on paper, he knew that he had to get along with the White House chief of staff.

Sam Ryan, a former B-52 pilot, who had made a name for himself giving briefings for the Joint Chiefs of Staff to the National Security Council. Sam didn't care what the weapon was, as long as we had it and the Russians didn't, and we could use it on them.

Jack smiled to himself. The report certainly would have to be a minor masterpiece to please this disparate group of forceful personalities. One thing was sure, the science would have to be relegated to a series of appendices. The decision makers would probably read only the executive summary, which Jack planned to take a strong hand in writing himself.

Finally, Jack's thoughts turned to the man who would be the hardest to please and, in the end, the most influential with the president.

Thomas Stratton, a former professor of political science at Harvard and now the secretary of state. Stratton was a master of geopolitical dialectic and international maneuvering and clearly the dominant intellect of the Leonard administration.

Jack's attention again focused on the agenda that lay before him on the desk, and he began to scan it yet another time. Monday and Tuesday would be entirely taken up with the transmitter/receiver screening experiments. The talks this morning would deal primarily with the physical characteristics of the equipment and what the doctors called protocols, the conditions and procedures under which the experiments were conducted. This afternoon, they would move on to presentations of the principal experimental results—compilations of the test scores of all the volunteers who had been examined, with primary emphasis on those people who had consistently shown well above chance performance in either transmitting or receiving thoughts.

Tomorrow morning would be devoted to a detailed discussion of the test results of the stars, those few volunteers who had achieved the highest test scores. Jack was particularly concerned that the review of these outstanding performances be conducted with sufficient depth that no doubt would remain that the high test scores resulted from genuine telepathic ability, and not from one of a myriad of more mundane possible causes—failure in equipment design, construction, or maintenance, careless test conduct, imprecise computer analysis, or, worst of all, some overt or subconscious form of cheating.

The specter of cheating had haunted Jack throughout the initial year of testing. Elaborate precautions had been taken to prevent it, but the possibility hung like the sword of Damocles over the whole endeavor. Jack was convinced that they had eliminated the most obvious and flagrant forms of deception. Volunteers who attempted to signal their partner by thumping their head on the glass separating it from its mate were embarrassed to find that the computer easily detected their chicanery through analysis of data from the vibration sensors and were rapidly given dishonorable discharges from further testing.

But Jack's nightmares resulted from far more subtle possibilities. Suppose that one of the scientists or computer programmers told a volunteer the type of algorithm used by the computer to generate the random sequence of numbers presented to the person who is trying to transmit his thoughts. Although the input quantities that control the random number generator were changed every day by the computer, the remote possibility existed, at least in Jack's worst dreams, that some subtle quirk in the software might allow a clever volunteer who was trying to receive thoughts to be armed by an unscrupulous mathematician with a rule that would produce more correct answers than expected from chance alone.

Suddenly, Jack's brooding was interrupted by a familiar greeting.

"Hi, old buddy, are you all set for the orgy? This is going to be a tough week for us high-school dropouts. But you science types should have a great time. Seriously, though, I hear that some of the results are really fantastic. Why, one of those guys got a twenty-seven the other day. You can't call *that* chance, can you?"

Jack smiled broadly.

"Remember, Bob, events of low probability do occur."

"Yeah, Professor, you keep telling me that. But, fortunately for us, I don't understand it. But I do recognize telepathic ability. And this guy's got it!"

"I hope you're right, Bob," Jack replied, nodding in the affirmative. "I really do. But suppose it turns out that all he's got is a friend on the programming staff?"

"What do you mean?" Green answered, with a twinkle. "It's against the law to be friends with a programmer."

"Yeah," Jack chuckled, "but it could be big trouble for us if one of the staff members gave a volunteer a clue, any kind of clue, about how to guess. It doesn't take much to make a volunteer look a little better than the laws of chance."

"Yeah, but not twenty-seven," Bob argued, a little defensively.

Jack had to admit that Bob was probably right. It might be possible for some subtle form of cheating to allow a volunteer to average perhaps twelve or fifteen or even seventeen correct answers out of a hundred rather than the expected ten. But for a person to consistently cheat his way into the middle twenties would require the assistance of a well-planned conspiracy involving at least two staff members. Data from each screening test run were recorded by the computer on a magnetic disk while the run was in progress.

Furthermore, the data file for a specific test run by a particular pair of volunteers was identified on the disk only by a serial number assigned by the computer. Even the statisticians and programmers who analyzed the test scores did not know which runs corresponded to which volunteers. This crucial information, the pairing of names with test scores, was known only to a small group of people who needed the information to do their jobs. Even Jack did not routinely have access to these records.

The faces of the people who did have access to these records flashed before his mind.

John Franklin, the head of the mathematical and statistical group, who prepared the reports summarizing the major conclusions to be drawn from each week's testing activity. *Phyllis Jackson,* who supervised the psychological testing of the people who were retained because of their superior test scores in the initial screening. *Barney O'Neil,* Jack's assistant and long-time friend.

Jack stared blankly past Bob and shook his head slowly from side to side. He could not believe than any of these people would even exaggerate, let alone falsify, test results.

"Come on, Jack, stop stewing," Bob injected, trying to cheer up his leader. "Things are going pretty well, and you know it. We're a hell of a lot farther along today than even I expected. And none of the key people are cheating. I can assure you of that. I gave them the lie detector tests myself. Now let's get a little fresh air before the orgy starts."

The week of seminars got off to a rocky start. They stayed in the conference room from nine in the morning until seven at night, with only a half-hour break for sandwiches. When the end of the long day finally came, their minds were numb and their energy for argument was dissipated. Worst of all, in spite of the marathon session, they had not completed all the presentations shown on the agenda. In an attempt to get back on schedule, Jack decreed that they would begin at eight A.M. the rest of the week.

By Friday, an amazing recovery had been made. About half the presentations had been written up, typed, proofread by the authors, and approved for inclusion in the report. Most of the discussion had ceased, and offices and conference rooms were filled with people hard at work writing the final sections. Over the weekend, the final version of the entire report was typed and a copy sat proudly in the center of Jack Mason's desk when he arrived on Monday morning.

When he entered the office and saw the report, Jack smiled with satisfaction at the Herculean task his staff had accomplished. Once again, he marveled at the fantastic group of people that the project had assembled and the incredible amount of work they could turn out in a short time when pressure was applied. And he took some personal satisfaction in having recruited most of them himself.

Jack pushed the intercom button and told his secretary to tell people that he was totally unavailable. He intended to spend Monday and Tuesday reading the report and writing the executive summary.

Late the following afternoon, Jack pushed away from his cluttered desk, leaned back in his padded chair, and began to reread the pages of a yellow legal pad on which he had written a paragraph or two about each of the major conclusions contained in the report.

1. During the period between July 1968 and May 1969, about 500 volunteers provided by several agencies (CIA, DIA, State Department) underwent an intensive two-day screening to determine whether or not they possessed any ability to transmit or receive telepathic signals. Specifically, they were tested in specially constructed, two-person chairs that allowed their brains to be in close proximity and, therefore, within each other's brainwave fields. However, the chairs were heavily padded, and physically and electrically isolated so that the volunteers could not signal to each other through any of the normal senses.

During each test run, the volunteer who was attempting to transmit his thoughts concentrated on a sequence of 100 digits, each presented to him on a screen for a period of ten seconds. Simultaneously, the volunteer who was trying to receive the thoughts attempted to perceive the digit that was being transmitted and recorded his choice by pressing a button. The numbers to be transmitted were selected at random by a computer, which also recorded the guesses of the receiving person and analyzed the test scores. Extensive precautions were taken to prevent all known methods of cheating.

2. Of the 487 volunteers initially screened as described above, 17 achieved test scores (as either transmitters or receivers of thoughts or both) that are extremely unlikely to have been the results of chance alone. The lowest score achieved by anyone in this group of 17 for a one-day testing period would be expected to occur by chance less than once in 100,000 test runs; the highest score would be expected to occur less than once in 1,000,000,000 runs. On the basis of these far-above-chance initial test scores, the 17 volunteers were retained for additional testing as described below.

3. Each of the 17 outstanding volunteers was subjected to a minimum of two weeks of additional testing, during which he or she completed at least 25 additional runs as a transmitter and 25 as a receiver. These additional screening tests have identified six individuals whose level and consistency of performance is so far above that which would be expected from chance that the only rational, scientific conclusion that can be drawn is that these individuals' brains are capable of transmitting and/or receiving telepathic signals over short distances.

The probability that the lowest average score achieved by any of these individuals over the two-week period occurred by the action of chance alone is less than one in 10,000,000,000,000. Three of the individuals achieved their phenomenal scores as transmitters, two as receivers, and one outstanding individual did so as both. On the basis of these test results, it is recommended that the six individuals be made permanent members of the Project Psi staff, so that they can undergo virtually continuous testing, with the aim of further understanding and developing their telepathic abilities.

4. Of the 17 volunteers initially identified by the screening tests described in paragraphs 1 and 2, nine achieve their high scores as transmitters. These nine individuals were subjected to an additional week of testing to determine whether or not their recorded brain-wave signals bore any consistent relationship to the numbers presented to them on the screen. Three of these people, including one who demonstrated exceptional abilities as a transmitter in the tests described in paragraph 3, showed correlations between the number presented to their eyes and specific

characteristics of their brain-wave signals. While preliminary, this evidence supports the conclusion that electrical signals in the brain are involved in the transmission and reception of the psi field. It also is recommended that the additional two outstanding volunteers identified by this test be made permanent members of the Project Psi staff, again to facilitate extensive investigation of their abilities.

5. Theoretical calculations, based on physiological, chemical, and electrical modeling of the brain, have determined that transmission of signals between two brains via the electromagnetic field should be possible if the brains are close enough together and if the background electrical noise is sufficiently low. The distance over which brain-to-brain communication is possible cannot be estimated precisely at present; however, distances of one to ten meters appear plausible.

In urban environments, the principal source of electrical interference with brain-to-brain communication is likely to be the electric power distribution system—generators, transmission lines, and large electric motors. In eventual espionage applications at conference tables or in crowded rooms, interference between the signals generated by many different brains may make precise communication between two specific brains difficult.

Coupled with the positive experimental screening results reported above, theoretical predictions of brain-to-brain communication over distances useful for the objectives of Project Psi are extremely encouraging.

6. A recent suggestion that placing the receiver in a state of hypnosis may reduce the extraneous signals generated within his own brain and thus enable it to receive better the signals generated in the brain of the transmitter has been tested on a limited number of volunteers. This effort will be continued, and a companion one will be initiated to explore the potential of drugs to improve both transmitter and receiver performance.

7. In summary, the first year of intensive effort by Project Psi has been extremely successful. Brain-to-brain communication has been predicted theoretically and demonstrated experimentally beyond any reasonable doubt.

The development of a man with psi now appears to be a rational scientific possibility, rather than just a fanciful desire. The route from here to the ultimate objective will be difficult and uncertain, but the summit is in sight.

Jack smiled to himself. The final prose was purple, but, considering the audience, he thought it was appropriate.

Several weeks later, Jack returned from lunch and scanned through the neat pile of telephone messages his secretary had arranged on his desk. One of them caught his eye.

Mr. Bennington's secretary called. He would like to arrange a meeting with you and a man from General Ryan's office as soon as possible. He suggests his office at 3 P.M. tomorrow. Please call.

"Hm," Jack said to himself. "I guess he's read the report."

The following afternoon, Jack pulled his car up to the main gate on the access road leading to CIA headquarters in Langley, Virginia. To the guard's inquiry, he responded:

"I'm Professor Mason. I'm visiting Mr. Bennington. He's expecting me."

"Who did you say you were visiting?" the guard responded dumbly.

"Mr. Bennington. Mr. Stuart Bennington," Jack repeated with a smile.

"Oh," the guard exclaimed, finally making the connection. "You mean the director."

"Yes," said Jack with unconcealed amusement.

At this, the guard retreated into his shelter and made a hurried phone call. He returned shortly and addressed Jack in an official tone.

"The director is expecting you, sir. Do you know the way, sir?"

"No," said Jack, still smiling.

The now attentive guard instantly produced a map from his clipboard and began to explain.

"We're right here, sir. At the main gate."

He drew an X and then a line on the map and then tilted the clipboard so that Jack could see it.

"Just go straight ahead until the road bears left around the main building. You'll see a driveway on the left that leads to the garage under the building. Just drive down there, and the guard will tell you where to park."

120

Stuart Bennington greeted Jack with the Ivy-League charm he naturally employed to disarm visitors.

"Professor Mason. I'm really glad to see you again. Thanks for coming on such short notice."

Bennington led the way into his inner office and then spoke to the secretary who had followed them.

"Elizabeth, would you be so kind as to get us some coffee?"

The Director of Central Intelligence gestured toward a pair of leather-upholstered wing chairs on each side of a walnut butler's table, and they sat down. Shortly, Elizabeth returned with a small silver tray on which were a pair of white china cups and saucers and a gleaming pot of coffee.

"Well, Professor," Stuart Bennington began, as if they were academic colleagues seated at the faculty club, "I'm sure you must have known how impressed we would be with your report. I've been in this business for a long time. Ever since I left Yale. And I can honestly tell you that Project Psi is one of the most exciting developments that I've seen. You may not realize it, but the intelligence business has become pretty mechanized and automated.

"Most of the new developments in the last ten or twenty years have been high-technology stuff. Radars and computers and satellites, and that kind of thing. But the human side hasn't really changed much. It hasn't kept pace. Real spies are about the way they always were. Hard to recruit, difficult to train, and impossible to trust. Paranoids, every one of them. And egomaniacs. And to top it all off, just about the time you get a good one, who starts to produce really useful information, you lose him. They grab him, or they buy him off, or he just gets scared or tired or . . . "

Jack attempted to appear nonchalant, but his face revealed his puzzlement at this down-to-earth description of the secret world of espionage from the man at the top. Bennington detected his visitor's uneasiness and turned his discourse back to praise for Project Psi.

"So you see, Professor, this telepathic capability that you are developing will be the most fundamental change in human espionage since it all began."

121

Jack tried to nod knowingly. With this slight encouragement, Stuart Bennington reverted to his rambling description of the problems of the chief of American intelligence.

"Our biggest problem is to get someone near the top. Where we can find out what their intentions are. Not just what they're doing in the laboratories and on the military bases and in the factories, but what the leaders are really trying to achieve. Are they building up their forces to start something? Or is it just their paranoia left over from World War Two? You know, fear of another invasion by the Germans. Or consider détente. Do they take it seriously? Or is it just a ploy to keep us talking while they're building?"

Jack's continued unease was obvious by now, and Stuart Bennington smiled, got to his feet, and changed the subject.

"Pardon me, Professor, it's hard not to get excited. This end of the business has been waiting so long for a fundamentally new technique to be developed. But, enough of that. Let me get to why I asked you to come over this afternoon."

The look of relief on Jack's face pleased his host, and the latter resumed his chair before continuing.

"I sent the executive summary of your report over to the White House. To Sam Ryan. Sam was just as impressed as I had been, and he had one of the cleared people on his staff prepare a one-page summary for the president. Sam got it back the other day with a scrawled comment saying, 'Sam: I want this thing given top priority. I want to see a plan to push it hard. Really hard!' So you see, Professor, your achievements have received some pretty high-level attention."

While Jack was absorbing the fact that his report, or at least a summary of it, actually had reached the president, a flashing light on the telephone console behind his desk beckoned to Stuart Bennington. The Director of Central Intelligence excused himself, crossed the room, and took the call.

"Mr. Bennington, Colonel Damon is here. Shall I send him in?"

"Give us a few more minutes, Elizabeth. I'll call you when I want him to come in."

Bennington returned to his seat across from Jack and spoke in a confidential tone.

"The man from the White House is outside. Colonel Richard Damon. He started out as Sam Ryan's aide, but now he thinks he's an advisor to the president. He's here to talk about the plan that the president asked Sam for. But I want to have an understanding with you first. What do *you* think should be done next? More testing? More people? More money? A new facility?"

Jack had finally succeeded in at least partially collecting his thoughts.

"Well, I've been giving those possibilities considerable thought lately," he said with a small smile. "We certainly should do more testing. But I don't think that it will change the fundamental answer. We've shown that telepathy is possible. That the phenomenon exists. That two brains can communicate directly."

As he spoke, the thought flashed into Jack's mind that this conclusion, properly documented in a scholarly article, would surely bring the Noble prize. But his vision of grandeur was fleeting, and he quickly returned to reality.

"The problem is that there's a tremendous gap between feasibility and practicality. All we've shown, after a year of hard work, is that when two brains are as close together as possible, they can communicate a small amount of information about single numbers that a person concentrates on one at a time. The difference between that and a spy who can discern the motives of world leaders at the conference table is like the jump between Goddard's rocket and Neil Armstrong's step onto the moon. Goddard knew that travel to the moon was possible. But it took NASA ten years and fifty billion dollars to get there."

Stuart Bennington smiled broadly.

"Good, I'm glad to see that we're in agreement. You're going to need a lot of money and a new facility and a larger staff."

A look of surprise and concern instantly returned to Jack's face. *Things were going too fast again. Sort of half out of control,* he thought. But Stuart Bennington continued without waiting for Jack to reply.

"Let me tell you how I want to handle this. I'm sure it will seem a little spooky to you, but it's the way you have to do things in this business."

The Director of Central Intelligence rose and moved to the bookcase-lined wall at the far end of his office. He pressed a hidden button and a concealed door faced with a stack of shelved books swung open noiselessly.

"Through this door you'll find my private study," Bennington said, pointing through the opening. "Make yourself comfortable. You'll find pads and pencils and whatever else you may need. What I want you to do is to sit down and write out a skeletal draft of a plan. How much money you think you'll need. How big a facility. How many people. How long you think it will take."

The color drained from Jack's face as he began to comprehend the task, but Stuart Bennington continued matter-of-factly.

"There's a dictating machine on the desk too, if that's easier for you. When you're finished, just push the call button and Elizabeth will come and get it from you and type it up. And when you think it's in reasonable shape, she'll bring you in through the front door again to talk to Damon and me. You pull the plan out as if you brought it with you, and I'll be surprised. And I'll have reservations about whether we should go that fast. But Damon won't. He'll urge us to go even faster and tell himself that I'm kind of conservative. And that it's certainly lucky for Sam and the president that they have him around to push me."

Jack got up and crossed the room in a daze to where Stuart Bennington stood before the open hole in the bookcase. Bennington again gestured toward the hideaway office and Jack passed through the door in the wall of books and found himself in what could have passed for the comfortable den of an expensive home in the Washington suburbs.

The Director of Central Intelligence pushed a second hidden button, and the door swung closed behind his bewildered visitor. Bennington returned to his desk and picked up the telephone.

"Elizabeth, will you please send in Colonel Damon."

Richard Damon looked the part. Although he was dressed in civilian clothes, the fact that he was a military officer was obvious to any perceptive observer. His gray hair was crew cut, he stood unusually erectly, and his gut revealed not the slightest trace of the bureaucrat's paunch. Damon came almost to attention in front of Stuart Bennington's desk and greated him respectfully.

"Good afternoon, Mr. Bennington. It's an honor to see you again. I appreciate your finding time for this meeting on short notice. As you know, General Ryan and the president have given this matter top priority."

Bennington motioned to the colonel to be seated in the chair beside his desk, while Elizabeth surreptitiously removed the tray that was the only remaining evidence of the previous meeting. After she left the room, Stuart Bennington leaned forward toward his visitor and began in a confidential tone.

"I've asked Professor Mason to be here in about an hour. I thought that you and I should talk before he arrives."

Richard Damon nodded knowingly and then unzipped a thin plastic briefcase and handed a sheet of paper to the man behind the desk. It was a copy of the one-page summary of Project Psi accomplishments on which the president had written his instructions. Stuart Bennington smiled and casually flipped the sheet of paper into one of the mahogany letter boxes on his desk. He thought to himself that the president's endorsement of their activities would make a fine addition to his collection of memorabilia. But his response to Damon was unrevealing.

"I see that you are aware of the president's interest. I discussed the progress with him a week ago, and he expressed a strong desire to be kept informed."

"It's more than just informed, sir," Richard Damon responded. "As you can see from what he wrote on the summary, the president really wants this thing pushed. He has told General Ryan to make sure that Project Psi gets the highest priority and all the funding it needs. And the general has asked me to work with your people to come up with a plan."

Stuart Bennington smiled benignly, and Richard Damon persisted, oblivious of the true situation.

"I'll bet that guy Mason will really be surprised when he finds out how hard we're pushing this thing. You know how those college professors are; they'll screw around forever if you let them."

Stuart Bennington's gaze drifted from the colonel seated erectly beside his desk to the wall of books separating his office from the study. He visualized Jack hard at work, while Damon continued to talk enthusiastically.

12

Exotic Chemicals Research

Only a little more than a year has elapsed since Jack Mason secretly prepared the plan for Project Psi expansion in Stuart Bennington's hideaway office. But the changes have been profound. The tight-knit group of old friends and academic colleagues has grown by leaps and bounds to a sometimes disorganized staff of hundreds. The budget that was unspendable when measured in millions now seems tight at ten times the amount. And the spartan anonymity of a nondescript, glass-and-steel office building in a suburban mall has given way to a hastily constructed private campus isolated from nosy neighbors and aggressive attachés. The search for the man with psi has become a big business.

The new Project Psi facility was located in the rolling Virginia countryside between Dulles Airport and the historic Civil War battlefields surrounding Manassas. The only evidence it presented to local residents or adventuresome tourists was a series of signs at intervals along a chain-link fence proclaiming ominously:

> American Chemical Company
> Exotic Chemicals Research Facility
> Keep Out for Your Own Safety

Jack Mason wheeled his new Porsche Targa through the main gate without stopping; the guard recognized the car and waved a greeting. Jack took the turns of the winding road leading to the laboratory at high speed, hoping to momentarily experience the exhilaration of the Porche's performance. The road was empty in the early morning haze, and he rapidly arrived at a second fence surrounding a group of low buildings. This barrier was topped by rows of barbed wire slanting both inward and outward, and the signs it bore were more ominous:

American Chemical Company
Exotic Chemicals Research Facility
U.S. Government Jurisdiction
Authorized Personnel Only

Jack stopped the Porche at the gate and handed his badge to the guard, who smiled his acknowledgment of the boss's identity. The sentry inserted the badge into a slot in a box in his shelter and then returned it to Jack. Instantly and silently, a computer in Building A added a record to the perimeter entry file: 5 Oct 70, 0737, Mason, J.W., 070–41–9165, Technical Director.

Jack drove the short distance to Building A and parked in his reserved space next to the entrance. Inside the lobby, he again presented his badge to a guard and engaged in pleasantries while the computer updated the Building A entry file.

Once settled in his office, Jack scanned his calendar for the day and confirmed that Brian MacFarland, the deputy director of the CIA, would be visiting them later that morning to hear about the project's latest achievements. Although they had rehearsed several presentations that might be given to MacFarland, Jack still had not decided what the best mix of people and topics might be. He began to play over in his mind how he wanted the session to go and exactly who should take part in the discussion. The problem was to convey the exciting scientific progress that had been made without leaving MacFarland with the impression that the operational product—the man with psi—was just around the corner. Brian was a nice guy, Jack thought with a smile, but not technical. And because of his background, first as an agent, and then as an agent handler, all Brian really knew or cared about was the end result—a productive spy in place.

Jack concluded that Barney O'Neil was the right person to summarize the recent testing results. Barney came across as being enthusiastic and genuine. Now for the cold water. Who should he use for that? Walter Patton? Based on an analysis of sources of noise that would interfer with brain-to-brain communication, Walter was afraid that the most that any person would ever be able to do would be to transmit or receive a few numbers at close range. *Or Phyllis Jackson?* Jack thought. *She was so sensible and pleasant, and concerned that under the stress of a real espionage situation, any telepathic ability that a man with psi had might be completely suppressed. On Anton Start?* Jack thought, with a smile. *Anton was sure that human subjects could be taught to do anything. Just like rats.*

Jack finally decided on Barney and Walter for the initial discussion. Barney for the enthusiasm and Walter for the caution. Jack would personally start out neutral and then swing whichever way was necessary. And as a safety valve, if Brian got too excited, he and Phyllis would take him to lunch and try to calm him down.

A little after ten o'clock, Brian MacFarland entered Jack's office in his usual jovial manner.

"And how's my favorite professor? Have you had any strange dreams lately? In Russian, I hope."

Jack smiled, and MacFarland continued in the same vein.

"Let me tell you one that I heard at a barbecue last night. From my neighbor who works for the Fat Boys' Institute. What's the Polish plan for winning the Vietnam War?"

Jack's smile broadened into a grin of anticipation.

"They're going to do it the same way the Americans did."

Jack laughed out loud, and MacFarland joined in, always pleased when his humor struck a responsive chord. When he finally recovered, Jack addressed his visitor seriously.

"Brian, I think we're at a turning point in the project. And I think you'll agree with me after you have heard what Dr. O'Neil and Dr. Patton have to say this morning. But first, I'd like to put it in context for you myself."

"Context," repeated MacFarland with a grin. "You sound like an attorney about to explain why his client was under the other guy's wife's bed, or like one of my station chiefs about to begin a long, sad story about why their man got our man first."

Jack smiled and tried to respond in kind, but in a way that would get his real point across.

"Well, it's something like that. Only better. It's sort of like the Wright brothers. We've gotten off the ground a couple of times, but not for very long. So we know it's possible. But it's going to take some time and a lot of hard work before we have a commercial airliner or, more to the point, a U-2."

"I get it," MacFarland responded with a broad grin. "You think you've got it by the balls, but I shouldn't go off half-cocked or get Stuart or Sam too excited."

"Right," said Jack with obvious relief.

A half an hour of bantering later, Barney O'Neil and Walter Patton entered Jack's office, and Brian MacFarland jovially greeted Barney.

"Oh, I see we're going to get a touch of the blarney this morning."

"Yeah, but we'll have Scotch for lunch. That is, if you can wait that long."

MacFarland grinned broadly, and Barney was pleased that his rejoinder had been taken good-naturedly.

Jack motioned for them all to take places around the conference table and then seated himself at its head.

"As I've told you, Brian, I'd like Barney and Walter to bring you up to date. We've made a lot of progress recently that you should know about. Why don't we start by having Barney summarize the experimental results."

"Lay on, MacDuff," said MacFarland with a simulated flourish of a cape.

"Well, Brian," Barney began, "let me try to tell you the most important things first. Basically, I believe that we have proven beyond any doubt that under ideal circumstances two brains can communicate directly via the electromagnetic field."

"Those are strong words, young fella," said MacFarland, with obvious good humor, and O'Neil continued.

"The strongest evidence we have for this conclusion is the performance of our two best pairs of volunteers. All four of these people have been permanent members of the staff for at least nine months and have taken part in test runs almost every working day. So we have a tremendous amount of experimental evidence on their performance. At first, we were testing them with different partners and alternately asking them to both transmit and receive digits. We were trying to see which role each person was best at and which pairs worked best together. And we were also using them to screen new volunteers. But, for the last three or four months, the pairings of the four people with the most telepathic ability have remained the same, and each person has had a fixed role as either a transmitter or a receiver of thoughts."

Brian MacFarland nodded with genuine interest, and Barney continued the description enthusiastically.

"We arranged the four people in the best pairs we could, based on statistical analyses of their test scores on the computer. For the last three months, each of the pairs has done five to eight runs per day, five or six days per week, for a total of four or five hundred runs. Thus, over this period, each of the two transmitters has attempted to send over forty thousand digits to his companion receiver. Truly a massive amount of data from a statistical standpoint."

MacFarland nodded again, hardly interrupting O'Neil's stream of consciousness.

"The performance of the two people who have been receiving the digits is so far above that which would be expected on the basis of chance alone that we are convinced beyond any shadow of a doubt that real telepathic transmission and reception has occurred. The average score for all the test runs these four people have made is twenty-three correct answers out of one hundred, as opposed to the ten that would be expected from chance alone. The probability of this average score occurring over so many runs due to a colossal run of good luck is so microscopically small that I'm not sure it would mean anything if I wrote it down for you. It's ten to the minus one hundred and sixty-nine or something. Walter will give you more of the details later."

As Barney continued to speak, a frown slowly developed on Brian MacFarland's face. As if by telepathy, Jack anticipated his concern.

"I know what you're thinking, Brian. That they're cheating. I was afraid of that, too. And I'm still concerned. But I think we can convince you that it's very unlikely."

"When you've dealt with agents as long as I have," MacFarland replied, his frown turning to a grin, "cheating is certainly the first thing that comes to mind."

Jack nodded and then began his explanation.

"Basically, we've done two kinds of things to try to prevent cheating. I think you know about all the technical precautions. The screening and padding between the chairs, the microphones and vibration sensors, the coding and password protection of the computer records, and those sorts of things. If you'd like to hear any more about any of that, Barney and Paul Rosenfeld can fill you in."

The thought of being subjected to further abstruse technical presentations did not thrill Brian MacFarland. His doleful expression was all the hint that Jack needed to proceed to something that his guest was likely to find more interesting.

"Recently, I took an entirely different approach to the problem. I told Bob Green that it was his responsibility to find out for certain whether or not any cheating was occurring, to use whatever techniques he saw fit as long as they were reasonably legal and ethical. Furthermore, I told him that I didn't want to have anything to do with the investigation while it was in progress. All I wanted to do was read the report when it was finished. Let me say for now that the report convinces *me*. And I've arranged for Bob to talk to you privately about the subject later and to show you the report, so you can judge for yourself."

Brian MacFarland's glum expression turned to a broad smile. At least, he thought, he'd hear some good stories from Bob. Like which volunteer was screwing which secretary or which of the crazy scientists beat his wife or preferred young boys or whatever.

With their visitor's good humor restored, Jack motioned to Barney to continue.

"We've got two other secondary, but important, pieces of experimental evidence confirming that telepathy is really taking place," O'Neil began again. "First, we tried increasing the distance between the brains of the people who are transmitting and receiving the digits. As you know, we attempted to get them as close together as possible for the initial screening tests. About two inches between the heads and less than a foot between the brains. Well, recently, we tried increasing the distance, in steps, up to about ten feet between heads. And just what you would expect happened; the scores went down as the distance between the heads increased. Walter will show you some nice curves comparing the test scores with theoretical predictions."

Again Brian MacFarland nodded, although he was less than sure that he understood why decreasing test scores with increasing distance between the brains was a satisfying result to Barney. But the latter continued, oblivious to his listener's perplexity.

"The second important result comes from those experiments where we try to find indications in the brain-wave signals of the transmitter that are related to the digits presented to his eyes. Researchers call them evoked potentials. The results are still preliminary, but we have found a correlation. It's weak, but it's definitely there. Again, Walter will show you a comparison with theoretical predictions. So, based on all of this, we are convinced that brain-to-brain communication via the electromagnetic field really exists. The sixty-four-million-dollar question is, can it be exploited in any practical way?"

Brian MacFarland was roused from his confusion by the mention of exploitation. He visualized a man with psi peering into the brain of a chunky Soviet general using a combination of Superman's X-ray vision and the Shadow's power to cloud men's minds so that they cannot see him.

"Well," Jack interjected, "I guess that's your cue, Walter. Why don't you start by describing to Brian the estimates your people have made of the possible performance of a man with psi based on extrapolations from our present test results."

Walter Patton unfolded his six-foot-four-inch frame from the confinement of his chair and loped to the blackboard. He was dressed informally in an open-necked shirt accented by a striking Hopi Indian bola tie. Now standing before them, Patton began in a low-keyed, almost apologetic tone.

"Any predictions we make now are really wild-assed guesses. Some people dignify them by calling them SWAGs—scientific wild-assed guesses. You've got to understand what a gulf there is between two specially selected people with their heads close together in a laboratory successfully transmitting and receiving single digits and a spy at a conference table groping to receive and unscramble the sophisticated and jumbled thoughts of unfamiliar adversaries thinking in a foreign language.

"The things we can put numbers to are the easy parts of the problem. That's the way we physicists are. We work on the aspects of the problem that we know how to handle and ignore the parts we don't. Like the story about the drunk who was looking for his car keys under a street light. A friend asked where he had lost them and the drunk answered, 'In the parking lot.' 'Then why aren't you looking for them in the parking lot?' the puzzled friend enquired. 'Because it's dark over there,' the drunk replied with twisted logic. And that's the way physicists are. We work on the easy stuff and hope that the hard stuff doesn't matter."

Bryan MacFarland smiled and added the joke to his collection along with a mental note that Walter Patton might not be such a bad guy after all, at least for a scientist.

Having warmed up a bit, the lanky physicist continued more confidently.

"We've tried to quantify three things. The way in which the ability to receive telepathic signals lessens as the distance between the two brains increases. The increased difficulty of receiving words or phrases as opposed to just single digits. And the problem of receiving signals from a particular brain in a crowded conference room, where interfering signals are present from other brains and electrical equipment."

Brian MacFarland looked perplexed.

Walter Patton scrawled cryptically on the blackboard: "decay law, information content, background noise."

An hour later, all the blackboards in Jack's office were filled with equations, sketches, curves, and cryptic words and phrases. On several occasions, when Walter Patton had run out of space to write, he simply erased a small portion of the board with his clenched fist and continued the lecture. Barney O'Neil had followed the thread through the forest enthusiastically, offering comments, suggestions, and leading questions. But Brian MacFarland had been mesmerized. In the end, he was reduced to staring, head in hands, at the jumble of hieroglyphics on the blackboards and the strange, gangling creature who was writing them. And Brian thought, ruefully, that his fleeting concession that Walter was a regular guy certainly had been naive.

But Jack Mason was secretly pleased. He thought that Walter had conveyed just the right impression. On the one hand that the project's staff was supremely competent, but on the other hand that the problem they were attacking was extremely difficult. When Patton at last had wound down and MacFarland was sufficiently impressed and confused, Jack summarized as if the ultimate truth had been lucidly revealed.

"So, Brian, I think that you now understand why we are so excited about the progress that has been made lately, and yet, why we want to emphasize how far there still is to go."

MacFarland nodded numbly, and Jack accepted his silent concession of defeat and changed the subject.

"Why don't we get some lunch? I've asked Phyllis to join us."

Brian MacFarland perked up instantly as the image of Phyllis Jackson flashed before his eyes. He prided himself on not missing an opportunity to be with a charming woman.

13

The Command from on High

The loud, incessant ringing of the secure telephone jolted Jack upright in his chair. He glared at the demonic instrument demanding to be answered and then lifted the receiver.

"Mason speaking."

"Good morning, Professor Mason, just a moment for Mr. Bennington."

Elizabeth's pleasant voice soothed Jack's jangled nerves, but his anxious mind raced with speculations. Why was the Director of Central Intelligence calling at 8:30 in the morning? Jack rapidly concluded that someone above had made some kind of decision. He only hoped that it wouldn't be too disruptive.

"Good morning, Jack," boomed the voice of Stuart Bennington. He sounded as if he were at the bottom of a rain barrel, the way all deep voices do over the secure telephone.

"Good morning, Stuart," Jack responded warily. "What can I do for you?"

"From what Brian has told me, it seems that you've done quite a lot already," Bennington began in a laudatory tone. "We're pretty impressed over here with the progress you've been making."

Jack's thoughts raced ahead, anticipating the worst. Clearly, Brian had told an enthusiastic story to Stuart, and Stuart to Sam, and, God knows, probably Sam to the president.

"I'm glad you're pleased, Stuart," Jack responded truthfully. "We're pretty encouraged ourselves. But there's a long way to go. We're just at the beginning. You and General Ryan have got to understand that—"

"Look, Jack, I know what you're trying to tell me," Bennington interrupted. "But it's too late. The president has made up his mind."

A sudden chill enveloped Jack, and the muscles in his gut tightened. He groped for a response, but, before he could utter a word, Stuart Bennington continued in a confidential tone.

"I'm going to give you some background that very few people are aware of. But I think you should know so that you'll understand why all the pressure is being put on. But you must not tell a soul, or we'll both be in the doghouse. The president wants to have a summit meeting with Sherkov before the end of his second term. He's aiming for the spring of 1972."

Jack's sense of panic intensified, and his stomach was gripped by real pain. But Stuart Bennington continued inexorably.

"And he has ordered that a man with psi be ready to accompany him."

Jack's head spun. What was this mad man saying? He tried to visualize the months. It was the end of November now. What did spring mean? April? May? Hope for the best. Suppose it's May. How many months? December, January, February, Jack frantically counted on his fingers. *Eighteen months!* To do the impossible! A year and a half. To go from people babbling numbers to a spy in a conference room. *It's crazy! What do they think . . .*

Even at the other end of a poor-quality, encrypted telephone conversation, Stuart Bennington could sense Jack's shock and dismay. Lacking any other palliative, Bennington tried to employ the lure of power to turn the discussion in a more positive direction.

"Look, Jack, it's not all bad. You've certainly got visibility, all the way to the top. And the clout that goes with it."

Clout! Jack thought and the image of a major-league batter at the plate flashed before his eyes. Clouting the ball out of the park. And the ball had a face, Stuart Bennington's face. And the hitter had a face too, Jack Mason's smiling face.

Oblivious of his listener's Freudian hallucination, the Director of Central Intelligence continued enthusiastically.

"The president has directed that the project shall have an unlimited budget and maximum cooperation from other government activities. Not just within my agency, but others too, if they can help. Why, we haven't had a project with this kind of priority since we started Purple Flash!"

Purple Flash! Jack thought. And the image of a Louisville Slugger swatting the skull of Stuart Bennington returned for an instant.

"Look, Jack," Bennington persisted, "I realize that this has hit you pretty suddenly. Why don't you take some time to think about it before responding. Talk it over with your key people. You can tell them roughly what the deadline is. Just don't mention the summit meeting."

Jack nodded numbly to himself, and Stuart Bennington went on thinking out loud.

"Let's see, what should we use as a cover story with the key staff people? How about this? Let's tell them that the secretary of state wants to start testing a man with psi in discussions with the Soviet ambassador about a year from now. How does that sound to you?"

Now eighteen months is down to a year, Jack thought, and the panic returned. *And the secretary of state is in the act. And the Soviet ambassador! How does it sound to me? Crazy!*

"Look, Stuart, you're right," Jack finally responded, trying to control his emotions. "You'll have to give me some time to think about it. Because, if I tell you what I'm thinking now, you won't like it. And neither will Ryan and the president. People don't like to be told that—"

"Okay, Jack, I get the message," Bennington interjected. "Call me tomorrow, and we'll arrange a meeting for next week."

Stuart Bennington hung up abruptly, and the receiver blasted a loud rush of noise in Jack's ear as the secure telephone tried in vain to decode the voice that was no longer present. The stabbing sound brought Jack to his senses, and he hung up, too. He looked silently around the room, wondering what to do next, then impulsively pushed the button to call his secretary.

"Joyce! Find Bob and Barney, and tell them to come over right away!"

The three old friends and coconspirators huddled behind closed doors in an atmosphere of crisis. Jack paced frenetically back and forth, reviewing out loud the impossible list of things that had to be accomplished in the next twelve months. And he always came back to the same conclusion: "It's impossible!" This forceful repetition of the obvious was usually followed by some sort of epithet, much to Barney O'Neil's amusement.

"What do those fucking idiots think they're up to?" Jack shouted for the third or fourth time.

Barney slouched in an overstuffed, leather chair with one of his legs draped casually over an arm. From time to time he tried to offer Jack suggestions, some serious and some not. "We probably could screen twice as many volunteers if we worked around the clock." "You might resign; that would get their attention!"

But Bob Green could hardly contain his excitement. He leaped from his chair periodically with outbursts of enthusiasm. "It's the best thing that's happened to the spy business since the phone tap!" "We're at the center of this thing! We're driving it!" "And we've got an unlimited budget!"

To a remote viewer, the three men appeared to be actors in a mime play repeatedly rehearsing the same scene without noticeable improvement. The hours ground on, and they wearied inexorably without reaching a conclusion.

The unproductive and seemingly endless discussion was finally interrupted when Joyce entered the room.

"I don't know about you guys, but I'm going home," she announced firmly. "Have you got anything that you want me to lock up?"

The three exhausted thespians stared dumbly back at her as though their springs had finally wound down. At last, Jack spoke absentmindedly.

"Just this stuff on the desk, thank you, Joyce. How about you guys?"

"Uh, I've got to go back and lock up in my own office," Barney responded, as if in a daze.

"Me, too," said Bob. "But I'll be back in a minute. Let's get a drink."

"Okay," Jack agreed wearily. "I think I need one."

Jack and Bob engaged in an impromptu road race from the Project Psi facility to the Sheraton Hotel in Reston. Bob squealed out of the parking lot and down the winding drive to the main gate in the lead. But, once on the open road, the aging Fiat Spyder was no match for the new Porche Targa.

Jack was pleased to be comfortably installed in a booth at the rear of the dimly lit bar when Bob arrived out of breath.

"Hey, old buddy, that thing really moves. How fast were you going on the Dulles access road?"

"Not over a hundred," Jack said, with a smile. "I ordered you a gin and tonic."

"Sounds good," Bob responded, settling in. "But you'll have to start getting used to drinking vodka—straight! I don't know how the KGB trains their guys, but when I was in the embassy in Moscow ten years ago they could drink you under the table and then just walk away smiling. It was kind of scary. You were never quite sure the next day what you might have told them."

Jack smiled momentarily, but then his expression became more serious.

"Look, Bob, all joking aside. This thing is just moving too fast. Like I was on the access road. And now those guys want to step on the gas instead of the brake. I'm telling you, there's going to be a crash. A really bloody crash. And it won't be Stuart or Sam or the president that gets picked out of the wreckage and scooped into a rubber bag. It'll be some poor volunteer who happens to have extraordinary telepathic ability. And whose bad fortune it was to run into us."

Bob Green nodded his understanding and then tried to deflect his friend's concern.

"Look, Jack, they're all big boys. Most of them are spooks, and they know it's a rough game. You can get killed on the highway or in a plane crash or, most likely, by a heart attack. So why not have some fun before you go."

So that's what it is, Jack thought, *fun! It's a game. Like cops and robbers when you were a kid. Only now the kids are grown up, at least physically, and the guns are real.*

Jack and Sue Mason sat in the darkness on the deck of their home overlooking Lake Anne. It was cool, but not cold, and the lights of the houses around the lake twinkled through the clear

140

November darkness. Jack was pensive, and Sue sensed that something was the matter.

"What's the trouble, Jack? Did something go wrong at the lab?"

"Well, it's funny," he responded with a wry smile. "If I told it to you one way, you'd wonder why I'm not celebrating."

"Try me," she said, "and maybe it will help."

"Suppose I told you that the president got a report on our project and was so pleased that he has ordered that we be given an unlimited budget and complete cooperation from other agencies."

"I'm impressed," Sue said half seriously. "You must be doing something pretty big if that guy Leonard is interested. I can't imagine him giving a damn about science unless it could do something to enhance his political image. Do you remember that book I gave you to read before the election in sixty-four?"

Jack marveled at how close to the mark Sue had come without knowing exactly what the project was doing.

"Well, you're certainly on the right track. I guess the question is: Is he making a responsible decision? Have the people between me and him given him the straight story? Or have they each embellished it a little along the way?"

"Of course they have," she said incredulously. "They're politicians, too! And if they make you look good, they look good also. I'm not sure that Leonard would know or care about the truth if he heard it, but if you want him to, you had better tell him yourself."

Tell him myself? Jack repeated silently. He had never really thought about talking to the president himself. How could he do it? He couldn't just walk up to the White House gate. He'd have to arrange it through Stuart and Sam, and they would never agree. Jack stared blankly at his wife through the darkness for a moment longer and then responded unenthusiastically.

"You may be right, but it doesn't sound very practical."

"Why not?" Sue persisted. "If this thing you're doing is as important to Leonard as you say it is, he'll talk to you. The people between you and him won't like it. And they'll try to destroy you. But if you've got something that Richard Leonard wants, he'll talk to you."

"Uh-huh," Jack said, with a laugh, "That sounds good sitting here on the deck, but I doubt if it would cut much ice with the White House switchboard."

"Okay," Sue conceded, "if you can't call him, write him a letter. Dear Mr. President: I'm the guy who's in charge of that project that you're so excited about. And I'm afraid that people have exaggerated the prospects to you. So I'd like to come and tell you the straight story myself."

Jack looked out across the lake in silence. Reversing the president's decision sounded so simple to Sue, or at least she said it did. But somehow Jack knew that Project Psi now would continue inexorably to a final climax.

Much later that evening, Sue Mason lay wide awake in bed listening in terror as her husband twisted and turned beside her, mumbling back at the pursuing demons of his nightmare. Finally she could stand it no more.

"Jack? Jack! Wake up! What's the matter?"

Jack was roused to consciousness by the sudden feeling that someone was shaking him. When he finally realized where he was, he groggily swung his feet to the floor and sat on the edge of the bed. He was dripping wet with perspiration. The nightmare's last image was still vivid before his eyes, and the characters spontaneously began to replay the scene in his mind.

A man lay on a table in the center of a stark room, surrounded by a group of agitated people. A tall figure in a white coat stared down and addressed the supine figure authoritatively.

"Repeat it slowly for Professor Mason."

A strange, gurgling sound began in the prostrate man's throat and then slowly emerged from his mouth.

"Gar, ad, as, rowl, scld, ker."

"Again!" the interrogator commanded.

"Gar ad as rowl scld ker," the supine form repeated.

All the faces in the room suddenly turned toward Jack, and the white-coated figure intoned solemnly:

"Well, Professor Mason, what does it mean?"

The stares intensified, and the voices asked in chorus:

"Professor Mason! What does it mean? What does *garadas-rowlscldker* mean?"

Sue Mason sat up in bed and hugged her husband from behind. She was shocked to find his pajamas soaking wet.

"Jack, what's the matter?" she asked with renewed terror. "You must have had a terrible dream."

Jack turned slowly on the bed and returned his wife's hug. He sighed deeply and shook his head slowly from side to side as if attempting to dispel the terrifying latent image.

"What is it, Jack?" Sue persisted with a frightened voice. "Can you remember?"

Jack held his wife tightly again, then subsided onto the bed and stared wide-eyed at the ceiling. The faces from the dream stared back, and, through the mocking smiles, he could hear them saying: "What does it mean, Professor Mason? What does it mean?"

Jack arrived at the Project Psi facility early the next morning and immediately called a meeting of his key people. By a little before nine, Joyce had rounded up most of them, and they milled around the conference table in Jack's office talking and drinking coffee while waiting for the stragglers. Finally Jack closed the door and announced loudly:

"Well, let's get started! I think we're only missing Paul and Ken, and we can bring them up to speed when they get here. Most of you know that something big has happened, but I think that only Bob and Barney know any of the details. I'm going to tell you everything I know, but you've got to keep it quiet, at least until we get a chance to do some planning. So, for the time being, I don't want you discussing it with anybody except the people who are in this room."

The serious tone of Jack's preamble terminated the numerous private conversations, and people took seats at the conference table or in the chairs around the room. Jack sat on the edge of his desk and addressed his colleagues informally.

"Yesterday morning I got a call from Stuart Bennington. I think you all know that he's the Director of Central Intelligence and the person through whom our progress is reported to the White House. Bennington talks to Sam Ryan about the project on a weekly basis, and also discusses it with the president from time to time. Ryan is an ex-air-force general who functions as a mixture of senior aide and chief of staff to the president."

People around the room nodded their understanding, and Jack continued his explanation.

"As well as I can reconstruct it, what happened is something like this. Last week, as you all know, Brian MacFarland, Bennington's deputy, spent a morning over here getting an update. I thought we had pitched it just about right, but apparently I was wrong. I cautioned Brian about being too enthusiastic in his report to Bennington, and Barney and Walter told him in detail how much more we have left to do. About how we're just at the beginning. And that all we've done is proven feasibility. But I guess that all Brian heard, or chose to report, was the good news. My impression is that by the time the story got to Ryan and the president, it sounded like we've got the problem licked."

The faces around the room registered his staff's disbelief, and they all looked intently at their leader.

"Anyhow," Jack continued, "let me get to the bottom line. The president has ordered that the project be given the highest priority, an unlimited budget, and full cooperation from other agencies."

Some of the faces brightened, but the more experienced people waited for the other shoe to drop.

"The catch is," Jack concluded, "that we've got to have a man with psi ready for field testing in about twelve months."

Stunned silence gripped the room. The younger staff members stared incredulously, but the older hands shook their heads and smiled wryly at the all-too-familiar turn of events.

"Look, I know it sounds crazy to you," Jack acknowledged. "I told Bennington that myself yesterday. But his attitude seems to be that one just has to live with the whims of the White House."

"You mean," said a sarcastic voice from the back of the room, "that we can't tell the king that he isn't wearing any clothes!"

Jack smiled broadly, and several others laughed out loud. The tension was broken.

"Well, I think it's a little more sophisticated than that," Jack responded. "I gather that Bennington's experience in government has been that the time when a project is ready to go technically, and the time when the politicians want it and can pay for it, almost never coincide. So he's come to the conclusion that you've got to take the money when they offer it, even if you're not ready."

"It's better to make a false start than not to be allowed to start at all," someone else injected.

"Yes," Jack agreed. "I think that's about the most charitable interpretation you can put on Bennington's motivations. The way I left it with him was that we would get together today and do some brainstorming and planning. And if it still looks crazy at the end of the day, I'll tell him so in no uncertain terms."

Jack got up from his perch on the desk and moved toward the blackboard at the head of the conference table. He picked up a piece of chalk and continued speaking.

"Why don't we begin by listing all the major steps that would have to be accomplished to get from where we are now to having an operational man with psi. I suppose the first thing would be to continue the screening tests on an accelerated basis."

The group was still too stunned to respond constructively, but Jack persisted by starting a list at the top left-hand corner of the blackboard:

1. Accelerated Screening Tests

"What would we do here?" Jack continued, trying to stimulate discussion. "More of the same? Or something different?"

"Well," said Ken Anderson, who had just arrived, "we're between a rock and a hard place! We're doing the best experimental screening tests we know how to do. And we've found a number of volunteers who clearly have telepathic ability. But we'll never get to a man with psi in a year, or even two or three, if we just keep doing what we're doing now."

Jack's eyes scanned the faces, and they silently agreed with Ken's gloomy summary.

"So we've got to do something new," Jack concluded. "What could it be? Let's try to list some possibilities."

He turned back to the blackboard and began a list under the first major item.

1. Accelerated Screening Tests
    —more chairs, more volunteers

"We could do the same tests, only with more chairs and more volunteers," Jack said, explaining the obvious.

From the back of the room, John Franklin, the project's senior mathematician, joined the discussion.

"That may not be as stupid as it sounds. I've been doing some numbers while you were talking. Suppose we say that we've found two excellent subjects in the last three months by operating five sets of chairs, five hours per day, five days per week. It would take us some time to build more chairs, but we could start using the ones we have at least two shifts per day, seven days per week. That alone should double our number of star subjects in about a month."

Barney O'Neil nodded his head in agreement.

"John's suggestion has got to be a good way to start. It's something we know how to do, and we're bound to find some additional people with telepathic ability while we're trying to think of some better approaches."

Bob Green could restrain himself no longer. He felt impelled to inject a note of both enthusiasm and practicality.

"We ought to start testing these guys for ability to speak and think in Russian! We've got to keep the ultimate objective in mind. We'd look kind of stupid if we developed a guy with a lot of psychic ability who couldn't learn the Cyrillic alphabet!"

Suddenly, the shrill, incessant ringing of the secure telephone silenced the conversation. Jack moved behind his desk and lifted the appropriate receiver. He held the instrument away from his ear until the blast of noise ceased, indicating that his phone had become synchronized with the one at the other end. When he did put the receiver to his ear, a clipped, military voice had already begun to speak.

" . . . Major Burns at the White House. General Ryan would like to speak to Professor Mason."

"This is Professor Mason," Jack responded a little testily.

146

"Good morning, sir," the major continued, "just a moment for General Ryan."

Jack nodded, but said nothing.

"Good morning, Mason," Sam Ryan began loudly. "How are you? Let me get right to the point. Bennington has told you about the president's decision. But I want to be sure that you understand how important what you are doing is to us and how committed we are to it. The president has ordered that this thing be given top priority, an unlimited budget, and full cooperation from other agencies. And I am personally responsible to him for monitoring your progress. I want to have weekly meetings with you and Bennington. We'll do it Friday mornings after Stuart gives me the weekly intelligence wrap-up. At the first meeting, next Friday, I want—"

"Hold on, General!" Jack interjected. "Didn't Bennington tell you that I have serious reservations as to whether or not this thing can be done at all? Let alone on the insane schedule that has been proposed."

Sam Ryan was not used to being interrupted. And certainly not by a subordinate in the field telling him that his orders to attack were insane. The color rose in his ruddy Irish face, and the anger spilled out in his voice.

"Don't give me that reservations shit! You've received a direct order from your commander in chief, and you're going to obey it. Or I'll get someone else who will!"

Jack was taken aback at the sudden vehemence and vulgarity of Ryan's reaction, but he persevered in trying to get the truth across.

"Look, General, it's not a question of insubordination. It's a question of the laws of nature. They may not let us achieve what the president has ordered. No matter how hard we try. Or how much money you give us. Or how much cooperation from other agencies."

Sam Ryan could sense fear, even over the secure telephone. He had seen it so often in men in combat, especially before a big operation. His tone changed abruptly to that of a tough, old coach giving a halftime pep talk to a demoralized quarterback.

"Look, Mason, we've got the utmost confidence in your ability to do the job. And you've got a great team! All hand picked. Why, we got you anyone you asked for."

147

"I'm not saying the team isn't good," Jack replied defensively. "What I'm trying to tell you is that the problem is tough. Tougher than you and the president think."

"You know the saying, Mason," Sam Ryan responded firmly. " 'When the going gets tough, the tough get going!' That was a favorite of President Kennedy, and you ought to to think about it. Now, let's get back to next Friday's meeting. I want a number of things from you. First, a one-page summary of recent accomplishments. Second, a plan and schedule leading up to the field demonstration of a man with psi in twelve months. Third, a list of the other agencies from whom you want cooperation, and the specific tasks they must accomplish and the schedules they must meet. Fourth, a budgetary breakdown of the additional funding you will require. Is that all clear?"

Jack considered arguing further, but wisely concluded that it would be pointless. He simply answered, "Yes," and abruptly hung up the receiver, hoping that the blast of noise as the secure phones' lost synchronization would convey his feelings to the general. Rather like telling him to go fuck himself without being so uncouth.

Jack turned back to the people in the room and found all eyes concentrated on him, seeking amplification of the one-sided conversation they had heard.

"Well, I'm sure you got the gist of it," he said, with a wry smile. "They're pretty serious about crashing ahead. I guess that before we submit our resignations, we might as well try to come up with a plan. And whatever way it comes out, that's the way I'll present it."

14

The Psionauts

A month has elapsed since the president's decision, a month of frenzied activity for Project Psi. The testing facilities are used sixteen hours a day, six days per week to screen a greatly increased flow of volunteers hastily rounded up by the CIA and several other government agencies. Each volunteer undergoes four eight-hour periods of testing on successive days.

The first day, his ability as a receiver of thoughts is tested, using the best transmitters that the project has found.

The second day, the subject's ability to perceive artificially generated brain-wave signals is tested. These signals are modeled on those detected in the brain waves of the best human transmitters when they concentrate on each of the digits.

Psychological screening occupies the third day and attempts to answer two questions: Is the volunteer strongly motivated to succeed as a receiver of psi signals? and, Does the volunteer have the emotional stability to withstand the stress of life as a spy?

The final day of testing measures Russian language ability, beginning with basic oral and written exams. Later, those who do well are given word association tests by a native-born psychologist to measure their ability to think and perceive subtle ideas in Russian.

The results of the first few weeks of accelerated testing were disastrous. The two star transmitters were exhausted from working ten-hour days, with only Sundays to rest. The staff was discouraged, absenteeism was on the increase, and several junior people had quit. In spite of the heroic effort, only five people had been found who scored significantly above the chance level on either of the thought reception tests. And only two had scored well in receiving both real and artificial brain signals.

The psychological testing had gone just as badly. More than half of the volunteers believed that they had some sort of psychic ability. Unfortunately, the personality tests indicated that many of these true believers had highly emotional and potentially unstable personalities. Most of the rest of the volunteers had been shanghaied into the testing program by the agencies for which they worked. This group contained a higher percentage of stable personalities, but few people with any belief in psychic phenomena or much desire to succeed as a man with psi. Bob Green had summed up the dichotomy succinctly: "The *nuts* are sure they can do it, and the *squares* are sure they can't!"

The only tests in which a substantial percentage of the volunteers routinely succeeded were those of basic Russian language ability. But this isolated success was not surprising, because a speaking knowledge of Russian was one of the criteria used by the agencies in rounding up volunteers.

Phyllis Jackson's face and voice betrayed her concern. She and Jack sat at the conference table in his office, and he listened intently as she spoke.

"I guess you know that one of my hobbies is watching the way people behave around here. Normally, it's a harmless professional amusement—a busman's holiday. But recently I've been seeing things that worry me. Major mood swings. Not just in individuals, but in the whole staff. First enthusiasm and activity, then depression and lethargy."

Jack silently nodded his agreement with Phyllis's clinical observations, and she continued earnestly to describe the symptoms.

"It's gone through several cycles since the president made his decision. You know how depressed people were after the meeting where that Neanderthal Ryan called you on the secure telephone. Everyone moped around for a couple of days and said how crazy the White House was. But then the accelerated screening tests got started. And people got caught up in the activity. They worked long hours and forgot about the fundamental problem. And, for a couple of weeks, spirits were pretty high. But, about that time, the trend of the results began to become clear—we weren't really finding any terribly useful subjects. You know how it is; it takes a while for a conclusion like that to diffuse through the staff. The people directly doing the testing and the analysis are the first to know, and then the senior managers, like yourself. Finally, everyone in the place knows that something's wrong, even the computer operators and the guards. And then a sort of group depression settles over the place."

Jack again nodded his agreement with a serious expression. But then he gave her a small smile.

"Well, Phyllis, you're the doctor. What do you recommend?"

Phyllis Jackson smiled, too. Both of them were glad that the tension generated by her persuasive description of their group neurosis had been relieved. Phyllis began again, but this time a little less seriously.

"I've been talking the problem over with Dick Sterling. He was actually a practicing clinical psychiatrist before he joined the staff. So I think that he's a better judge of the seriousness of the problem than I am. Is it just an annoying group neurosis? Or has it gotten bad enough in the most seriously affected people that it's beginning to degrade their on-the-job performance?"

Jack continued to nod without speaking, and Phyllis went on earnestly.

"Since I first talked to him about it a week ago, Dick's been doing some informal psychological interviewing. And yesterday he came and told me that he thought the problem was serious enough that we should bring it to your attention. He believes that several fairly senior people are beginning to be noticeably affected by the stress. You know that we can't tell you their names, but I think you can imagine that they are people who feel a major responsibility for the success of the testing. They know it's going badly, and they desperately want it to succeed, but they don't know what to do to improve the results. And that's what leads to the anxiety."

Jack again nodded his agreement and then, uncharacteristically, made a personal confession.

"I guess I can sympathize with them. I've been pretty discouraged recently myself. Right after the president's decision and Ryan's call, I thought pretty seriously about resigning. Perhaps Sue has talked to you about it. She thinks I should quit. To bring them to their senses. Or at least to get me out of this madhouse. It's been pretty hard on her and the kids. I spend most of my time over here, but I can't tell them what I'm doing. She knows a little and probably suspects the worst. It's not a very good situation."

Phyllis nodded understandingly.

Having temporarily unburdened himself, Jack gave another little smile and returned to the problem at hand.

"Well, anyhow, enough of *my* troubles, Doctor. What do you recommend for the rest of the staff?"

Phyllis Jackson was secretly amused at Jack's reticence to discuss his own feelings in spite of their long friendship. But, nevertheless, she was pleased that he was seeking her advice about the staff. She began again in a professional tone.

"I think we can divide the people roughly into two groups so far as possible actions are concerned. The first group, the great majority of the staff, are just a little nervous or anxious about what's happening. Their reaction is completely normal. You and I feel the same way. This is the group that we can give you some advice about.

"The second group, and we're not really sure that anyone falls into it yet, would be individuals who are seriously psychologically disturbed. If Dick or I think that anyone is degenerating into this category, we will speak to them and strongly recommend that they seek professional help. But I don't think that *you* should worry about this potential second group. It won't do any good. If a person is emotionally disturbed, he was probably that way long before this project, and he'll probably still be that way long after it's over. So you and I can sympathize with him as a human being, and I can recommend that he seek professional advice, but there isn't much we can do personally to help him."

Jack's look was now very serious indeed, and Phyllis hurried on to the crux of her advice.

"So let's talk about the first group, the *normal* but *anxious*. Dick and I think there are several things that *you* can do to help them. First and foremost, they want to think that someone that they trust has a plan to make this thing come out right. This makes the situation doubly difficult for you. You've got to suppress your own natural anxieties and convince the staff that you have a rational plan that they can understand and follow. Even if you, yourself, have doubts."

Much to Phyllis's relief, Jack nodded his understanding vigorously.

"Yes, you're certainly right. I can't blame them for feeling anxious when they hear about the president's decision and Ryan's call, and then see the helter-skelter way that we're reacting. The problem is, of course, that we really don't have a very good plan. It's hard to make a plan to do the impossible," he concluded with a chuckle.

Phyllis Jackson smiled thinly, and Jack continued his explication.

"I guess what you're saying is that I've got to act like I have a plan. Even if I don't!"

Phyllis was pleased at Jack's frankness, and her smile broadened perceptibly.

"I'm not saying that you have to deceive them," she said firmly. "But you do have to lead them."

Jack's look suddenly turned cold, but, before he could respond to the criticism, Phyllis continued matter-of-factly.

"Get them together at staff meetings and discuss the problems frankly. And then lay out a plan and some assignments that everyone can understand. That way, people will feel that they know what's going on and what each of them is supposed to do. It doesn't have to be a perfect plan, just something that people can understand and use to see where they fit in."

Jack slowly began to smile again, and, after a moment more, he interrupted her nervous explanation.

"Okay, Phyllis, I get the point. I've kind of let them down lately. Like a general hiding in his tent when the attack is on. I'll take your advice and call a staff meeting for tomorrow morning. And get all the problems and concerns out on the table."

A loud knock on the door of Jack's office disturbed their concentration. He and Phyllis turned toward the noise. The door opened, admitting a smiling Bob Green.

"Joyce was afraid to interrupt you. She thought you might be doing something personal. But you know me, I'm never afraid to join the party."

Jack and Phyllis laughed out loud, and Bob joined them at the conference table. He handed Jack a Xerox copy of what appeared to be a newspaper clipping.

"Have you seen my ad for volunteers?"

Jack took the sheet of paper, and he and Phyllis read it with astonishment:

WANTED
People with Psychic Ability
Must be Highly Motivated
Unusual Opportunity for Income and Adventure
Russian Language Ability Desirable
Call 351–1100

"I'm running it that size all week in the *Post* and the *Star,* and larger on Sunday."

Phyllis looked at Bob as though he was a prime candidate for admission to the second psychological group—the truly emotionally disturbed. But Jack began to smile, having recognized the telephone number.

"What do you think the CIA switchboard will do when all the nuts start calling in?"

"Don't worry. I've headed that one off," Bob responded jovially. "I sent a copy to Stuart by courier yesterday."

Jack began to laugh uproariously.

"That's great! He'll have a fit! An absolute shit fit!"

Phyllis began to laugh too, but she was still not certain that the clipping was a joke.

"Bob, you didn't really run that ad, did you?" she asked incredulously

"Sure I ran it, Phyllis," Bob replied with a twinkle. "I just limited the distribution. Here and in Stuart's office!"

The long overdue staff meeting started off on a positive note, with Jack giving a subtle pep talk along the lines that Phyllis had suggested the previous day. But, perhaps inevitably, things had gone downhill from then on. Jack had suggested that each of the senior people describe the major problems they were facing. This was followed by group discussion and an attempt to formulate a plan. The trouble was, as Jack had suspected it would be, that a group of intelligent people cannot convince themselves that they have made a rational plan to accomplish something they fear is impossible. Fortunately, however, Barney O'Neil's unfailing good nature allowed him to summarize their desperate situation with a note of humor.

"The answer is," he proclaimed loudly, "we can't get there from here! At least not on the road we've been taking. We need something new. A new idea or a new technique."

The room quieted down, and serious faces nodded their agreement.

"As I see it," Barney continued, "there are are only two possibilities. One is to screen even more people even faster and just hope, like the sucker at the track, that we'll hit a winner. A guy who scores fifty out of a hundred. A statistical or telepathic freak. The other possibility is to find some way to improve the modest ability of the people we're already found. To help them to learn how to do it better. If we only knew what the *it* is that they do."

The normally serious face of Hermann Anton Stark was crossed by a mischievous smile. Stark was not given to humor or frivolity, but Barney's play on words sparked his fertile imagination.

"I know what I'd do if they were rats!" he injected forcefully.

Stark's sudden outburst silenced the discussion. Eyes and heads turned toward him.

"If they guessed right, I'd give them some cheese, and if they guessed *wrong,* I'd give them a *shock!*"

The room filled with laughter. and Bob Green chimed in.

"I bet *that* would get their attention!"

Bob visualized a white-coated staff member jabbing the bare ass of a hapless volunteer with an electric cattle prod, and he laughed uncontrollably. He vividly described his mental image to the assembled group and depression momentarily gave way to hysteria.

Several minutes later, when the remnants of laughter had finally died away, Barney O'Neil picked up the discussion again.

"Your suggestion might not be as crazy as it sounds, Anton. Think of the amazing things that people have taught chimpanzees and gorillas to do. Some push buttons with pictures on them

155

to make sentences, and others converse with their trainers in sign language. If they make a complete, correct sentence, they get what they want. Like a hug or a banana or whatever. But if they leave out the subject or the verb or something, they don't get anything. And they've learned a fantastic amount that way—several hundred words or signs. So perhaps we should seriously consider rewarding the volunteers for correct answers."

Bob Green started to chuckle again. When Barney had said reward, Bob has visualized Alice, the buxom, short-skirted programmer, being vigorously screwed on the computer room floor by a smiling volunteer. But he decided against sharing his second mental image with the group for fear of further degrading what he suspected was their already low opinion of his character.

Silence fell over the room and brows wrinkled. No one spoke immediately, but it was clear that the concept of training the volunteers had captured their thoughts. Finally, pleased at its impact, Anton Stark began to pursue his own suggestion.

"I can conceive of two different time scales for rewards and, with them, two different approaches to training. If we simply used the record of a volunteer's scores to reward him for good performance at the end of a day or a week, we would motivate him with the desire to do better, but probably not train him in how to do better. On the other hand, if we gave him something pleasant, like a kiss, right after each correct answer, and something unpleasant, like a shock, right after each wrong answer, we might conceivably help him learn how to do better."

Little by little, the idea was catching hold, gaining momentum. Ken Anderson, who headed up the group doing the actual testing of volunteers, made the first really practical suggestion.

"Let me try this on you. It's a combination of some things that we could do relatively easily, and it seems to fit Anton's suggestion. First of all, suppose that during the ten-second interval between the displays of digits to the person who is trying to transmit his thoughts—the time when we now let the person who is is trying to receive the thoughts rest—we gave the receiver a stimulus indicating whether his last answer was right or wrong. We could easily flash some sort of message on his display screen, like the words, 'Right' or 'Wrong.' And we could give him an auditory stimulus, too. For example, a voice that would say, 'Correct, keep up the good work' or 'Incorrect, try to concentrate harder.' I think these things might fill the bill for Anton's category of immediate feedback that tells the subject whether he was right or wrong while he can still remember what he was thinking when he performed well or poorly."

"Like whacking a horse on the ass with your crop while he's still standing on your toes," Bob Green quipped.

But this time Bob elicited no laughter. The idea of training someone to receive thoughts was too important. Instead, people just nodded their agreement with Ken Anderson's suggestion, and he continued enthusiastically.

"The other category, rewards for good longer-term performance, is easy to handle. We keep complete histories of every volunteer's performance on every run on disk right now. So all we would have to do is decide what kind of reward or penalty we wanted to give them. For example, we could set up a bank account for each person in the computer. And credit the account with nine dollars for each correct answer he gives, and debit the account by one dollar for each incorrect answer. That way, a volunteer who was just guessing or had no telepathic ability would come out even. But someone with performance consistently above that expected from chance would see his computer bank account growing steadily."

The faces around the room smiled their tacit approval of the idea of financial rewards, and, thus emboldened, Ken Anderson concluded with a stunning example.

"Let's see, the best guy we've got now averages about twenty-five correct answers per run. So he would make a bonus of about one hundred and fifty dollars per run. And right now he's doing about five or six runs a day, six days a week. So he'd earn a bonus of about five thousand dollars a week. That ought to motivate anybody!"

"I know we have this rule about staff members not becoming test subjects," said Bob Green with a broad grin, "but for that kind of dough, I'd sure like to sign up. I tell you what, Ken, I'll come around in a wig on Monday with the new crop of volunteers, and you pretend that you don't know me."

Bob's humor finally drew a smattering of chuckles, but, through all the banter, Jack could tell unmistakably that the idea of people learning to receive psi signals was being taken seriously.

"I think you've really hit on something, Anton," Jack said, with sincere praise. "Why don't you and Ken and Barney get together and work out the details of something that we could try fairly quickly on a pilot basis."

It was three weeks since Anton Stark had made the suggestion that rewards and punishments be employed to train people to transmit and receive psi signals. Thinking about it later, Jack wondered, with some amusement, whether B. F. Skinner, the controversial behavioral psychologist and Stark's mentor at Harvard, would approve of this ultimate clandestine application of the technique he had pioneered.

In the rooms used to measure the telepathic ability of the most talented volunteers, modifications to allow training experiments had proceeded frantically, without second thoughts. The receiver's side of one of the two-person chairs had been equipped to indicate to the subject after each guess whether or not he had selected the proper number. Correct answers were rewarded by the steady display of the word "RIGHT" in a pleasant pale blue and by a soothing woman's voice saying, "Good work, you are improving, keep it up."

In contrast, incorrect answers were penalized by the flashing display of the word "WRONG" in brilliant red, and a stern man's voice saying, "Try harder, concentrate more, don't guess." In addition, computer bank accounts had been established for the two people who were the subjects of the pilot training program. These two star subjects each had been making about five training runs a day for the past two weeks, and Jack called a meeting to discuss the results.

The conference room was dark, and Ken Anderson was gesturing with a long pointer at a jagged line that sloped slightly upward across the screen.

"There's no doubt about it," Anderson said enthusiastically. "He actually seems to be learning. Over here on the left, I've plotted his average scores for the ten days before the training

158

started. They bounce around from a high of twenty-seven to a low of nineteen, but there's no trend. His average score over the ten-day period is about twenty-three.

On the other hand, over here on the right, I've plotted his average scores for the ten days since he began the training runs. You can see that, initially, his performance actually got a little worse. I guess the lights and voices distracted him. But after about three days, he was back up to his normal performance, and he's been getting better ever since. For the last three days, his average score is twenty-nine, and one day he got a thirty-one. That's the best daily average performance we've ever had!"

"The curve looks pretty ratty to me, Ken," Barney interjected, playing the devil's advocate. "How can you be sure that he's really learning? And that it's not just a statistical accident that his scores have gone up a little in the last week or so?"

"I was worried about that too, Barney," Anderson agreed, nodding his head. "Because this thing is so important to all of us. So I asked John Franklin to have a couple of his people look at the data completely independently. And I think that John should tell you himself what they found."

Anderson turned off the viewgraph projector and sat down. Someone flipped on the room lights, and they all turned to face John Franklin. The kindly, gray-haired mathematician began to speak deliberately, without rising from his place at the end of the conference table.

"We subjected the data that Ken showed you to a variety of statistical tests. I won't bore you with the details now, but they are written up in this report."

Franklin held up a document that must have been at least a quarter of an inch thick, and then continued his explanation.

"The basic conclusion is that the hypothesis that no learning took place and that the scores just got better by accident is extremely unlikely. Less than one chance in a thousand. So we've concluded that, beyond any reasonable doubt, learning really did take place. Determination of the *rate* of learning is, of course, much more uncertain. And forecasting whether or not the apparent rate of learning will continue is impossible. But to us in the statistical group, there seems to be no doubt that we should continue and even expand the training program."

The room was filled with silent, smiling faces and nodding heads. Without speaking, people expressed their confidence that the breakthrough they so desperately needed had been made. Jack tried to sum up the shared enthusiasm, tempered with a note of caution.

"It certainly looks like the quantum jump in performance that we've all been searching for. But there's still a long way to go and not much time. Remember, he is still just receiving *digits,* not even words, let alone phrases or thoughts. But it's certainly a giant step in the right direction. And we've got to follow it up aggressively."

Jack rose from behind his desk and moved through the crowded room to the head of the conference table.

"Let's try to list the things we should do to exploit the breakthrough. Both in the near term, the next few weeks, and in the longer term; that is, the next several months."

There was general, nodded agreement with Jack's suggestion, and he continued.

"The first thing seems to be obvious. We've got to modify more of the two-person chairs to provide feedback for training. But exactly what should the modifications be? Are flashing lights and soothing voices really the best things? Or would more subtle forms of feedback work better? Barney, why don't you be the secretary and start listing our ideas on the board."

Barney O'Neil rose from his chair, ambled to the front of the room like a good-natured bear, picked up a piece of chalk, and theatrically held it poised inches from the top, left-hand corner of the blackboard.

"While I've got the floor," Jack continued, "I've got a couple of thoughts in the longer term category. First, we ought to start thinking about having them try to transmit and receive simple words in addition to, or in place of, the numbers. If we don't get started in the direction of phrases and thoughts soon, we'll never get there in anything like the eight months or so that we've got left—at least according to the crazy schedule they've given us."

Smiles and nods around the room indicated concurrence both with Jack's suggestion that words should soon replace numbers in the testing and with his characterization of the schedule imposed on them from on high.

"The other idea is much more mundane," Jack said, adding one last thought. "We've got to arrange some dormitory facilities here in the laboratory. So that the best subjects can live right here during the week when the training gets really intense."

Almost a month had elapsed since the first jubilant reports of success with feedback training. Bob Green sat at Jack's conference table, drinking a cup of coffee and waiting for his boss to arrive. Bob's normally cheerful expression was absent. Before him on the table ominously lay a report he dreaded to deliver—documentation of the first serious case of cheating his security people had discovered. Even though the scheme had been detected only weeks after it began, the fact that it had functioned successfully, even for a short time, hurt Bob's professional pride.

Jack strode cheerfully into the room, greeted his friend matter-of-factly, and began to scan the telephone messages neatly arranged on his desk.

"Hi, Bob. What's up?"

"Well, old buddy," Green began in an uncharacteristically serious tone, "it's not a very good day for us security beagles. We've got some people cheating on the training tests and I'm ashamed that we didn't spot them sooner. The best we can tell, it's been going on for about the last ten days."

Jack's face turned ashen. He sat down behind the desk expecting the worst. *He's going to tell me that all the positive results are bullshit,* he thought despondently.

"How extensive is it?" he finally inquired numbly.

"Well, that's the good part, if there can be one to a story like this," Bob responded weakly. "As far as we can tell, just three people are involved. One of the subjects, one of the computer programmers, and a lab technician who works on the training tests. Apparently they agreed to share the bonus money that is credited to the volunteer's account in the computer."

"But how are they doing it?" Jack blurted out incredulously. "I thought we had pretty extensive procedures to detect things like that?"

"We do," Bob agreed a little more cheerfully, "and that's how we caught them. But that's getting a little ahead of the story.

161

Let me summarize it for you, and then you can read the details in this report. As I understand it, and you sure know that I'm not a technical guy, the way they're doing it goes something like this. The lab technician finds out a day ahead of time when and in which chair the subject is going to act as a receiver. Then the technician tells the programmer, who somehow manages to reset the random number generator in the computer just before each of the subject's training runs. And that makes the sequence of numbers the subject is asked to receive the same for every run during the day. Apparently the programmer can do this because we only change the input conditions to the random number generator once a day. But during the day, it just runs on. Which is okay as long as no one resets it. But if it is reset, then it starts giving the same sequence of numbers all over again."

Jack shook his head. The trick was so obvious. At least to someone familiar with computers and random number generators. He silently wondered how many more chinks in their supposedly impenetrable armor were waiting to be exploited by a clever but dishonest programmer or engineer.

"Now, the next part goes something like this," Bob said, continuing the story. "The technician arranges to be on duty in the receiving room during each of the runs the subject makes. That way, the technician can be sure that no one but him sees that the subject has a pencil and paper, and writes down whether he guessed right or wrong on each number in the run and what the correct number is for the ones he got right. Then, on the next run, the subject only guesses on the numbers he got wrong before. But on the ones he got right, he just repeats the number he wrote down that he guessed before. That way, his performance gets better on every successive run during the day!"

Jack smiled and then laughed out loud. He had to admire the ingenuity and simplicity of the scheme. And he anticipated the denouement of Bob's tale.

"I bet I know how you caught them. The volunteer's scores got too good. He was learning too fast."

"Yeah, that's right," Bob said, amazed. "How did you know? Why, one day the guy went from a twenty-one on the first run to a sixty-nine on the last! The training people were ecstatic!

162

But John Franklin didn't believe it, and so he started to investigate. And he found that the subject's performance went right back down again at the beginning of the next day. So he was a super student during the day, but forgot everything he learned overnight. And that's what led John to how they were doing it—to the resetting of the random number generator. It's all here in the report."

Jack continued chuckling to himself, and then inquired sardonically:

"Well, other than firing these people, what do you recommend that we do?"

"Maybe you should fire me, too," Bob said, only half smiling. "I've been giving you all kinds of assurances that nothing was going on."

Jack smiled wryly at Bob's mea culpa, and the latter continued without giving his boss a chance to reply.

"We've got a bunch of recommendations in the report. Basically, they fall into two categories. Technical things, and administrative and security changes. In the technical area, John Franklin is going to institute a group of additional statistical tests on the results of the training runs. He feels that these new tests should flag successful cheating almost automatically. If there are any unusual patterns or changes in the data for any person or test or chair or day of the week or whatever, the computer will call our attention to them for further investigation. And on the administrative side, I'm going to have better records kept of which technicians are present during what tests and which programmers work on what data and that kind of thing."

Jack nodded his agreement, and Bob continued, but with obvious hesitation.

"There's really only one controversial recommendation, and I'd like to discuss it with you. It concerns more frequent lie detector tests."

Jack's brow wrinkled and Bob hastened to explain.

"As you know, everyone takes one once a year around here. But I'd like to do spot checks more often, particularly of people who work in sensitive areas—with the subjects or with the data. I know that people will scream that it's a further invasion of their privacy and an additional stress on them at a time when they're working extremely hard. So I would keep the spot tests short and simple. Just a few questions like, 'Are you involved in any scheme to falsify results?' "

Jack's face took on a truly sad expression, and he shook his head slowly from side to side. The project was taking on more and more aspects of a Kafka novel.

Bob sensed his old friend's discomfort, but the explication he offered only deepened Jack's feeling of descent into the depths.

"I think that if we gave the spot check to about ten percent of the people every month, it would be enough to put the fear of God into them. That way, each person could expect to be spot-checked about once a year. In addition to the more extensive regular yearly check, of course."

Of course? Jack thought and frowned deeply.

"Isn't there any other way to do it?"

"There are other ways," Bob acknowledged, "but I suspect that you'd think they're worse. Like taps on the phones and hidden microphones and TV cameras and security spies on the technical staff."

Jack closed his eyes and silently shook his head in agreement. He certainly did think the alternatives were worse.

The gentle rolling pastures and wooded hills surrounding the Project Psi facility lay gray and dormant in the last chill winds of February, silently awaiting the cue of March's first warm days to burst forth with the new green of spring. But within the double barbed-wire fence, inside the mysterious, low laboratory buildings, a rebirth of sorts was already taking place. Much to everyone's surprise, the training program actually seemed to be working. Four volunteers had consistently scored better than forty out of one hundred on training runs, and one record score of fifty-nine had been achieved. The four star subjects had been given overnight living quarters in Building C—small rooms with a bed and a bureau and a chair, such as medical residents would be pleased to receive—so that their training could continue on an around-the-clock basis. In addition to the training runs, these four virtual prisoners were being given individualized instruction in spoken Russian, extensive psychological interviewing and counseling, and background briefings on Soviet history, culture, and political leaders.

The four psychic stars were treated like crosses between visiting royalty and sideshow freaks. The staff had taken to calling them *psionauts,* and one of the secretaries had had T-shirts made that said across the chest: WATCH WHAT YOU'RE THINKING! The psionauts' computer bank accounts had been growing steadily, and one of the mathematicians had predicted—not entirely facetiously—that they had a chance to become millionaires before the training program was completed. The depression and disorganization created by the president's decision had given way to the mania of twelve-hour days and the euphoria of unexpected success.

Barney O'Neil had come to Jack's office to discuss the most recent spurt of progress and to plan where they should go from here. With him was Dina Friedman, the newly recruited head of the project's expanded Russian-language program. Dina was concerned that the gap between transmitting and receiving numbers and perceiving Soviet thoughts was so great that it was imperative for the psionauts to begin to practice receiving Russian words immediately. But, as was his wont, Barney began the discussion facetiously.

"Dina thinks that the transmitters should sit in their chairs and read *War and Peace,* and the receivers should try to list each character's diminutive names."

Both Jack and Dina smiled, and, having broken the ice, Barney continued.

"Seriously though, Jack, she's got a good point. The same one that you made at the meeting a few weeks ago. Now that we've got the scores on numbers up to the point where there's no doubt that the feedback training is working, we really should begin to have them try to transmit and receive something more realistic."

Jack vigorously nodded his agreement, and Barney kept talking.

"As a start, I asked Dina to come up with a list of ten simple, often-used, well-differentiated Russian words. That way, we can easily substitute one of the words for each of the digits we're currently using. We'll display the word in Cyrillic letters on the transmitter's screen and have Dina's voice say the word to him through his headphones. And on the receiving side, we'll have all ten words displayed and ask the psionaut to point to the one he thinks is being transmitted with a light pen. Dina, why don't you show the list to Jack."

The small, dark-haired, twinkly-eyed woman handed a Xerox copy to Jack. He began to read the Russian script haltingly and was relieved to see that the translations had been included.

Russian Word Transmission Tests
Initial Vocabulary

Russian		English
один	(odin)	one
дба	(dva)	two
чёрный	(chernyi)	black
белый	(belyi)	white
бóльшй	(bol'shoi)	big
маленький	(malen'kii)	small
мальчик	(mal'chik)	boy
девочка	(devochka)	girl
любовь	(lyubov')	love
ненависть	(nenavist')	hate

Dina Friedman waited for Jack to look up from the paper and then began speaking with a noticeable accent—Polish? Jack asked himself, or perhaps Czechoslovakian?

"The idea we have is to start with words that are almost as simple and easy to tell apart as the numbers from zero to nine. In fact, we have included two numbers on the list. Then, as the students make progress, we will gradually increase the size and complexity of the vocabulary. In the end, of course, they must arrive at least at phrases if they are to communicate thoughts of any subtlety. But, right now, my fear is that we will not make the deadline if they do not begin soon with real Russian."

Jack nodded his agreement, and Dina continued more confidently.

"Initially, I think that the performance of the psionauts will decline drastically when the change takes place from ten numbers to ten words. Even to the simple words on this list. Because, as you well know, Professor Mason, the mind and the way it learns are so complex. While the transition from ten numbers to ten words does not appear to be much of a step, sitting here in this office, I believe that for a psionaut struggling to receive the message, it will seem like being snatched from a Sunday afternoon walk in the valley and forced to join a climb of Gerlachovka."

While Jack was mentally trying to place Gerlachovka on a map of mountainous eastern Europe, Barney O'Neil brought the conversation back to the gentle foothills of northern Virginia.

"Dina's made a good point about the rewards too, Jack," he interjected. "She thinks that the psionauts will do so poorly on the words at the beginning that they'll get discouraged at not earning as much bonus money as they've gotten used to in the last few weeks. And that will give them a negative attitude toward the shift from numbers to words. So Dina thinks that in the beginning we should up the reward they get for correct answers. At least until they begin to show some learning progress again."

Dina Friedman vigorously nodded agreement with Barney's explanation of her idea, and Jack smiled his acquiescence.

"Why not! They're already richer than any of us will ever be."

PART IV
THE COMRADE AND
THE SECRETARY

15

The Seeds of Suspicion

Viktor Leonidovich Grechko was perplexed. He stroked his goatee and stared pensively at the far wall of his large, ornate office. Before him on the massive, inlaid desk lay a report from the Soviet Embassy in Washington. What is MacFarland up to? Grechko mused. Why would the deputy director of the CIA visit an Exotic Chemicals Research Facility? Was it part of the CIA's drug research program? That did not seem likely to Grechko. The facility was out in the Virginia countryside and was not connected with any hospital. Was the Agency getting into chemical warfare? Or could it be the new defector debriefing center for which Grechko's own KGB had been diligently searching without success?

The thoughts of the Russians' greatest master of intelligence analysis were interrupted by the tentative voice of an assistant standing in the open doorway at the far end of the room.

"*Tovarishch* (Comrade) Grechko, may I enter? We have some new information from the embassy on the chemical facility."

Viktor Grechko nodded his assent, and the thin, bespectacled man approached and stood dutifully before his leader's paper-strewn desk.

"This supplementary report arrived by diplomatic pouch this morning, Tovarishch Grechko."

The aide bent forward stiffly, handed the document to Grechko, and then retreated a few paces to wait respectfully while his chief read.

Years of experience allowed Viktor Grechko to scan the report rapidly for new or unusual pieces of information.

... Signs on the outside fence proclaim, "American Chemical Company, Exotic Chemicals Research Facility." However, additional placards on a second interior barrier add, "U.S. Government Jurisdiction." ... Inquiries by a member of the Soviet delegation at the United Nations to the New York headquarters of the American Chemical Company were met with the uninformative statement that: "The facility is involved in research and development on a variety of exotic chemicals on behalf of the American Chemical Company and its subsidiaries." Requests for additional information brought forth only evasive replies. ... Surveillance by attachés reveals that about 150 people enter the facility regularly between 0800 and 0900 each morning from Monday until Friday. The times of leaving vary greatly, but about the same number of people exit between 1600 and 2000 in the evening. ... Brian MacFarland, the deputy director of the CIA, has been identified positively in recent photographs taken of automobiles entering the outer gate of the establishment.

Viktor Grechko put down the report, folded his hands, and leaned forward on the desk. He then stared at the nervous aide with a penetrating scowl.

"Well, Tovarishch, you are supposed to be an analyst; what do you make of this?"

The uneasy assistant shifted his weight from one foot to the other, hesitating to reply.

"Come now, Tovarishch," Grechko growled, "what malevolent activity is the CIA undertaking?"

The mounting displeasure conveyed by the guttural tones issuing from the massive form behind the desk compelled the sallow, moustached man to answer, but his voice was weak and his response tentative.

"Well, sir, we are not certain. Some say it could be a place for training agents, while others favor a laboratory for experimenting with drugs or poison gases. And a third group is of the opinion—"

"You should have stopped when you said, 'We are not certain,'" Grechko interjected. His voice was stern and his rebuke incisive. "You really do not have any idea what is the purpose of the facility, do you, Tovarishch? And, greatest failing of all, you do not have even a plan to find out."

The now thoroughly frightened assistant retreated a few more paces and glanced toward the door as if he were considering fleeing the room. But Viktor Grechko continued the lecture unrelentingly.

"Let me give to you some thoughts, Tovarishch. They might do to you some good. First, let us consider the purpose the Americans have proclaimed. Exotic chemicals research—do you think that anyone with half a brain would build such a laboratory in the Washington countryside?"

The aide stared blankly and then, finally, nodded his head from side to side almost imperceptably.

"How many members of President Leonard's cabinet, his closest political associates, live within a twenty-five-kilometer radius of the CIA facility? You do not know, do you, Tovarishch. But *I* do. The answer is three of them. And you and your wooden-headed helpers believe that the Agency is taking the chance of killing all of them with exotic chemicals? Not very likely, is it, Tovarishch?"

All remaining color drained from the frail man's face and he instantly took on such a look of panic that Grechko thought he might actually bolt from the room. Abruptly, the old spy master grinned broadly and switched to a fartherly approach.

"Now, Tovarishch, come over here and sit down. And I will instruct you how we are going to uncover the real purpose of this mysterious CIA establishment."

The assistant approached again obsequiously, took a seat at the corner of the massive desk, and, with noticeable relief, prepared to copy his instructions on a pad of paper.

Viktor Grechko began again in a mellow tone. He thoroughly enjoyed playing the role of master detective.

"Now, Tavarishch, here is what I want you to have them do. First, I want every person identified whose face is visible in any of the photographs that the attachés have taken. Second, I want more photographs taken, with greater clarity in the faces. That means larger lenses. Be sure that those clods in the embassy have them. And, for each automobile they photograph, they must take also a picture of the license plate. They always forget to do this. The simplest method for determining the identity of the driver is to place a telephone call to the registry of motor vehicles of the state of Virginia."

Viktor Grechko laughed throatily in appreciation of his own cleverness and the aide nervously joined in.

"Telephone to the registry of motor vehicles. That is very clever, Tovarishch Grechko. I never would have thought of it myself."

Viktor Grechko's scowl returned.

"That is the trouble with this bureau. It is full of people like you. People who never think of anything themselves. They all just sit and wait for me to tell them what to do. Now, Tovarishch, what point had I reached in your instructions?"

The assistant consulted his pad and then responded dutifully.

"You had just finished instructing me to tell them to call the American registry of motor vehicles. Very clever, Tovarishch Grechko."

"Stop being such a bootlicker," Grechko growled. "I know it is clever. What I would like you to do is to have some clever ideas of your own. Now, what was I saying?"

"You were about to give the third instruction, sir," the aide responded eagerly, glad he could give at least one answer correctly.

"Yes," Viktor Grechko acknowledged. "The third action I want you to have them take is to get someone inside that facility."

"You mean climb over the fence or something like that?" the thin man replied incredulously.

"No, you fool!" Grechko shot back. "The alarms would be triggered, and the dogs would be on him before he reached the ground! I want them to do something subtle. If they can understand what that means. They should get one of their well-covered agents to apply for a menial job. As a groundskeeper or a janitor or something like that. Some job for which the Americans are not likely to give him a lie detector test. Or do a very complete job on his background investigation."

The assistant grinned thinly, visualizing a helpless agent, wired to a massive lie detector, being browbeaten under bright lights.

Viktor Grechko instantly detected the smile, correctly surmised its origin, and once again, deftly skewered the hapless lackey.

"Would you like to know how a lie-detector interrogation feels, Tovarishch? I can have our local experts over in D Building give you a personal demonstration!"

Once again the color drained from the aide's face instantly.

"Oh, no, sir," he stammered. "Nothing of the sort. I was just concerned about what might happen to the unfortunate agent."

"The unfortunate agent?" Viktor Grechko shouted. "What do you think agents are for, Tovarishch? They are to be used! Used to protect the soil of Mother Russia and spread the word of the glorious October Revolution!" *And,* Grechko thought silently, *to enhance the reputations of the masters of the KGB.*

16

What Will Historians Write?

Richard Hart Leonard was in an expansive mood. He had just
finished a hearty dinner with Thomas Stratton, his secretary
of state, and Sam Ryan, his trusted aide, in the salon of the
presidential yacht *Sequoia*. It was a pleasant evening in early
April and the stately old motor vessel glided noiselessly down
the Potomac past Mount Vernon. The president called for Cuban
cigars and French cognac and then pushed his chair back from
the table, inviting the postprandial conversation to begin.

"The story you were telling me about that Project Psi this
afternoon is pretty amazing, Sam," the chief executive began,
exhaling a cloud of forbidden smoke. "Do you think they've really
found some people who can read minds? Or are they just giving
you the usual Washington sales pitch?"

"Well, Mr. President," Sam Ryan replied, while lighting up
himself, "you can never be sure around this town. But I think
they actually have found a mindreader or two. Psionauts, they
call them. I meet once a week myself with that professor who
heads the thing up—Mason—and I visit their lab once a month.
They've shown me a lot of their data and let me talk to the
psionauts and the people on the staff. They'd have to be a damn
well-organized bunch of liars if it's all a hoax."

He concluded his answer with a cloud of Cuban smoke.

The president responded by jabbing at the swirls between
them with his own cigar.

"That's what Washington is full of, Sam—damned well-organized bunches of liars!"

Richard Leonard laughed heartily at his own joke and then
turned to his secretary of state.

"What do *you* think, Thomas? Can this psi thing be real?"

"Well, Mr. President, I've asked myself that same question," Thomas Stratton began rhetorically, as if leading a graduate seminar in political science. "Can they really develop the ultimate negotiating weapon? A man who can read the minds of one's adversaries across the conference table. Such an achievement would revolutionize the conduct of international diplomacy. The negotiator, the head of state, the nation that possesses this weapon would totally dominate the international scene. Historians would marvel at his prescient insights. His iron nerve at calling bluffs. His remarkable ability to discern the minimum concessions necessary for agreement."

"You like the idea, don't you, Thomas?" the president said, with a smile, goodnaturedly interrupting the secretary of state's enthusiastic recitation. "But let's be sure we don't get mousetrapped. You know, like the old draw play. Suck 'em in, and then lay 'em flat from the blind side!"

Richard Leonard grinned broadly and accepted a fresh snifter of brandy with one hand and another large cigar with the other.

"Let's go out on deck and get some fresh air," he proposed, with the unmistakable hint of a royal command.

The three men rose from the table, and white-coated stewards appeared from the shadows to remove their chairs. The president led his guests to the aft end of the salon and strolled through the sliding glass and mahogany doors onto the observation deck. The night was clear and the protective canvas had been furled to give an unobstructed view of the heavens above. Richard Leonard moved to the aft rail and gestured expansively with his snifter of cognac toward the lights of the capital city in the distance.

"You know, Thomas," the president began almost philosophically, "if the people out there knew half of what we do, they wouldn't sleep at night. They'd be too excited. But somehow, *we* just take it all in stride. The threat of war one day and the reality of famine the next. Like this psi thing. The public would never believe it. But to *us*, it's just another tool. In our endless battle with the Russians and the others out there who want to destroy the American way of life—the French who criticize everything we do, and the Africans who settle things by killing each other and anyone who gets in the way, and the Indians who spend their time screwing in alleys, and the—"

"Yes, Mr. President," Thomas Stratton interjected, trying to head off a familiar diatribe, "it certainly is a troubled world in which we live. And that's why it's so important for us to continue the quest for world order and stability. And a *man with psi,* if one can be created, could make all the difference in our level of success. The leaders with whom I negotiate around the world are always so unreasonable. They always ask for everything and offer nothing in return. My skill, if I may be so presumptuous as to say so, is in divining what they will settle for when push comes to shove. But, with a man with psi at my side, I wouldn't be guessing. I'd know what they need to keep from getting thrown out by a coup or a vote and what they are willing to give up to keep the same thing from happening to some other world leaders. It would seem strange to common people, but, despite all their power, the name of the game with world leaders is really *survival.*"

The president turned from the rail, the cigar and the snifter still in his hands, and faced his secretary of state.

"Very eloquent, as usual, Thomas. But I have a more personal goal in mind for Project Psi. That bastard Sherkov! He thinks he's so tough. With all those World War Two stories. He was in the tank corps or something. And the last time we met, he spent an hour telling me about the battles around Stalingrad or Leningrad or some damn place. He said that after those experiences, being a world leader was easy. That conceited bastard!"

"He certainly is conceited, Mr. President," the secretary of state agreed. "But, I don't think you should discount the effect of wartime experiences on his character. The Russians lost a million people in the 900-day siege of Leningrad, and I can imagine that anyone who fought there would be inured to almost anything."

"Damn it, Thomas!" the president shot back furiously, again jabbing with his cigar. "I'm not discounting anything! But, I *am* going to grind that bastard Sherkov into the ground! I'm tough myself too, you know. It hasn't been easy going through all those damn campaigns. And putting up with all that liberal crap from that bunch of eggheaded senators. And—"

"I know you're tough, Mr. President," the secretary of state responded in a fatherly voice, stroking the ego of his enraged chief. "And so does Sherkov. He *must* know after the way you've handled him at the summit meetings."

"Yes, I guess I have handled him pretty well, haven't I?" Richard Leonard agreed, seeking reassurance. "Remember the time that he tried to get me to back off on the missile limit that you and Gersky had agreed to? And I just held firm. I said, 'That's the deal you agreed to. And you're not going to change it now. Where I come from a man's word is everything. And Stratton has Gersky's word on this. And if you go back on it now, that's the end. We'll never trust you again!' "

"You certainly were tough with him, Mr. President," Thomas Stratton agreed. "Poor old Gersky told me the next day that Sherkov gave him an awful dressing-down—for not having been more ambiguous in his negotiations with me. But Basov told me later, back here in Washington over a drink one evening, that the idea of trying to get a last-minute concession had been all Sherkov's. He invented it on the spur of the moment, without telling anyone, not even Gersky."

"That's what I mean," Richard Leonard concurred, his anger rising anew. "He's irresponsible! And I owe it to the world to show him up. To let everyone see what a conceited, cowardly faker he really is! And that's where the man with psi comes in. With him at my side, I'll be invincible! Like a poker mechanic playing at an Elks Club picnic. I'll know all the cards, mine and his, too!"

"It certainly does open up some interesting possibilities, Mr. President," the secretary of state agreed, with a smile. "Men with psi could be tremendously useful even in more mundane situations. Like my weekly meetings with Basov. I am never completely certain when he's being sincere or when he's just earnestly putting forward a line he's been sent from Moscow."

"Men?" the president responded with belated enthusiasm. "Do you think they can develop more than one? A group of them? An army of them! Think of the possibilities. We could use them in trade negotiations, in the Middle East talks, in—I guess you'd have to have different ones for different languages. Wouldn't you?"

"Yes, I suspect you would, Mr. President," Thomas Stratton said with only partially concealed amusement. "I've only known a few exceptional people who could think in more than one language. And it would be truly remarkable if such a person also turned out to have telepathic ability."

"That's all right," Richard Leonard continued, oblivious in the darkness of his secretary of state's condescension. "Let's have separate ones for different languages. Clearly, Russian is the one to start with. But what should be next? Arabic, for dealing with OPEC? Or Chinese, for getting behind those inscrutable smiles? Or perhaps it ought to be English, for handling those damned congressmen!"

"Those are certainly interesting possibilities, Mr. President," the secretary of state agreed, but then he subtly deflected the path of their conversation. "Perhaps we should talk a little about what should be the first test of their initial product. I have told Bennington and Mason that you want a man with psi ready to accompany us to the summit meeting in Moscow next spring. But we don't want to take un untried agent with us. The danger is too great that he might get us into difficulties."

"Yeah," Richard Leonard concurred, "we certainly wouldn't want a thing like that to backfire. Sherkov would never let us hear the end of it! And world opinion! Those yammering monkeys from the Third World would talk about it for years. And the *New York Times*! I can see the headline. 'Psychic Spy Revealed, President Flies Home Disgraced.' We've got to be damn sure nothing like that happens."

Richard Leonard wagged his finger in Thomas Stratton's face and continued vehemently.

"Thomas, I want you personally to be responsible for the testing of this guy. Really wring him out. Put him under stress! And only when you're satisfied will I consider using him at the summit meeting."

"A very wise decision, Mr. President," Thomas Stratton concurred disingenuously, having drawn his chief to the desired conclusion. "Both the potential rewards and the risks in this thing are so great that we must proceed with the utmost caution. I think that it might be best to test the man with psi first in a mock negotiation between two Russian-born members of my staff. That way, if he fails or reveals himself, nothing will have been lost. If he gets past that first test, I might put him on my staff and start bringing him to some meetings with Basov. So the ambassador will get used to seeing him around. Also, I could test the thoughts he says he is receiving against other intelligence we get about what Basov's really up to. And then, if he passes muster with Basov, I might take him with me to some of the pre-summit negotiations in Moscow. That way—"

"Right, Thomas," the president agreed distractedly. "You work out the details. I just want to be sure that when I call him off the bench, he's ready to play."

Richard Leonard handed his empty snifter to a waiting steward and again strolled to the aft railing. The president stared pensively at the yacht's wake for a time and then gestured expansively at the starry heavens.

"Our astronauts have conquered space. Now my psionauts will conquer the world! Diplomatically, of course. In the name of peace and international order and the American way of life. Think about it, Thomas. Think what historians will write about us. 'President Richard Hart Leonard, aided by his able secretary of state, Thomas Stratton, achieved an unprecedented level of world order during the last quarter of the twentieth century through his astonishing skill as a summit negotiator.' "

Stuart Bennington picked up the beige handset of the internal secure telephone and pushed the button marked "B.MacF." on the console. The phone rang several times and then a familiar voice responded:

"Hello, Stuart. What can I do for you?"

"Hello, Brian. I am just reading that report about the surveillance of the Project Psi facility by the Soviet embassy. It sounds like their curiosity really is aroused, and I think we should do something to throw them off the track. I'd like you to come over and talk about it, if you're free right now. I'm sure that Sam will hear about their snooping. He'll be calling to ask me what we're doing about it."

"Okay, Stuart," the deputy director of the CIA responded. "I'll be right over. I agree with you. We should head this one off before it becomes a big pain in the ass."

About fifteen minutes later, Brian MacFarland entered Stuart Bennington's office carrying a disorganized collection of papers and folders.

"Here's everything we've got on what the attachés have been up to," MacFarland began, without waiting for his boss to ask. "Basically, they've been driving by the place and taking pictures while people go to work in the morning and leave at night. Between identifying faces and getting the names of car owners from the license plates, they'll probably get a pretty good idea of who's on the staff. And then they'll start looking at the scientific journals to see what kind of work the technical people have done in the past. And pretty soon they'll figure out that we've got an awful lot of psychologists and very few chemical engineers for an exotic chemicals research facility."

"I'm sure you're right that they may come to that conclusion in time," Stuart Bennington agreed. "Particularly if we don't do anything. But I think that if we take some steps to shore it up, the cover story should last a lot longer. We need something to convince them that the place really is doing research with dangerous chemicals—like an accident or something."

Brian MacFarland's eyes began to twinkle.

"Now you're in my ball park. I've arranged so many accidents in my time that I'm beginning to think that some of them were acts of God."

"That's why I called you, Brian," Stuart Bennington continued, with a hint of uneasiness in his voice. "You've always handled that side of the business. And, frankly, I like it better that way. At least when some congressman asks me about one of your capers, I can honestly say that I don't know anything about the details."

"Right," Brian MacFarland agreed jovially. "I guess that's why we work so well together. You charm the White House and the congressmen, and I get the dirty jobs done."

Several weeks later, while scanning the paper at the breakfast table, Jack Mason was surprised to read, in a small article buried in the back pages of the *Washington Post,* that several head of cattle had been found dead in a field near the exotic chemicals research facility of the American Chemical Company.

The story went on to say that toxic wastes from the facility were the primary suspect in the deaths and that an investigation was continuing.

As soon as he arrived at the Project Psi facility, Jack called Bob Green to his office and asked him about the story. Bob shifted his weight nervously from one foot to the other and answered evasively.

"Uh, yeah, old buddy, I did see something like that in the paper. I asked our people to check to see if we've been dumping anything and the report came back that we're clean."

Jack stepped out from behind the desk, closed the office door, and motioned to Bob to sit down.

"Come on, Bob. Come clean! You know more about what's behind that article than you've told me, and I'm not going to let you out of here until I know the whole story."

"Look, old buddy," Green responded, "sometimes there are things that you're better off not knowing. Things that guys like me can take care of and you can honestly deny knowing anything about."

Jack sat down in the chair next to Bob's, scowled directly at his old friend, and wagged his forefinger.

"Look, Bob, I'm the director of this project. And, for better or worse, I'm in it for the duration. So if we're killing cattle, I want to know about it."

"Okay, okay, Jack," Green came back, resigned to the inevitable. "You asked for it. But you may regret later that you pushed me."

"If I'm going to hell," Jack replied vehemently, "I'd at least like to know the reason why!"

"Okay, old buddy," Green continued in a conciliatory tone. "I'll give you the whole story. But don't tell *anyone* about it. Not a soul. Or Brian will never trust me again."

"Brian!" Jack shouted involuntarily. "I should have known that that overgrown college prankster was behind this thing. God knows why Stuart lets that maniac and his troop of James Bond thugs run around loose. I'll bet they're more dangerous to our own country than they are to the Russians!"

"Look, Jack, don't get too excited until you've heard the whole story," Bob Green pleaded. "It's not as bad as you're probably imagining. It all started when we began to get reports that

183

some attachés from the Soviet embassy had been photographing our people coming and going. So Brian decided that we should do something to boost the credibility of our cover story. To convince the Russians that this is really an exotic chemicals research facility. But it had to be something subtle, so that they won't guess that we're feeding them a line. Well, anyhow, Brian decided that having some cattle die near our fence would be just the kind of bait they'd bite at. So that's all there is to it. A couple of his guys put a highly toxic, but very short-lived, chemical poison into the stream that flows behind the south fence. And they made sure that some cattle were around to drink the water before the poison degraded to something harmless."

Jack shook his head slowly from side to side. *What have I gotten into?* he thought. *What have I gotten into! These guys would do anything to perpetuate the lies they've already told.*

Jack continued staring at Bob without speaking.

17

Jason Star

At the Project Psi facility, an unbelievably hectic five months flashed by since Anton Stark first suggested using feedback training with rewards and punishments to teach volunteers to receive thoughts. For the last two months, the elite group of people who have demonstrated the greatest psychic ability—the newly anointed psionauts—have been transmitting and receiving a ten-word Russian vocabulary. To the amazement and relief of all concerned, three of these psychic wonders repeatedly scored better than fifty percent in perceiving the words on which their partner who was transmitting his thoughts was concentrating.

The best of the psionauts, Jason Star, an athletically trim man, had achieved such high scores, frequently above eighty percent, that his vocabulary had expanded to twenty-five words. In a further attempt to enhance the realism of the training, native-born Russians were being employed as the transmitters of thoughts.

It was a beautiful spring morning in early May. The Project Psi facility was surrounded by newly verdant woods and placidly grazing cattle standing motionless on rolling green hillsides. But inside the mysterious, low laboratory buildings, the euphoria of unexpected success mated with the adrenaline of an approaching deadline to spawn a heightening tension.

Jack Mason had called a staff meeting to assess the project's most recent progress and to plan the first demonstration of a man with psi, in anticipation of the scheduled demonstration to be given in less than three months. When most of the key people were assembled in his office, Jack closed the door, moved to the head of the conference table, and began to speak in a loud voice.

"The reason that I asked you all to get together this morning is to plan how we get from where we are now to an initial demonstration of Jason's abilities in about ten weeks!"

The intensity of Jack's delivery and his emphasis on the deadline quieted the private conversations almost immediately. Anton Stark was the first to respond, raising his voice to be heard from a chair in the back of the room.

"I believe that it depends crucially on what kind of demonstration you have in mind. If they will be satisfied to see Jason receiving a twenty-five-word Russian vocabulary through a thin wall while seated in a two-person chair, we could give the demonstration next week. But if they want to see him read the mind of some stranger they bring in, I think that we are courting potential disaster! We could not be sure how Jason would perform, and we would have no way of knowing objectively whether or not the person they brought it was being honest in reporting his thoughts."

"I think you've hit the key point, Anton," Jack said, shouting back across the room. "The trouble is that what seems to *us* to be a controlled demonstration will seem to them to be a put-up job! What would seem to them to be a fair test, we would know is a totally uncontrolled experiment. Our problem is to try to find some compromise that will convince them and yet not be completely out of our control."

There was general, nodded agreement around the room and Barney O'Neil joined the discussion from his place at the conference table.

"I think the key is to try to get them to accept one of our native Russians as the transmitter. Someone whose thoughts Jason is used to perceiving. They could tell our person what thoughts he should concentrate on during a mock negotiation. Whether he should lie or be truthful or hostile or whatever. That way, only they would know what thoughts he had been told to concentrate on. But we would have someone whose thoughts we know Jason can receive and whom we can trust to tell us later what thoughts he was told to transmit. Do you think they'd go for that, Jack?"

"It sounds fair to me, Barney," Jack replied with a broad smile. "But you never know with Ryan and Stratton. If they

186

think that we're trying to pull a technical trick on them, they'll just arbitrarily change the ground rules to throw us off balance. So all I can say is that I'll try to talk them into it. In the meantime, why don't we do our planning on the basis of that kind of demonstration. Dina, how many words do you think Jason would need for a demonstration like that?"

"Well, I'm not sure that learning more words will be his biggest problem," Dina Friedman began tentatively. "The important new thing he's got to learn to perceive is some minimal amount of syntax. You know, so that he can tell the difference between 'I hate you,' and 'You hate me.' It sounds laughably simple when I say it that way, but I'll bet that it will prove maddeningly difficult for Jason to learn."

"That's a good point, Dina," Jack concurred. "What do you think we should do? Start him on a simple set of phrases?"

"Well, I've been giving some thought to that," the small, twinkly-eyed woman replied. "And, frankly, I believe that syntax perception is going to be extremely difficult. If the subject always came first, it might not be so bad. You know, if people always thought, 'I hate you,' and never 'You are the one I hate,' everything would be a lot easier."

There was general laughter around the room led by Barney O'Neil, and the tension was relieved. Dina Friedman chuckled to herself then continued more confidently.

"It seems to me that we have two choices. We can either make a major effort to teach the psionauts to perceive simple syntactical forms—probably from Russian case endings—or we can ignore syntax, train them to remember the sequence in which they perceive words, and hope that we can piece together the proper syntax later."

"Wouldn't it be risky to pursue only the first alternative if you think that syntax perception is going to be so difficult?" Phyllis Jackson asked, quietly joining the discussion from the rear of the room. "Our psychological tests indicate that most of the psionauts have remarkable memories. So it probably would not be too difficult to train them to remember the exact sequence in which they perceived a group of words."

"I think you're probably right, Phyllis," Dina agreed. "Teaching them to memorize the sequence of the words they perceive should be relatively straightforward, and I think that we should start on that kind of training immediately. A person like Jason, who now scores as high as sixty percent on a twenty-five-word vocabulary, could be asked to write down the words he perceives in five-word groups. And later, perhaps, in variable length groups that he thinks make sensible phrases."

"But what about syntax perception?" Jack interjected firmly. "I think it's a very fundamental issue, and we shouldn't just duck it. I agree with you that we should start with training in word-order memorization immediately, but I think that we also should do some pilot tests of syntax perception. Perhaps it won't turn out to be as difficult as you think."

"How about this, Dina," Barney O'Neil suggested. "Suppose that you took a small number of words that Jason perceives very well and made them into pairs of short sentences or phrases that differ only in syntax. Like your 'hate' example. That way, Jason wouldn't have much trouble with the words, and he could concentrate solely on perceiving the differences in case endings and any other clues to syntax."

"I think you're on the right track, Barney," Dina replied, nodding her agreement. "In fact, I've started to write down some phrases now. Why don't we talk about it after the meeting?"

"That sounds like a good suggestion to me," Jack concluded, signaling an end to that discussion. "Why don't Dina and Barney work up a pilot syntax perception test and present it to a group of us in a few days."

There was nodded concurrence from most of the participants, and Jack changed the subject.

"Now, I think there's another point we ought to discuss. One that Anton brought up implicitly at the beginning of the meeting. The fact that Ryan and Stratton will think that we're crazy if we propose to do the demonstration in a two-person chair! Or even, perhaps, here in our own facility. I think they are likely to insist on doing it sitting around a conference table at the State Department or in the White House basement. And that's going to pose a number of very serious problems for Jason. Most fundamentally, his head won't be as close to that of the transmitter as it normally is in the two-person chair. On top of that, there will be other brains in the room whose thoughts may interfere with those of the transmitter. Let's start with the fundamental question of distance. Ken, what do our latest results look like?"

Ken Anderson moved to the blackboard and began to draw a graph.

"We've done the distance tests with the smaller, ten-word vocabulary. If I plot Jason's average scores vertically and the distance between his brain and that of the transmitter horizontally, it goes something like this." Anderson marked some X's on the board and connected them with a line. "At the shortest distance, less than half a meter, Jason scored over ninety percent. When we increased the distance to about a meter, his average score dropped to about eighty percent. At two meters, it was down to fifty percent, and at three meters, less than twenty percent. Beyond three meters, Jason scored so near the ten percent level that you'd expect from chance that you might as well say that his perception was zero. So I guess the bottom line is that Jason had better sit damn close to the transmitter during the demonstration."

"That may pose a problem," Jack said with a frown. "If Jason and the transmitter sit right next to each other, Ryan and Stratton are almost certain to think that they're signaling each other under the table. I don't know how we'll handle it. Perhaps someone could sit between them, if he wasn't too fat," Jack concluded with a chuckle.

"And if he promises not to think in Russian," Barney O'Neil interjected. As usual, Barney's humor brought welcome laughter to the room and dispelled the tension.

"Well, look," Jack said, groping for a conclusion, "I think that at the very least we should set up a mock conference room for Jason to practice in. And suppose we build a portable screen that fits between Jason and the transmitter and extends both over and under the table. That way, Jason wouldn't be able to see the display that presents the words to the transmitter, and yet the whole thing would be portable enough that we could volunteer to take it over to the State Department or the White House or wherever. And once Jason gets used to the new setup, we can start moving his chair farther down the conference table away from the screen to see how much his performance drops off."

"Okay," Ken Anderson agreed. "We'll put together some plans for the mock conference room setup and bring them in to you."

People began to push their chairs back from the table and the meeting was about to break up, when Dick Sterling raised his voice and addressed the group unexpectedly.

"I've got an idea that I'd like to try out on you before we disperse." Heads turned toward him and he continued. "It comes from my clinical experience in treating psychiatric patients. A considerable number of them show a remarkably increased ability to remember and describe past events or repressed feelings when placed under the influence of hypnosis or drugs like sodium pentothal. What I'm wondering is whether the performance of the psionauts might be improved substantially if, after a test run was over, we asked them to recount the sequence of words they had perceived while under the influence of a drug or hypnosis?"

The room fell silent and people gradually took their seats again. The idea clearly was worthy of serious consideration. And, after a moment of thought, Anton Stark was the first to follow it up.

"That is an extremely potent suggestion, Dr. Sterling. I wish I had made it myself. As you have said, it might result in a quantum leap in performance. I have read clinical reports about patients who apparently could recall minute and seemingly complete details of events that occurred years before."

"It's more than just events," Dick Sterling continued enthusiastically. "What has fascinated me in my own practice and leads me to think that the procedure might work here is that patients seem to recall the feelings they perceived on the part of others during stressful situations. It's even conceivable to me that these reports are in fact clinical evidence of the psi ability that has gone unnoticed by the medical profession!"

Silence again spread over the room. The awed silence that so often greets the lucid exposition of a great idea. They all knew that Sterling's suggestion was so powerful that they should begin to test it immediately.

Jason Star awoke suddenly, uncertain of where he was. He groped for a light switch, and finally found one on a lamp on a table beside his bed. Instantly, brilliance flooded the room and his eyes closed automatically. But the blinding flash that preceeded their reaction further confused his already disoriented brain. Jason covered his face with his hands and then slowly peeked between his fingers at his surroundings. As his eyes gradually became accustomed to the light, Jason slowly concluded with great relief that he was in his room at the Project Psi facility. He shook his head and smiled wryly at his own fear and confusion. Jason still was not fully accustomed to sleeping at the laboratory after a long evening of training. But he was doing it more and more often now, as it became increasingly evident that he was the star psionaut and the prime candidate to become the first man with psi.

Realizing that Jason embodied their only chance to conduct a successful demonstration of a man with psi on the president's impossible schedule, the staff had repeatedly intensified his training. Jason was now working at least ten hours per day, six days per week. And he often put in eighteen hours at a stretch when the scientists wanted to try some new training technique or evaluation scheme. As it became clearer and clearer to Jason that he was the chosen person, the project's messiah if there was to be one, his sense of responsibility and commitment deepened. He was doggedly determined to improve his performance on every new vocabulary run. Each word perceived correctly was a minor triumph, and each wrong answer, particularly as they became increasingly rare, was a stab at his ego.

Jason Star turned out the intruding light and flopped back onto the bed. He stared at the darkened ceiling for a moment, as the shrinking residual spot of light faded from his retina, and then closed his eyes. As he slowly descended from consciousness to the welcoming arms of Morpheus, a scene from his undergraduate days at Princeton gradually materialized.

As the dream unfolded, Jason found himself walking across the campus toward the library. He concluded that the season was early fall, because the ground was strewn with golden leaves and a group of properly sweatered young men were playing touch football. Jason waved to the one with the ball and then started to run. The pigskin arched through the air and, despite a final frantic sprint, sailed past Jason's outstretched fingertips.

He made a final lunge, lost his footing, and crashed to the turf. Fortunately, Jason did not recall the pain.

The dream scene disappeared as rapidly as it had appeared. But, awake again, Jason shook his head slowly from side to side, recalling the aftermath. A broken arm that had been in a cast for six weeks and had prevented him from playing basketball or going skiing for the entire winter. But it hadn't been a total disaster. He had certainly gotten a lot of sympathy from the girls on weekends. He thought of one of them, Mary what's-her-name. The blond with the big tits he loved to kiss. Her smiling face and bulging breasts appeared for a moment and then, as quickly, vanished.

I've certainly come a long way since Princeton, Jason thought. *The years in the air force—mostly wasted, but not entirely. I guess I was a fool to join ROTC. But the Korean War was on, and I didn't want to peel potatoes. The year at the language school in Monterey was pretty good though. Lots of time for sailing and diving. And the trips to San Francisco on weekends. And learning Russian hadn't been a waste. God knows, I'm using it now.*

Jason smiled to himself in the darkness and slowly returned to the land of dreams. In the wrinkled recesses of his brain, the repressed remembrances of things past began to prowl. When his mind's eye again came into focus, Jason found himself in full scuba gear, silently searching the depths of Monterey Bay. Suddenly he spotted his prey and energetically he began to pry a reluctant abalone from its rocky perch. Jason was having trouble getting the long, screwdriverlike tool beneath the shell and was gasping great clouds of bubbles from the effort.

He finally forced the bar under the tenacious mollusk and positioned his flippers on the rock for leverage. With a final heroic heave on the tool, Jason at last broke the suction of the abalone's foot. The sudden release of tension caused him to spring back from the rock through the water as the dislodged abalone plummeted from sight into the murk below. Jason quickly regained his composure and, with strong kicks of his fins, followed the prize in its downward plunge. Reaching the bottom of the bay, he began a methodical search for his quarry;

but, despite repeated crisscrossing, he was rewarded only by vast expanses of rippled sand. Jason swam on in vain until the dream again faded and sleep overcame him.

18

The Bluebirds

The sterile telephone on the credenza behind Joe Scali's desk began to ring. This frequently changed, unlisted number was called only by CIA agents reporting from the field when time or circumstances did not permit the use of a more secure means of communication. Despite his years in the business, the ring of one of these special phones still made Joe Scali's gut tighten. He always expected the worst and, often, was not disappointed. Scali swiveled his chair toward the sound, looked at the phone apprehensively, and then placed the receiver to his ear but did not speak.

Without waiting for acknowledgment, an excited voice began its report.

"This is Bluebird Three. We've got a problem. The accident got a little out of hand. The big, four-footed things conked off right on schedule. But later on, a bunch of little, two-footed things showed up unexpectedly and one of them took a drink before we could stop him. Now he's in the hospital!"

"Return to the nest immediately," Joe Scali said impassively. He put down the black handset, reached for the beige one, and punched the button marked "B.MacF." on the secure internal telephone console.

After several rings, a familiar voice answered:

"MacFarland."

"Brian, this is Joe. The Bluebirds just called in and we've got trouble. They've had a problem with the latest accident that we staged near the Project Psi facility. The idea was just to poison a few more cattle. But apparently a bunch of kids showed up and one of them drank some of the water. I guess that the poison had pretty well degraded by the time the kid drank it, because it didn't kill him outright, but he's in the hospital."

"Oh, shit!" Brian MacFarland shouted at no one in particular. He knew that his troubles had just begun. "Get those assholes back here as fast as possible. And give me a call as soon as you have debriefed them." MacFarland slammed down the receiver and stormed out from behind his desk.

Jack and Sue Mason were enjoying an unaccustomed evening together at home. With dinner over and the children dispersed to other activities, they sat in the living room reading to a soft background of harpsichord concerti. A little before nine, the peaceful atmosphere was shattered by the ringing of the telephone followed by a bellowed message from their eldest son:

"Dad! It's Mr. Green calling you."

A frown crossed Jack's face and he closed his book and made his way to the telephone in the study.

"Sorry to bother you, old buddy," Bob Green began in a voice than clearly betrayed his concern, "but we've got a serious problem. I think you'd better meet me over at the facility as soon as you can so that we can discuss it."

"Can't it wait until morning, Bob?" Jack asked with unconcealed annoyance. "Sue and I are enjoying the first quiet evening at home that we've had in a long time."

"I don't think it can wait," Green insisted somberly. "If we're going to do something, it's got to be done this evening."

"What is it, Bob?" Jack enquired anxiously. "Give me a hint."

"It's that caper of Brian's that you pried out of me," Green confessed in a falling monotone.

"Oh my God," Jack said with a shudder. "I'll be right over."

He hurriedly hung up the receiver and returned to the living room.

"I've got to go over to the lab," Jack announced to his wife with obvious nervousness in his voice. "We've apparently got a serious problem. It's some of Bob Green's crazy friends and I just hope that they haven't hurt anybody."

Sue Mason looked up from her book with a frown.

"What do you mean, hurt anybody? Bob may believe some pretty crazy things, but I don't think he'd purposely hurt anyone. Did they have an accident?"

"Something like that," Jack agreed disingenuously. "It's not really Bob, but some of the crazy people he associates with."

Jack headed for the kitchen door leading to the driveway, and Sue was left with a perplexed look on her face, trying to decipher the cryptic conversation.

Even the Porsche's steel-belted radial tires squealed occasionally as Jack maneuvered at breakneck speed over the bumpy, winding back roads leading from Reston to the Project Psi facility. Despite his dangerous haste, Bob Green's Fiat Spyder was already there when Jack reached the parking lot in front of Building A. Jack scrambled out of the Porche and sprinted into the lobby, where the guard greeted him with a concerned expression.

"Is something wrong, Professor Mason? Mr. Green said to tell you that he would meet you in your office."

Jack hurried down the hall and found Bob Green seated at the conference table in his office. Bob's look was uncharacteristically serious, and his customary cheerful greeting was not forthcoming.

"Thanks for coming in," Bob said in a monotone. "I need some help."

Jack closed the door and seated himself at the table across from Bob.

"What happened? Let's have the whole story. Is anyone hurt badly?"

"Well, let me give you the worst first," Bob began emotionally. "There's a kid in the hospital, and he may die! And those bastards at the Agency won't do anything to help him."

"What do you mean, 'help him'?" Jack responded incredulously. "It sounds as though they've done enough already. You had better tell me the whole story. From the beginning."

Bob Green nodded sheepishly and began his tale of CIA enthusiasm gone wrong.

"Well, about a week ago, Brian decided that it was time for toxic chemical wastes from our facility to kill a few more cattle. In case the people at the Soviet embassy who go through the newspapers didn't pick up the story the first time. Or even if they did, in case it wasn't enough to convince their bosses back

196

at KGB headquarters to call off the attachés. Anyhow, this morning, a couple of operational types went out and put some poison in the same stream they used last time, after being sure that some cattle were drinking from it. Three or four cows died pretty quickly, and the spooks were waiting around in a grove of trees for somebody to show up and find the carcasses.

"And that's when the trouble started. A group of kids came walking across the field and found the dead cattle. Unfortunately, though, one of the kids took a drink from the stream. The spooks hoped that the poison had been washed away or had degraded to something safe, the way it's supposed to, by the time the kid drank the water. So they just kept waiting until the kids brought a crowd of people to see the carcasses. After a while, the agents could see that one of the kids was on the ground, and pretty soon an ambulance came and took him away. The CIA guys followed the ambulance to the hospital and found out that the kid was still alive, but in serious condition. And I guess that's when they called their controller and he called Brian. I don't want to tell you who called me, because he'd lose his job for sure, and maybe worse."

Jack began to feel nauseous. His head became light and started to spin, and his stomach tightened and began to churn. *I've truly thrown in with the Mafia,* he thought. *And now they're killing children and I'm part of it.* Jack stared at Bob in disbelief for a long moment and then finally managed to ask weakly:

"What did you mean when you said that they won't do anything to help the kid?"

"Well," Bob Green continued sadly, "my informant is sure that they have an antidote for the poison or at the very least a recommended medical treatment. He thinks that if one of the Agency's docs was advising the people who are treating the kid, he'd have a much better chance. But my guy can't get his bosses to move. They're afraid that it will blow their cover, and ours, too. So they're just going to sit it out and hope that the kid doesn't die."

"Those fucking sons of bitches!" Jack shouted. "If it's their cover they're worried about, I'll get them moving!"

He leaped to his feet, sprang behind his desk, and attacked the pop-up index of telephone numbers. Jack found the desired target, "Bennington, Stuart (home)" and began dialing violently.

"Wait a second, Jack!" Bob Green reacted with concern. "Who are you calling? You've got to be careful. This thing is very sensitive. If it gets out, a lot of people could be hurt."

As he listened to the phone ring, Jack thought emotionally that one helpless, innocent person had already been hurt badly, and he was going to do something about it.

At last the ringing ceased and a pleasant woman's voice answered:

"Hello."

"This is Professor Mason," Jack began, trying to conceal his agitation. "I'm sorry to bother you this late in the evening, but I must speak with Stuart Bennington."

"What did you say your name was?" the woman enquired cautiously.

"Mason," Jack replied firmly. "Jack Mason. He knows who I am."

"Just a moment," the woman concluded with a hint of annoyance. "I'll get him."

While Jack was talking to Mrs. Bennington, Bob Green had written a message on the blackboard so that his voice would not be heard over the telephone.

"Bennington probably doesn't know the story," the chalked scrawls advised.

Jack nodded his understanding to Bob as Stuart Bennington came on the line.

"Hello, Jack. How are you?"

"I'm okay, Stuart," Jack began coldly. "And I'm sorry to bother you at home. But some of your boys have done something pretty bad, and you're going to have to do something about it quickly—this evening."

"Well, look, Mason," Stuart Bennington dissembled, "I'm sure I don't know what you are talking about. And this is hardly the way or the time for me to find out. Why don't you come around to my office first thing in the morning and we'll talk about it."

"That won't do, Stuart," Jack came back, raising his voice. "There isn't time. They've put a kid in the hospital and now they won't help him survive. And if you don't—"

"Hold on, Mason," Stuart Bennington interjected. "I haven't the slightest idea what you're talking about. And I don't intend to listen to you any longer. If you want to talk about it in the morning—"

"God damn it, Bennington!" Jack shouted vehemently. "If you hang up, I'm going to call the *Washington Post!* Now just sit your ass down and listen to me. There's a kid in the hospital, on the critical list. And he's there because a couple of your thugs poisoned him. And his doctors don't know the right treatment, because it's some sort of exotic brew that your witches cooked up. You have doctors who know how to treat it, but they're sitting on their asses. Because somebody told them that maintaining your cover is more important than a kid's life! Now, I'm telling you, Stuart, if that kid dies, and I find out that your people didn't try to help him, I'm going to take the whole story to the *Post* and the *Star* and the *Times* and whoever the hell else will listen! Do you understand me?"

"Yes, I understand you," the Director of Central Intelligence replied softly, and Jack heard a click as Stuart Bennington put down the receiver. Jack turned back to the conference table and found Bob Green grinning broadly.

"Boy, you sure burned his ass! If that doesn't get them moving, nothing will."

"Seriously, Bob," Jack enquired, "do you think he'll do something?"

"Yeah, I think he will," Green answered, nodding his head. "I think you've convinced him that the danger to him if he does nothing is greater than the risk of exposing one of his docs to save the kid."

"Are you sure?" Jack persisted emotionally. "If you're not, I'll call someone else. Like Sam Ryan."

"Oh, no," Bob responded white-faced. "Don't do that. Sam would just fuck it all up. He'd blow the cover and end up not helping the kid. And then he'd start a witch hunt at the Agency to hide his own bungling. No, don't call Sam."

"Well, if not Sam, who?" Jack continued, almost relishing his newly found power.

"Look, Jack," Bob pleaded, "I think you've done enough for a while. Why don't you go back to reading your book and listening to the harpsichord concerti. And I'll call you again in a few hours, unless my informant says that they've started to do something."

Jack suddenly looked relieved and got to his feet.

"Okay, that sounds reasonable to me," he agreed. "I probably won't be able to pay much attention to the reading, but it will beat rolling around in bed thinking about that kid. Maybe it's a good night to start on *War and Peace*. Now, you be sure to call me if you have any doubt that they are doing something."

"Right, I'll call you," Bob confirmed dutifully. "And I'll stay right here and keep on top of what they're doing."

Jack spent a sleepless night on the living room sofa, alternately reading and trying to rest. When he did doze off, he was shortly awakened by the nightmare vision of a child writhing in agony in a high-sided hospital bed. Sue was up and down most of the night trying to calm him with cups of warm tea and snifters of a 100-proof brandy. At last, at about four A.M., Jack began a few hours of uninterrupted sleep.

When he arrived bleary-eyed at the office again next morning, Jack was surprised to find an unshaven, but smiling, Bob Green seated at his conference table. Bob's cheerful greeting told Jack in advance that things must have taken a sharp turn for the better.

"How did you sleep, old buddy? I found your sofa here pretty comfortable?"

"You got some sleep?" said Jack accusingly. "I didn't."

"Well, not really very much," Bob replied half apologetically. "I've been on the phone most of the night. But it's all over now but the shouting. Get a cup of coffee and I'll tell you about it."

Jack poured himself some warm brew from the carafe on the table and slumped wearily into the padded chair behind his desk. Bob Green smiled broadly and seemed genuinely eager to recount the remainder of night's events.

"About an hour after you blasted Bennington, my informant called back and said that they had gotten the word from MacFarland to do something," Green began with a hint of amusement in his voice. "Then, things were quiet for about three hours. I was getting nervous and was about to call some people to try to get a few details about what they were up to. But, about two A.M., the guy I had stationed at the hospital called me.

"He said that two sleepy-looking doctors with black bags had shown up and said that they were from the American Chemical Company and thought that they had some information that might help the doctor who was sitting up with the kid. Apparently the three docs had a conference, and at about two-thirty they all came back in hospital coats and started giving the kid a series of injections and intravenous solutions. Whatever it was, it must have worked. By six A.M., my guy called back for the last time to say that the kid was out of the coma and the witch doctors had disappeared as mysteriously as they had come."

Jack nodded with satisfaction and gave Bob a broad smile.

"Those bastards backed down!" he said jubilantly. "We backed the fucking Agency down! And made them do what's right for once. Even though we can't tell anyone about it, I think we've got a right to feel pretty good. Or at least not as bad as we might have."

Bob Green grinned in agreement.

"It isn't often that you can do something that you're proud of in this business," Bob said, "but I'll remember this one when the next load of horseshit comes along."

19

The Audition

The day had arrived when Jason Star's psychic powers would be demonstrated to the secretary of state and the president's chief of staff. Jack Mason had come to the Project Psi facility at a little after 6:00 A.M., mostly out of nervousness, but ostensibly to check on the last-minute preparations. The demonstration would be conducted late that morning in a secure conference room in the basement of the State Department. Much to Jack's surprise, Sam Ryan and Thomas Stratton had been remarkably agreeable to the final arrangements he had proposed.

A native Russian from the project's staff would engage in a mock arms control negotiation with General Ryan and would attempt to transmit his thoughts to Jason. The Russian transmitter would be given instructions by one of the secretary of state's aides right before the negotiation. He would be told when to be sincere and when to bluff, when to express strong emotions that were genuinely grounded in national interest and when to use feigned emotion as a negotiating ploy.

In the interest of objectivity, the briefing from the aide to the transmitter would be recorded for later comparison with Jason's perceptions. In the State Department conference room, General Ryan and the Russian transmitter would be seated opposite each other across a negotiating table, and Jason would be seated next to the transmitter. Aides to the general and the secretary of state would watch Jason and the transmitter continuously, like nervous officials at an international bridge tournament, seeking to detect the slightest attempts at nonpsychic communication.

At a little after seven o'clock, Barney O'Neil and Bob Green came to Jack's office with a status report. Bob ticked off the schedule for the morning's events like the countdown for a moon shot.

"We just woke Jason up, and he's showering and getting dressed. He'll be through eating by 0745 and will start his warm-up session with the transmitter at 0800. It will be a series of fifteen-minute mock negotiations. After each one, there will be a fifteen-minute debrief, and then a fifteen-minute break before the next one. That way, Jason can go through three practice negotiations by ten o'clock. At ten-fifteen, the people who are going to the State Department will start leaving the facility, each principal in a separate car driven by one of my security people. Here's the list of who's going. Jason, of course. The transmitter, Yuri Andromov. And the three of us. And that's it. I've tried to keep the group as small as possible to limit our exposure."

Jack nodded his agreement, smiling at Bob's efficiency, and Green continued the rundown.

"I'll drive you, Jack, and one of my guys will drive Barney. The cars will leave at five-minute intervals and take different routes into town. We'll be able to park in the garage under Old State and go directly to the conference room without being observed. The secretary and General Ryan and their people will meet us there at eleven-thirty. Stratton and Ryan normally have a working lunch every Thursday anyhow, so no one will be surprised when the general shows up at the State Department."

Jack nodded again to Bob and then turned to Barney with a look of concern.

"What do you think? Is he going to get a hit?"

A broad smile crossed O'Neil's Irish face.

"Well, if I go by what I've seen him do around here, he'll tear the cover off the ball. Knock it out of the park. But, frankly, I think this is a new ballgame. Like going up to the majors from the Pony League. A lot of guys who hit like Babe Ruth in Buffalo look pretty sad striking out in Yankee Stadium."

Jack smiled wryly, nodding his agreement, but then persisted.

"Seriously, Barney, what do you think his chances are?"

"If the demonstration goes the way we've planned it, he should do pretty well," O'Neil replied. "What I'm afraid of is that something will go wrong. Or that the ground rules will get changed or something. Like, the room won't be the way it was when we inspected it last week. Or Stratton or Ryan will change the format at the last minute. Or bring in a lot of strange people. You know, something that will throw Jason off his stride."

"Uh," said Jack with a frown, "you think they're going to throw us a curve ball."

"Well, I'm not sure," Barney admitted. "It's just that we're playing with some pretty important people. And I'm always suspicious when guys like that are so agreeable."

Jack nodded his concurrence.

"You may be right, Barney. I've got an uneasy feeling myself."

The ride from the Project Psi facility to the State Department was one of the strangest of Jack's life. At about ten-fifteen, Bob Green arrived in Jack's office wearing a mustache and a fedora and looking for all the world like a Mafia enforcer. He was carrying a blond, shoulder-length wig and a pair of granny glasses. Jack began to laugh and could barely speak through his chuckles.

"Come on—Bob—who do you think you're fooling—with that stuff?"

"It may not fool 'em," Green responded jovially, "but it'll sure slow 'em down, and give the guys in Moscow looking at the photographs something to scratch their heads about."

Bob held out the wig to Jack and continued in a way that made clear that it wasn't just a joke.

"Let's see how it fits, Goldilocks; I had it made specially."

Jack retreated behind his desk, and his laughter increased.

"You don't think you're going to get me to wear that thing do you?"

"Come on, old buddy," Green pleaded, "it's all part of the game. Now hurry up, and get it on. We've got to leave in five minutes. With the glasses and your raincoat, you'll look like something I picked up in Georgetown."

When the two oddly dressed characters reached the parking lot, Jack was surprised to see Bob head for a new sedan rather than his aging Fiat Spyder. Jack frowned quizzically as they entered the car, and, as Bob wheeled down the drive, his curiosity finally got the better of him.

"Did you get a new car?"

"No, I just left mine at the airport and rented this one," Bob replied with obvious self-satisfaction. "When the attachés call the registry, they'll find out that it belongs to Hertz."

Bob drove on winding back roads for about twenty minutes, passed a couple of large, new developments, and then finally pulled into the parking lot of a suburban shopping mall. Having remained silent throughout most of the ride, Jack no longer could restrain his curiosity and impatience.

"Come on Bob, what are you up to now? It's getting late, and I want to be there on time."

"Don't worry, old buddy," Green replied nonchalantly, "we're right on schedule. We've just got to do a little quick shopping."

Before Jack could respond, the car was parked and Bob had jumped out and headed toward the entrance to a large department store. Jack hustled after him, self-conscious in the strange disguise, his curiosity rapidly turning to annoyance.

"Come on, Bob, cut out the spy shit," Jack said in a stage whisper to Green's fleeing form in front of him. "What are you up to?"

"Just trust me, old buddy," Bob gasped back over his shoulder and continued his frantic pace. "Remember, this is my side of the business."

Green elbowed his way through the docile crowd of late morning shoppers in the aisles of the ground floor of Woodward and Lothrup. He emerged shortly from the door on the far side of the store with a bewildered Jack still in tow. Bob continued at jogging speed into the parking lot and, to Jack's consternation, approached another new sedan. As Jack finally caught up with him, Bob, checking the license number with the tag on a set of keys, motioned to his boss-cum-hippie to get in.

"This is it, old buddy. Hop in, and we're on our way."

As he swung the car out of the parking lot and back onto the roadway, Bob explained the caper with obvious satisfaction.

"If anyone was following us, we'll be long gone by the time they get back to their car."

Jack smiled his agreement and then shook his head in resignation.

The remainder of the trip was uneventful. They swung into the underground garage at the State Department at eleven-fifteen. Bob pulled up to the guard and spoke with a phony Latin accent.

"We have come for the luncheon conference on Central American Trade."

"Yes, sir," the guard responded. "Your name?"

"Lo-pez," Green replied affectedly. "Roberto Lopez."

The guard scanned a list on a clipboard and checked off the name.

"Go straight ahead to the end of the garage, sir, and then turn left. You'll see a set of spaces marked 'Visitor, Reserved.' Take any one of them. There are signs that will lead you to the elevator."

As soon as he had parked the car, Bob removed the fedora and the mustache and then with a grin, turned to Jack.

"Okay, Blondie, you can remove the tresses."

Jack took off the glasses and the wig and, following Bob's example, stashed them under the front seat. They got out of the car and were about to follow the signs to the elevator, when they were joined by one of Bob's assistants.

"I'll watch your car," the man said cryptically. "Do you know the way to the conference room?"

"Yeah, if it's still the same one we checked out yesterday," Bob replied, heading for the elevator.

"Right, that's it," the man called after them. "And you'll find Mark standing guard in the hall outside with one of the regular State Department types."

When Jack and Bob entered the conference room, they found Jason Star and Yuri Andromov already seated on the far side of a long mahogany table.

"Where's Barney?" Jack inquired nervously.

"He's off with one of General Ryan's assistants discussing the procedure they're going to use to brief Yuri," Jason responded.

"I think that Barney wants to be sure that they don't try to confuse me and then blame the bad results on Jason," Yuri said with a smile.

Several minutes later, Barney O'Neil reentered the room, followed by a short, wiry man with a crew cut. Although they had not met and the stranger was dressed in civilian clothes, Jack immediately presumed from his appearance that he was one of Sam Ryan's military assistants. Barney moved to Jack's side and bent down and spoke in a whisper.

"They've gone back on the agreement to record the briefing that they give to Yuri. They say that recording conversations has gone out of style around here."

Jack smiled thinly and then turned from Barney and addressed the crew-cut officer.

"General Ryan agreed that the briefing given to Mr. Andromov could be recorded."

"That may well be, sir," the aide responded deferentially. "Of course, I have no knowledge of your conversations with General Ryan. All I know is that the general told me this morning that the secretary of state has decided that no recordings of any kind are to be made. The security risk is simply too high."

Jack knitted his brow, suspecting some kind of skullduggery. He motioned to Barney to join him at the far end of the room for a private conversation. When O'Neil reached his side, Jack inquired in a low voice:

"What do you think they're up to?"

"I think they're just scared," Barney whispered back. "They're afraid that if their voices are on tape somewhere it will get used against them somehow in the future."

"Well, what do we do?" Jack persisted. "We can't let them be the only ones who know what they tell Yuri. It will be his word against theirs, and they will always say that he is the one who doesn't remember quite right."

"The only way out that I can see is to insist that one of us listen to the briefing," Barney suggested. "That way, at least we'll be sure of what was said, even if they don't believe us."

Jack nodded in agreement, walked back to the center of the room, and again addressed General Ryan's aide.

"If we can't record the briefing, I insist that Dr. O'Neil be allowed to listen in. In order to evaluate Mr. Star's performance scientifically, it is essential that we have independent corroboration of the instructions that are given to Mr. Andromov."

"I see," said the wiry man with a worried look. "I'll have to check that out with General Ryan. Please excuse me."

The aide left the room, presumably to call Sam Ryan. Jack and Barney seated themselves at the table and began to banter with Yuri and Jason. In less than five minutes, the general's assistant returned and indicated concurrence with Jack's demand.

"General Ryan agrees to have Dr. O'Neil listen to the instructions that are given to Mr. Andromov by Mr. Cabot. The general says that we should get started with the briefing now and that he and Secretary Stratton will be down in about fifteen minutes."

"Fine," said Jack, with a hint of triumph in his voice. "Why don't you go and do it."

"Please come with me, Mr. Andromov," the aide said in a tone that sounded like an order. "And you too, Dr. O'Neil." The officer in mufti led the way out of the conference room, and Yuri and Barney rose and followed. As he reached the door, O'Neil did a little skip and a jump and looked back and winked at Jack.

The secretary of state was in a serious mood. As soon as he and president's chief of staff had joined the group in the conference room and they had all seated themselves around the negotiating table, Thomas Stratton rose and began to deliver a soliloquy.

"Gentlemen, the demonstration we are about to witness, if it is successful, may well be the first practical test of a capability that will revolutionize international diplomacy. I believe that you are aware of the intensive efforts I have made, through negotiations with both our allies and our adversaries, to establish a structure of alliances and treaties that foster world order. In my view, only through such order can lasting world peace be ensured."

The secretary of state surveyed the group at the table, like a mighty professor scrutinizing cowering sophomores at a tutorial, in search of a spark of recognition of the import of his words. They all stared back earnestly, acknowledging his unquestioned mastery, and Thomas Stratton began again, addressing Jason with utmost seriousness.

"You, Mr. Star, if your capabilities are a fraction of what I have been told they are, will have an unique opportunity to contribute, perhaps immeasurably, to my quest for world order and enduring peace."

Thomas Stratton looked at Jason intently, apparently expecting an acknowledgment of this implied partnership, and the man with psi finally weakly nodded his understanding. The bargain sealed, the secretary of state gestured expansively to the group as a whole and continued in a confidential tone.

"The president has asked me to convey to all of you his deep personal interest in your work. Because he shares my belief in the importance of the quest for world order, he has given Project Psi the top priority backing it now enjoys. Needless to say, I hope to be able to report to him after this demonstration that his confidence and commitment have been justified."

Thomas Stratton again surveyed the room in silence, making sure that the import of his remarks had been fully appreciated. Finally, he turned to Jack with a theatrical gesture.

"Now, Professor Mason, please describe the illusion we are about to witness."

Jack rose at his place, turned toward the secretary of state, and began as matter-of-factly as he could.

"Well, Mr. Secretary, it's relatively simple. In the interest of making the demonstration of Mr. Star's ability to receive psi signals as realistic as possible, General Ryan graciously has agreed to engage in a mock negotiation concerning strategic arms with Mr. Andromov. Mr. Andromov is one of the native-born Russians on our staff who has an exceptional ability to transmit brain-wave signals, and we have been using him to train Mr. Star and the other psionauts. Mr. Andromov has just been briefed by Mr. Cabot of your staff on the positions he should take and the emotions he should feel during the negotiations. General Ryan is unaware of these instructions, as are the rest of us, with the exception of Dr. O'Neil, who witnessed the briefing."

Thomas Stratton nodded, acknowledging his familiarity with the arrangements, and Jack resumed his description.

"My understanding is that Mr. Cabot has instructed Mr. Andromov to give truthful answers to General Ryan's questions concerning certain weapons and issues and to give untruthful answers concerning others."

Jack paused for confirmation of what had transpired at the briefing, and Barney O'Neil nodded his agreement. Thomas Stratton turned toward the far end of the table and fixed his gaze on Livingstone Cabot II. The latter nodded weakly and Jack continued.

"Mr. Star will attempt, by receiving Mr. Andromov's brain waves, to determine which of his answers are truthful, and which are not. During the negotiations, Mr. Andromov will take strong positions on certain issues, again following Mr. Cabot's instructions. In some cases, he will truly be expressing the adamant position of his country, while in others, he will be bluffing to see if he can obtain additional concessions from General Ryan. Again, by receiving psi signals, Mr. Star will attempt to perceive when Mr. Andromov is serious and when he is bluffing."

Jack paused, and again Thomas Stratton signaled his understanding.

"In order to prevent Mr. Star from receiving visual cues from Mr. Andromov, Mr. Star will wear a blindfold throughout the negotiation. While he would not be so handicapped at an actual conference table and might receive additional useful information from the facial expressions of Soviet leaders, we thought it best to blindfold him at this demonstration for two reasons. First, it will force him to concentrate solely on receiving psi signals. And, second, it should help to alleviate any concern that you may have that Mr. Andromov might be signaling to Mr. Star by some prearranged set of facial expressions."

Jack hesitated momentarily, allowing time for Thomas Stratton to raise an objection, but, uncharacteristically, none was forthcoming. The secretary of state simply nodded again solemnly, and Jack concluded the introduction with great sincerity.

"Let me assure you, Mr. Secretary, that this demonstration is being conducted as honestly and carefully as possible, given your desire for a negotiating table environment. In the interest of allaying any residual doubts you may have, all of us have agreed to take lie detector tests concerning the truthfulness of the demonstration if you feel that would be appropriate."

Thomas Stratton smiled.

"I don't think that will be necessary, Professor. Somehow, lie detector tests seem out of place at the negotiating table."

Having begun to put them at ease, the secretary of state turned his humor on the president's chief of staff.

"Well, Sam, let's see you in action. I have never thought of you as the negotiating type, but if this audition goes well, I might take you on my next trip."

Thomas Stratton chuckled at his own joke, and the others joined in timidly. Even Sam Ryan seemed to take the kidding good-naturedly.

"Well, Mr. Secretary, I've been trying to be a bit more diplomatic since I've been over at the White House. Professor, are we ready to begin the demonstration?"

"Just about, General Ryan," Jack responded. "But there are a few things that I should say about the seating arrangements."

Jack turned toward Thomas Stratton and continued earnestly.

"Mr. Secretary, because the psi field decays rapidly with distance, we have asked that Mr. Star be allowed to sit next to Mr. Andromov at the table. Your aides may watch them both to ensure that no signaling is taking place."

Thomas Stratton nodded his concurrence, but then responded with a hint of annoyance.

"Professor, you seem obsessed with the idea that I should believe that you are cheating me. If I were meeting you across the conference table, your protestations would indeed convince me that you probably were trying to cheat me. I know that you are an honest man, and you don't have to keep trying to convince me."

"Thank you for your confidence, Mr. Secretary," Jack replied sheepishly and then sought to explain. "The reason that I am so preoccupied with the possibility of fraud is that our investigations have shown it to be a ubiquitous constituent of most previous ESP research. For that reason, we have taken the most careful and continuous precautions to prevent it from intruding into Project Psi."

"Very laudable, Professor. Very laudable," Thomas Stratton said perfunctorily. "But time is fleeting, and I have other meetings to attend. Let's get on with the show."

211

"Yes, sir," Jack replied deferentially. "We'll begin as soon as people have taken their places. I'd like General Ryan to sit on one side at the head end of the conference table, and Mr. Andromov on the other side opposite him. Mr. Star will sit next to Mr. Andromov. The rest of us should sit at least two or three seats away from them, so as to minimize the interfering brain-wave signals we present to Mr. Star. Mr. Secretary, why don't you sit there," Jack said pointing, "three chairs down from General Ryan."

Thomas Stratton nodded his agreement and moved to his appointed chair. The others filled in between him and Jack, who remained standing at the foot of the table, giving final directions to the cast.

"General Ryan, I believe that it was agreed that you would begin the negotiations by asking Mr. Andromov some questions."

Jack sat down and all eyes riveted on the three people isolated at the head of the table. Sam Ryan began, somewhat uncertainly, like a first-time actor auditioning for the local community players.

"Good morning, Mr. Andromov. It is, ah, a pleasure for me to meet with you this morning to, ah, discuss matters of great importance to our countries. My government has asked me to ask you to clarify your government's position on several subjects. The first, ah, issue we seek clarification on is the purpose of the new missile silos we believe, ah, we know you are building along the Trans-Siberian railroad."

Yuri Andromov smiled benignly across the table, and Sam Ryan continued with somewhat increased confidence.

"We believe that these new silos are much larger than any you have built before. This is a cause of great concern to my government because your largest missiles are already much larger that ours. What can you tell me about the purposes of this new silo construction?"

Yuri Andromov smiled again and began to speak in a steady, clear voice, the same one he had practiced so often with Jason.

"Good morning, General Ryan. It is indeed a pleasure for me to meet with you this morning on behalf of my government. Unfortunately, with regard to the specific question that you have raised, I can provide no information. May I suggest that you reconsult your intelligence analysts. They apparently have been reading more in their tea leaves than is present on the ground. We are building no new missile silos, either along the Trans-Siberian railroad, or elsewhere for that matter."

Sam Ryan appeared genuinely disturbed and responded with noticeable emotion in his voice.

"Come now, Mr. Andromov. You know as well as I do that it is hard to hide something as large as a missile silo. What are those holes for if not for new, larger missiles? You are not going to try to tell me that your government is going to put oil or grain in them, are you?"

By now, the two-man play had totally captured the tiny audience. All eyes turned toward Yuri Andromov waiting for his reply. Jason held his head in his hands, seeking to exclude all disturbances save the psi fields. The tension continued to build, and, finally, Yuri responded in his best diplomatic tone.

"I assure you, General Ryan, that the Soviet Union is not constructing any new missile silos along the Trans-Siberian railroad. Whoever has told you this fanciful story is simply wrong. Now, may I suggest that we go on to another topic?"

"I don't want to go on," Sam Ryan said, almost shouting. "I want to get a straight story out of you about those silos!"

Yuri Andromov stared placidly across the table at his red-faced adversary.

"General, I do not know what your analysts have been drinking. If they were ours, I would suspect that it was vodka."

Thomas Stratton laughed out loud and could no longer resist chiding the president's chief of staff.

"Now you're getting a feel for what it's like to deal with a Russian, Sam. I think you'd better go on to the next question."

Sam Ryan looked chagrined but accepted the secretary of state's advice.

"Very well, Mr. Andromov," the general concluded sternly. "I hope that you will be more forthcoming on the next subject."

Yuri only smiled again, and Sam Ryan hurried on to his next prepared question.

"My government would like clarification of your government's recent demand in the SALT negotiations that tactical nuclear weapons stationed in Western Europe be included in the

213

overall totals of strategic nuclear forces. In view of the fact that tactical nuclear weapons have long been excluded from SALT, we do not understand your recent demand to blur the distinction."

Yuri Andromov began speaking again in a measured tone, and Jason Star appeared as though in a trance.

"My government has no desire to blur the distinction between strategic and tactical weapons. The definition of a strategic weapon is clear. It is any weapon possessed by either of our countries that can strike the other country. The nuclear weapons that the United States has deployed in Western Europe unambiguously fall into the strategic category because they can, according to the boasts of your fellow generals, strike the Soviet Union."

Sam Ryan's face and voice again revealed his rising anger—not the result of method acting.

"Dammit, Andromov, you know very well why we have tactical nuclear weapons in Western Europe. To keep your tanks from rolling across Germany and France. So if I accept your argument that our tactical nuclear weapons are really strategic, then your tanks must be strategic, too!"

Yuri Andromov smiled involuntarily in instant recognition of Sam Ryan's blunder. He waited a moment to be sure that the audience had grasped the inconsistency and then delivered a lightning thrust.

"But, General, you have forgotten the definition of strategic. Our tanks surely cannot strike New York!"

Thomas Stratton began to chuckle audibly and then, mercifully, ended Sam Ryan's brief career as a summit negotiator.

"So much for your audition, Sam. I think I'll take Andromov here along instead. But, seriously, let's take a break and hear Mr. Star's impressions."

Sam Ryan looked relieved. Jason Star slowly removed the blindfold and smiled at the group that was staring at him from the other end of the table.

"Well, Mr. Secretary," Jason began forthrightly, "let me start at the beginning and give you all my impressions, just exactly as they came to me. General, you'll have to pardon me.

The first impression isn't very flattering. But I'm sure that it wasn't intended personally."

Sam Ryan frowned and Jason Star continued.

"From the moment that Mr. Andromov sat down, and from time to time during the negotiations, I received clear psi impressions—*'fool,' 'you fool,'* and even the entire phrase *'think you fool.'*"

Sam Ryan turned and glared at Thomas Stratton's assistant at the far end of the table. Livingstone Cabot's face turned white, and Barney O'Neil could hardly conceal his amusement.

"What the hell kind of instructions did you give that guy, Cabot?" the irate general demanded.

Livingstone Cabot II could barely speak. His short State Department career appeared headed for an untimely demise. What could he say? How could he apologize? Or rationalize? It had seemed so clever. So Harvard clever.

"But, General it, ah, as he said, ah, wasn't meant personally. We, ah, er, tried to think of, ah, something he wouldn't guess in a million years."

Ryan continued glaring, and Cabot squirming and babbling.

"You're, ah, er, so imposing, sir, it's, ah, the last thing we thought he would ever guess. We really didn't think he could, ah, read Mr. Andromov's—"

Ever adept at calming stormy waters, Barney O'Neil tried to intercede on behalf of the hapless assistant.

"I think it really was a pretty good test phrase, General Ryan. It's the kind of emotion that a Soviet leader might feel, and yet one that Jason would be very reluctant to report unless he received a really strong psi signal."

Sam Ryan continued to look at Livingstone Cabot as if visualizing him before a firing squad. The offender appeared about to faint and slide beneath the table, when Thomas Stratton intervened.

"Very good, Mr. Star! Let's hear your next impression."

The tension in the small, poorly ventilated room was relieved noticeably. Jason continued eagerly before the general could press the confrontation.

"The next psi signals came during the discussion of missile silos, Mr. Secretary. I received the impression *'no'* and *'no new'*

215

several times. I'm not certain if I ever received the entire phrase *'no new silos'* or if my own mind added the object 'silos.' "

"Well, Cabot," Thomas Stratton said sternly. "What did you tell Mr. Andromov about the silos?"

Livingstone Cabot was sufficiently recovered to shake his head in amazement.

"That's *just* what we told him! That there *weren't* any new silos. And that despite any supposed evidence that the general presented, he should vehemently and genuinely deny that any new silos were being built."

Jack and Barney began to grin broadly at Jason's success. Although it was only the first-act curtain, they thought it likely that the most influential circle was about to leave the theater and write a rave review.

"Well, Mr. Star, that's two out of two!" said Thomas Stratton, obviously understating his enthusiasm. "What's next?"

"Well, sir," Jason replied, "the next psi signals came while General Ryan was pressing Mr. Andromov about the silos. I got the impression 'wrong' several times. And once, I received the phrase 'American wrong.' "

"I think we'll have to rely on Yuri for this one, Mr. Secretary," Barney O'Neil interjected. "Mr. Cabot simply told him to continue to honestly and vehemently deny that any new silos had been built. What were you thinking, Yuri?"

Yuri Andromov turned toward Thomas Stratton.

"Well, Mr. Secretary, I decided to repeat over and over in my mind in Russian the phrase 'intelligence American wrong.' Apparently Jason received the words 'American' and 'wrong,' but not the word 'intelligence,' which hasn't been in any of our vocabularies."

"Well, Mr. Star, at last you have stumbled, if only slightly," Thomas Stratton said with a chuckle. "Your performance is truly amazing. At least with your friend Andromov. Tell us what you got about the tactical nuclear weapons."

"Well, sir," Jason responded confidently, "those signals were very distinct. I received one Russian word clearly, over and over again—'bluff.' "

"That's right!" Livingstone Cabot blurted out without waiting to be asked. "I told him to be sincere and forceful in presenting the case, but to continually think about the fact that he was bluffing."

"Point, set, and match to Mr. Star!" exclaimed Thomas Stratton. But then he added more ominously, "Are you game to try a tougher opponent?"

A sudden chill flooded through Jack's chest and gripped his stomach. He had suspected that Stratton or Ryan would spring something on them, and this apparently was it. The room was silent, and all eyes turned toward Jack. He stared back in confusion verging on panic and finally managed to respond tentatively:

"What do you have in mind, Mr. Secretary?"

"Well," said Thomas Stratton jovially, "since Mr. Star has played so well against his friend, Mr. Andromov, I thought that he might be ready for a match with a stranger."

The room was silent again; everyone was waiting for Jack's response. His mind raced and fear engulfed him. To accept this unknown challenge seemed mad. After Jason's successful performance with Yuri, they had everything to lose and little to gain. But could one successfully refuse a suggestion from the secretary of state? Before Jack could mentally resolve the dilemma, Thomas Stratton spoke again.

"Come now, Professor, it's only sporting. In the first match, you selected both of the players, and I only got to pick the court. Since you won that one, I think it only fair that I be allowed to select Mr. Star's next opponent."

Jack capitulated without knowing why.

"Whom did you have in mind, Mr. Secretary?"

"A young man on my staff who speaks Russian," Stratton responded matter-of-factly. "A Mr. Stephen Janek. He's been participating behind the scenes in the grain negotiations, and having a hard time with the Soviets, I might say. Sam, if you think that Andromov was tough on you, I suggest that you talk to Janek sometime. He says it's like trying to carry on a conversation with the Kremlin wall. But I'm getting off the subject. What I propose is the following. I'll have Stephen come down here and play a Soviet grain dealer. And I'll be his American counterpart. And we'll see if Mr. Star can perceive how badly Stephen wants the grain and what he's willing to pay for it."

The results of the second match were disastrous. Stephen Janek claimed to have repeatedly lied to the secretary of state during the mock grain negotiation. Although Jason had difficulty perceiving any words distinctly, his overall impression of Janek was one of sincerity. Afterwards, Janek ridiculed Jason's perceptions, much to the amusement of Sam Ryan. In the end, Thomas Stratton excused himself with a seemingly callous parting remark:
"That's the way the ball bounces on the court of international diplomacy."

Jack and Bob drove out of the State Department garage in silence. Finally, as they were crossing the Potomac on the Fourteenth Street bridge, Jack could no longer contain his anger.
"That bastard Stratton crushed us for no reason! With some ringer from left field. Why did he do it? We give him a nice, well-planned, successful demonstration and he isn't satisfied. So he brings in some kid with an accent and they talk about wheat for a while, and then the kid announces that Jason didn't get the message. It's like a kangaroo court! The kid was the prosecutor and the witness, and Stratton was the jury and the judge. We didn't have a chance!"
"Yeah, old buddy, they sure did spring one on us," Bob responded disconsolately.
But Jack continued his rambling discourse without acknowledging Bob's comment.
"I still can't figure out why he did it? Why would he want to make us look bad? To make that asshole Ryan feel better? Or does he really think we're frauds?"
"I don't think it's that," Bob said. "I think he's seen an awful lot of people fold up under the pressure of international negotiations. Maybe he just wanted us to get a taste of what the real ball game is going to be like."
Jack sat back in silence pondering Bob's suggestion. Perhaps Stratton's action made some sense after all. Even their

218

most recent conference room training was certainly a far cry from the environment Jason would encounter at a real summit meeting. Slowly, Jack's thoughts shifted to a potentially more serious problem, and finally he articulated his concern to Bob.

"Why didn't Jason perceive any of Janek's thoughts clearly?"

Green shrugged his shoulders.

"I don't know. Maybe Janek's got funny brain waves. He sure talked like a wild man."

Jack chuckled, glad that Bob had relived the tension, but then became serious again.

"Well, if that's the case, it's not so good for us. If some people's brains emit signals that are substantially different from those of our transmitters, how are we ever going to be sure that Jason is ready to read Sherkov's mind?"

"We could always send Jason to the Black Sea for the summer as a valet or something," Bob responded facetiously.

"Seriously, Bob," Jack persisted, "it could be a real problem. Worst of all, suppose that some people's brains don't emit any psi signals at all."

"Come on, Jack," Bob replied sardonically. "You don't believe that. Even a dumb guy like me can understand Walter Patton's explanation about how the currents in the brain produce magnetic fields and the magnetic fields propagate through space and the other person's brain—"

"Yeah, that's just standard electromagnetic theory," Jack broke in despondently. "But what if it has nothing to do with psi perceptions?"

For a while they rode on in silence, enduring the muggy August afternoon in the rolling Virginia countryside. Then, abruptly, Jack again began to ruminate.

"The key thing is to determine why Jason didn't perceive any of Janek's thoughts clearly. We should concentrate on that during Jason's debriefing."

20

"He's a Hungarian!"

When Jason Star returned to the Project Psi facility, he went directly to the new debriefing room. It had the appearance of a small hospital operating theater complete with a central padded table and resuscitation equipment against one wall. Although Jason had been debriefed while under the influence of sodium pentothal before, he still was not entirely accustomed to the procedure. When Jason entered the debriefing room, he found Phyllis Jackson and Dick Sterling already there, looking quite medical in white hospital coats. Dr. Paul Berman, the new full-time anesthesiologist, was working over a cart of bottles and hypodermic syringes. Jason eyed the cart nervously, boosted himself up onto the table, and began to banter with Dick and Phyllis to bolster his courage.

"Well, I guess I was doing pretty well until they brought in that ringer."

"You really did phenomenally well, Jason," Phyllis said. "We all were amazed when we heard about it, truly amazed."

A warm glow of pride engulfed Jason Star. *Phyllis is such a kind person,* he thought. *She is trying to cheer me up.*

Paul Berman turned from his cart and faced his patient with a warm, open smile.

"Well, Jason, I'm ready to go any time you are."

Jason nodded resignedly and swung his feet up onto the table and lay down. Phyllis and Dick raised the restraining railing on each side of the table to prevent Jason from rolling off, and Paul placed a small pillow under his head. Next, Phyllis clipped a small microphone to Jason's shirt and taped the cable to one of the railings to prevent the microphone from being pulled loose. Finally, all the preparations being in order, she addressed the supine figure in a soothing tone.

"If you're comfortable, Jason, please say something for us so that Ken can adjust the tape recorder."

"This is Jason Star, ladies and gentlemen," the man with psi said, mimicking a television newsman, "reporting to you in a pentothal trance on mysterious events that transpired today in the basement of the State Department."

Barney O'Neil began chuckling and the others joined in. A moment later, Ken Anderson's voice was heard from a loud-speaker in the ceiling talking to them from behind the sound-proof glass panel separating the recording studio from the debriefing room.

"That's fine, Jason. Now let's hear Phyllis so that I can set her mike, too."

Phyllis Jackson raised her clipboard and began to read.

"As soon as Yuri came into the room, what was the first psi signal that you received?"

"Ryan is a fool. Ryan is a fool," quipped Jason, and the room again dissolved into laughter. Barney O'Neil could hardly control his guffaws, and Paul Berman had to put down his syringe to keep from dropping it.

When the mirth finally subsided, Phyllis Jackson tried to bring them back to reality.

"Well, gentlemen, shall we proceed? Or should I call the producer of *Laugh-In*? Jason, are you ready?"

"As ready as I'll ever be, Phyllis," Jason replied with resignation, and he laid his head down on the pillow.

Paul Berman grasped Jason's outstretched right forearm with one hand and deftly inserted the needle with the other.

"It'll be just like last time, Jason," Berman advised soothingly. "You'll feel a little light-headed and euphoric and talkative. But you've got nothing to worry about. I'll be right here all the time, monitoring your condition."

Jason Star stared at the ceiling above him and it slowly began to rotate. His eyes tried to follow it, but his head didn't move. The next sensation he experienced was like slipping beneath the surface in his scuba gear. The room slowly receded and darkened as he plunged deeper into the murk below. He swam on with powerful kicks of his fins and finally emerged from a jungle of giant kelp into clear blue water over sparkling white sand. Slowly, as if from another world, Phyllis Jackson's ethereal voice filtered down to him.

"Jason? Can you hear me?"

"Sure I can, Phyllis," Jason responded with a silly smile.

"All right, Jason," Phyllis continued, "take your thoughts back to the State Department conference room this morning."

Jason nodded slightly in the affirmative, and Phyllis began the questioning.

"As soon as Yuri came into the room, what was the first psi signal that you received?"

"*Think you fool general*. Think you fool, General," Jason repeated slowly but clearly.

Yuri Andromov peered with wonder from the foot of the operating table at Jason's prostrate form.

"Those are the exact words that I repeated over and over to myself," he said incredulously.

Phyllis Jackson nodded approvingly and moved on to the next question.

"Jason? What impression did you receive while General Ryan was asking Yuri about the missile silos?"

"*No new silos*. No new silos," the man with psi intoned.

"That's fine, Jason," said Phyllis reassuringly. "What was the next signal you received?"

Jason Star was swimming through the blue water, following a small, multicolored fish. A faint voice filtered down to him from the surface and Jason smiled up at it.

"Jason? Can you hear me?" Phyllis Jackson repeated.

"I hear you, Phyllis," Jason answered in a singsong voice. "It's beautiful down here."

"He's all right, Phyllis," Paul Berman interjected. "Just hallucinating a little. Keep repeating the question."

"Jason? What impression did you receive next? After Yuri stopped thinking 'no new silos.' "

Jason Star's drugged mind slowly began to concentrate again on Phyllis Jackson's questioning. All of a sudden, he clearly remembered the next psi signal.

"American wrong. Intelligence American wrong."

"Incredible!" said Yuri Andromov, shaking his head. "Again he perceived the exact words that I was thinking."

Barney O'Neil slipped out of the debriefing room to call Jack Mason. He found a phone in an unoccupied office, and as soon as Jack answered Barney began an enthusiastic report.

"Jack, things are going pretty well down here. Jason seems to recall the exact words that Yuri was thinking. And he's filling in words that he couldn't recall over at the State Department. Like 'intelligence' in 'intelligence American wrong.' "

"Sounds great, Barney," Jack responded enthusiastically. "That suggestion of Dick Sterling's to use sodium pentothal has certainly been a lifesaver. Apparently Jason receives a lot more psi signals than he can consciously recall. But the thing that's still really bothering me is that guy Janek. Why couldn't Jason clearly perceive anything that he was thinking? You should get Jason onto recalling the test with Janek as soon as possible. We know he does well with Yuri, so the thing you should concentrate on is finding out what the problem was with Janek."

"Right, Jack," Barney said, nodding to himself. "I'll go back and talk to Phyllis and get her to move on to the encounter with Janek as soon as possible. Berman doesn't like to keep Jason under too long, so we don't want to waste time proving to ourselves how well he does with Yuri."

"Right," Jack agreed. "Give me a call if you get a clue to the Janek problem."

Less than an hour later, Jack's phone rang and he discovered an excited Barney O'Neil on the line.

"He's not a Russian!" Barney shouted jubilantly. "Janek's not a Russian!"

"What do you mean, he's not a Russian?" Jack responded quizzically.

"That's the problem," Barney explained. "He's not a Russian. He's a fucking Hungarian!"

Jack began to smile. *A Hungarian!* he thought, shaking his head.

"How did you find out?"

"Dina doped it out," Barney replied triumphantly. "Jason was having so much trouble recalling any perceptions from Janek at all that we got her down here to talk to him in Russian. That didn't help much, but after a while Jason started to recall some funny sounds and words. And then, all of a sudden, Dina let out a shout: "He's a *Hungarian!* Janek's a *Hungarian!*" And then she started apologizing, and saying that she should have spotted it from the name right away. And we all just laughted and patted her on the back."

Jack leaned back in his high-backed swivel chair and chuckled at Barney's tale.

"Tell Dina that she certainly has made everyone's day. And then come on up here. We've got to think of an appropriate way to tell Professor Stratton that his Eliza Doolittle has been exposed."

After discussing several amusing, but potentially embarrassing, alternatives, Jack and Barney and Bob finally decided that a straightfoward, Boy Scout approach was probably best when dealing with someone as egotistical and powerful as the secretary of state. It was now approaching nine P.M., hopefully past Thomas Stratton's dinner hour, yet well before he was likely to retire for the evening. Jack dialed the number that Bob had provided while the others watched with nervous excitement.

"The Stratton residence," said a voice that sounded like a butler.

"This is Professor Mason," Jack began. "I have some information that I believe the secretary would like to receive. May I please speak with him?"

"Will you please repeat the name, sir?" the butler's voice requested.

"Professor John Mason. M A S O N," Jack said emphatically.

"Just a moment, sir," the servant responded. "I'll see if the secretary is receiving calls."

Jack covered the mouthpiece and repeated, in a highfalutin tone:

"Just a moment, sir, I'll see if the secretary is receiving calls."

Bob Green smiled and Barney O'Neil began to guffaw. Jack motioned to Barney to be quiet and then replaced the handset at his ear.

"Secretary Stratton will be with you in a moment, Professor," the butler's voice was saying.

"Thank you," Jack replied, trying to keep from laughing.

Several minutes passed in silence, but at last Thomas Stratton's well-modulated voice came over the line.

"Good evening, Mr. Secretary," Jack responded deferentially. "I'm sorry to bother you at home, but we discovered something very interesting during the debriefing after today's demonstration. It concerns your Mr. Janek."

"Yes, Professor," said Thomas Stratton, without a hint of concern in his voice. "What did you discover?"

"He's not a Russian, is he, Mr. Secretary?" Jack said in a voice that clearly revealed his satisfaction. "He's a Hungarian. So he was thinking in Hungarian today, not in Russian."

"Very astute of you, Professor," Thomas Stratton replied curtly. "Perhaps you should teach Mr. Star Hungarian."

"But you knew that Mr. Star didn't—"

"Thank you for calling, Professor," said the secretary of state matter-of-factly. "Now I think that I had better return to my guests. Good evening."

Thomas Stratton hung up abruptly and Jack was left holding a dead receiver. His face made clear his frustration as he explained the conversation to Barney and Bob.

"That smooth bastard. He wouldn't even admit that he tricked us and we found him out."

"I guess that's why he's secretary of state," Barney chortled. "Those diplomatic types never call a cow flop *shit*. They allude to an unpleasant smelling substance on the ground having a curious round, flattened shape."

"But you'd think the least he would have done would have been to apologize," Jack said earnestly. "Or to claim that he hadn't known that Janek was a Hungarian. Or that he didn't realize that it would make any difference to Jason."

"I think that you're missing the point, old buddy," Bob Green interjected. "He knew perfectly well what he was doing. We were ahead five to nothing late in the game, and he didn't want us to blow his team out of the ballpark. So he brought the old spitball artist in from the bench to fan the side."

21

The Acid Test

Several weeks had passed since the successful demonstration of
Jason Star's psychic powers at the State Department and the
unnerving encounter with Stephen Janek. Jack Mason was
seated at his desk, unenthusiastically taking care of some routine paperwork, when his senses were jarred by the shrill, repeated ringing of the secure telephone. He reached for the heavy,
black receiver, waited for the rush of noise to subside as the
phones synchronized, and then responded:

"Mason speaking."

A businesslike female voice announced:

"Secretary Stratton is calling for Professor Mason."

"This is Professor Mason," Jack replied with a hint of annoyance.

"Just a moment for Secretary Stratton, Professor Mason,"
the secretary replied mechanically.

Jack's mind raced trying to guess what new trick Thomas
Stratton might have up his sleeve. *Perhaps he's got a Lithuanian
or a Pole this time,* Jack thought with amusement. *He must have
some new test in mind for Jason. I wonder—*

"Good morning, Professor Mason," said the voice of Thomas
Stratton above the background noise. "How is our star, Mr. Star?
I hope he's in good form. I have in mind a little workout for him."

Jack's worst fears were realized and a sudden chill swept
through him.

"Good morning, Mr. Secretary," Jack said, slowly, trying to
give himself a few more seconds to think. "I'm sure that you
realize that Jason still needs a lot of training. What do you have
in mind?"

226

"My proposal should fit right in with his training program, Professor," Thomas Stratton said, not to be denied. "I'm going to give him some realistic exposure—to the Soviet ambassador."

"But, Mr. Secretary!" Jack protested. "Don't you think that's a bit premature? As you know, Jason hasn't yet tried to read the mind of anyone except the native Russians on our staff."

"Don't forget Stephen Janek, Professor," Thomas Stratton interjected. "Has Jason learned Hungarian yet?"

Apparently the secretary of state had a sense of humor after all, Jack thought, and he decided that there was no percentage in trying to fight the inevitable.

"When is this, er, encounter going to take place, Mr. Secretary?"

"Tomorrow at lunch. That's why I'm calling now to give you some advanced notice."

Advanced notice! Jack thought. *Twenty-four hours advanced notice for a test with the Soviet ambassador!*

"But, Mr. Secretary," Jack finally managed, almost pleading. "Wouldn't you be taking a substantial risk in exposing Jason to the Soviet ambassador before he's had some field training?"

"That's a well-taken point, Professor. One that I have already considered," Thomas Stratton said curtly. "Now, let me tell you how the encounter, as you call it, will be handled. Basov is coming to see me tomorrow at ten o'clock to present some new Soviet ideas on a total ban on nuclear testing. It's an important issue and an important meeting, but not supremely important. Just the right circumstance to give Jason a realistic test. If he can provide some insight into the ambassador's thoughts and feelings, his perceptions will be very valuable to me. On the other hand, if Jason fails completely, nothing will have been lost."

Jack listened in blank-faced silence as Thomas Stratton described with Machiavellian enthusiasm the web into which Ivan Aleksandrovich Basov would unsuspectingly be drawn.

"Now, Professor, let me tell you how I plan to introduce Jason. Basov and I will talk in my office until about noon or twelve-thirty and then go down to my dining room for lunch. I normally invite one or two of my key aides to join us, and, tomorrow, Jason will be the guest. His name will be David Brentwood.

He majored in economics at Princeton and is one of my advisors on the economic implications of disarmament. Close enough, I believe you'll agree, to Mr. Star's actual background that he shouldn't have much trouble carrying it off. I've dispatched a courier to your facility with an entire Brentwood dossier. Be sure that Jason studies it carefully."

Jack found himself dumbly nodding his understanding of the secretary of state's instructions to the empty room, and, oblivious of his listener's almost catatonic state, Thomas Stratton continued his monologue.

"This afternoon, I'll send someone over to brief Jason on recent topics in the economics of arms control. Just in case Basov should ask him a question. Now, about tomorrow morning. I want you and Mr. Star to be in the conference room in the basement by nine-thirty. I'll come down and chat with you for a few minutes before I go up to meet with Basov. And then, while I'm talking to the ambassador, I've arranged some additional background briefings for you and Mr. Star. By the way," the secretary of state concluded emphatically, "I don't want any of your other people coming along. Just you and Star, and your security people if necessary."

Jack nodded again and was about to respond when Thomas Stratton abruptly ended the conversation.

"Well, Professor, I had better let you go and start getting Jason prepared."

The secretary of state hung up without waiting for Jack to reply. The rush of noise in his ear jolted Jack to his senses. He hung up the receiver, not sure whether he was mostly depressed or excited. After a moment of reflection, his normal enthusiasm regained the upper hand and he pushed the intercom button and spoke to his secretary.

"Joyce, please find Dr. O'Neil and Mr. Star and Mr. Green and ask them to come over here as soon as possible. And if Jason is in the middle of a training run, tell them that I said that it should be interrupted."

About ten minutes later, Barney and Jason and Bob assembled in Jack's office with perplexed looks on their faces.

"Thanks for getting me excused from class, Professor,"Jason quipped. "I was doing syntax drills and they give me an awful headache. But Dina just persists. She and John Franklin are convinced that I'm getting better at it, although it sure doesn't feel that way to me. But I guess that John's fancy statistics say that I'm making progress."

"What's up, old buddy?" Bob Green asked, suspecting that orders had come from above. "It sounds like something important."

"It is," Jack confirmed. "I just got a call from Secretary Stratton on the secure phone. He wants Jason to have lunch with him and the Soviet ambassador—tomorrow!"

"He's certainly full of surprises, isn't he," said Barney, with a chuckle.

"Lunch with the Secretary of State," Jason mused. "I'm certainly moving in rarefied circles these days. I don't know if I should continue to associate with a rowdy group like this."

"Don't forget, Jason, without *us* you'd still be a normal human being," Barney retorted.

Eventually they all sat down at the conference table and Barney continued in a somewhat more serious tone.

"Well, Professor, what do we do now?"

Jack smiled and shook his head.

"I'm not sure there is much we *can* do in the way of last-minute preparation. Let me tell you what the plan that Stratton has in mind looks like. First of all, he's sending a courier over this morning with a dossier on the fake identity that they've established for you, Jason. Your name is David Brentwood."

"It's an honor to meet you, Mr. Brentwood," said Barney with mock seriousness.

"Dr. O'Neil, I presume," Jason responded with a slight bow.

"Seriously, Jason," Jack interjected, "you'd better plan to study that stuff pretty carefully. We wouldn't want Basov getting suspicious the first time he meets you."

"You're telling *me*," Jason agreed. "Suppose he asks me a question or wants to engage in small talk about some simple diplomatic topic, like the Middle East peace negotiations. He'll find out in five minutes that everything I know comes from the *Washington Post*."

"Stratton thinks that he's got that point covered, too," Jack replied. "He's sending a guy from his staff over here this afternoon to give you a background briefing on what he called 'recent issues in the economics of arms control.' You're supposed to be, I mean, David Brentwood *is* his staff expert on the economic implications of arms control."

Jason raised his hand and waved it like an anxious grade-school student.

"Professor? Can I go back to my syntax class? Economics was never my strong suit."

"I don't know," said Barney, with a smile. "A guy who's made a million dollars guessing words and numbers must have some talent for economics."

"Come on, gentlemen, let's get back to the problem at hand," Jack said with a note of irritation. "Barney, I want you to arrange to record the background briefing that the State Department guy gives Jason this afternoon. That way we can play it back this evening in case Jason's opinion of his economic abilities turns out to be right. Now, the rest of Stratton's schedule goes like this. Jason and I are to be in the conference room in the basement of the State Department at nine-thirty tomorrow morning. Stratton doesn't want anyone else coming along, just the two of us and the security people who drive the cars. Bob, who do you recommend?"

"I'll drive you like I did last time," Green responded "and I'll have Joe Cap drive Jason. Joe just came back from kidnap-prevention school and he should be able to protect Jason against almost anything."

"I can see who's important around here," Jack said. "Jason gets the athletic, young guy who's just come back from kidnap-prevention school, and I get the flabby, aging ex-lieutenant commander."

Jack waited for the chuckling to subside and then continued more seriously.

"Stratton has planned the actual meeting between Jason and Ambassador Basov like this. He, Stratton, will talk to the ambassador privately from about ten o'clock until about noon. They'll be discussing some new Soviet proposals on a total ban on nuclear testing. While they're talking, some of Stratton's people will give Jason additional background briefings down in the basement conference room. Then, when Stratton and Basov adjourn to the secretary's dining room for lunch, Jason will join them. Apparently, the secretary normally invites one or two of his key aides to join him and the ambassador for lunch. So Basov won't be surprised to find a guest at the table. I take it that Stratton will carry the ball during the lunchtime conversation with Basov and let Jason concentrate on trying to receive psi signals."

The small group around the table was silent and Jack surveyed their pensive faces.

"Well, this is our first big-league game," Jack concluded. "Can anyone think of anything beyond the normal conference-room training sessions that we should do to help Jason prepare?"

The silence continued. Wry smiles revealed the lack of great ideas. Finally, Jason himself ventured a suggestion.

"Do you think that Stratton might possibly have any recordings of his previous meetings with Basov?"

Bob and Barney turned toward the man with psi with surprised looks on their faces, and Jason continued with an explanation.

"Perhaps listening to them would help me get accustomed to Basov's voice and personality. So that tomorrow he won't seem like a total stranger."

They all nodded agreement with Jason's brilliant suggestion. Jack turned to Bob with the crucial question.

"Do you think that Stratton's got recordings, Bob?"

"I'd bet my life he does," Green replied, "but I doubt that he'll admit to it. And even if he does, he might not be willing to let you listen to them. But it's worth a try if you're game to risk his wrath and call and ask him—on the secure phone, of course."

Jack looked at Barney and Jason, and they nodded their agreement.

"All right, I'll call him," Jack concluded. "The worst he can do is have me replaced! And I need a vacation anyway. Any other bright ideas?"

His three coconspirators at the table shook their heads slowly from side to side, and Jack decided that the meeting was over.

"Okay, let's get back to work. We've got a long afternoon and evening ahead of us. Bob, can you find the Stratton's secure telephone number?"

The little group left Jack's office, but Bob Green returned momentarily and handed a slip of paper to his boss. Jack sat down behind his desk and began to dial the secure telephone. When the phones had synchronized, a voice responded officially:

"Secretary Stratton's office."

"This is Professor Mason," Jack began. "May I please speak with the secretary? It's quite important."

"The secretary is in conference at the moment," the voice responded almost automatically. "May I take your name and number and ask him return the call?"

"Professor John Mason," Jack answered, raising his voice. "M A S O N. I'm calling concerning the subject he called me about a few hours ago. We need his assistance to prepare for a meeting tomorrow. You have my number."

"I'll give Dr. Stratton the message, Professor Mason," the secretary, cum answering machine, concluded. "Thank you for calling."

Several hours passed before Thomas Stratton returned the call. When Jack responded to the incessant ringing of the secure telephone, a clipped voice, clearly different from the one before, announced authoritatively:

"Secretary Stratton is calling for Professor Mason."

"Mason speaking," Jack said, while wondering idly how large an army of secretaries Thomas Stratton had.

"Just a moment for Secretary Stratton, Professor Mason."

Jack laid down the receiver momentarily and closed his office door. When he put the handset to his ear again, Thomas Stratton had already begun speaking.

". . . Professor. What can I do for you?"

"We had a meeting right after you called, Mr. Secretary," Jack began innocently, "to determine what additional preparation we should make for tomorrow. And Jason had the idea that it would be extremely helpful to him if he could hear the ambassador's voice so that Basov wouldn't seem like such a stranger when Jason meets him tomorrow. So we were, er, wondering if you might possibly—"

"I can't imagine what you're driving at, Professor," Thomas Stratton interrupted. "But if you're concerned about the adequacy of Jason's preparation, so am I. You and Mr. Star had better be here earlier than I had indicated so that I can personally evaluate his readiness. Shall we say eight A.M. in the conference room?"

"But Mr. Secretary," Jack stumbled, "it's not that we're concerned about Jason's preparation. It's just that we thought that if he got a chance to hear Basov's voice before the meeting it would help to put him in a more receptive frame of mind."

"I'll see you at eight A.M. in the conference room, Professor."

Thomas Stratton hung up as abruptly as he had done that morning. And again the blast of noise from the secure phone added insult to injury. Jack shook his head and wondered why he had bothered to call Stratton in the first place.

Early the next morning, when Jack and Bob entered the conference room in the basement of the State Department, they found that Jason had arrived before them and was already seated at the table conversing with the infamous Stephen Janek. The latter greeted them cheerfully and remarked:

"I've been teaching Jason a little Hungarian while we were waiting so that he can say good morning to the Secretary."

They all chuckled, and Bob and Jack helped themselves to coffee from a carafe at the far end of the table and then sat down. There was a portable tape recorder on the table in front of Stephen Janek. Jack was puzzling about its purpose when the closet Hungarian explained.

"The secretary won't be able to join us until about nine-thirty. But he asked me to come down and to give Jason a little background information on Ambassador Basov. You can hear it too, Professor Mason, but I'm afraid that I'll have to ask Mr. Green to wait outside. I'm sure that you can understand that material of this kind is pretty sensitive. The secretary personally controls who has access to it."

"No problem," said Bob Green with a knowing smile. "You're just following good security procedures. I don't have a 'need to know.' I'll just shoot the bull with Joe and your guys out in the hall."

233

Stephen Janek was obviously relieved as Bob headed for the door.

"There's another conference room just across the hall," Janek hastened to offer. "Please make yourself comfortable. This may take a while."

When Bob Green left, Stephen Janek reached into his briefcase, pulled out two sheets of paper, and handed one to Jack and the other to Jason.

"This is just a formality," he said nervously. "A security oath you've got to sign before you hear the material. The secretary insists on it."

Jack picked up the sheet and began to read:

TOP SECRET—SBB

Security Oath

Special Background Briefing

I, <u>John William Mason</u>, Social Security No. <u>070-41-9165</u>, acknowledge that on <u>16 Sep 71</u> I received Special Background Briefing <u>Su-46</u>.

I solemnly swear that I will not reveal to any person, organization, or government any of the following information:

1. That I received this briefing.
2. The subject of the briefing.
3. The name(s) of the person(s) who gave me the briefing.
4. Anything concerning the contents of the briefing.
5. That I have signed this security oath.

I understand that violation of the provisions of this security oath may result in grave damage to the United States and may expose me to administrative sanctions and/or criminal penalties.

_____   _____
Witness   Signature

TOP SECRET—SBB

"I trust they've spelled your names correctly," Stephen Janek said nervously. "Just check your Social Security numbers and sign at the bottom."

Janek looked greatly relieved when Jack and Jason took out their pens and began to write.

"Three years ago I would have thought this was crazy,' Jack said "but now I've signed so many of these damned things that I can't even keep count."

Stephen Janek managed a small smile.

"I guess you've been around this spook stuff longer than I have. It still makes me a little nervous every time I have to sign one of these oaths."

Janek retrieved the signed pledges, hurriedly returned them to his briefcase, and then began to manipulate the controls of the tape recorder.

"I think that when you hear this you'll understand why we don't want the whole world knowing of its existence," he offered by way of explanation.

The tape began to move and a quiet hiss of background noise issued from the machine's built-in speaker. As Jack and Jason stared intently at the revolving reels of tape, a voice that was unmistakably Thomas Stratton's began speaking in the distance.

"Good morning, Ivan Aleksandrovich. It's a pleasure to see you again. Let's sit over here where it's comfortable."

Muffled noises gave the impression of people moving through a room and then a second voice responded more clearly than the first.

"Good morning to you too, Thomas. It is always a pleasure to visit with you. The discussion is usually on such a lofty intellectual plane."

Despite the perfect English, the hint of a Slavic accent made Jack and Jason certain that the second speaker could only be Ivan Aleksandrovich Basov, the Soviet ambassador. Jack shook his head in amazement at the secretary of state's Byzantine way of satisfying the request he had pretended not to understand. But Jason continued to stare intently at the machine in the center of the table as if trying to receive a psi impression from the tape recording.

"I have some Turkish coffee this morning, Ivan," Thomas Stratton's voice continued. "May I tempt you?"

"If is it strong," the Basov voice responded, "the temptation is overwhelming."

"Two strong Turkish coffees, please," said Thomas Stratton, apparently speaking to a steward.

There were more muffled noises and then the secretary of state again addressed the Soviet ambassador.

"Now, Ivan, what is the topic of our intellectual fencing match this morning?"

"You know that I would not feint and parry with you, Thomas," the voice of Ivan Basov responded. "My government has simply asked me to ask you to clarify your government's position on the Helsinki accords. I know that you understand that we are fully in compliance with what your press likes to call the human rights clauses of the agreements. However, recent remarks on the floor of your Senate indicate that some of your colleagues may have a less perceptive view than your own."

"You would not, of course, care to mention any of my congressional colleagues by name," the Stratton voice said with a hint of humor. "So, in their anonymous absence, let me ask you what inferences they should draw from the way your government has recently been treating those whom I believe your press is fond of calling disloyal and wrong-thinking scientists?"

"Surely, Thomas, you of all people have the political perception to recognize that the carping criticism of a few dissident misfits does not represent the true feelings of a great people," Basov responded with unmistakble irony. "Why, I would not degrade this discussion by asking you about the recent comments of certain black leaders concerning your government's dealings with the racist dictatorship in Rhodesia."

The sword play continued for more than an hour, interrupted only by the necessity of turning over the tape, and Jack began to amuse himself by trying to anticipate the attacks, parries, and ripostes. But Jason Star remained motionless, like a man in a trance. Elbows on the table, head in hands, he stared intently at the recorder, concentrating on Basov's every word. Finally the tape ran out. Stephen Janek turned off the machine and addressed the man with psi.

"Well, Jason, I hope that's been of some help to you. You can see that Ambassador Basov is an extremely clever debater and seems to have a very complex personality. I have great difficulty, myself, telling when he's serious and when he's just arguing. But that's why you're going to be so valuable to us."

Janek paused to look at his watch and then continued hastily.

"The secretary will be down at nine-thirty. That only gives me about ten minutes to get this tape locked up again. I'll have to get moving." He removed the tape from the machine, placed it in his briefcase, and prepared to leave the room.

"If the secretary arrives before I return, please tell him that I'll be right back."

The door closed behind Stephen Janek, and Jack and Jason were left in silence. They stared at each other for several moments, exchanging amazed smiles, until Jack finally asked rhetorically:

"Well, what do you think?"

"Basov's going to be a challenge," Jason responded, shaking his head. "He's so different from Yuri. I get the impression that Basov's mind is constantly darting from one approach to another, probing for an advantage. Whereas, in our practice sessions, Yuri concentrates on a single thought for a considerable period of time."

"Don't worry, Jason, it's just the first time," Jack said reassuringly. "And everyone realizes how tough it is on you to do this on such short notice."

Jason Star chuckled.

"I'm not sure that more notice would do me any good."

The two friends' idle bantering was interrupted by a knock on the door. When Jack opened it, one of the State Department guards reported dutifully:

"Sir, the secretary will be here momentarily."

Jack stepped out into the hall to greet Thomas Stratton, and they returned to the conference room together.

"Good morning, Jason," the secretary of state said heartily. "How are you feeling? Ready for my friend Ivan Aleksandrovich, I trust."

Jason Star rose and returned the salutation.

"Good morning, Mr. Secretary. I'm sure that you realize that Ambassador Basov is going to be a real challenge for me. He seems to possess a very facile and active mind."

Thomas Stratton motioned for them to be seated and when they had complied he began confidentially.

"If the truth be known, Ivan is one of the most competent people in this city. Frankly, I find talking with him exhilirating and if I may say so, I am confident that he would return the compliment."

Thomas Stratton paused, as if reconsidering the wisdom of this revelation of his inner feelings, and then changed abruptly to a more serious tone.

"But, of course, one must always remember who and what he represents. And that he has been steeped in Marxist dialectic as surely and as long as we have been taught to sing the praises of liberty and free enterprise."

Having thus extricated himself and delivered a capsule lesson in East-West politics to boot, Thomas Stratton rose again at his place at the table.

"Now you will have to excuse me, gentlemen. I must go and prepare for my meeting with the ambassador. Remember, not a word about what has transpired here this morning to anyone. Not anyone! See you at lunch, Jason."

The secretary of state left as rapidly as he had come and a breathless Stephen Janek returned to the conference room shortly after his boss had departed.

"Did you tell him that I would be back momentarily?"

"He didn't ask," Jack said with a chuckle.

Janek's face fell and Jack continued more sympathetically.

"He hardly acknowledged my presence either, Stephen. Jason is the one he's interested in."

Stephen Janek continued to look disconsolate and Jason joined the effort cheer him up.

"You guys can say you knew me back when," the man with psi quipped.

"Yeah, and that and a quarter will get us a cup of coffee," Jack rejoindered.

Stephen Janek smiled weakly and then sat down, but a few moments later, he began the conversation again in a business-like tone.

"We've got about three hours before you meet Basov, Jason. And I've got some guys lined up to give you background briefings on recent developments in arms control. Professor, you are welcome to listen in and so is Mr. Green. The briefings should take a couple of hours. After that, I'll take Jason on a short tour of the secretary's area of the building so he'll know where the dining room is and the secretary's office and the men's room. And then, Jason and I will wait in my office until the call comes to go down for lunch. I won't stay; Jason will be the only guest. You wouldn't want any of my crazy Hungarian thoughts confusing you, Jason."

Jason Star was nervous. He knew that he could not remember half the facts that had been thrown at him during the background briefings on economic factors affecting arms control. The man with psi sat pensively in Stephen Janek's office awaiting the call that would summon him to join the secretary of state and the Soviet ambassador in the dining room. Janek was making small talk in a vain attempt to dispel Jason's anxiety.

"Don't worry, Jason. The first time I had lunch with them, I was scared to death and dumb as a mute. They like to do all the talking themselves anyhow."

Jason Star smiled and thought to himself that Stephen Janek was not such a bad fellow after all, particularly for a Hungarian.

Thus encouraged, Janek continued with a somewhat altered approach to distracting Jason from fretting about the encounter to come.

"Tell me, Mr. Brentwood, what branch of economics is your specialty?"

Jason looked surprised, hesitated for a moment, and then responded as the Brentwood dossier had instructed him.

"I did my thesis on the American aerospace industry. And now the secretary has me looking at the potential impact on this segment of our economy of various arms control proposals."

"Including general and complete disarmament?" Janek interjected, simulating a Basov thrust. "That would certainly have a devastating impact on your merchants of war, would it not?"

The man with psi was startled and groped for a reply. The background briefings had instructed him to be deferential to the Soviet envoy and to avoid heated or protracted discussions. But Jason's problem at the moment was to think of anything at all to say.

"That's certainly correct, Mr. Ambassador," he finally responded feebly. "Complete disarmament would have quite an effect on the economies of both of our countries, I suspect."

The newfound friends continued the rehearsal goodnaturedly until a light began to flash on the call director behind Stephen Janek's desk. He lifted the receiver, listened for a moment, and then spoke to Jason.

"You're on, Mr. Brentwood. I'll walk down the hall with you."

An uneasy chill settled over the man with psi as they walked briskly down the marble hall toward the secretary of state's dining room. Jason had not felt this way since waiting for his bride to come down the aisle in the little church in Carmel. Quite irrationally, he feared that Ivan Basov would instantly divine his clandestine purpose and loudly denounce him and his mentor. When they arrived at the dining room, a white-jacketed steward opened the door and Stephen Janek patted Jason gently on the shoulder and whispered,

"Good luck."

Jason strode silently across the vast Oriental carpet toward the secretary and the ambassador, who were engaged in animated conversation in front of an open French window. Thomas Stratton smiled as the man with psi approached. He gestured toward him while speaking to the ambassador.

"Ivan, I would like you to meet David Brentwood. David is a very bright young economist who has recently joined my senior staff. David, you have the distinct honor of meeting Ivan Aleksandrovich Basov, the Soviet ambassador."

Jason approached Ivan Basov and bowed his head slightly. "It's a very great pleasure to meet you, Mr. Ambassador."

Ivan Basov extended his hand and responded heartily:

"The pleasure is mutual, Mr. Brentwood. I am always eager to meet someone who is an expert in what, I believe, has been called the dismal science!"

Jason shook the ambassador's hand firmly and noted the strength of his grip.

"Will you join us in a glass of sherry, David?" Thomas Stratton, the affable host, continued. "It's there on the table."

"Thank you, sir, I will," Jason said, thinking that he needed it. He walked to the ornate French provincial buffet and poured himself a small glass of fino from one of the elaborate decanters. When he returned to the windows, Ivan Basov addressed him pleasantly.

"The secretary has been telling me that you are particularly concerned with the economic impact of arms control. I have an interest in that subject myself."

Jason smiled and strained to detect a psi signal that would confirm or belie the ambassador's apparent sincerity. He stepped closer to Basov and employed one of the opening lines he had been given in a background briefing.

"I have recently been studying the effects of arms acquisitions on the economies of the major countries in the Middle East. As you know, both Israel and several of its Arab neighbors spend much larger fractions of their gross national products on weapons than do either of our countries."

"And have you discovered who is the major supplier of weapons to the Middle East?" Basov interjected, unable to resist an easy rapier thrust to his opponent's vitals.

Jason blanched, but Thomas Stratton chuckled.

"Come now, Ivan, it's not sporting for the principals to wound the seconds. David, here, is an academic economist, inexperienced in the rough-and-tumble of the world of diplomacy."

"Well, then, Thomas," said Basov with a twinkle, "consider the gauntlet hurled in your direction."

Thomas Stratton beamed, relishing another intellectual skirmish and the first real opportunity to test Jason's psi perceptions.

"Do I hear the lament of the losing salesman? Driven from the marketplace by dissatisfied customers. Or are these the crocodile tears of the representative of a country that pretends to give away arms but later extracts concessions that money could not buy?"

Ivan Basov continued smiling, but Jason detected a distinct impression of hostility. He turned his eyes from the Soviet ambassador to the secretary of state in an attempt to avoid being deceived by Basov's facial expression.

The ambassador returned to the attack with only the slightest trace of acidity in his voice.

"Unlike the representatives of your military-industrial complex, my country has no international arms salesmen. In the Middle East, we simply support the legitimate right of Arab peoples to resist Zionist expansionism. I would think that you would agree with me, Thomas, that in the last half of the twentieth century no nation should be allowed to seize by war the sovereign territory of its neighbors."

Jason Star closed his eyes momentarily and strained to perceive Ivan Basov's true purpose in pursuing the debate. Was he simply sparring harmlessly with Thomas Stratton to stimulate their stomach juices in preparation for the coming repast, or was he sincerely expressing a deeply held personal or governmental position? In spite of his intense concentration, no Russian words flashed into Jason's mind. The only sensation he continued to receive was a diffuse aura of hostility.

Perhaps sensing the man with psi's anxiety, Thomas Stratton ended the debate as abruptly as it had begun.

"Would you care for another glass of sherry, Ivan? Or shall we sit down?"

The ambassador accepted the secretary's veiled suggestion that their verbal chess game be adjourned, and the Russian looked with genuine interest toward the luncheon table.

"I believe that I am ready to eat, if you are, Thomas."

The secretary of state and the Soviet ambassador strode toward an elaborately set table facing another set of French windows. Jason followed dutifully in their wake, waiting for them to select their places. The secretary motioned expansively to the ambassador indicating that Basov should take the seat facing the windows. Jason allowed the two older men to be seated and then took the remaining place himself.

The table setting was the most elaborate that Jason had ever seen. Two silver knives, three forks, and two spoons, three plates with elaborate gold decorations, three crystal glasses, and an immense folded napkin. Jason surveyed the dazzling array of implements before him, unsure as to which to first employ. He decided to fold his hands and wait patiently for a cue from the host.

Thomas Stratton detected his disguised guest's discomfort and, in the sliest form of deception, remarked upon it jovially to the ambassador.

"David finds the table setting a little more elaborate than what he is used to in our cafeteria, Ivan."

"Enjoy the fruits of capitalism while you can, David," said Basov with a twinkle. "Your studies must tell you that its days are numbered."

"You'll find when you visit the Soviet embassy," the secretary of state interjected, "that the ambassador does not believe in bourgeois ostentation. The elaborate display he puts on for his guests is only part of his attempt to behave in the manner of his host country. At home in Russia he would never think of consuming vast quantities of Beluga caviar and Stolichnaya vodka. He secretly prefers tepid borscht and stale black bread."

Thomas Stratton chuckled at his mildly insulting rejoinder, and even Ivan Basov smiled pleasantly enough. But again Jason clearly received the psi signal of hostility. He strained to define it further and thought that he perceived the Russian word "derz-kii" (disrespectful).

"As the secretary has said, David, you will certainly have to visit us at the embassy," Ivan Basov continued, outwardly registering no afront. "Thomas, you should bring him to the dinner next week. And let him taste really fine cuisine."

"Well, David, you're not such a political neophyte as I thought," the secretary of state said with a smile. "You've hardly begun lunch and you've wangled yourself an invitation to dinner."

Jason smiled silently, uncertain as to how to respond to the ambassador's invitation, but Thomas Stratton came to his rescue.

"That's a splendid idea, Ivan. David accepts with thanks. He's simply too modest to say so."

"Yes, Mr. Ambassador, it would be a privilege for me to attend," Jason concurred with momentary relief. But, immediately, his mind began to struggle with the implications of the commitment he had made. A second field test within a week, and this time at the Soviet embassy. Much to his own surprise, Jason's feelings slowly turned from anxiety to exhilaration. He would soon get a second chance at the enigmatic target sitting to his right. *I'll get to the bottom of this man Basov,* Jason thought.

The remainder of the luncheon was uneventful. Thomas Stratton and Ivan Basov sparred and bantered, apparently good-naturedly, and Jason Star received no distinct psi signals. At a cue from the secretary of state, Jason excused himself from the table, on the pretense of being late for a meeting, and returned to Stephen Janek's office. After a few minutes of whispered conversation, Jason and Stephen descended to the conference room in the basement where Jack and Bob anxiously awaited them.

When the soundproof door had closed, Jack was the first to express their bursting curiosity.

"Well, Jason, how did it go?"

"All right, I think," Jason responded tentatively. "At least Basov didn't appear to suspect anything."

Bob and Jack looked relieved, and Jason continued with a broad grin.

"And I even got invited to dinner at the Russian embassy next week."

"The Russian embassy? Next week?" Jack repeated excitedly. "Whose idea was that? Basov's or Stratton's?"

"It just sort of happened," Jason answered sheepishly. "They were bantering about the relative quality of the food here and at the Russian embassy. And Basov said that Stratton should invite me to come with him to a dinner the Russians are giving next week. And Stratton accepted for me before I could say a word."

Unnoticed in the pell-mell questioning, Bob Green produced a slim pocket tape recorder from inside his jacket and placed it on the table in front of Jason.

"Hey, guys!" Green interjected. "Let's do this in a little more orderly fashion."

"Bob's right, Jason," Jack agreed. "I'm sorry I got excited and had you start in the middle. Let's sit down and let you go through your impressions right from the beginning, just the way they occurred at lunch."

The four men sat down, two on each side of the conference table, and Bob Green switched on the recorder and began to speak in a monotone.

"This recording is classified Top Secret—Psi. This is the record of the debriefing of Jason Star that occurred at 1330 hours on 16 September 1971 in a conference room in the basement of the State Department. Also present are Jack Mason and Bob Green. Okay, Jason, it's all yours."

"Well, ah," the man with psi began a little self-consciously, "the first impression that I recall occurred while the secretary and the ambassador were talking in front of the French windows while drinking glasses of sherry. They began to spar rather aggressively about which of their nations was principally responsible for the arms race in the Middle East. Although Basov continued smiling throughout the debate, I detected a strong feeling of hostility. I continued to perceive this hostility until Stratton led us to the luncheon table."

"Did you receive any specific Russian words?" Jack interjected.

"No, not at that time," Jason responded, shaking his head. "I just perceived an intense feeling of hostility."

"Were you looking at Basov?" Jack said, pursuing the questioning. "Did his face appear hostile? Or the tone of his voice?"

"No, he didn't look particularly upset," Jason replied. "And I tried not to look directly at him most of the time, anyway, so as not to be misled by his facial expressions. I just tried to concentrate on receiving psi signals."

The debriefing continued for almost an hour, interrupted only when Bob Green had to turn over or change the tape in the recorder. Still, the only Russian word that Jason could consciously recall having received was *"derzkii."*

Several hours after returning to the Project Psi facility, Jack Mason received a call indicating that Jason Star was about to begin his formal debriefing under the influence of sodium pento-thal. By the time Jack reached the debriefing room, Phyllis Jackson had already begun to talk to the man with psi, lying supine, using questions she had prepared after listening to the tape Bob Green had made at the State Department.

"Jason?" Phyllis asked, as Jack joined the group "when you perceived this hostility on the part of Basov, did you receive any Russian words?"

"No words, Phyllis," the supine form answered apologeti-cally, "tried hard, believe me, really tried hard."

"We know you tried hard, Jason," Phyllis said soothingly. "You always do. But try hard again now. Try to remember, Ja-son. What was Basov thinking?"

"Trying hard, Phyllis, really am, but don't—"

"We know you're trying, Jason," Phyllis said with an un-characteristic hint of frustration. "But we think that you per-ceived some words. Try to recall the Russian words. What were the words, Jason? What were the Russian words?"

Jason Star's brow wrinkled deeply and his head rolled from side to side on the pillow involuntarily expressing his mental turmoil.

"Can't remember clearly. Think it was 'nenavizhu.' Think he was thinking, 'hate you.' 'I hate you.' That's it, Basov was thinking, 'I hate you.' "

"Wonderful, Jason," Phyllis said with exhilaration. "You've done it again. Just keep concentrating. What did you perceive next?"

"Nothing more while drinking."

"Are you sure?" Phyllis Jackson persisted. "Concentrate hard. Like you did before. What other words did you perceive?"

"No more words, Phyllis," Jason said with childish annoy-ance. "Just drinking. Drinking sherry. And Stratton and Basov arguing. About Middle East. And Basov thinking 'I hate you' and—istreblyayu, 'I destroy you.' "

"Excellent, Jason," Phyllis said enthusiastically. "You've re-membered another phrase. Tell us again, Jason. What was Ba-sov thinking after 'I hate you.' What came after 'I hate you.' "

"I destroy you," the supine man with psi responded. "Basov thinking, 'I destroy you.' "

Jack Mason had heard enough, enough to convince him that they had struck it rich, a vein of pure gold—incontrovertible proof that the man with psi could read the mind of a senior Russian official. Jack headed out of the room and motioned to Barney O'Neil to join him in the hall. When the soundproof door had closed behind them, Jack put his arm around Barney's shoulders and spoke to him confidentially:

"Talk to Berman and find out how long he's willing to keep Jason under. Phyllis really has him recalling words well right now and I don't want to take a chance that we'll draw a blank when Berman puts him down again tomorrow. So ask Paul how long he can stretch it today without taking any risk. And tell him that we'll forgo another session tomorrow if that will make him feel better about extending this one."

"Okay," said Barney nodding his understanding. "I'll get back in there and talk to Paul and Phyllis."

Jack waited restlessly in the hall until Barney returned with the answer.

"Paul is willing to keep him under for another hour if necessary. And Phyllis thinks that's more than enough time. We'll bring the tape up to your office as soon as we've made a copy for transcription."

Jack Mason hustled back toward his office full of enthusiasm. Jason had really perceived Basov's thoughts. *The man with psi had perceived the thoughts of the Soviet ambassador! We've really done it,* Jack thought, exhilarated. *We've done the impossible! Created a man who can read other men's minds!*

"How's Jason doing?" his secretary asked anxiously as Jack entered the office.

"Fantastically, Joyce, just fantastically! Jason actually perceived Basov's thoughts. We've done it! We've really done it!"

Jack strode on past her desk and entered his office, and Joyce stared after him, shaking her head. *The strain is really getting to him,* she thought sympathetically.

Jack, Barney, Bob, and Phyllis stayed in Jack's office until almost midnight listening to the tapes of the pentothal debriefing. Jason had wanted to join them, but Paul Berman had insisted that the exhausted man with psi have a good dinner and get to bed. The four coconspirators were now listening to the last tape for the second time and beginning to show the cumulative effects of having been awake since four A.M. The room stank from the sickening combination of the still pungent aroma of cold pizza and the acrid stench of half-smoked cigarettes.

When the tape finally ended, Jack dully repeated the rhetorical question they had so often asked themselves during the evening.

"Is there any doubt in anyone's mind that Jason actually perceived the ambassador's thoughts?"

Jack looked at the other three for a long moment, silently polling his board of directors.

Tired heads slowly confirmed their lack of reservations and, at length, Jack expressed their implied conclusion.

"So we're all agreed that Jason really read Basov's mind."

This time the nodding was affirmative and a little more vigorous.

"Do you think that I should call Stratton and tell him the news?" Jack continued earnestly.

The exhausted faces looked at him quizzically, and Phyllis Jackson finally verbalized the obvious.

"Isn't it a little late, Jack? It's almost one A.M."

"She's right, Jack," Barney agreed, joining the side of rationality. "Get some sleep and call him in the morning. You'll feel better, and so will he."

They all chuckled and, eventually, even Jack saw the wisdom of the suggestion.

"Okay, sold! I'll call him first thing in the morning. Let's get these tapes locked up and get out of here."

Despite having had less than five hours' sleep, Jack Mason had sprung from bed at his usual early hour, hurriedly showered, shaved, and dressed, and was now pushing his Porsche at too high a speed, fueled by fresh enthusiasm for Jason Star's achievement. As he roared, top down, through the early morning sunlight, breathing deeply of the first cool air of September, Jack pondered the proper approach to bringing the news of the man with psi's success to Thomas Stratton. On the one hand, the

248

conclusion that Jason had actually perceived the Soviet ambassador's thoughts was of inestimable importance. It truly portended the radically altered world of international diplomacy that the secretary of state had envisioned. On the other hand, Basov's thoughts about Thomas Stratton, the man, were deeply disturbing. Would the secretary of state believe that his seeming colleague in intellectual debate actually harbored the deepest hatred and the direst intentions?

Jack was seated in his office, still mulling over possible approaches to the Basov dilemma, when his time for further contemplation was suddenly cut to zero by the stark ringing of the secure telephone. Jack reached for the ominous black handset, held it from his ear until the noise had subsided, and then responded guardedly:

"Mason speaking."

"Good morning, Professor Mason," a cheerful secretary's voice replied. "Secretary Stratton will be on the line momentarily."

He's certainly anxious to hear the results, Jack thought. *That's an encouraging sign.*

"Good morning, Professor," the well-modulated voice of Thomas Stratton began. "What do you have to report?"

"Good morning, Mr. Secretary. I was just about to call you, but you beat me to it," Jack said, not untruthfully. "Jason recalled a great deal more under the influence of sodium pentothal than he did at the preliminary debriefing in your conference room."

"I'm glad to hear that, Professor," Thomas Stratton replied with more than a hint of sarcasm. "The report that I received from Stephen yesterday afternoon wasn't very informative. I don't need a mind reader to tell me that Basov is antagonistic."

Clearly, the secretary of state was more aware than Jack had realized of the Soviet ambassador's malevolent predisposition. Jack reached for the sheaf of papers on his desk and, with a little less trepidation, began his report of the man with psi's ominous perceptions.

"Jason recalled a number of specific Russian words and phrases that he received as psi signals. Let me give you a summary in chronological order. When Jason first joined you and

Basov at the windows for a glass of sherry, Basov was thinking 'I hate you.' Later in the same conversation, Jason perceived him thinking 'You are arrogant.' I know that the words are strong, Mr. Secretary," Jack offered by way of apology, "but we're quite certain that Jason really did perceive them. Frankly, I was a little hesitant about reporting—"

"Nonsense, Professor!" Thomas Stratton interjected firmly. "You and I have got to understand one another. Your regard for my feelings should not enter into our relationship. I want to know exactly what Jason perceives at all times. I don't want the slightest bit of glossing over or interpretation. If Basov hates me, I want to know it!"

"Yes sir, Mr. Secretary," Jack said with obvious relief. "I'm glad that you feel that way. It's much easier for me as a scientist to simply tell you the truth."

"The truth, Professor. That's what I want from you," Thomas Stratton said theatrically. "The truth and nothing but the truth, so help you . . . now, please continue."

"Later on, while you were having lunch," Jack began again, "Jason perceived Basov thinking 'We will destroy you.' And, further on in the same conversation, 'You are a fool and we will destroy you.' Then a little later on—"

"I think I get the gist of his sentiments, Professor," Thomas Stratton interjected sarcastically. "When can you bring the tapes and the transcripts to my office? I suggest at the end of the afternoon. Say at about five-thirty?"

"That sounds fine to me, Mr. Secretary," Jack agreed. "We began typing the transcripts last night and certainly should have them finished by noon. So I could come any time this afternoon that is convenient for you."

"Thank you, Professor," the secretary of state concluded. "I'll see you at five-thirty. Stephen will meet you in the same conference room at five-fifteen and bring you to my office. And give Mr. Star my compliments. You've all done an outstanding job."

Thomas Stratton hung up abruptly, as was his wont. But for once the secure phone's rude noise did not offend Jack's sensibilities. He glowed with the satisfaction that the secretary of state had clearly acknowledged their monumental achievement.

Jack and Stephen Janek had been in Thomas Stratton's office for more than an hour. The secretary of state seemed totally absorbed in listening to the tape recordings of Jason Star's debriefing under the influence of sodium pentothal. Stratton repeatedly requested the replaying of segments of the tapes where Jason recalled perceiving specific Russian words. Finally, when the stupefied voice of the man with psi had ominously intoned, "You are a fool and we will destroy you," for the fourth or fifth time, Thomas Stratton abruptly turned off the tape machine and firmly addressed the room as if Jack and Stephen Janek were merely additions to the furnishings.

"We'll see who destroys whom, Ivan Aleksandrovich! We shall see who dominates summit diplomacy! Who is remembered by historians as the architect of global order and lasting peace! And who receives barely a passing footnote as a dutiful, but uninspired, spokesman for the outmoded policies of an anachronistic dictatorship."

The secretary of state gripped the edge of the conference table and glared triumphantly across the vast expanse of his office. Jack and Stephen Janek were nonplussed by his vehemence and gave the impression of wishing that they could discreetly disappear beneath the table. But Thomas Stratton's wrath dissipated as rapidly as it had crested. His stern stare turned slowly to an expansive smile and in another moment he addressed the distressed onlookers as if the outburst had not occurred.

"Well, gentlemen, let's discuss Jason's next encounter with Ivan Aleksandrovich. The ambassador has been so kind as to arrange it for us himself. He has invited David Brentwood to the dinner he is giving next week for the Ukranian trade delegation. Frankly, I was planning to be busy that night. But now the opportunity is too good to be passed up."

22

A Hint of Dissension

Jason Star devoured a thin slice of black bread spread with butter and mounded with caviar. The reception at the Soviet embassy for the Ukranian trade delegation was all that he had anticipated and more. Jason raised his crystal shot of Stolichnaya in a salute to an imaginary companion, and was about to toss the fiery liquid down, when the voice of Ivan Basov suddenly captured his attention.

"Good evening, Mr. Brentwood. I am happy to see that you were able to join us this evening."

Jason turned toward the voice and the ambassador continued.

"I would like you to meet Mr. Sergei Dolgin of our staff. He is an economist, as you are." Basov gestured toward the man at his side and completed the introduction. "Sergei, this is David Brentwood. David is an assistant to Secretary Stratton."

Sergei Dolgin was a thin, middle-aged man wearing a dark blue, double-breasted suit that appeared to Jason far too heavy for early October in Washington. Dolgin smiled thinly, made the slightest bow, and extended his hand to David Brentwood. As they shook hands, Jason had the distinct impression that Dolgin's grip was that of a military officer.

"A pleasure to meet you, Mr. Dolgin," Jason said, and then added, "Have you been working with the Ukranian trade delegation?" employing one of the safe queries he had been given at a background briefing that afternoon.

"Yes, I have," Dolgin responded in nearly unaccented English. "I have been assisting them in meeting with American businessmen and trade associations."

Jason was surprised to receive the strong psi impression that Dolgin was lying. While the man with psi pondered this telepathic revelation, the enigmatic Russian skillfully changed the subject.

"Ambassador Basov tells me that you are the secretary of state's expert on the economic implications of arms control. That is a subject about which I am totally ignorant. But I would be interested in learning of it, if you are in the mood for a pupil."

Sergei Dolgin smiled as much as his face would allow, but the psi impression that Jason was receiving distinctly changed to one of hostility, and the man with psi strained to perceive a word or phrase that would define its thrust. After an awkward moment of silence, David Brentwood finally returned the smile and responded:

"Yes, I'm particularly interested in the Middle East."

Dolgin's curiosity was obviously aroused and he continued aggressively.

"Very interesting, Mr. Brentwood. Very interesting. What specific aspects of arms control in the Middle East are you studying?"

Jason concentrated again and finally perceived the Russian pronunciation of 'Israel.' Sergei Dolgin was obviously not what he purported to be and Jason groped for a way to deflect or end the conversation.

"Oh, I really don't deal with the weapons themselves," David Brentwood offered by way of exculpation, "only with the economic impact upon the countries that purchase them."

Dolgin would not be denied and bored in for further information.

"Which countries are of particular interest to you?"

Jason nervously downed the shot of vodka in his hand and was considering feigning ill effects when a familiar voice came to his rescue.

"Good evening, David," said Stephen Janek. "I see that you've met my old friend Sergei."

Surprised, Dolgin turned sharply toward the voice as if to repel an attack. But, almost instantly, he recovered his composure and extended his hand.

"Good evening, Stephen. Are you and David colleagues?"

"We both work for the same stern taskmaster," Janek said with a smile. "And a few minutes ago he asked me to find David. So you'll have to excuse us, Sergei."

Dolgin bowed slightly again, indicating that he knew that the encounter was terminated.

"A pleasure to see you, gentlemen. Please pay my respects to the secretary of state."

Stephen Janek smiled benignly at Sergei Dolgin, and then turned and led a greatly relieved Jason Star across the room. On the way, Janek took two shots of vodka from a passing waiter and handed one of them to Jason. Leaving the main reception hall with the man with psi following close behind, Stephen Janek led the way into a smaller room that appeared to be a library. Finding a corner devoid of other guests, Janek at last turned and clinked his glass against Jason's.

"Here's to your first encounter with the GRU (Soviet Military Intelligence)" Stephen proclaimed with a grin. "Did Dolgin give you a hard time?"

"Is Dolgin GRU?" Jason asked nervously. "I certainly detected a lot of hostility."

"Right," Janek responded matter-of-factly. "He's an air force colonel. And Basov probably told him that you had been studying arms sales in the Middle East."

"Yeah, that's what he said," Jason confirmed. "And I got the psi signal that he's interested in Israel."

"Not surprising," said Stephen nodding. "Well, anyhow, I'm glad that I could help you get away from him. No sense taking any chances. And Stratton really does want you to join him and Basov."

Their tête-à-tête concluded, Stephen Janek led the way from the library back through the main reception hall to a smaller salon where Thomas Stratton and Ivan Basov were the focus of attention. Stephen and Jason approached the group surrounding the principals and stood innocuously at the rear attempting to gather the gist of the conversation.

Thomas Stratton was expounding professorially on the necessity for world order as the basis for lasting peace, and Ivan Basov was smiling the smile of a generous host who cedes the center of attention to an honored guest. Finally, when Stratton at last paused for breath, Basov raised his glass and proposed a toast.

"To world peace through general and complete disarmament!"

Thomas Stratton raised his own glass, touched it to Basov's, and repeated the toast with a twist of his own.

"To world peace through stable world order!"

On cue, the senior officials present, both Russian and American, raised their glasses and intoned enthusiastically:

"To world peace!"

At the back of the crowd, Jason and Stephen also raised their shots of vodka, and Jason emptied his in one searing swallow while nervously recalling the stressful encounter with Sergei Dolgin.

Emboldened by the fire in his gullet, Jason used the momentary lull in the conversation to squeeze through the encircling crowd to a position closer to Stratton and Basov. The secretary of state noticed his approach and smiled in greeting.

"Good evening, David. The ambassador told me that he saw you deep in conversation with his economist, Dolgin."

"Good evening, Mr. Secretary. Good evening, Mr. Ambassador," Jason responded, and then added with double entendre, "I had a very stimulating discussion with your Mr. Dolgin."

"I am glad to hear that, David," Ivan Basov said jovially. "I like to see our staff people engaging in working-level interactions with their counterparts."

Jason strained to receive a psi signal confirming what he knew to be Basov's insincerity. No perception was forthcoming, so the man with psi attempted to move closer to his quarry. Ivan Basov turned to face Thomas Stratton for renewed debate and Jason casually took a position at the ambassador's shoulder. The secretary of state sensed that his man with psi was in an ideal position and began a subtile probing of their prey.

"As you know, Ivan, I have great hopes for the forthcoming summit meeting between President Leonard and General Secretary Sherkov. I believe that we are living during an unique period in history. A time when proliferation of nuclear weapons on the one hand and improvements in communications and transportation on the other make a stable system of agreements among the major powers both essential and attainable."

Ivan Basov listened with seeming attentiveness to Thomas Stratton's rhetoric and then responded in kind.

"Your expectations are shared by my government, I assure you, Thomas. As you know, the leaders of the Soviet Union have long expressed the conviction that war in the nuclear age is a madman's folly and that peace and prosperity for the working peoples of the world can only follow from general and complete disarmament."

Suddenly, without warning, Jason received a rush of distinct psi impressions.

. . . pompous fool . . . hate you . . . destroy you . . .

The strength and clarity of the signals astounded him and the man with psi searched the ambassador's face for confirmation of his antagonistic thinking. But Ivan Basov wore the glowing smile of the experienced diplomatic host and continued his enthusiastic endorsement of Thomas Stratton's optimism.

"Foreign Minister Gersky asked me today by telephone to convey to you, Thomas, how anxious he is to meet with you to begin planning for President Leonard's visit to Moscow. The foreign minister would be delighted to have you visit him or to come here to Washington himself if you prefer."

The next psi signals Jason received were both clear and astounding.

. . . Gersky fool . . . why Gersky . . . why not me . . . Gersky fool . . .

Jason Star's face instantly revealed his consternation and Thomas Stratton sensed that something was amiss. The secretary of state stepped toward a hovering waiter and took a glass of vodka for himself and one for the ambassador. Thus distracted, Ivan Basov moved away from the man with psi and accepted the proffered refreshment. Thomas Stratton raised his glass theatrically and proposed a toast to the room in general.

"To a successful summit conference under the inspired leadership of President Leonard and General Secretary Sherkov!"

The crowd of senior officials again surrounded the secretary and the ambassador and raised their glasses in ceremonial ratification of Thomas Stratton's pronouncement.

"To a successful summit conference!" they echoed.

"To President Leonard!"

"To General Secretary Sherkov!"

Jason Star, who had remained where he was originally standing, now found himself outside the circle of sycophants. The man with psi was still disturbed by his perceptions of Basov's ominous thoughts and concerned that his own mind might be playing tricks. Perhaps the shots of Stolichnaya he had unwisely consumed were distorting his perceptions of psi signals. Or, worse still, creating psi impressions where no Russian thoughts really existed. Abruptly, Jason decided to leave the reception and temporarily retreat to the van where his Project-Psi colleagues were hidden.

The contrast was striking between the noisy, smokey reception and the quiet, cool evening outside. Jason Star inhaled deeply as he briskly walked the several blocks to the side street where the van was parked. By the time he knocked on the vehicle's rear door, Jason's mind was clear and he was certain that the startling psi signals had been real.

"Who is it?" a muffled voice from inside responded.

"Hank Aaron," Jason replied, using the signal they had agreed upon.

The door swung open, and the man with psi clambered into the dark interior and groped for a seat. When the door was closed again, someone turned on a dim light, and Jason was greeted by the concerned faces of Jack Mason and Barney O'Neil.

"What's the matter, Jason?" Barney asked anxiously. "Did something happen?"

"No, I think everything is okay," Jason responded tentatively. "I just had a couple of strange experiences. The first was with a guy called Sergi Dolgin. Basov told me that Dolgin was an economist, but he looked like a military type to me. And Dolgin started quizzing me about the Middle East. And then I got the psi impression that what Dolgin was interested in was Israel. That made me pretty nervous, but Stephen Janek rescued me. And then Janek told me that Dolgin was a GRU man. An air force colonel!"

"That's right," confirmed Bob Green who had entered the blacked-out rear portion of the van from the driver's compartment. "Dolgin probably thinks that you know something about upcoming U.S. arms sales to Israel."

"Well, Jason," Jack said with relief, "that encounter doesn't sound too bad. What upset you so much?"

"After I got away from Dolgin," Jason continued, "I had a couple of vodkas and then went over and stood next to Basov while he talked to Stratton. And I got those same threatening psi signals from Basov again: 'pompous fool,' and 'hate you,' and 'destroy you.' The same intense hostility toward Stratton that Basov was transmitting when I had lunch with them at the State Department."

Jack and Barney silently nodded their understanding, and the man with psi continued with increasing emotion.

"But then, a really incredible thing happened. Basov was saying that Gersky, the Russian foreign minister, had called him from Moscow with a message for Stratton. About wanting to meet with Stratton to arrange President Leonard's trip to Moscow. And Basov sounded so sincere while he was saying it. But, I got distinct psi signals to the contrary: 'Gersky fool,' and 'why Gersky,' and 'why not me.' As if Basov hates Gersky too! And thinks that he should be the foreign minister instead of Gersky."

"That's pretty heady stuff, Jason," Jack said, shaking his head with incredulity. "Are you sure that your imagination wasn't working a little overtime after your encounter with Dolgin?"

"That's what I was afraid of," Jason agreed. "Particularly after a couple of vodkas. So I thought that I'd better come out here and talk it over with you people."

"I think you did the right thing, Jason," Jack said. "Bob, get Phyllis and Paul over here from the other van. I think they should check Jason over. Barney and I will take a walk to give them some room."

Jack turned out the light and then opened the door and climbed down into the darkness. Barney O'Neil followed him and they walked in silence for several blocks in the opposite direction from the embassy before beginning a whispered conversation.

"Do you think we can talk here?" Barney began hesitantly.

"Yeah, I think so," Jack ventured. "If we keep it down. What do you make of Jason's story about Basov having a thing about Gersky?"

"It sounds like something out of a Russian novel," Barney quipped in a whisper. "But I don't think Jason made it up. At least not consciously."

"That's what I hope Phyllis and Paul can determine," Jack responded. "If it's real, we probably should send him back to the embassy to try to get some more. But if he's imagining things, we should get him back to the facility and into bed before he gets any more disturbed."

Barney nodded his agreement in the darkness, and the two old friends strode on in silence.

When they returned to the van, Phyllis Jackson joined them for another walk and whispered conversation. As soon as they were again a safe distance from the embassy, Phyllis began her report earnestly.

"Paul and I have talked to Jason and checked him over physically. He's not drunk, and we don't think that he is imagining things. As far as we are concerned, he's fit to go back to the reception."

Jack nodded his understanding and mentally made the decision to tell Jason to return to the embassy. The chance to confirm jealousy and dissension in the highest echelons of the Soviet hierarchy was a heady experience.

When the man with psi next found Ivan Basov, the ambassador and the secretary of state were standing in a corner of the embassy grounds having a private conversation. Jason Star smiled to himself as he remembered Bob Green saying that the hardest place to bug was a garden. Hesitating to approach Basov and Stratton directly, Jason waited with a small knot of people where the secretary of state would be sure to see him. After several minutes, Thomas Stratton casually strolled in the direction of Jason's group and Ivan Basov followed, continuing their conversation.

As the pair came within earshot, Jason heard the ambassador say:

". . . and thus you understand in greater detail why Gersky feels that a preliminary meeting between you and him is essential to the smooth conduct of the summit conference."

Thomas Stratton nodded his comprehension and then smiled as though he had just noticed David Brentwood.

"David, I thought you might have left. Ivan has just convinced me that I should visit Moscow again in the near future. Perhaps I should take you with me in view of the growing importance of economic issues in the relationship between the two countries."

"A splendid idea, Thomas," Ivan Basov agreed enthusiastically. "David is just the kind of intelligent young man that our people in Moscow like to talk with."

By now, Basov was close to Jason and the man with psi received another distinct signal.

. . . KGB . . . Brentwood . . .

A sudden chill swept through Jason's body and he strained to control its effect on his facial expression.

Thomas Stratton and Ivan Basov continued their leisurely stroll across the garden and Jason followed at the ambassador's side, now a legitimate auditor of their conversation. As if by way of explanation to David Brentwood, the secretary of state casually recounted part of his private discussion with the Soviet ambassador.

"Foreign Minister Gersky apparently agrees with me that President Leonard and General Secretary Sherkov should discuss and attempt to resolve a broad range of issues at the summit meeting. Accordingly, there is a need for one, or perhaps more, preliminary meetings between Gersky and me to formulate the issues and alternatives that the heads of state will consider."

From his position close behind Ivan Basov, Jason suddenly received more clear psi signals:

. . . Gersky fool . . . Sherkov . . . say . . .

The man with psi was perplexed. Was Basov thinking that Sherkov had said that Gersky was a fool? While Jason was still pondering these latest psi revelations, Ivan Basov obligingly continued the description of the private conversation.

"I have been telling the secretary of state, David, of the great importance that General Secretary Sherkov attaches to his forthcoming meeting with President Leonard. As you know, the general secretary has repeatedly called for general and complete disarmament as the essential step along the road to world peace. The general secretary feels that he and President Leonard have an historic opportunity to end the arms race."

Jason detected a clear psi impression of insincerity as the ambassador spoke. He leaned closer as Basov continued, hoping to receive some specific Russian words.

"As I told you, Thomas, my government will make every effort to facilitate the successful outcome of the summit conference. We stand ready to participate in any preparatory discussions and meetings that the general secretary and the president may feel are desirable."

Jason's diligence was rewarded amply with an additional burst of psi signals.

. . . Stratton . . . Gersky . . . fools . . . destroyed.

By now, the ambassador and the secretary of state had reached the stone steps leading up to the terrace overlooking the garden. They mounted the steps together and then Thomas Stratton turned back to face the small knot of senior aides who stood in the garden below. The secretary of state spread his arms wide in an expansive gesture and addressed the group in the garden in a theatrical tone.

"Gentlemen, someday you may be able to tell your admiring protégés that you were present in the garden of the Soviet embassy in Washington when Thomas Stratton and Ivan Basov set in motion preparations for the summit conference that achieved enduring peace in the last quarter of the twentieth century through détente between the superpowers."

Thomas Stratton struck a Shakespearean pose and waited for the grandeur of his words to move the impromptu audience. After a moment's hesitation, someone cried:

"Hear, hear!"

A polite riffle of applause spread across the garden. Thomas Stratton beamed with satisfaction and Ivan Basov felt impelled to respond in kind.

"On behalf of the Soviet Union, I would like to express to all of you the profound commitment of the great Russian nation to the continuing search for world peace through general and complete disarmament and our unfailing support for the struggles of working-class people everywhere to throw off the yoke of imperialism and the oppression of neocolonialism and to achieve the ultimate goals of socialism: equality, prosperity, and peace."

It was Basov's turn to beam and, as if on cue, a chorus of cheers and a round of loud applause issued from the Russians present. The ambassador bowed slightly, like an actor embarrassed by an overly demonstrative audience, and then called for vodka all around. When the drinks were in hand, Ivan Basov mounted to the topmost step of those leading from the terrace into the embassy, raised his glass high in the air, and loudly proposed a toast.

"To the success of the summit conference and the achievement of world peace!"

"To world peace!" responded the officials below, and the call echoed from the walls of the embassy above.

Even Jason Star was caught up in the enthusiasm of the moment and he raised his glass high and then downed its fiery contents. But the thoughts of the man with psi were still preoccupied with the ominous signals he had received.

23

"The Ultimate Weapon!"

Jack Mason had been in Thomas Stratton's office since a little after eight that evening. Jack stole a bleary-eyed glance at his watch and thought that it said a little after twelve-thirty, but the secretary of state seemed oblivious of the hour. Still dressed in the formal attire he had worn to a reception, Thomas Stratton sat at his conference table in a ruffled shirt adorned with gold studs and cufflinks, looking much the part of the prince of the past he yearned to be. Jack had played the tapes of Jason Star's pentothal debriefing completely twice through, but, unsatisfied, the secretary of state was now concentrating on particular Russian words and phrases that he found especially vexing.

"What right does that insignificant messenger Basov have to conspire against my plans for world peace?" Thomas Stratton inquired rhetorically.

Jack stared blankly in reply and the secretary of state continued with rising emotion.

"The man is deranged! It's bad enough that he denigrates me, the American secretary of state, but he goes further, this audacious knave; he has insulting and disloyal thoughts about his own foreign minister."

Jack nodded in a vague attempt to convey understanding, but his thoughts were on sleep. He had been awake for most of the last two days and nights, and could concentrate only with extreme difficulty.

Thomas Stratton did not seem distracted by Jack's lack of responsiveness and continued his soliloquy in impassioned tones.

"In times past, such disloyalty, once discovered, would have been ended summarily—by the sword! But in our modern civilized world, obsequious bureaucrats shuttle from office to office and country to country pretending to do their principal's bidding, while in reality scheming his downfall."

"It certainly is surprising," Jack finally managed to offer, "that a country as authoritarian as the Soviet Union would have an ambassador who is disloyal to his own foreign minister."

"It's not surprising at all!" Thomas Stratton responded vehemently. "It happens to us all the time. I've got more than one ambassador who thinks that he should be sitting here instead of me. Just because he's an old college chum of Dick Leonard or gave a lot of money to his campaign. And some of them are so dumb. I've got one who has been in a Spanish-speaking country in South America for more than a year and hasn't learned a word of the language. I've sent the best tutor we have down there, and she just comes back shaking her head. She finally told me, 'Some people are just too stupid or stubborn to learn, and he's one of them.' And I've got another one in the Middle East. He shows our classified messages to their foreign minister. And the CIA tells us that the foreign minister is on the KGB payroll. I don't know how many times we've told the ambassador, but he can't get it through his thick skull. He just keeps telling me what a nice friendly guy the foreign minister is."

Jack shook his sleepy head with genuine sympathy.

"I see what you mean, Mr. Secretary. It certainly must be difficult for you having people like that as ambassadors."

"Difficult!" Thomas Stratton exploded. "It's impossible! They screw things up faster than I can fix them. If I leave a country alone for a while, I come back and find things in shambles. And some of them don't even tell me what they're up to. One guy, who served with Leonard in the navy, gets his foreign-policy guidance by going to football games with the president."

Jack chuckled and Thomas Stratton smiled too, his angry mood broken.

"You'll have to excuse me, Jack, for letting my hair down a little. Needless to say, you should keep my remarks in the strictest confidence."

Jack nodded solemnly.

"Of course, Mr. Secretary."

The uncharacteristic outburst over, Thomas Stratton's usual composure returned and he picked up the discussion of Jason Star's psi perceptions.

"Let's go back to the point where I have just suggested that David Brentwood accompany me to Moscow and Basov agrees and says that Brentwood is the kind of intelligent young man that their people would like to talk with. Jason got the distinct psi signal that Basov wants him to talk to the KGB. What I want to be sure of is that Basov is thinking only about David Brentwood, the expert on Middle-East arms sales, and not something more sinister. I don't want to risk taking Jason with me if the Russians are at all suspicious. It would be better to save him for the main event."

Jack rewound the tape and, after several false starts, found the conversation that the secretary of state wanted to hear.

"... and now, Jason," the gentle voice of Phyllis Jackson issued from the portable tape recorder, "let's go on to the signals you received after Ambassador Basov said that David Brentwood is the kind of bright young man that people in Moscow would like to talk with. What Russian words did you receive, Jason?"

"KGB, Brentwood, KGB talk with Brentwood," the ethereal voice of Jason Star responded.

"Can you remember any other words, Jason?" Phyllis Jackson's voice continued. "Try hard to concentrate, Jason."

"Arms, Israel."

"Excellent, Jason. You keep remembering more. What else was Basov thinking?"

"No more words, Phyllis. Can't remember any more words."

"Okay, Jason. Let's go on. Stratton and Basov continued to stroll across the garden and you followed them. What psi signals did you receive—"

Thomas Stratton had motioned to Jack to stop the tape recorder and now stared pensively at the silent machine.

"What do you think, Jack?" Thomas Stratton asked collegially. "Does Basov have any suspicions that Jason isn't David Brentwood?"

Jack stared dumbly and didn't respond.

"Professor!" Stratton said, raising his voice. "Did you hear me?"

Jack's dull head gave a quick, violent shake and his bleary eyes blinked.

"I'm, ah, sorry, Mr. Secretary. I must have dozed off."

Thomas Stratton at last looked at his watch and then smiled and spoke to Jack in a fatherly tone.

"I can see why. I imagine that you've been up for a couple of days now. Why don't you go home and get some sleep. You can take the tapes with you, but leave me a copy of the transcript. I want to prepare a summary for the president."

General Sam Ryan sat in a straight-backed chair at the corner of the president's massive desk, facing his commander-in-chief. Richard Leonard hung up the phone and returned to the conversation with his trusted assistant.

"What have you got for my meeting at ten with Stratton? I'll bet that he's sent over a bunch of position papers that he'll expect me to have read. That guy is a frustrated author. He's always writing. And the worst of it is, he sends it all to me."

Sam Ryan smiled furtively at the president's characterization of the secretary of state and then responded in a dutiful tone.

"There is one thing I think you should read, Mr. President. It's a summary of the debriefing of the man with psi after his test at the Soviet embassy last week."

Richard Leonard sat up in his chair, his face expressing both surprise and interest.

"Test at the Soviet embassy? Why wasn't I informed?"

"Uh, you were, sir," Sam Ryan responded with a hint of embarrassment. "I told you myself, about ten days ago. Just after we discussed the report of Star's successful performance when Stratton had Basov to lunch at the State Department."

"Well, I don't remember being informed," the president said with finality. "Of course, I'm not doubting your word, Sam, but you can't have made a very big point of it. In the future, I want you to be sure that I personally approve every use of a man with psi. I don't want Stratton and Bennington running off and doing something that we'll all regret later."

"Yes, sir, Mr. President," the general said firmly. "I'll make certain that you personally approve each proposed use of Star, and that you are kept up to date on the results and any intelligence on possible Soviet reactions."

"You make sure you do," said Richard Leonard, shaking his finger. "These men with psi are the most important weapon to come along since the H-bomb. And I'm the only one who has them. It's like being the first coach to have a T-formation quarterback while the other teams are still using the single wing. For a few years, you kill 'em, until they figure out how to do it themselves. I've got the secret advantage, and I intend to use it in my own way and not let Stratton and Bennington go and blow it in some silly experiment at the Soviet embassy."

"Yes, Mr. President," Sam Ryan nodded. "I'll impress Secretary Stratton and Director Bennington with your desire to personally deploy the men with psi."

"Good!" said Richard Leonard with a look of self-satisfaction. "Now, where's that report that you want me to read before Stratton gets here?"

Sam Ryan fumbled through the stack of papers in his lap and extracted a folder marked "TOP SECRET—PSI" in large red letters. He opened the folder and passed a typewritten memorandum to the president.

"This is a summary that Secretary Stratton prepared of the signals that our man with psi, Jason Star, received from Ambassador Basov while Basov and Stratton were talking at a reception at the Soviet Embassy last week."

Richard Leonard took the paper and began to scan it.

". . . Top Secret–Psi . . . Eyes Only . . . Memorandum for the President . . . Test of Man with Psi at Soviet Embassy . . . KGB Colonel Boris Karpov (alias Sergei Dolgin) . . . Basov was thinking . . . 'you (Stratton) (are a) pompus fool . . . Gersky (is a) fool . . . why (is) Gersky (Foreign Minister) . . . why not me (Basov)' . . ."

The president looked up with a smile.

"It seems that Basov doesn't think much of either Stratton or Gersky. I wonder what Sherkov would think of that? Maybe I'll have the opportunity to tell him sometime."

Sam Ryan looked at his commander-in-chief with a puzzled expression and the President went back to reading.

. . . 'KGB talk (to) Brentwood (Star). . . (about) Israeli arms (sales) . . . Gersky (is a) fool . . . Sherkov told (him what to) *say . . . Stratton* (and) *Gersky* (are) *fools* . . . (they will be) *destroyed'* . . .

The president looked up again, his face wrinkled in a thoughtful frown.

"This is pretty heavy stuff, Sam. That fellow Star would have us believing that the Soviet ambassador is plotting to destroy both the American secretary of state and his own foreign minister. Are you sure this guy Star hasn't wandered off the reservation? You know, maybe all this training they've been giving him just has been too much and he's gone off his rocker. I mean, the Russians are schemers, but this is a little wild, even for them."

"I knew you'd be concerned, Mr. President," the general agreed. "That's why I thought that you should read it before Stratton gets here. I think he's worried about it, too, and that's why he wants to talk it over with you."

"What's there to talk about?" Richard Leonard said gruffly. "I think we should send Star on a vacation."

The president tossed the memorandum back to Sam Ryan and rose from his chair.

"What else have you got in your pile, Sam? I've got some senators coming in five minutes."

Later that same morning, Thomas Stratton paced slowly up and down in front of the president's desk with his hands clasped behind his back. Richard Leonard leaned back in his massive padded chair, hands behind his head, only half listening to his secretary of state.

". . . and so you see, Mr. President, why I feel that this is a very delicate time in the initial testing of the man with psi and why I feel that we and we alone should deeply consider his next employment."

Basov's right, thought Richard Leonard, *you are sort of pompous, Thomas.* But the secretary of state continued his professorial recital, unaware of the president's mental derision.

"Already we have learned several things of inestimable value through Mr. Star's extraordinary parapsychological abilities. First, we know of Basov's dislike for me and Gersky. Second, we know that Basov is thinking about, or perhaps even planning, an attempt to destroy us in some unspecified way. And, third, we know that Basov, at least, is insincere about the forthcoming summit conference."

Richard Leonard halfheartedly nodded his agreement with Thomas Stratton's summary and the secretary of state went on with his lecture.

"In addition, we have the disquieting fact that Basov has already sicked his GRU man, Dolgin né Karpov, on Brentwood né Star. While all indications are that Basov's interest is only in Brentwood's supposed knowledge of impending U.S. arms sales to Israel, there is always the possibility that Ivan Aleksandrovich suspects that David is not what he appears to be. Furthermore, Basov already has told us that if I take Brentwood to Moscow with me for the preliminary negotiations, they will have KGB people swarming all over him. So the question is—"

"The question is," Richard Leonard said forcefully, after sitting upright in his chair and folding his hands on the desk, "whether I want to let my only man with psi go to Moscow with you to talk to Gersky, or whether I want to save him for my summit meeting with Sherkov."

The president's assertion of his obvious authority stopped Thomas Stratton in mid-stride and sentence. The secretary of state rapidly and silently reorganized his thoughts and began again in a somewhat more deferential tone.

"Very succinctly summarized, Mr. President. As I see it, what you stand to gain by allowing Jason Star to accompany me to Moscow is possible prior knowledge of true Soviet intentions for the summit conference. On the other hand, what you risk is increased Soviet suspicion of David Brentwood. It seems to me that you should consider—"

"I have, Thomas," Richard Leonard injected. "The answer is no! Star stays here! I've only got one man with psi and I don't intend to let you blow his cover in second-rate discussions with Gersky."

Thomas Stratton sat down in a wing chair along the wall of the Oval Office and mentally counted to ten. He told himself once again that successfully manipulating Richard Leonard was one of the essential elements in his quest for world order and historical immortality.

"A very wise decision, Mr. President," the secretary of state finally offered, "at least for the moment. However, with your permission, I will have a plan prepared for guaranteeing Mr. Star's complete security should you later desire to consider, in changed circumstances of course, his accompanying me to Moscow."

"Fine, Thomas, fine," said Richard Leonard with obvious exasperation. "Go ahead and make your plan. But I've told you my answer. Star is staying here! Sending him to Russia would be like sending your best pitcher to play in the All-Star game when you're two games out of first place. And he comes back with a sore arm and you kick yourself in the ass when you lose the pennant. And then the owner fires you, and you wish you hadn't been such a stupid shit!"

Thomas Stratton's eyes rolled upward, but he smiled benignly.

"Very apt analogy, Mr. President. We certainly wouldn't want to risk exposing Mr. Star to any danger. And now, if I may, I'd like to raise one additional concern that arises from Mr. Star's perceptions. While Basov and Gersky have both expressed to me high hopes for your summit meeting with General Secretary Sherkov, and Sherkov himself has made similar assertions to you in writing, the sum of Mr. Star's impressions to date casts doubt on the sincerity of the Soviet leaders. While Jason has not yet perceived any word or phrase specifically indicating their intention to sabotage the conference, Basov's hostility cannot be regarded as a favorable omen."

"Basov's not against the summit meeting, Thomas," the president replied with a chuckle. "He just thinks that you and Gersky are pompous fools!"

Thomas Stratton smiled weakly and told himself again that being subjected to Richard Leonard's supposedly amusing insults was a cross he must bear.

"Yes, Mr. President, I know that Basov hasn't expressed hostility to the summit meeting itself in so many words, but the implication is clear that he believes that they can deceive and destroy us. We must, therefore, always be aware that Russian interest in summit diplomacy may be less than genuine."

"I think you're taking a much too pessimistic view, Thomas," the president said, sensing a rare opportunity to lecture the professor. "I, myself, see their antagonism and scheming as a positive advantage to us, now that we know of it. When I meet with Sherkov, he will be so preoccupied with his own plans and schemes that he will be oblivious to my secret weapon—the man with psi. And then, when I spring a dazzling array of new and comprehensive proposals on him, Sherkov, will be as startled and confused as a lonely cornerman suddenly facing two wide receivers. He's screwed before the ball is thrown. Whichever one he covers, the other one will catch it."

Thomas Stratton chuckled somewhat more genuinely. At least, he thought, football was a subject that the president knew something about.

Richard Leonard noticed the subtile change in his secretary of state's mood and continued enthusiastically.

"And think of how Sherkov will feel when he tries to respond to my brilliant thrust with one of his schemes and we are ready and waiting for him, because Star has told us all about it. Sherkov will be like the quarterback who gets up off his ass after being sacked and decides to show up the defense by calling a draw. But they ignore him completely and stop the runner cold. And then he's faced with third and twenty and has to try to pass again and they really bust his ass!"

Thomas Stratton smiled and mentally decided that now was not the time to pursue further serious discussion.

"Your enthusiasm is certainly heartening to me, Mr. President. If the American people knew of the importance that you place on our quest for world peace, I'm sure that they would have renewed confidence in the mandate they gave you."

The president beamed, gestured expansively around the Oval Office, and went on enthusiastically.

"They should have confidence, Thomas. In Richard Leonard they've got the toughest damned fighter for peace they've ever had. I've been committed to stopping Russian expansion ever since I was a freshman in the House. In those days all I could do was talk. A voice in the wilderness. But now I'm here in the White House. And I've got the weapon. The ultimate weapon! The man with psi! I'm going to put those damned Russians in their place and show them up to the world for what they really are, a bunch of damned, scheming, Communists."

Even Thomas Stratton had a limit when it came to enduring Richard Leonard's vituperative ramblings.

"I think, Mr. President, that I've taken up too much of your valuable time this morning with Project Psi. Perhaps we should get on to some other issues. Do you have any comments on the material that I prepared for your discussions with the king of Jordan when he comes here next week?"

24

The Puerto Rican Connection

Viktor Leonidovich Grechko paced slowly back and forth across the large Uzbek rug in front of his desk. Grechko had just finished reading the most recent message from the Soviet embassy in Washington about their surveillance of the American Chemical Company's Exotic Chemicals Research facility. The report highlighted several recent incidents—another group of cattle killed by toxic wastes, and a demonstration by local mothers and remnants of an antiwar group.

Viktor Grechko ended his pacing in front of the large windows overlooking Kirova Ulitsa and stared at the scene below, gently pulling at his goatee. While the recent incidents appeared to confirm the facility's advertised purpose, Grechko's suspicious mind, molded by years of experience with facts that belied clandestine activities, sifted through the information he had received for a clue to the real purpose of this intensive secret effort by his counterparts at Langley. Why had Brian MacFarland, the deputy director of the CIA, repeatedly visited the facility? Why did some of the laboratory's regular employees occasionally use switches of rented cars to elude surveillance? Could it be, as Grechko had speculated from time to time in the past, the new defector debriefing center that he knew the CIA had established somewhere near Washington?

Viktor Grechko continued his pensive observation of the scene in the street below. The bright Red Flags were already in place for the imminent November 7th celebrations and they flapped in vivid contrast against the gleaming white background of the winter's first dusting of snow. At last Grechko slowly turned from the windows and ambled toward the large door to his outer office. Standing in the open doorway, he addressed his secretary in a firm but detached manner, still engrossed in his previous thoughts.

"Sasha, get Tovarishch Borodin and Tovarishch Talko up here immediately. Tell them to bring all the information they have on the American exotic chemicals research facility."

Viktor Grechko reentered his office, closed the massive door, and retraced his steps to the windows. Below in the street, and on down to the right in Dzerzhinskaya Ploshchad, lines of cars and knots of people were the subjects of his stare and contemplation.

Who knows what any of them are doing or planning, Grechko thought. *Certainly not me, even though I am near the top of the largest and most effective intelligence apparatus in the world. And if I am uncertain as to what is really going on in the street outside my office in Moscow, how much more tenuous is my grasp of the true purpose of a mysterious laboratory in the countryside of the American state of Virginia.*

Returning to the chair behind his desk, Viktor Grechko began to reread the report from the Soviet embassy in Washington. Grechko was deep in thought when his secretary's seemingly tiny head peered in at him through the narrow opening she had created between the massive door and its jamb.

"Tovarishch Grechko? Tovarishch Borodin and Tovarishch Talko are here."

Viktor Grechko looked up from the report and silently motioned to the secretary with his massive head to the effect that the aides should come in.

Talko, the analyst, was young, tall, thin, and businesslike. But Borodin, the agent-master, was different. His rumpled clothes, tousled mane, and ever-burning pipe gave him the appearance of an aging history professor.

Talko stopped stiffly in front of Grechko's desk, made a slight bow, and formally greeted his chief.

"*Dobroe utro* (Good morning), Tovarishch Grechko. What may I do for you this morning, sir? I have brought my entire file on the American research facility for exotic chemicals."

Grechko nodded toward the ornate conference table and Talko scurried to take a seat at one side of the massive chair that was at the head of the table and reserved for its owner. Borodin had already slouched into the chair opposite Talko's and was endeavoring to light his pipe. Viktor Grechko rose from behind his desk and greeted his aging comrade from struggles past.

"*Kak dela* (How are you), Zdenek Ivanovich?"

"Tolerable, Viktor Leonidovich. What do you make of this chemical thing?"

Grechko seated himself at the head of the table and smiled at the rumpled figure.

"That is just the question I was going to put to you."

Borodin exhaled a cloud of smoke and Grechko turned to the nervous Talko.

"What about you, Tovarishch Talko? You are the analyst."

Talko sat erect in his chair, nervously facing the older men and, after a moment's hesitation, began his report.

"Well, sir, we have, ah, considered a number of possibilities. The first is that it could be what it seems to be an, ah, exotic chemicals research facility. That interpretation is supported by the three incidents that we know about in which cattle grazing on land near the laboratory have died mysteriously after drinking water from a stream that passes through the fenced area."

"So you believe the story that the Americans have put forward, do you?" said Grechko with a scowl.

"Oh no, sir, not necessarily. I was just, ah, saying that we have to consider it."

"Good!" replied the massive head with obvious impatience. "What other explanations have you considered?"

Talko squirmed in his seat, shuffled through the folders on the table in front of him, apparently found the one he was looking for, and opened it with obvious relief.

"Well, sir, we have considered the possibility that that facility might be the new defector debriefing center for which you have asked us to search."

"Why do you believe that?" Grechko growled. "Because it will solve two problems I have given you at the same time?"

"Oh no, sir. Not for that reason, sir. We only wanted to consider all possibilities."

Talko glanced furtively at the top sheet in the open folder and then continued in an uncertain voice.

"The explanation that it is a defector debriefing center is supported, we believe, by the fact that the deputy director of the CIA, Brian MacFarland, has been observed visiting the facility."

"How many times has MacFarland visited the facility?" Grechko probed. "And when?"

Talko consulted the folder again, turned several sheets of paper, and then responded hesitantly.

"Two times of which we are certain, sir. But perhaps several times more."

"What do you mean, perhaps? Do you have any evidence?"

"Nothing concrete, sir. Only that on several other occasions MacFarland was observed leaving the CIA headquarters in Langley in an official car and driving in the general direction of the chemical facility."

"The general direction!" Vicktor Grechko said angrily. "Did it ever occur to you that he might have been going to Dulles Airport? Or to Camp David? Or to Mount Weather? Or to a thousand other places in that general direction?"

Talko appeared genuinely shaken and replied meekly.

"Yes, sir. We, er, did consider that he was, ah, likely to have gone to some other place. That is, ah, why we have listed only two visits as positively confirmed."

"And out of two visits by the deputy director of the CIA you have made a defector debriefing center?" Viktor Grechko shook his massive head slowly from side to side unmistakably conveying both incredulity and extreme dissatisfaction.

"It is not, ah, only the visits, sir," Talko responded hesitantly. "There is, ah, some other evidence that seems to fit. There is—"

"So we finally get to some other evidence!" Grechko interrupted loudly. "Tell us, Tovarishch analyst, what is this other evidence."

Talko's faced turned ashen and he shuffled his papers frantically. Finally, he began again in the weakest voice.

"Well, sir there is, ah, the fact that we have, ah, positively identified two medical doctors as regular members of the staff from photographs taken by our attachés. One, a Phyllis Jackson,

276

is a psychiatrist and, ah, the other, a Paul Berman, is an anesthesiologist. We, ah, think that such specialists would be likely to be found on the staff of a defector debriefing center."

Grechko silently nodded his agreement with the struggling aide's conclusion and Borodin gave forth another dense cloud of smoke.

"He makes a reasonable point, Viktor Leonidovich."

Grechko nodded again, and the struggling Talko continued with slightly more confidence.

"And then, sir, there is this man John William Mason. We think that he is quite high up in the organization because of the way the guards wave him through the outer gate. He was formerly a professor of electrical engineering at the Massachusetts Institute of Technology."

"Hmm, that is interesting," the rumpled form said and issued two short bursts of smoke. "What was his specialty at the Institute?"

Talko's face brightened and, having the answer at hand, he responded quickly.

"The MIT catalogue says that his title is Professor of Electrical Communications and that he is on a leave of absence. Also that he teaches a graduate-level course called Neural Signal Processing."

Viktor Grechko knitted his brow and stared intently through the smoke at his old friend Zdenek Borodin.

"Neural signal processing? Could the Agency have discovered a new technique for interrogating defectors that combines the administration of drugs and the recording of brain waves?"

"It is possible, Viktor Leonidovich," Borodin responded quietly. "Anything is possible in the war for the minds of men."

Grechko turned back to the young assistant and, for the first time, invited him in a friendlier tone to continue.

"That is interesting, Tovarishch Talko. What other possibilities have you considered?"

Talko's relief was obvious and he hastened once again to consult his papers.

"Well, sir, the only other possibility that is supported by any concrete evidence is that the CIA is developing some new type of computer or communication equipment. We know that they have a number of electrical engineers, programmers, and computer operators on the staff. And photographs have shown trucks marked with the names of several computer and electronic equipment companies entering and leaving the facility. But we do not have any clues as to what the Americans might be doing with the equipment."

Viktor Grechko pushed his massive chair back from the conference table and smiled benevolently at the still-nervous aide.

"*Spasibo* (Thank you), Tovarishch Talko. You have provided us with some interesting information. Now, if you will leave us, Tovarishch Borodin and I have other matters to discuss."

Talko hurriedly gathered up his papers, stood at his place, and bowed slightly to Grechko.

"*Bol'shoi spasibo* (Thank you very much), Tovarischch Grerchko. I will try, sir, to have new information and a more organized analysis the next time."

"An excellent plan, Tovarishch. Get started on it immediately!"

Thus dismissed, Talko hurriedly retreated from the room. When the massive door had closed behind him, Viktor Grechko addressed the slumped figure shrouded in smoke.

"What do you know about Professor Mason, Zdenek Ivanovich?"

Borodin puffed again, removed his pipe, and began slowly.

"One of my agents in Boston posed as a visiting researcher from Poland and talked to some of Mason's former colleagues." He exhaled another cloud and then continued. "Apparently Mason used to head a research project that was investigating the structure of the brains of animals by means of electrical measurements. But, about four years ago, he began to spend more and more of his time in Washington. And then, about two years ago, Mason took a leave of absence from the Institute and moved his family to Virginia." More clouds of smoke. "No one that my man talked to knew exactly what he was doing, but they all thought that he was working for the government."

Viktor Grechko nodded his head slowly up and down, savoring and evaluating each morsel of information offered by his friend.

After several more leisurely puffs, Borodin continued his narrative in almost inaudible tones.

"Apparently Mason took several of his colleagues with him to Washington. A Professor Barney O'Neil and a Dr. Paul Rosenfeld. And probably also some graduate students. O'Neil was an assistant professor of electrical engineering and Rosenfeld was the assistant director of the computation center."

Viktor Grechko rose from his chair and again began to walk back and forth across the worn Uzbek rug. Zdenek Borodin smoked on in silence, knowing that Grechko was attempting to place the new facts in their proper locations in his mental picture of the puzzle. After several minutes of pacing, Grechko stopped, grasped the back of his chair at the head of the conference table, and addressed his friend quietly.

"What else have you found, Zdenek Ivanovich?"

"I have an agent making the rounds of the bars and restaurants near the chemical research facility in the evening," Borodin responded and then paused to relight his pipe. "And he has heard some strange stories. A man at a bar told a woman that he had been paid a large amount of extra money by his agency for being a subject in a special test conducted at the facility." Borodin puffed again. "But, unfortunately, they left the bar before he said anything about the nature of the test."

Viktor Grechko knitted his brow and looked intently at Zdenek Borodin. The latter exhaled another cloud of smoke and then slowly shook his head from side to side.

"I am sorry, Viktor Leonidovich. That is all that I have."

Viktor Grechko began to pace again and, after a while, Zdeken Borodin rose and joined him at the window.

"I hope to have an additional source of information in about a month," Borodin said in a barely audible voice. "I have ordered an agent in Puerto Rico to send two recruits to Washington with instructions to attempt to get jobs at the facility as gardeners or janitors or something. The recruits think that they are secretly helping the Puerto Rican Communist Party uncover a CIA plot against their island. Therefore, even if they fail a lie detector test or are caught snooping, the trail will not lead our friends from Langley back here, at least not directly."

Viktor Grechko smiled and nodded his agreement and then put his large right arm around his friend's shoulders and hugged him with genuine affection.

"Thorough and professional as always, Zdenek Ivanovich. Try to get as much information as you can. I have a feeling that this is a big one."

PART V
THE SUMMIT

25

The Infamous KGB

The Moscow summit conference—the ultimate challenge for the man with psi—was rapidly approaching. At the White House and the State Department, aides scurried frantically about, making endless changes in the details of schedules and arrangements, while unnamed senior officials jockeyed for position in the president's entourage. At the Project Psi facility, activity had reached a fever pitch and the staff was working around the clock in a vain attempt to accomplish an ever-expanding list of action items:

Monday, 7 February, 1430:
   5th package of computer tapes must be ready for pickup by State Department couriers for shipment to American Embassy in Moscow via diplomatic pouch.

Tuesday, 8 February, 0900:
   Demonstration of Mr. Star receiving 50 phrases from Mr. Andromov in simulated summit conference room.

Tuesday, 8 February, 1400:
   Progress Review by Technical Director for Secretary Stratton and General Ryan in Technical Director's conference room.

Tuesday, 8 February, 1600:
   Final staffing rosters for Moscow embassy facility must be submitted to . . .

Jack Mason shook his head in dismay as he read through the weekly list of deadlines and thought of the heroic efforts that would be required to come even close to meeting them. He told himself that he should feel exhilarated—by his coming trip to Moscow, the summit conference, and most of all, by the part that *his* man with psi was going to play in the making of history.

But Jack's body and mind were tired from the sixty-hour weeks and the endless meetings and the building tension. Would Jason Star be a successful hero or would Project Psi turn into the ultimate nightmare? Thankfully, Jack's disconsolate musing was interrupted by the cheerful voice of Bob Green.

"Hi, old buddy! Are you ready? We don't want to be late for the show."

Jack looked up from the papers on his desk at Bob's grinning face, framed in the doorway, and felt better already.

"Late for what show, Bob? Is Jason giving some sort of demonstration that isn't on these damn lists?"

"No, no," Green replied, shaking his head. "Don't you remember? Today is the day that we go over to headquarters for the defensive briefing."

"Defensive briefing?" Jack repeated quizzically. "I thought I told you to turn that bullshit off!"

"Well, uh, I tried," Bob answered unconvincingly. "But the people in security were adamant. They say that even Bennington and Stratton get updated before each trip abroad."

"Good grief!" Jack said, grimacing. "What do they think is going to happen? The KGB is going to snatch me off the sidewalk in front of the embassy or something?"

"Yeah, something like that," Bob replied, nodding. "We've had a lot of trouble, you know."

"What do you mean, *trouble?*" said Jack, frowning. "I've never heard anything about it."

"Right, it's pretty tightly held," Bob responded. "The story usually doesn't get into the papers. Or if it does, it's something innocuous, like 'Soviets insist that official at U.S. Embassy leave Russia. State Department contemplates retaliation against known Soviet agents on United Nations staff in New York.'"

Jack smiled at Bob's recitation but persisted in his derision.

"Come on, Bob! You've been reading too many spy stories and having too many bull sessions with your friends in the DO (Directorate of Operations). I'll bet the stories get better every time they tell them."

"Yeah, well, we sort of thought that you felt that way," Green demurred. "So, after the regular briefing, I've set up a little session that may change your mind."

Bob Green's face showed the sly, rascally grin that Jack had come to know meant that he had something up his sleeve.

"Okay, what can I say?" Jack capitulated. "When does this show, as you call it, begin?"

"Well, I told them we'd be there by two o'clock," Bob replied. "And since it's almost noon now, why don't we get something to eat on the way. We have to pull the car-switch business, and I have it set up for that mall with the good delicatessen."

Jack grinned broadly. He rose from his chair, his palms outstretched in resignation.

"Lead on, I'm in your hands. It will probably be more fun than sitting here and reading about how far behind we are."

Bob Green drove the Hertz car down the ramp to the underground garage at CIA headquarters with the nonchalance of a frequent visitor. Just inside the entrance they encountered a guard, and Bob rolled down the window and spoke cheerfully to him.

"Hi, my name's Bob Green. We're here to see Frank Alvisi. He's expecting us."

The guard consulted his clipboard, found the appropriate listing, and motioned to them to proceed.

Bob circled through the first floor of the large garage, searching for a spot near the elevator, without success. Finally, he resigned himself to the only space available, in a far corner.

"It looks like a busy day at the spookworks!"

"Yeah," Jack responded half-heartedly. "I wonder if they're mostly buying or selling?"

They entered the elevator lobby and displayed their CIA badges to yet another guard. He nodded perfunctorily as they passed, and Bob pressed the elevator call button before resuming the conversation.

"We'll meet Frank in a small conference room first, and one of his security guys will give us the latest version of the standard defensive briefing. It's all canned on a set of slides, and they just

285

kind of mumble through it. They're as bored giving it as we'll be sitting through it."

Jack nodded in agreement as the elevator door opened and they stepped inside.

After they left the elevator, Bob Green led the way through the corridors of the fifth floor of the sprawling CIA headquarters building with the confidence of an old hand. But, after several wrong turns, Bob, reduced to reading the room numbers next to successive closed doors, was perplexed. From time to time, he consulted a small slip of paper on which was scrawled cryptically: "5C37." Finally, in desperation, Bob knocked on one of the cipher-locked doors.

After a few moments, the door opened slightly, and a stunning blonde peered out at them quizzically.

"Do you work here?"

"No," said Bob, holding up his badge to allay her fears, "but I wish I did! We're lost, and we need some help."

The blonde grinned broadly and, thus encouraged, Bob continued jovially.

"We're looking for five-cee-thirty-seven. It's supposed to be a conference room. But this is thirty-six and the next door is thirty-eight. What happened to thirty-seven?"

"It's still here," the blonde replied with a smirk. "Right through that wall. But they moved the door around the corner." She stepped into the hall and pointed down the corridor. "Take your next left, and it's the first door on the left."

"Thank you, ma'am," Bob said with a broad smile and a slight bow. "I hope our next meeting will be under more exciting circumstances!"

The blonde smiled again, retreated inside, and closed the door.

"Oh, well," Bob signed, "another passionate affair nipped in the bud."

Bob and Jack made their way around the corner. Bob knocked on the door of the elusive 5C37, and it was opened by Frank Alvisi.

"Good to see you, Bob. Did you have any trouble finding the room?"

"No, not after we got some help from a good-looking blonde next door."

"Oh," Alvisi said knowingly, "that must have been Carol. She's the most popular new staff member we've had in a long time. Speaks Russian fluently and Polish, too. But she's so good looking that some people have trouble taking her seriously."

Bob grinned lasciviously, thinking that he would take Carol any way he could get her, and Frank Alvisi winked his appreciation.

Jack and Bob stepped inside the conference room, and, once the door was closed, Frank Alvisi addressed Jack in a more official tone.

"It's a pleasure to see you again, Professor Mason. Bob tells me that you're going to a scientific conference in Moscow, so I've asked Jimmy, here, to give you our standard defensive briefing."

Alvisi gestured toward a man at the end of the conference table who was adjusting a magazine of slides on a projector.

"Jimmy, I'd like you to meet Professor Mason. Professor, this is Jimmy Cone, one of our counterespionage specialists."

Cone looked up from the projector with a smile and extended his hand to Jack.

"A pleasure to meet you, Professor."

Jack glanced at Bob furtively, hoping for an explanation of Alvisi's less-than-truthful introduction. Bob nodded his head ever so slightly from side to side, and Jack suddenly realized what should have been obvious—Cone was not, of course, privy to the activities of Project Psi.

"Pleased to meet you, Mr. Cone," Jack finally said, trying to recover nonchalantly. "This business of defensive briefings is all new to me. Do you people really think that the Russians might bother me or my colleagues at the meeting in Moscow?"

Jimmy Cone smiled condescendingly.

"Well, Professor, we just don't want to take any chances. If you'll pardon me, our experience is that you academic types are so naive and friendly that the Sovs pump you for everything you know. And then you come back and tell us how nice everyone was and how interested they were in your scientific work."

Jack smiled, but Frank Alvisi didn't.

"I'm sure, Jimmy, that Professor Mason is well aware of his obligation to protect the classified information to which he has had access."

Cone's face fell as a hint of the reality of the situation dawned on him.

"Of course, sir, I'm sure he is. Please excuse me, Professor. I didn't mean anything personal. It's just that we've had so much trouble—"

"Let's get on with the briefing, Jimmy," Frank Alvisi said with growing annoyance. And then, in an abrupt change of tone, he addressed Jack deferentially.

"Professor, why don't you and Bob take the front two seats on the left, where you'll have an unobstructed view of the screen."

Jack and Bob sat down, and Jimmy Cone flipped a switch that caused a projection screen to descend in front of the blackboard facing the head of the conference table. When the screen was in position, Cone dimmed the room lights and projected the first slide.

The background was bright blue and the title was in large, silver block letters.

DEFENSIVE BRIEFING FOR
OFFICIAL TRAVELERS TO THE SOVIET UNION

Jimmy Cone pushed the control button he held in his hand and the second slide flashed on the screen. The background was still blue and the lettering silver but smaller in size.

Classification

The material contained in this briefing is classified SECRET-SENSITIVE and must not be revealed to any person, organization, or government without specific prior written approval and verification of appropriate clearance and need to know.

As Jack was trying to decipher the slide's tortured syntax, Jimmy Cone mercifully pushed the button again. A view of the

Kremlin as seen from Red Square appeared and, below it, a chilling admonition.

The Seat of Soviet Power

From these buildings the lives of every Russian and visitor to the Soviet Union are monitored and controlled.

Jack frowned in disbelief, and Jimmy Cone smiled weakly. "We just put that one in as an attention grabber, ha, ha, Professor." He quickly pushed the button again.

A street scene of a Moscow café appeared and, at a table in the foreground, a good-looking woman and a serious man were conversing tête-à-tête. The subtitle menacingly warned:

Beware of Entrapment

Even the most casual contacts with seemingly innocent Soviet citizens may well be approaches of the KGB—the infamous Soviet internal security police.

Jack frowned again and swiveled in his seat to appraise Bob's reaction. Green sensed his boss's dwindling patience and gave a reassuring wink that seemed to say, "Just grin and bear it, it'll all be over soon."

Jack turned back toward the screen and found that the café had been replaced by the interior of a hotel room. A perplexed guest was being shown what was apparently a microphone that had been hidden in the base of a table lamp. The caption stated with conviction:

Ears Are Everywhere

While in the Soviet Union, the official traveler must assume that his every conversation is overheard and recorded.

289

Fifteen minutes and twenty-three slides later, the briefing finally came to an end. Jimmy Cone turned up the room lights and smiled embarrassedly at Jack.

"Well, Professor, that should give you a feeling for what you'll be up against. We just want to be sure that you'll keep your guard up and not—"

"Thank you, Jimmy," Frank Alvisi said curtly. "I'm sure that Professor Mason understands the message."

With that, Frank Alvisi stood up and addressed Bob Green.

"Well, Bob, it's been nice to see you again, but I'm told that you've got another meeting to attend at 1500."

Bob and Jack rose and stretched, and Bob picked up on Frank Alvisi's cue.

"Right, we do. A technical discussion with some of the people that the professor consults for. So I guess we'd better get going."

Bob and Jack moved toward the door, but Jimmy Cone pursued them nervously with some sheets of paper.

"Excuse me, Professor. Just a formality. I need your signatures on these briefing statements."

Cone spread the sheets out on the table, and Jack noticed that one of them had already been filled out with his name and Social Security number.

Acknowledgment of Defensive Briefing

I, John William Mason, Social Security No. 070-41-9165, hereby acknowledge that on 7 Feb 72 I received a defensive briefing prior to a forthcoming trip to the Soviet Union. As a result of this briefing, I understand that while I am on Russian soil every attempt may be made by Soviet secret police and intelligence agents to extract from me classified United States government information of which I have knowledge. I further understand that Soviet agents will use any and all techniques available to them in the pursuit of their nefarious goals, including: surreptitious observation and photography, eavesdropping and hidden microphones, apparent friendliness of scientific colleagues, romantic advances of attractive women, offers of copies of underground literature, and appeals for assistance to Soviet dissidents. I further understand that I must be constantly vigilant and steadfastly resistant

to these approaches if I am to succesfully complete my visit to
the Soviet Union without compromising the interests of the
United States.

| _____ | _____ |
| Witness | Signature |

Jack frowned and shook his head at the document, but Bob
Green poked him in the ribs indicating that he should sign it.
Jack shrugged with resignation and affixed his signature with
a flourish.

Jimmy Cone smiled weakly, collected the signed statements, and began a fumbling attempt to remove the magazine
from the slide projector.

The *pro forma* ordeal over, Bob Green shook Frank Alvisi's
hand and led the way to the door.

"See you around the campus, Frank. Keep your microfilm
dry!"

"Right, Bob," Alvisi said with a smile. "Don't do anything I
wouldn't do. Unless you get paid an awful lot!"

Bob Green led the way to another elevator and, when he
and Jack had boarded, pressed the button marked 'B2.' When
the door opened again, they faced a short corridor terminated
by a guard station. Bob approached the desk and held up his
badge, and Jack followed suit.

"We're here to see Vincent O'Brien. I'm Robert Green and
he's John Mason."

The guard took each badge in his hand and carefully inspected it, comparing the photograph with the wearer. Only
when he was satisfied with their identities did he proffer a clipboard holding a sheet on which their names and Social Security
numbers were already inscribed.

"Please sign your names and the time in," he said in a
monotone.

When the clipboard had been returned, the guard dialed a
telephone behind his counter as Bob and Jack looked on.

"Mr. O'Brien? I have Mr. Green and a Mr. Mason at the
desk. Will you send someone to get them? Okay, I'll tell them."

The guard hung up the phone and turned back to Bob and
Jack.

"Mr. O'Brien will be out to get you himself in a minute," he said in an expressionless voice and then turned back to the television monitor screens on the console behind him. Jack noticed that one of them displayed the very counter at which they stood, allowing the guard to monitor his own activities in a caricature of Orwellian self-scrutiny.

At length, Jack's musing was disturbed by the opening of the vault door beyond the guard and the emergence of a smiling, ruddy-faced Irishman who could be none other than Vincent O'Brien.

O'Brien grasped Bob Green's outstretched hand and shook it vigorously while slapping his old friend jovially on the shoulder with his other giant paw.

"Hey there, Robert! You're lookin' pretty good for a man in your condition! How are things in the erotic chemicals business?"

Bob Green smiled broadly and returned O'Brien's shoulder-pounding.

"Well, now, old buddy, I'm just fine, if I do say so myself. And seeing you again makes me feel even better."

"And this must be the magical Professor Mason you've told me about," O'Brien continued, with a broad, toothy grin. "An honor to make your acquaintance, Professor. Welcome to our humble abode."

O'Brien bowed in mock ceremony holding the vault door open with one hand and motioning them inside with a sweeping gesture of the other. The guard observed this comical display, not live before his eyes, but rather in the safety and anonymity of instant replay on the screen before him.

Vincent O'Brien led the way through the internal corridors of the vault and they arrived shortly at his office. The door had a push-button lock, which O'Brien manipulated to allow their entrance.

The interior of Vincent O'Brien's office was decorated in a way that Jack had neither experienced nor, in his wildest dreams, could have imagined. One entire wall displayed a collection of small arms ranging from rather conventional-appearing revolvers and automatics through several compact machine guns to what seemed to be a space-age version of a high-powered rifle. O'Brien grinned expansively at his new visitor's incredulity and motioned for them to sit down on a sofa facing the display of weapons. After pouring coffee from a carafe for his guests, O'Brien gestured toward the wall and commented theatrically for Jack's benefit.

"Those are a few mementos of my service in the field, Professor. Bob's heard all the stories a hundred times before, but I'd be pleased to spin a yarn or two for you if you like."

Jack's gaping gaze appeared to focus on the weird ray gun. O'Brien seized the opportunity to indulge his passion for reliving past adventures.

"That baby zapped Colonel Mugabi of Zaoufoo in the black of night at two-hundred yards. His bodyguards fired every round they had and only succeeded in killing a couple of dozen of their own people! My guy didn't even have to run hard! Lucky too, carrying that thing."

Vincent O'Brien watched his one-man audience with the perception of an experienced actor. When the expression on Jack's face indicated that the image of the shocking deed and the subsequent violent reaction had sunk in, the raconteur continued.

"It's got a light-amplifying sight that shows things clear as day in just the slightest moonlight. And it fires a thirty-caliber expanding bullet at almost five thousand feet per second. The trajectory is flat to a foot out to three hundred yards! And that muffler on the front is just what it looks like, a very effective silencer."

Jack shook his head from side to side with incredulity, but Vincent O'Brien beamed with the satisfaction of an actor who has grabbed the vitals of his audience and squeezed.

While Jack was still agape at the story and vaguely wondering whether to question its veracity, Bob Green brought the conversation around to the original purpose of their visit.

"Well, Vincent, enough of your war stories! As you know, the reason I asked you to talk to Jack is that he thinks that we're overemphasizing the potential danger he'll face when he visits Moscow. He thinks the Sovs are gentlemen about spying."

O'Brien, the inveterate storyteller, instantly perceived the improvisation that Green's introduction requested.

"Ah, so he thinks they're gentlemen, does he! Perhaps I should show him some of my souveniers of their gentlemanly activities!" O'Brien gestured theatrically like the prince in a Shakespearian play and Green nodded the servant's dutiful encouragement.

The prologue over, Vincent O'Brien moved behind his desk, picked up a manila envelope, and returned to the sofa. He opened the envelope ceremonially, extracted a set of photographs, and handed them to Jack.

"You may find these interesting, Professor. In more ways than one!"

The prints that O'Brien handed Jack appeared to be enlargements made from small negatives. They were grainy and somewhat blurred, but nevertheless clear enough that people and objects could be identified. The first photograph showed a man and a woman in heavy coats mounting the steps of a nondescript apartment building. In the second, Jack was surprised to see the woman seated on a bed in the process of removing her blouse, while the man sat next to her leering expectantly. Jack turned to the third print with the hesitation of a surreptitious reader of *Penthouse* and found the couple naked with the man firmly mounted between the upraised knees and spread thighs of his partner.

Jack's face flushed with embarrassment, and he stole a glance at Vincent O'Brien. The Irishman feigned a psychiatrist's clinical stare, but the slightest twinkle in his eyes revealed his amusement.

"Go on, Professor. They get better!"

Jack nervously flipped to the next print and found the roles reversed. The man was supine on the bed and the woman was vigorously fucking him from above with a purposeful look on her face.

Still red-faced, Jack put down the photographs and tried to look at O'Brien seriously.

"I think I get the message, Mr. O'Brien. But what's the point?"

"Sorry to shock you, Professor," Vincent O'Brien responded, his tone now serious too. "But the point is painfully relevant to your forthcoming trip to Moscow. The hapless fellow you see

294

enjoying himself in those photographs was, until recently, our expert on the biophysical effects of microwave radiation at the embassy in Moscow. You may have read in the papers that the Soviets have been bombarding the embassy with high levels of microwave radiation for years. We became quite concerned about it a while ago and started monitoring the health of all embassy employees. You know, blood tests, urine tests, eye examinations, and the like. Well, about a year ago, the Russians stepped up the level again after having cut it back for several years in response to our protests. So we sent Doctor X, the fellow in the photographs, over there about six months ago to head up an intensified health monitoring program. We thought that we had him well covered, but apparently the KGB found out what his function was and didn't like it. So they put that woman onto him and those photographs were the result. One day our ambassador got called in by the Soviet foreign minister, who indignantly threw down those photographs and demanded that Doctor X leave the country within twenty-four hours or face arrest on a morals charge."

Jack nodded numbly, the color now drained from his face.

"Do you know what you can get on a morals charge in Russia?" O'Brien continued rhetorically. "The rest of your life in a labor camp, or worse if they think that no one cares about you! So we got the doctor out on the next flight to Helsinki, before the Russians could change their minds and decide to pick him up at the airport."

Jack looked at Vincent O'Brien soberly and again nodded his head slowly.

"I guess I'm a little naive about how tough the cold war really is in the trenches. You never hear this kind of story in those glowing articles about détente in the *New York Times Magazine*. Why don't you tell some reporters what's really going on?"

"We do tell a very few of them that we can trust," O'Brien responded with conviction. "But most of them are so blabbermouthed and scatterbrained that we'd lose all our sources and half our agents if we had anything to do with them."

Jack again nodded his understanding, and Vincent O'Brien, apparently satisfied that he had made the point, poured another round of coffee. And, after a moment of sipping his brew, his Irish smile restored, their host jovially began again.

"Well now, Professor, if you don't think that I'm overdoing it, I'd like to show you another little item."

Jack's look of dismay revealed his uncertainly, and O'Brien hastened to explain.

"Nothing as sordid as those photographs, but in its own way perhaps more shocking."

Jack's curiosity was arroused, and he nodded his agreement weakly.

"While you're initiating the new pledge, you might as well go all the way."

Vincent O'Brien moved to the far wall and slid open a small hidden panel revealing a movie projector. He flipped a switch, and a motor whirred, causing a screen to descend from the ceiling behind his desk.

"We got this bit of film and the story it tells by a truly remarkable stroke of luck," the raconteur began his tale. "Two of our attachés were returning to the embassy after a photographic expedition, when they spotted a commotion in front of the gates. They stopped their car at the end of the block and managed to take the film you are about to see without being spotted by the KGB."

O'Brien dimmed the room lights and turned on the projector. The initial scene was blurred, apparently because the driver was still maneuvering the car as the photographer began to shoot. The lens zoomed in on a knot of people in front of the embassy and focused on a uniformed policeman who appeared to be arguing with a hatless, crew-cut man in a trench coat. The disagreement grew more heated and finally the trench-coated man turned abruptly on his heels and strode purposefully toward the open embassy gate. As if on cue in a Mack Sennett comedy, two burly men in fur hats and heavy overcoats blocked his path. He froze for an instant and was overtaken from behind by the uniformed policemen.

Jack's eyes bulged and a sudden chill swept through his chest and landed convulsively in his stomach.

The film blurred again as if the photographer was repositioning the camera to shoot through a different window. When relative sharpness returned, the screen revealed a black van racing down the street toward the embassy. It lurched to a stop opposite the group on the sidewalk, and its rear doors flew open, disgorging uniformed reinforcements. A small, thin man, also in fur hat and heavy overcoat, stepped from a sedan at the curb and directed the police as they muscled their hapless victim into the van. As it drove away, the lens zoomed to telephoto, following the van's disappearance around the corner. The image blurred again, and when it refocused on the scene in front of the gates, the slender man, flanked by his oversized copies, appeared to be lecturing a surprised and frantic knot of people who had emerged from the embassy. The marine guards watched warily from inside the fence, powerless to intercede outside the embassy property. The scene blurred again, and the screen went white when the film ran out.

Jack sat pensively with head in hands staring at the blank screen. Bob Green also seemed moved, and Jack concluded that he had not seen the film before.

"As you said, Professor, they don't play by the Marquis of Queensberry rules in the trenches," Vincent O'Brien said, after waiting for the film's full impact to affect his guests. "That fellow you saw hustled away was an assistant naval attaché. They planted microfilm of blueprints for an ancient diesel submarine on him while he was in the van and then discovered it with great fanfare during his questioning at KGB headquarters. They know it's a put-up job, and we know it's a put-up job, but they'll hold him forever unless we trade him for one of the real spies we've caught. It's a dirty game, and the Russians are past masters of it."

Jack Mason lay down on one of the living-room sofas after dinner. It wasn't so much that he was tired, although God knows he was, but more because Vincent O'Brien's revelations of KGB ruthlessness had left him with pervasive feelings of depression and foreboding. For a while Jack stared blankly at the ceiling, but finally he closed his eyes and drifted off, only to be seized by a nightmare more terrible than reality.

Jack was running at top speed down a dark cobblestone street in a light rain, frantically trying to evade the pounding boots of an army of faceless pursuers. He gasped for breath, and his heart pounded. Jack glanced furtively from side to side seeking a place to hide or an avenue of escape. But, as far as he could see, the dark houses on either side were separated from the roadway by tall iron fences. Suddenly the terror of his situation multiplied. The street ended abruptly at a fence like all the others, leaving Jack no alternative but to stop and face his pursuers.

On they came like a cattle stampede, each several times his own size and all dressed in identical black fur hats and overcoats. They were shaking their fists menacingly and shouting incomprehensible epithets as they bore down on him. In stark terror, Jack turned again to face the final fence and, fortified by fear with strength he did not possess, began to climb. The rails of the tall iron barrier were damp and cold and the toes of his shoes alternately jammed and slipped between them. Below him, the black-coated men began shaking the fence like a mad mob of prison inmates seeking their freedom.

The higher Jack climbed, the more wildly his tenuous perch gyrated until at last his grip failed, and he toppled backward toward the shrieking crowd below. As he fell, weightless and suspended in time, his pursuers magically moved aside to avoid cushioning his impact, and, after exaggerated seconds of accelerating terror, Jack struck the cobblestones with his head and back simultaneously. A blinding light flashed before his eyes, and all was over.

Jack was vaguely aware of a dull thud in the distance as his head thumped against the living-room rug. He awoke to find himself awkwardly wedged between the sofa and the coffee table and his wife staring down at him with a look of barely concealed amusement.

"You fell asleep on the sofa," she said by way of explanation. "You were snoozing so peacefully that I left you alone. But then, all of a sudden, you began frantically flailing your arms and legs and finally did a flip onto the floor!"

Jack climbed uncertainly back onto the sofa and then looked up at his wife with a sheepish grin.

"I guess I was dreaming about some of the things they told me this afternoon at the defensive briefing."

"Defensive briefing?" Sue repeated with a frown. "What's that?"

"Oh, it's nothing," Jack replied unconvincingly. "They just try to scare you a little before you go to Russia."

"What do you mean, *scare you?*" Sue persisted. "What is there to be scared about?"

Sue's voice betrayed her mounting concern, and she sat down on the other sofa opposite her husband.

"It's got something to do with the crazy work you're doing, doesn't it?"

"Yes," Jack agreed, nodding seriously. "I guess they're afraid that if the Russians knew what I'm doing they'd try to get at me somehow."

"*Get at you?* You sound like a character in a Kafka novel. You're doing something important that you can't talk about. But if the Russians knew that you were the person doing the thing that you can't talk about, they'd try to *get at you?*"

Jack smiled at her fondly and shook his head slowly up and down.

"That's about the size of it. It's about as crazy as it sounds. And I'm in the middle of it."

"Well perhaps you should get out, while you have the chance," Sue responded with uncharacteristic vehemence. "If you ask me, this crazy work is consuming you! For four years you've been a secret man doing a secret job. And now you tell me that at a secret briefing, a bunch of other secret Americans so terrified you with the thought that some secret Russians might try to get you that you're having nightmares on the living room sofa!"

Jack got up and then sat down next to his wife and hugged her to him.

"Don't worry, Sue. It'll all be over soon. After the Moscow summit, I'm going to submit my resignation, and we'll all go back to Boston. And I'll just be dull old Professor Mason again. The guy whose students fool with cats and monkeys and get in trouble with the Antivivisection League."

26

The Die Is Cast

The band struck up "Hail to the Chief" as Richard Hart Leonard stepped from his limousine and strode toward the outdoor podium set up in front of a hanger at Andrews Air Force Base. To one side, Air Force One stood gleaming and ready to wing the president away on the first leg of his historic journey to Moscow. Thomas Stratton hurriedly alighted from the second limousine in line and hustled to join his principal on the podium. Ivan Aleksandrovich Basov was already standing in the front row of the diplomatic delegation that was seeing the president off, and the ambassador led the applause as the music stopped. Richard Leonard advanced toward the microphones and acknowledged the greeting with upraised arms and a broad smile. Only when the last clapping had ceased did the president begin his prepared remarks.

"I speak to you today with a great measure of humility and an extreme sense of responsibility as I embark on this historic trip to Moscow for the summit conference. I believe that you all are fully aware that this administration has placed the highest possible priority on the search for world peace through a stable system of agreements among the major powers."

Thomas Stratton beamed from behind the president as Richard Leonard's voice intoned the words he had written. Stratton told himself once again that moments like these were his reward for countless hours of behind-the-scenes labor. And, as the secretary of state dreamed of grander things to come, the president continued like an animated ventriloquist's dummy.

"The road to world peace is not an easy route to travel. It is strewn with the boulders of national self-interest and pocked with the potholes of envy and suspicion. But, through continuing dialogue at the highest levels, the obstacles to agreement can, one by one, be rolled aside until the ultimate objectives of stable international order and lasting world peace are attained. I take leave of you today very mindful that without your efforts in the cause of peace and your prayers and good wishes in the days to come, the successful completion of my mission would not be possible. I can only assure you that in all my dealings with the leaders of the Soviet Union I will be guided first and foremost by the principles of freedom and democracy that have made this country great and the desire for peace that always has dominated the thoughts and prayers of the American people."

Richard Leonard stepped back from the microphones indicating that his speech had ended and waited for the applause. When the acknowledgment had reached a suitable crescendo, the president again raised his arms above his head and smiled broadly at the officials and reporters below.

Throughout Richard Leonard's speech, Jason Star stood in the crowd behind Ivan Basov straining to perceive the ambassador's mental reactions to the president's remarks. Jason had been amply rewarded with psi signals, but they were fragmentary and confused. He could not even be certain that all the psi impressions had come from Ivan Basov, because several Russian aides stood between Jason and the ambassador.

The first clear words that the man with psi had received were *Moskva* (Moscow) and *sem'ya* (family), probably, he thought, from the brain of a homesick member of the Russian embassy staff who was getting the opportunity to visit his family as a result of the summit conference. As Richard Leonard had stepped to the microphones and acknowledged the greeting of the crowd, Jason had perceived what seemed to be a single thought from one Russian mind: *'politics, American, strange.'* The naivete of the reaction seemed more appropriate to a junior official than to the worldly Soviet Ambassador.

Later, while the president was speaking, a torrent of Russian words and phrases had flashed before Jason's mind, some so fleeting or unintelligible that they did not register on his conscious thoughts. Jason had tried desperately to remember the most distinct signals in the order that he had received them: "*day ... airplane ... woman ... beautiful ... president ... antenna*

*... communications ... Sherkov ... secret ... fool ... Moscow
..."*

When Richard Leonard's speech had ended, and the crowd
had begun its applause, the man with psi had used feigned enthusiasm to elbow his way between two Russians to a position
directly behind Ivan Basov. Jason's brain had immediately been
accosted by a sequence of sinister thoughts: *"president ...
puppet ... Stratton ... behind ... throne ... unaware ... Sherkov. ..."*

The man with psi strained for more, but Ivan Basov stepped
forward in a visible display of enthusiasm for the president's
remarks, and the ambassador's aides again closed in behind
him. Jason was left bewildered by the deluge of psi perceptions
and struggled desperately to memorize their sequence by repeating them in his mind: *"Moscow ... family ... politics
... American ... strange ... day ... airplane ..."*

A hand on Jason's shoulder broke his concentration, and he
turned to face an air force major consulting a list on a clipboard.

"Mr. Brentwood?" the officer inquired.

Jason appeared startled and then finally responded.

"Yes, I'm David Brentwood."

"You'll have to board now, Mr. Brentwood," the major continued authoritatively, "so that the aircraft can leave as soon as
the president is ready. Give your name to the captain standing
inside the door, and he will direct you to your seat."

The major placed a check next to the name David Brentwood
on his list, and Jason started to walk toward the gleaming white
aircraft. He wondered idly how the accommodations would differ
from the commercial version of the same plane, the venerable
Boeing 707, in which he had flown countless times. As Jason
reached the foot of the boarding stairs, he found himself in the
company of a select group of White House and State Department
aides who were about to experience the ultimate Washington
status symbol—a flight to Europe and on to the Moscow summit
conference with the president and the secretary of state.

In spite of the mild April weather, a chilly feeling of unease
slowly crept over him as Jason realized that he was about to
enter a world of ego and power, where, outside of his strange
gift, he was ill prepared to cope. When he reached the top of the

stairs, the man with psi glanced back at the podium and saw Richard Leonard heartily shaking the hand of Ivan Basov as Thomas Stratton looked on with a cherubic smile. The president and secretary of state began to stroll toward the aircraft, and a voice inside the cabin jolted Jason back to reality.

"Please step inside, sir. We must prepare to depart immediately."

Jason turned and found himself facing the captain that the major had described.

"Your name, please, sir?" the officer demanded.

"Brentwood. David Brentwood," Jason responded nervously, and then added, "I'm a special assistant to the secretary of state," momentarily fearing that he might be denied admittance.

"Yes, *sir,* Mr. Brentwood," the captain replied. "You will be sitting in the aft cabin on the starboard side, next to Mr. Janek."

Jason's face brightened. At least he would have a companion who presumably knew the ropes of travel with the big wheels. Like which john you're allowed to use and how much it's wise to drink.

"Go through the presidential compartment and the conference area to the third cabin," the captain continued. "Your seat is 12C, the third row on the left."

Jason stepped into the presidential area and was surprised to find that it appeared much as he had seen it on television news reports. The compartment was dominated by a massive, high-backed, padded chair for the president, which faced aft, presumably as a safety precaution in the event of the necessity of an emergency landing. A work table faced the chair, and numerous telephones were grouped at its side. The purpose of each of the communications circuits was apparently identified by the color of the telephone handset—red, white, beige, green, and black—but the significance escaped the man with psi. A colorful, sculptured presidential seal was mounted on the bulkhead behind the massive chair, and Jason thought that it must appear like a gaudy halo over the head of the chief executive.

"Please step to the rear of the aircraft, gentlemen," the captain pleaded. "The secretary of state is boarding."

Jason hurried through the conference area into the aft cabin and found it appointed the same as first class in a commercial airliner. He was pleased to find Stephen Janek already seated at a window and headed for the aisle seat beside him.

Janek smiled at Jason as he approached and greeted him cheerfully.

"I see you found the right airplane, *David!* That's a good start."

Jason grinned broadly and then sat down and nervously fastened his seat belt.

"That's about all I'm sure of, Stephen. Traveling in these rarefied circles is all new to me."

"It's still pretty new to me, too," Janek confessed. "But you get used to it fast! Just enjoy the food and drink and be ready whenever the president or the secretary calls."

The cabin was now mostly filled, and Stephen Janek leaned toward the man with psi and continued in a whisper. "Be careful what you say. I'm about the only person in here who knows about your mission."

Jason nodded slightly and then looked slowly around the cabin at his traveling companions. They all seemed to be attired in the uniform of diplomatic Washington—a conservatively cut, three-piece suit of dark-blue, brown, or gray pin-striped cloth. Jason's own navy-blue blazer with brass buttons suddenly seemed strangely out of place, and he made a mental note to switch to more conservative garb during the stopover in London for the president's presummit meeting with the British prime minster.

"Gentlemen, the president is boarding," a voice from the loudspeakers overhead interjected. "Please check your seat belts. We'll be rolling as soon as the president is seated."

Jason instinctively tugged at his seat belt as a faint thud and slight shudder indicated the closing of the outside door. Almost immediately, the whine of the engines increased slightly and the plane began to roll, gathering speed as it turned onto the taxiway. With other aircraft shunted aside, *Air Force One* rolled directly onto the active runway and immediately began to accelerate for takeoff. Shortly after the landing gear had been retracted, the pilot banked gently to the left to give the president an unobstructed view of Washington as they began the climb to their chosen cruising altitude.

"This sure beats being number nine for takeoff at National on Friday evening," Stephen Janek quipped.

Jason smiled and nodded as he peered out the window across the aisle at the gleaming Capitol dome in the distance.

Thomas Stratton sat facing Richard Leonard as they both gazed out at the seats of power they knew so well receding in the distance. The secretary of state spoke with a hint of theater in his voice.

"Well, Mr. President, we are embarked on an historic journey. The next two weeks may well mark a turning point in the history of the atomic age. If we can successfully negotiate a reduction in nuclear weapons on terms favorable to the West, the tide of Soviet expansion may again be stemmed."

Richard Leonard smiled at Thomas Stratton and responded sardonically.

"You make it all sound so historical and impersonal, Thomas. For me, it's simpler. I'm going to put that bastard Sherkov in his place! He's like a two-bit gangster who's risen to the top of the mob. And now he's got the leaders of the world so scared that none of them will stand up to him. They all come sniveling around and kiss his ass to try to get a few favors. And all because he acts so tough. And what do we get in comparison, for feeding and clothing and defending the world? I'll tell you what we get. A lot of shit! Insulted in newspapers around the globe, outvoted by a bunch of monkeys at the UN, and advised by our so-called friends to give the Russians anything they want at the conference table because Sherkov is so damn tough! Well, I'm going to show them who's tough! And when I'm through with Sherkov and his buddies, they'll wish they'd been killed at Stalingrad or Leningrad or whatever the hell grad it was!

"Very well said, Mr. President," Sam Ryan injected enthusiastically from across the aisle. "It's about time someone made those Russians understand that we're just as tough as they are and we're willing to prove it if we have to!"

The president beamed at them with self-satisfaction. Sam Ryan stared back intently at his commander in chief with childlike respect, but Thomas Stratton smiled wryly, thinking again of the seemingly endless sequence of unreasoned diatribes that

305

he had had to endure during the arduous climb to a secure spot on a pinnacle of history.

After basking in self-congratulatory silence for a moment, Richard Leonard continued his monologue enthusiastically.

"That's why the man with psi is so important. He's the key to putting that Russian bastard in his place. I bet that Sherkov's bluffing most of the time. Like a lot of supposedly tough guys. You know the kind. They bet big with a pair of sixes and take the pot because everyone else is chicken. But when Sherkov bluffs me, Star's going to catch him. And then I'll pounce and grab him by the balls and squeeze until he screams uncle!"

Jason Star had just finished a delicious cold seafood platter accompanied by a glass of chilled white wine. He and Stephen Janek were bantering good-naturedly, when a young man in shirtsleeves entered the cabin and, after checking the seat numbers, leaned over and spoke to Jason.

"Mr. Brentwood?"

"Yes?" Jason responded hesitatingly, and the man in the aisle continued.

"The secretary would like to speak with you. He said to finish your lunch and then to join him in the conference compartment."

Jason looked surprised, but finally nodded his understanding.

"Don't keep him waiting," the aide whispered confidentially. "He's not very patient."

Jason smiled and nodded again, and the young man turned and retreated forward as if attempting to limit his exposure to the lower-class passengers in the rear.

"Well, David, I guess you shouldn't have drunk the wine," Stephen Janek quipped with a smile.

Jason smiled weakly in return, but his mind raced to remember the jumbled list of Russian words and phrases: 'Moscow . . . family . . . politics . . . American . . . strange . . . day . . .'

Stephen Janek noticed the concerned look on Jason's face and tried to allay his fears.

"Don't worry, David," he whispered. "The secretary isn't quite the ogre he appears to be."

The man with psi smiled weakly again and patted Stephen Janek on the shoulder. Then Jason released his belt, rose from his seat, and stepped into the aisle. He started to move forward, but suddenly stopped and turned and addressed Stephen Janek in a stage whisper.

"Which way is the john in this flying hotel?"

Janek laughed and pointed to the rear of the cabin.

"There are two back there and a private one in the conference area, if you think you can wait!"

Jason strode to one of the heads in the tail of the plane and energetically splashed cold water on his face in an attempt to dispel the glow of the wine and improve his recollection of the jumbled list of psi impressions. As he recited it again, Jason was suddenly overwhelmed by a new chill of doubt as he neared the end:

"... *President ... puppet ... Stratton ... behind ... throne ...*"

My God! Jason thought. *Can I tell Stratton that?*

The man with psi frantically splashed more cold water on his face, combed his hair, and returned to his seat.

"What do I do?" he whispered to Stephen Janek. "Just walk in?"

"No, the door's probably locked," Janek replied, shaking his head. "You had better knock, and someone will open it."

Jason rose again, moved to the door in the forward bulkhead, and followed the instructions. In response to his knock, the door opened part way and the young aide's face appeared.

"Come right in, Mr. Brentwood," he said and opened the door fully. "The secretary is ready to see you."

Jason stepped inside the conference area, and the assistant closed the door behind him. Thomas Stratton was seated in a chair similar to, but smaller than, the president's. On the forward bulkhead above Stratton's head had been hung the seal of the Department of State, and in front of him, a work table had been erected. The aide motioned to Jason to take one of two still smaller seats across the table from the secretary of state and then sat down himself in a similar seat across the aisle facing a small table strewn with papers and folders.

Thomas Stratton grinned knowingly at Jason Star, but greeted David Brentwood.

"Good morning, David. It's a pleasure to have you on board. How are you enjoying your first flight in a presidential aircraft?"

"Very much, thank you, Mr. Secretary," Jason responded. And then he added with some lack of sincerity, "It's rather more elaborate than I had expected."

"David, I'd like you to meet Charles Carter Hoving the third," the Secretary of State continued, gesturing toward the young man across the aisle.

Hoving stood hastily, papers sliding from his lap to the floor, and extended his hand to Jason.

"Pleased to meet you, Mr. Brentwood."

Jason rose, shook the aide's hand firmly, and then slid back into his seat.

"Well, David," Thomas Stratton began again, "how does it feel to be part of an historic adventure?"

Jason Star was suddenly confused. Was the secretary of state referring to his psi mission? Did he desire a candid reply? Or was he simply making high-powered small talk? Fortunately, Jason recalled Stephen Janek's admonition and answered innocuously.

"It certainly is exciting to feel that you have a part, however small, in the making of history, Mr. Secretary."

Thomas Stratton beamed with satisfaction at Jason's appreciation of the situation and then addressed his aide enigmatically.

"Charles, I'll have to ask you to leave us alone for a while. Please be certain the doors are locked."

Charles Carter Hoving III looked at the secretary of state with spaniel eyes, his ego crushed and his prestige score diminished.

"Yes, sir, Mr. Secretary," Hoving responded meekly and rose to check the aft door. Verifying that it was locked, he returned forward and spoke again quietly before disappearing.

"I'll be in the communications area if you need me, Mr. Secretary. The doors will be locked from the inside, so you'll have to let people in yourself."

"Thank you, Charles," Thomas Stratton responded matter-of-factly. But when the forward door had closed, he turned to the man with psi and smiled broadly.

"Well, Jason, we are truly embarked on a great adventure. And I do not use the royal we lightly. Make no mistake about it. The three most important people on this aircraft are the president, myself, and you!"

The warm glow that only generous flattery with an essential element of truth can provide spread over Jason Star.

"Thank you, Mr. Secretary. I must confess that I'm rather overwhelmed at the moment."

Thomas Stratton surveyed his gifted protege with a fatherly smile and continued.

"That's only natural. After all, you are rather a newcomer to the heady world of international diplomacy. But you'll get accustomed to it rapidly, I'm sure. Besides a sharp mind, which you clearly have, all it takes is a thick skin and a strong stomach!" Thomas Stratton chuckled to himself.

"I hope that you're right, Mr. Secretary. I'm just concerned that I won't be able to live up to your expectations."

"Nonsense, Jason! You have the most amazing ability the world has ever seen. The power to read other men's minds. In centuries past you would have been thought to be God incarnate! A messiah come to lead the sinful peoples of the world to the true perception of the righteous path to salvation!"

Jason looked at the secretary of state quizzically, and Thomas Stratton quickly returned to a more mundane plane.

"Well, now, what did you get from our friend Basov this morning?"

Jason felt curiously relieved and began anew to mentally rehearse the list of psi signals: . . . *Moscow . . . family . . . politics. . . .*

"Did you hear me, Jason?" Thomas Stratton persisted.

"Oh, yes sir, Mr. Secretary," Jason finally responded sheepishly. "I just was trying to organize my impressions for you. Things were rather confusing out there this morning. There were lots of Russians around, and sometimes I was close to Basov, and sometimes I wasn't."

309

"Well, let's just start at the beginning," said Thomas Stratton returning to the fatherly tone, "the way you do in the debriefings. Just pretend that I'm that woman with the sexy voice who asks you the questions."

Jason smiled and visualized Phyllis Jackson. *It certainly would be nice to have Phyllis here now,* he thought.

"Well, Mr. Secretary, the very first Russian words that I received clearly were 'Moscow' and 'family.' I got those signals even before you and the president arrived, and I think that they must have come from one of the people from the Soviet embassy who is getting a chance to travel back to Moscow for the summit conference."

Thomas Stratton nodded in agreement and wrote the words on a yellow legal pad.

> Departure Ceremony
> —Embassy Staff Member?
> —"Moscow"
> —"family"

When the secretary of state looked up again, the man with psi continued his recitation.

"I received the next signals while President Leonard was acknowledging the applause after he first stepped to the microphones. I perceived the phrase 'politics ... American ... strange,' and I think that all three words came from a single brain. I can't explain why, but that's the impression I had at the time."

Thomas Stratton again wrote on his pad and then addressed Jason with a twinkle in his eye.

"Whoever that Russian was, he's an astute observer of the contemporary Washington scene."

Jason smiled weakly, and Thomas Stratton continued.

"What did you receive during the president's speech?"

"Things were pretty jumbled," Jason responded, shaking his head. "There were a couple of Russians between me and Basov and a lot of different words and phrases flashed through my mind. I've tried to remember the ones that were distinct enough that I'm convinced that they were psi signals. Let me just recite the list to you."

Thomas Stratton nodded, pen poised, looking for all the world like a Freudian psychoanalyst.

"It goes like this," Jason continued. "Day, airplane, woman, beautiful . . . president, antenna, communications . . . Sherkov, secret, fool, Moscow."

Thomas Stratton dutifully recorded the words and then stared intently at his pad.

"It's a word association puzzle, isn't it?" the secretary of state asked. "Is the *day beautiful* or the *woman*? I'll guess the woman! And the *airplane* gets the *antenna* for *communications*. Now, are the *communications presidential* or *secret* or both?"

Jason rose from his seat, and Thomas Stratton turned the pad toward him so that the man with psi could see the circled groups of words. Jason nodded his understanding, and the secretary of state continued.

"If the *president* is using the *antenna* on the *airplane* for *secret communications,* that leaves *Sherkov* as the *fool* in *Moscow!*"

They laughed together for a moment, but then Jason suggested a chilling alternative.

"Perhaps *Sherkov* has a *secret* plan and is going to *fool* someone in *Moscow.*"

Thomas Stratton's expression became serious. He circled the combination of words that Jason had suggested and again stared intently at the pad. The man with psi sat back down in his seat apprehensively, unnerved by the secretary of state's abrupt change of mood.

Finally, Thomas Stratton began to nod his head slowly up and down.

"I believe that you're right, Jason. I think that Sherkov is laying a trap for us. But you are the scout who will find the pit and lead us safely around by another path."

Jason's attention now turned with dread to the phrases he would next have to report. How would the secretary of state react to Russian thoughts accurately reflecting his Svengali influence over the president?

The thoughtful frown disappeared from Thomas Stratton's face as rapidly as it had come, and he again began to question the man with psi matter-of-factly.

"Well, now, Jason, what did you perceive next?"

The look on Jason Star's face revealed his anxiety, and he answered with hesitation.

"Well, Mr. Secretary, at the end of the president's speech, during the applause, I managed to work my way through the Russian aides to a position directly behind Basov."

Thomas Stratton leaned forward with anticipation, his pen poised and his ears hanging on Jason's every word.

"I can't be certain it was Basov, of course, but I got the distinct impression that—"

"Come now, Jason, what is bothering you?" Thomas Stratton interjected. "Something Basov was thinking? Tell me what you perceived."

"Well, Mr. Secretary," Jason began tentatively, "I perceived three Russian phrases. *'President puppet, Stratton behind throne,* and *unaware Sherkov.'* "

The man with psi looked at the secretary of state anxiously. For a time that seemed to Jason endless, Thomas Stratton just stared back at him. Jason was about to offer an apology, when he noticed the faintest hint of a smile beginning at the corner of Thomas Stratton's mouth. Jason held his breath as the smile materialized and the secretary of state spoke again.

"Well, Jason, we've passed through out first small crisis together, you and I. You have perceived something you thought might be embarrassing to me and have told me the truth about it."

A great feeling of relief coursed through Jason Star's body, and his tensed muscles relaxed.

"There has to be complete trust between you and me," Thomas Stratton continued. "Otherwise, the gravest danger awaits us both."

The man with psi leaned forward in his seat again, intent on capturing the essence of the secretary of state's every word. Now Jason's feeling was one of genuine collegial interest, in sharp contrast to his near panic of a moment ago.

Thomas Stratton appraised his pupil.

"We will be like a single superperson, you and I. As the active and obvious part of us, I will stimulate Sherkov and his colleagues with feints and lunges, while you, the passive and unnoticed part of us, will perceive their thoughts, reactions, and plans. And then, armed with your insights, my attacks will grow bolder and my thrusts more telling. Finally, they no longer will be able to avoid the rapier's point, and I will drive it home to their vitals!"

Thomas Stratton's sudden vehemence surprised Jason Star, and he looked apprehensively at his mentor. But the secretary of state made no attempt to break the spell. Instead he basked in Jason's awe, much as he had done countless times in the past as a learned professor, after delivering a scholarly soliloquy to a quaking tutorial student. Finally, Thomas Stratton gestured expansively to the man with psi and resumed the interrogation.

"Well, Jason, what do you think that Basov's sinister thoughts mean?"

Jason Star squirmed in his seat, uncertain as to how to reply, but, mercifully, Thomas Stratton continued like a councilor leading a witness.

"You were quite perceptive about Sherkov's secret plan to fool us in Moscow."

The man with psi was grateful for the hint and gave the reply that Thomas Stratton obviously wanted to hear.

"Well, Mr. Secretary, Basov seems to be reiterating that we are unaware of the secret trap that Sherkov plans to spring in Moscow."

"Yes, unaware of its nature, but warned of its existence," Thomas Stratton interjected. "And before he gets to spring it, you will have discovered all its facets and I will have fashioned an artful escape and a slashing counterattack!"

A light began to flash on the white telephone at the secretary of state's side, which instantly commanded his attention.

"It's the president, Jason. You'll have to excuse me."

The man with psi rose to leave, but Thomas Stratton, as he lifted the receiver, motioned for him to be seated.

"Yes, Mr. President. Yes, Mr. President, he's with me now. We would be pleased to join you if you'd like."

The secretary of state hung up the receiver and grinned broadly at Jason Star.

"The president would like to hear about your latest psi perceptions."

A look of absolute panic came over Jason's face.

"Should—should I tell him about—"

"Of course," Thomas Stratton interjected emphatically. "I have no secrets from the president, and he has none from me."

The secretary of state rose from his chair and unlocked the forward door. He motioned for Jason to follow and stepped into the small communications space that separated the conference area from the presidential compartment. The communications area echoed with the clatter of teletype machines as efficient-acting army sergeants sent and received global messages. The spaniel-eyed aide gazed imploringly at the secretary of state as he passed, hoping to elicit an invitation to visit the president. But Thomas Stratton smiled at him benignly and tactfully denied the implied request.

"The president has asked to meet individually the senior staff people who are accompanying us. He already knows you, Charles, of course."

A sergeant perched on a jump seat at the door to the presidential compartment lifted a telephone handset from its cradle on the bulkhead as the secretary of state approached.

"Mr. President, the secretary of state is here. Yes, Mr. President, I'll ask him to come in."

The sergeant rose and opened the door to the presidential compartment, and Thomas Stratton stepped inside and motioned for Jason Star to follow. The secretary of state waited for the sergeant to close the door behind them and then addressed the president rather formally.

"Mr. President, it gives me great pleasure to present Jason Star, the man with psi."

Thomas Stratton smiled with satisfaction, and Richard Leonard rose and extended his hand to Jason.

"So you're the man with psi. I've heard a lot about you. You don't look, uh, as strange as I expected."

Jason clasped the president's hand and shook it enthusiastically.

"It's a great honor to meet you, Mr. President. I, er, only hope that I can, uh, live up to your expectations."

The president regained his high, padded chair and motioned for them to sit down. The secretary of state took the seat opposite

314

the president and indicated that Jason should sit across the aisle facing Sam Ryan. The general rose slightly and shook Jason's hand vigorously.

"Good to see you again, Star. You're our secret weapon on this trip, you know. The Sovs are sure to try to trip us up any way they can. And you've got to keep us informed about what they're up to."

Jason nodded his agreement silently and turned in his chair to face the president. To his surprise, the chair rotated like one at the barber shop and he found himself with his feet in the aisle facing the chief executive.

"The swivel chair fooled you, didn't it Jason?" the president said with a chuckle. "I had them installed myself. I hate talking to the side of someone's head. I like to look a man straight in the eye, to get the real measure of him."

Jason overcame his surprise and nodded enthusiastically at the president's remarks. An amused smile played across Thomas Stratton's face, and he waited a polite interval before attempting to get the conversation down to business.

"Mr. President, Jason received some interesting psi signals during your departure speech. I think you will be fascinated by them."

"I'm sure I will, Thomas," Richard Leonard responded enthusiastically. "This psi power of Jason's is the greatest new weapon against Communism that this country has developed since the H-bomb. And it could be just as important to our national security. Or even more important! You can only threaten people with H-bombs, but you can really use psionauts on them. Think what we could do with an army of psionauts. Several on the staff of every embassy. And at every international negotiation. Even at commercial trade deals. We'd always get the best price or terms or whatever. And as long as those damn commies don't find out about it and get psionauts too, we'll whip the pants off 'em!"

Thomas Stratton's eyes rolled ever so slightly toward the ceiling at the thought of enduring another of Richard Leonard's rambling diatribes. But, warming to the audience and the topic, the president continued vigorously.

"And that's why you're so damned important, Jason. Because, from what Sam and Thomas tell me, you're an army of one, right now, our *only* psionaut. The only man with psi. So we've got to be damned sure that nothing happens to you. Because if something did, where would I be? Out on a limb, that's where! At a summit meeting in Moscow without my secret weapon. What a hell of a mess that would be!"

The president pondered his own remarks for a moment and then shook his finger at Sam Ryan.

"Sam, you make goddamned sure that nothing happens to Jason! Do you understand me?"

"Yes, sir, Mr. President," the general responded. "I understand you completely. Mr. Star will receive the tightest possible protection."

Thomas Stratton frowned, and he spoke, as if thinking out loud.

"Of course, Mr. President, you don't intend that Sam make the security precautions so obvious that they will call the Russian's attention to Jason."

The president's look flashed his thanks to the secretary of state, and Richard Leonard again shook his finger at his chief of staff.

"And be damned sure that your gumshoes don't call attention to Jason, or the KGB will be all over him."

"Yes, sir, Mr. President. We'll make sure the security is as unobtrusive as possible."

"You've probably already thought of it, Sam," Thomas Stratton continued matter-of-factly, "but you might consider assigning a couple of the virgin CIA men in the press plane to Jason. Agents the Russians can never have seen or heard of."

The general nodded gratefully to the secretary of state for the suggestion and scribbled cryptically in the stenographer's notebook he always carried.

Thomas Stratton waited a decent interval to be sure that the president's preoccupation with the man with psi's safety had dissipated. But after the chief executive had beamed at them in royal silence for several moments, the secretary of state began anew.

"As I was saying, Mr. President, Jason received some interesting psi signals from Basov and his aides at Andrews this morning. The most important message seems to be that Sherkov is planning to trick us in some way at the summit conference."

Richard Leonard frowned deeply and looked intently at his secretary of state. Thomas Stratton allowed his elliptic words of warning to rest unembellished and waited for the predictable presidential reaction.

"That s.o.b. Sherkov intends to trick us? Who the fuck does he think he is? We're the ones who are going to trick him!"

The president swiveled his chair abruptly toward Jason and leaned forward, glaring menacingly at the man with psi.

"Is that true, Star? Did Basov really say that Sherkov was going to trick me?"

Jason recoiled from the harsh voice and violent facial expression. He fumbled for words to respond, but none came fast enough.

"Come on, Star!" the president almost shouted. "Did he say it, or didn't he?"

Jason's eyes flashed around the cabin, frantically looking for the nearest exit, but Thomas Stratton's level baritone voice again cleverly calmed the presidential tantrum.

"Of course, Mr. President, you didn't mean to suggest that Basov actually said these things; he merely thought them. Or at least Jason perceived that he did."

Jason smiled with relief and nodded enthusiastically in support of the secretary of state's explanation. The man with psi was finally able to speak coherently and followed Thomas Stratton's lead.

"That's right, Mr. President. What I perceived was Basov or one of his aides thinking that Sherkov had a secret that he would fool someone with in Moscow. In fact, all I really perceived were four words: *Sherkov, secret, fool, Moscow.*"

"Just four words?" growled the president. "And you've gotten me all excited over four words? The president of the United States! The man who holds the power of life or death for millions of people in his hands. You've gotten me all excited over four words?"

"Well, let's think of it this way, Mr. President," Thomas Stratton injected jovially. "Basov could have been thinking that Sherkov is a secret fool in Moscow, and that we are about to discover him."

Jason Star laughed weakly at the secretary of state's repetition of their private joke and then held his breath, hoping that the president would grasp the humor.

The chief executive swiveled toward Thomas Stratton as if in rage, but then responded heartily.

"Ha! That's a good one, Thomas. Basov thinks that Sherkov is a secret fool. And he's right. Only we're the only ones who know why!"

Having for once successfully matched wits with Thomas Stratton, Richard Leonard sat back in his chair with a satisfied grin on his face and jabbed a button on the console beside him with an exaggerated gesture. The forward door opened noiselessly, and a Filipino steward discreetly appeared.

"Yes, Mr. President?"

Richard Leonard swivelled his chair toward the steward and motioned at his guests as he spoke.

"Cognac all around, please, Miguel. We have a toast to drink to the success of the summit conference."

"Yes, sir, Mr. President," the steward said quietly and disappeared whence he had come.

And perhaps a toast to a special adversary in Moscow, thought the secretary of state. *To Vasily Sherkov, a man with a secret plan, from Thomas Stratton, a man with a secret weapon. May the greater statesman win and may history be the judge.*

A light blinked on the president's console, and he responded by pushing the steward's button. The forward door opened again and Miguel appeared, carrying a silver tray on which were four large snifters and a bottle of Courvoisier. The steward placed the tray on the president's table and filled the bottom of the chief executive's glass. The president cradled the snifter in his palms, raised it to his nose, and breathed deeply of the brandy's fragrance.

"Good stuff, as usual, Miguel. Pour some for my guests, please."

The steward filled the remaining snifters and passed the tray around. Jason took his glass and held it tentatively, waiting for a clue from Thomas Stratton as to how to proceed. The secretary of state mimicked the president's warming and smelling routine and then exclaimed with a smile:

"They say that cognac is the blood of diplomacy, Mr. President, and you certainly have a taste for the best."

"Thank you, Thomas," the president replied. "Perhaps that's why I selected you."

Thomas Stratton beamed beatifically, basking in the warmth of the president's praise. Richard Leonard sipped his brandy, and the others followed suit. The president surveyed his aides with a generous smile and raised his glass in a toast.

"To success in the most important negotiation the world has ever seen!"

"To success!" repeated Thomas Stratton.

"To success!" echoed Jason Star and Sam Ryan.

"We're making history here today," the president continued. "When children in the twenty-first century read of diplomacy in the nuclear age, the names of Richard Leonard and Thomas Stratton will stand head and shoulders above the rest for having achieved a stable international order and lasting world peace through their phenomenal skill as summit negotiators."

The president and the secretary of state smiled at each other in mutual satisfaction. And, across the aisle, General Sam Ryan nodded his head vigorously up and down in childlike adulation of the incomparable genius of his superiors. But Jason Star closed his eyes momentarily and shook his head imperceptibly from side to side, secretly hoping that he would shortly awake from a terrifying and unreal nightmare.

27

"Three Pertsovkas!"

The giant Rossiya hotel facing the Moskva River just off Red Square was one of the Russian capital's newest. Boasting more than 3,000 rooms, a concert hall, and two movie theaters, it often was used by the Soviet government for official American visitors—congressmen, trade delegations, state department advance men, temporary embassy employees, and the like. Rather than the faded prerevolutionary grandeur of the city's remaining fine old hotels, like the Metropole and the National, the reinforced-concrete construction of the Rossiya stolidly proclaimed the no-nonsense Marxist work ethic. The massive lobby was adorned with garish heroic murals portraying the triumph of the working class over the evils of bourgeois decadence. Despite the obvious differences in national style, the Rossiya might at a distance, or even at casual closer observation, have passed for the world's largest Holiday Inn.

After a seemingly endless wait in the lobby, Jack had been assigned a comfortable room on the seventh floor, overlooking the Moskvoretskya Naberezhnaya and the river. His suitcases had yet to be delivered to his room; when last seen, they also had been waiting in the lobby with a hundred others like them under the watchful eye of a stolid uniformed porter. Jack had been warned that his baggage might be searched in the course of its circuitous journey from the lobby to his room. Old hands had told him, he was not sure how facetiously, that they often carried toothbrushes, razors, pajamas and the like in their briefcases, because tales abounded of luggage selected for KGB inspection that took several days to complete the arduous trip from lobby to room.

Jack stared out the window in the fading late afternoon twilight at the vague shapes of buildings in the distance. He held the map that had been provided by the State Department and rotated it this way and that, trying to get his bearings. The only landmark he had positively identified was the onion dome of the Kremlin bell tower when a characteristic tap on the door buoyed his spirits with the knowledge that Bob Green undoubtedly was in the hall. Jack left the window, dropped the map on the bed, and opened the door. Bob entered with his usual greeting.

"Hi, old buddy! Welcome to the minimum security annex of Lubyanka! I've been assigned to take you on a guided tour of the facilities. In the gymnasium we have a variety of equipment to get you in shape—racks, pots of boiling oil, beds of nails, and the like! And, for your intellectual reeducation, we are featuring this evening, in theater number one, the heroic adventures of Tovarishch Ivan Ivanovich, the hardest working party member in Tractor Factory Number Seven."

"Hi, Bob," Jack said between his chuckles. "Come on in. I guess this place is old hat to you."

"No, this monument is brand new," Green responded. "At least since I last spent much time here. They used to put us up in a place near the railroad station—the Leningradskaya. It had practically no heat in the winter and one bathroom for every twenty people. You had to get a tee-off time from the *dezhurnaya* (floor concierge) to shave in the morning! By comparison, this place is palatial. There seems to be a john in every room and mine has a shower as well as a tub. I think they built this place to show western visitors that things are really up to date in Russia."

Bob noticed the map on the bed and picked it up and went to the window.

"You'll get a good view of the city from here; we're pretty high up. The Kremlin is off to the right and across the river in the distance. You should be able to get a glimpse of a lot of the city's old buildings when it gets light in the morning. You'll probably be able to see as far as Moscow State U.—it's the NYU of Russia."

Jack nodded and tried to note the general direction in which Bob had been looking.

"I'd like to get to know the city. Perhaps when we've got some time, you can show me around."

"Yeah, I'd enjoy it," Bob responded. "There have been a lot of changes since I was here ten or twelve years ago. They're putting up these reinforced-concrete beehives all over town."

Jack turned from the window and suddenly spoke in a disconsolate tone.

"Well, who are we kidding with all this tourist talk. We've got an impossible job to do, and time is running out. The president will be here in a few days and—"

Bob Green's face turned to stone. Without a word, he raised his finger to his lips and shook his head from side to side. Thus having silenced his loose-tongued compatriot, Bob moved to the wall opposite the bed, removed an innocuous picture, and carefully inspected its back and frame. Convinced that it contained no microphone or transmitter, he placed it silently on the bed and returned to the empty spot on the wall.

Jack's color gradually drained as he realized the importance of Bob's search and how perilously close he had come to casually revealing a clue to their clandestine activities.

Meanwhile, Bob was peering intently at the section of the wall that had been covered by the picture and was passing his fingers lightly back and forth across it searching for irregularities. After a while, Green smiled in triumph and began the conversation again in a voice that made clear to Jack that he was acting.

"I'll take you on a tour of the city by the Metro this weekend. And we'll try some of the restaurants I used to frequent, like the Ararat and the Uzbekistan. No matter what's happened to them, the food's got to be more interesting that what they'll serve us in one of the giant dining rooms in this place."

Bob continued to chat with feigned joviality while probing with the small blade of his pocket knife around the nail that had supported the picture. Jack peered intently over his shoulder like a new surgical intern watching the great man in action. Bob chipped away the plaster around the nail and then began to delicately extract it from the wall with the thumb and forefinger of his left hand while continuing to loosen it with the knife blade in his right. Jack held his breath as the nail came free of the wall followed by a pair of hair-thin wires. Bob let the tiny microphone hang by its umbilical cord and grinned broadly at Jack like a small boy displaying his pet snake to an astonished friend. Finally, satisfied with the audience reaction, Green cut the wires with a flourish of the knife and ceremonially deposited the microphone in Jack's hastily outstretched palm.

"One down and seventeen to go!" Bob said cheerily.

Jack inspected the microphone carefully in the light of the table lamp and was astonished to see tiny holes in the head of the nail to admit the sound. Shaking his head in amazement, Jack returned the ingenious bug to Bob. The latter nonchalantly held the nail-cum-microphone to the wall and pounded it back into the plaster with a convenient ashtray. Smiling with satisfaction, Green ceremonially rehung the picture and brushed his hands together as the sign of a job well done.

"Well, Jack, it's been a long day," Bob said with finality. "Let's get a drink!"

What little charm the Rossiya possessed was expressed in the bar and dining room in the basement. Tall, mustached bartenders stood at regular intervals behind a long, gleaming brass counter serving an eclectic mixture of drinks, ranging from American martinis on the rocks to neat shots of Russian vodka. As Bob and Jack approached, a rumpled man at the far end of the bar hailed them.

"Bob Green! How the hell are you! It sure has been a long time."

Bob smiled at the stranger in recognition and surreptitiously whispered to Jack.

"That's Len Goldstein of the *New York Times*. He must have gotten here early to try to dig up some background before the president arrives. Be careful. He'll pump you."

Jack nodded his understanding, and Bob strode down the long bar toward the reporter, returning his greeting.

"Hi, Len! Fancy meeting you here. What brings you to Moscow?"

Len Goldstein straightened himself up at the bar and moved down a couple of stools to make room for the new arrivals. He pumped Bob Green's hand vigorously and answered his facetious question in kind.

"Well, I was hanging around in New York not doing much, when I heard this rumor that a new traveling vaudeville team by the name of Leonard and Stratton, or was it Stratton and Leonard, was going to play a limited engagement in Moscow. So I thought, what the hell, the airlines need the money, and if I hang around the office, they'll think I'm not hustling."

Bob and Len thumped each other on the back, and Bob gestured toward Jack.

"Len, I'd like you to meet Jack Mason. Jack, this is Len Goldstein of the *New York Times*."

Jack extended his hand and paid the reporter a sincere compliment.

"Nice to meet you, Len. I've enjoyed reading a number of your articles. I take it you're here to cover the president."

"No, nothing like that," Goldstein responded with a broad smile. "I'm really here trying to negotiate the East Coast rights for *pepper vodka!*"

Bob and Jack laughed heartily, and Goldstein persisted.

"What'll you have, gentlemen? I've got a special on pepper vodka!"

"Sold!" said Bob enthusiastically. "And Jack will try one, too."

"Three Pertsovkas!" Goldstein shouted, first holding up three fingers and then pointing to the empty shot glass before them on the bar. The nearest bartender set up three new glasses and filled them to the brim with a clear brownish liquid from a bottle emblazoned with three red peppers. Len and Bob each grabbed a glass, and Bob handed the last one to Jack.

The two old hands held their shots high and clinked glasses in midair.

"To the summit!" said Goldstein enthusiastically.

"To the summit!" Bob Green repeated with a sly smile.

Jack had also raised his glass, but, before he could touch it to the others, Bob and Len tossed off their shots in a single gulp. They each exhaled audibly, and Jack's eyes widened.

"Down the hatch, Jack," Goldstein said jovially. "You've got to get in the swing of this international diplomacy."

Jack hesitated momentarily and then gulped the vodka down. Its first effect was what he had expected, a burning sensation in his throat reminiscent of a rapidly consumed vermouthless martini. But the taste that lingered was not the medicinal flavor of juniper berries; rather, it was the hot sting of Tabasco sauce. Jack gasped involuntarily and then exhaled a long breath as if attempting to expel the fire in his gullet. As Jack's eyes began to tear, Len Goldstein shook his head in mock discouragement.

"I guess you're telling me it won't be much of a hit on the Georgetown cocktail circuit."

28

The Greenhouse

A loud knocking on the door of his room awakened Jack Mason from a sound sleep. For one terrifying instant, he imagined that it was the KGB come to carry him off, but the rhythmic taps were repeated, and his bleary brain finally made the identification: Bob Green. Jack raised his left wrist to his face and peered molelike at his watch, but to no avail. Just enough light was filtering into the room around the heavy drapes drawn across the window to render the phosphorescent markings on the dial invisible, yet not enough to allow perception of the numbers themselves.

"Jack!" Bob shouted from the hall. "It's almost seven o'clock, and the first embassy bus leaves at eight. You'd better get moving if we're going to make it."

"Uh, thanks, Bob," Jack mumbled incoherently. "I'll, ah, meet you in the lobby in half an hour."

"What?" Green shouted back.

"I'll meet you in the lobby in half an hour," Jack repeated, raising his voice.

"Okay! I'll go and see if Goldstein is still in the bar!"

When Jack finally made it down to the sprawling lobby a good three quarters of an hour later, he had to search for several minutes before finding Bob Green in a corner reading *Izvestia*.

"Are you trying to pose as a local?" Jack inquired facetiously.

Bob lowered the paper and smiled.

"When I was stationed here, the standard Russian joke was: 'There's no news in *Izvestia* and no truth in *Pravda*!' So I'm just trying to get caught up and to see if anything has changed. So far, it looks like all the same old political steer excrement!"

Jack chuckled and sat down in the chair next to Bob's.

"Seriously, though," Green continued, "there is some interesting stuff in here. It's just hard to find. They have a couple of guys over at the embassy who read all the major papers every day and clip out the stuff they think is significant. They circulate Xerox copies of it around the embassy. I'll show you some of the daily issues when we get there. And later on, they translate the articles they think are important or that somebody asks for."

Jack nodded and then glanced at his watch and noticed that it was almost eight o'clock.

"Should we go outside and wait for the bus?" he inquired nervously.

"Yeah, might as well," Bob replied. "If there's a crowd and we're the last ones out, we might have to wait for the nine o'clock."

Bob rose and led the way across the lobby and through the main entrance. Once outside, they waited in the early morning sunlight with a knot of other Americans on the broad sidewalk in front of the Rossiya, and eventually a dilapidated bus of Russian manufacture pulled up opposite the group. Its only identifying marking was a dog-eared placard in a side window that proclaimed in English: "American Embassy Shuttle."

As they filed onto the bus, the driver halfheartedly asked for some form of American identification, a passport or a military ID card or the like. Jack wondered idly if the request was part of a *pro forma* effort to discourage KGB agents from riding the bus in the hope of picking up tidbits of information from unguarded conversations, or whether it was simply a bureaucratic attempt to prevent the Soviet nationals who worked at the embassy from getting a free ride across town. Bob and Jack took a seat together about halfway back on the side facing the river, and the bus soon was filled to capacity.

The short ride from the Rossiya to the American embassy was pleasant and uneventful. The bus moved away from the hotel along the broad Kremlyovskya Naberezhnaya between the south wall of the fortress and the Moskva River. It skirted the western wall as far as the Borovitsky Tower and then turned northwest, eventually reaching the embassy on Chaikovskovo Ulitsa.

When the bus stopped in front of the embassy, a more serious inspection occurred. A pair of burly, stone-faced men on the sidewalk eyed the stream of passengers alighting from the vehicle and filing through the gate. Ominously, the men appeared to Jack to be carbon copies of the heavies in Vincent O'Brien's film.

"Don't look like a defector," Bob Green quipped as they left their seat.

Jack smiled weakly for a second, but then strove to maintain a serious expression as he stepped off the bus and hurried through the embassy gate. Once past the first marine guards, Jack relaxed noticeably and began to smile again.

"They'll stop us in the lobby," Bob said from behind him. "We'll have to get fixed up with temporary badges, and then I'll show you around."

Bob Green began the tour of the American embassy on the upper floors. He showed Jack the ambassador's suite, the communications area, and the door to the secure conference room. They continued on to the reception and banquet areas below and were now in the cafeteria in the basement having a cup of coffee. Jack was surprised at how rapidly he had adjusted to the surroundings, probably because they differed so little from those in typical government office buildings in Washington.

"Well, old buddy," Bob Green inquired after they had sat for a while, "how do you like our home away from home?"

"Frankly, I'm surprised," Jack replied. "Somehow, I thought it would be different—more ornate or diplomatic or something."

"Yeah, I know what you mean," Bob agreed. "I felt that way myself the first time I came here. I don't know what I expected, but this isn't it."

Jack nodded and Bob pushed his chair back from the table.

"Well, old buddy, I've saved the best for last. Our space should be completed by now. They were still working on it when I was here six weeks ago, but the last message I got before we left said that everything is ready."

Jack felt growing excitement as they left the cafeteria and descended a flight of stairs to the subbasement. Bob led the way down a poorly lit corridor, which ended abruptly at a door protected by a cipher lock. Green manipulated the numbered switches in the box on the wall, but the characteristic buzz of the solenoid retracting the locking bolt failed to materialize.

"I guess they've changed the combination," Bob concluded as he reached for the buzzer that served to announce visitors.

Shortly the door opened, and they were greeted by the broad smile of Joe Cap.

"Hi, Bob! Glad to see you back. And Professor Mason! Welcome to the facility. Things must be heating up when the first team arrives."

Jack and Bob shook Joe's massive hand heartily. Jack felt reassured by his presence and manner. When Bob had first hired Joe as a bodyguard, Jack had called it unnecessary melodrama and had almost insisted on Joe's dismissal. But now, in the heart of Russia, haunted by the memory of Vincent O'Brien's movie, Jack was thankful that Bob had ignored his protests.

Once inside the outer door of the vault, they found themselves in a tiny anteroom, distinguished only by a second identical door and a one-way glass window with a hand-sized opening at the bottom.

"Pass your embassy badge through the hole, Professor," Joe Cap directed, "and the guard will exchange it for your project badge."

Jack followed the instructions, half expecting an unseen hand to grasp his as he slid the badge through the hole. He hastily withdrew his hand and, almost immediately, a pleasant female voice responded from a loudspeaker overhead.

"Good morning, Professor Mason. It's a pleasure to see you here."

Jack looked up toward the sound involuntarily and, when his gaze returned to the window, a Project-Psi badge bearing his likeness had appeared, as if by magic, on the small counter beneath the hole. As he took the badge, the ethereal voice continued.

"Please place the chain attached to the badge around your neck, Professor Mason, and keep the badge visible at all times while you are in the facility."

Bob Green and Joe Cap smiled with pride at the polite efficiency of their security system and exchanged their own badges.

Jack nodded his approval and decided to test how far they intended to carry the precautions.

"Do you have a badge for the president?" he inquired matter-of-factly.

"No," Bob responded with a chuckle, "but we're going to make Stratton wear one!"

Jack grinned broadly and again nodded his concurrence.

Once they had passed through the inner door, Joe Cap went about his business and Bob Green resumed his tour-guide role.

"As you remember from the plans, old buddy, we don't have too much space down here, and the computer and the isolated conference room ended up taking more room than we had expected. So some other things are pretty crowded, like the offices for key people like yourself and Jason and Secretary Stratton."

"That's no problem," Jack responded. "Jason and I are here to get the job done, and I suspect that the only time Stratton will come down here is to sit in the isolated conference room and hear what Jason has perceived."

Bob Green continued down the hall and opened a door on the left-hand side by manipulating a mechanical push-button lock.

"At least they haven't changed this one," he said with satisfaction. "Come on in; this is one side of the practice chair."

Jack found himself in a small room dominated by half of a two-person chair mounted against one wall. As they entered, a bearded young man, who was working intently on the display console over the chair, turned to greet them.

"Hi, Professor Mason. Glad to see you. I think we're just about ready for Jason."

"Hi, Stan," Jack responded. "I'm glad to hear it. Have you made any practice runs yet?"

"Yeah, Michael and Yuri made a couple of runs yesterday, and we ran them through the computer last night. From what I heard from Alice this morning, it sounds as though the equipment all functioned properly and Michael turned in some pretty good scores. If you want to hear more about where we stand, there's going to be a meeting in the greenhouse at one o'clock to discuss everyone's status."

"The greenhouse?" Jack repeated quizzically.

"Yeah," Bob Green responded. "That's what they call the isolated conference room. You'll understand when you see it."

Jack nodded skeptically, trying to visualize the design from the plans he had seen.

"Okay, Stan. Nice to see you again. I'll try to get to the meeting."

Bob and Jack reentered the hall, and Bob led the way, gesturing toward the next door.

"In there is the other side of the two-person chair. And here, across the way, is the debriefing room.

Bob opened the door across the hall, and they found Phyllis Jackson talking with a young women in a nurse's uniform. Phyllis smiled warmly and came toward them.

"Jack! I'm glad to see you. We've all been a little nervous waiting for you and Jason to arrive."

Jack clasped her outstretched hand and held it for a moment, and then, Phyllis turned back toward the nurse.

"Jack, this is Lieutenant Judy Pierson. She's an air-force nurse who will be assisting me at Jason's debriefings."

"It's a pleasure to meet you, Judy," Jack said, extending his hand. "You have a big responsibility helping Dr. Jackson with Jason. The pentothal debriefings always are where we get the best information."

"It's an honor to meet you, Professor Mason," the young officer responded. "I've heard so much about you since I joined the project. Everyone says that you're the man who invented the man with psi."

Jack glowed with the satisfaction that sincere flattery brings and was momentarily at a loss to reply.

"Don't butter him up too much, Judy," Bob Green interjected. "Or he'll be impossible to live with!"

They all smiled, and Jack regained his businesslike demeanor.

"Well, Phyllis, how do things look from the medical point of view? Are we ready to go?"

Phyllis Jackson nodded her pretty head affirmatively.

"Yes, I think we are. Or at least we will be by the time Jason arrives. I have a few remaining supplies coming in on tomorrow's courier flight, but other than that, the equipment and the people are all ready. We've scheduled a practice debriefing for tomorrow afternoon with one of the electronic technicians standing in, or I guess I should say lying in, for Jason."

"Sounds good," Jack said with a smile. "I never had any doubt that you'd be ready and well organized when the time came, Phyllis. But what I'm afraid to see is the computer room. I'll bet that Paul and his boys are pretty frantic right now."

The expression on Phyllis Jackson's face confirmed Jack's worst fears of the chaos he would find in the computer area.

"Come on, Bob!" Jack concluded emphatically. "Let's get out of here and let Phyllis and Judy get back to work. And what I want to do is find out where Rosenfeld stands with the computer."

They entered the hall again, and Bob gestured toward the door beyond the one leading to the second side of the two-person chair.

"The practice conference room is over here. Within the limits of the space we've got, it's laid out just like the one that Leonard and Sherkov will use in the Kremlin."

Bob opened the door and fumbled for the switch in the dark room. When the lights came on, Jack saw the end of a heavy conference table comically protruding from the far wall. There was only enough of it to allow three people to sit on either side in massive oak chairs. The table was covered with a green felt cloth, the floor was strewn with odd-sized Oriental rugs, and one wall was hung with incongruous dark red velvet draperies. All in all, it looked like a drawing-room set from a Victorian comedy.

"Where did you get this stuff?" Jack asked and chuckled.

"Oh, it's just some old junk the ambassador's wife wanted to get rid of," Bob responded cheerfully. "So I told her I'd get her a few bucks for it, and she was delighted to let me have it."

Jack smiled broadly and shook his head at this additional evidence of Bob's consummate skill at the midnight requisition.

"Well, enough of the show," Jack abruptly concluded. "Let's get down to that computer room and hear about the problems."

"Okay," Bob replied with an amused smile. "I just thought you'd like to save the laughs for last."

When they opened the door to the computer area, the scene was truly amazing to behold. Paul Rosenfeld and Ken Anderson were leaning on a table in the center of the room peering intently at a large electrical blueprint. Against one wall, a pair of programmers were frantically typing on input terminals. The displays on the television screens before them changed so rapidly that Jack found it hard to believe that they could comprehend the information.

Along another wall, an engineer and a technician appeared to be performing major surgery on one of the peripheral processors. Circuit boards were strewn on the floor around them and they were animatedly discussing the waveform displayed on a portable oscilloscope connected to the innards of the computer. In the far corner, another programmer stared, seemingly mesmerized, at the flying sheets of paper being ejected from the top of a high-speed printer. He appeared to be trying to read fragments of the results as the sheets arched up in the air and down into a stack behind the machine.

Jack and Bob entered unnoticed amid the din and approached Ken and Paul at the table. They stood and watched in silence for a moment, and then Jack announced their presence theatrically.

"I presume that you gentlemen have everything under control!"

The two shirtsleeved figures turned with a start and then smiled sheepishly.

"Hi, Jack. When did you get here?" Ken Anderson ventured weakly.

"We've, ah, got a little problem," Paul Rosenfeld chimed in. "But I think we've just about got it licked. It looks like one of the synchronizer boards was bad in the peripheral processor connected to the chair."

Anderson nodded his agreement, but the look on Jack's face clearly revealed that he remained unconvinced.

"Give us until this evening," Rosenfeld said, almost pleading. "And the whole place will look different."

"We've got some good results from Michael and Yuri," Ken Anderson offered enthusiastically, trying to change the subject.

"We're going to go over them in the greenhouse at two o'clock, after the status meeting. Why don't you join us?"

"Okay," Jack responded, with a smile. "Somehow I get the impression that you guys would rather we left you alone right now."

"Un, yeah," said Rosenfeld noncommitally, and he and Anderson both nodded.

"Okay," Jack agreed. "Come on, Bob, let's leave these mad geniuses to their work!"

The touring pair once again regained the hall, and Bob Green headed for the last door on the right.

"Well, this is the main attraction! The greenhouse that you've been hearing so much about."

The door to the room was secured by yet another cipher lock and a television camera peered down at them from the opposite wall. Bob pressed a button above the lock and spoke into a microphone recessed into the wall.

"This is Mr. Green with Professor Mason. I am about to open the outer door to the greenhouse. Please authenticate."

Bob manipulated the numbered switches in the box on the wall and, at the central guard desk, an unseen hand did the same, but with a different combination. Satisfied with their actions, an electronic circuit withdrew the bolt barring the door with the characteristic buzz.

Bob pulled the door open, and they stepped inside. The lights were on for the benefit of the television cameras, and Jack was immediately dazzled by the scene. Within the outer room, another complete interior chamber had been constructed. Its floor, walls, and ceiling were made entirely of transparent plexiglass that seemed suspended in space from the normal room around it. A set of plexiglass stairs led to yet another door through which one gained admittance to the inner sanctum.

Bob presented his main attraction with a ringmaster's flourish, and Jack shook his head in amazement.

"It looks like something out of *2001*! Or *Alice in Wonderland*!"

Bob grinned broadly, taking Jack's awe as a compliment.

"It's what you have to do if you want real security," he said proudly. "You'll notice that there's not a piece of metal or a wire anywhere. And we sweep it both visually and electromagnetically every day. There's just no place for a bug to be hidden."

Bob beamed with the true believer's enthusiasm, but Jack was still smiling and shaking his head with incredulity.

"As you can see," Bob continued, gesturing animatedly, "even the conference table and chairs are made of plexiglass. And everything that people carry in with them to a meeting is inspected by one of the guards—pads, pencils, briefcases, computer printouts."

"Perhaps you should make everyone take off their clothes," Jack injected with mock seriousness, visualizing a group of naked Thurberesque characters in animated conversation in the plexiglass showcase.

Bob stared at his boss, his brow furrowed for a moment, not knowing if Jack was kidding.

"Uh, I never thought of that. I wonder if they ever do that at headquarters?"

29

Sherkov's Plan

After politically successful stopovers in London and Paris, Richard Leonard and Thomas Stratton were airborne again on the final leg of their journey to Moscow. General Sam Ryan entered the presidential compartment through the forward bulkhead door with the latest report on *Air Force One*'s progress.

"Colonel Bronson tells me that we'll be landing in Moscow at four-ten P.M. local time. That's nine-ten in the morning back in Washington."

The president nodded his understanding.

"Thanks, Sam."

"The Russian navigator says we've got a straight-in descent and approach from way out here," Ryan continued. "They must have told every aircraft for miles around to get out of our way."

Richard Leonard beamed with self-importance, and Thomas Stratton smiled wryly.

"Well, Sam, a midair collision wouldn't be a very good way to start a summit conference."

The president snickered momentarily, but then addressed the secretary of state.

"Well, Thomas, this is it. The start of a week that will make history. And you and I are the ones who will make it."

"You are certainly right, Mr. President," Thomas Stratton concurred in sonorous tones. "The results that will flow from your achievements at this conference are destined to change the course of history. The arms race will be stemmed and, with it, the expansion of Soviet military power. And the world will recognize that all of this was achieved by your consummate skill as a summit negotiator."

Richard Leonard nodded his agreement with Thomas Stratton's flattery as if he considered it a mere statement of acknowledged fact. He then distractedly tossed away a crumb of royal largess.

"Uh, of course, I'll have some help from you and Jason."

The president stared pensively out of the window for a while and then continued with more emotion.

"And best of all, I'll put that bastard Sherkov in his place. I'll show him up in front of the world. For what he is—a big, bragging bully who'll cut and run when the going gets tough."

Richard Leonard turned to the window again, and Thomas Stratton decided not disturb his brooding. After a while, the president turned back to his secretary of state.

"I've got a duty to the world, you know, Thomas," he continued seriously, wagging his finger. "To keep it out of the hands of men like Sherkov. Men whose only motivation is power. Power over the people. Men who don't love freedom and democracy the way I do."

Richard Leonard ended his soliloquy in a firm voice tinged with patriotism, and Sam Ryan's chest swelled visibly with pride.

"If I may say so, Mr. President, that's what makes a military career like mine worthwhile. Serving a commander in chief like you! A man who is dedicated to the preservation of freedom and democracy, and is willing to stand up to those Russian bastards!"

The president looked at his chief of staff approvingly, and even Thomas Stratton nodded his agreement without visible sign of condescension. He felt like a coach in the locker room, before the big game, listening to his star player whip up the moral indignation that would justify their team's savage treatment of the opponents.

Colonel Al Bronson drew the throttles back gently, and *Air Force One* settled without a jolt onto runway 27 at the Shermetevo International Airport, north of Moscow. Bronson and his copilot, Lt. Col. Dan Gibbs, smiled at each other with professional pride. They had, in flying parlance, "greased it on." Since the runway was long and all the taxiways were clear, Bronson applied only a minimum of reverse thrust and wheel braking, slowing the presidential aircraft as smoothly as possible.

The Soviet Air Force navigator, who had joined them in Paris, was already speaking to ground control and confirmed in English that they were cleared to use the taxiway of their choice. As Bronson turned the big jet off the runway, a Russian version of a "follow-me" jeep raced up to lead them to the reviewing stand and the official reception party.

Richard Leonard swiveled nervously from side to side in his high-backed chair as the plane rumbled toward the waiting crowd of Soviet dignitaries. Sam Ryan stood, precariously maintaining his balance, overcoat already on, consulting a clipboard.

"You'll be the first one off, of course, Mr. President. Followed by Secretary Stratton, Jack Stewart, the interpreter, and myself. When you step out onto the boarding platform, a Russian band will strike up 'Hail to the Chief.' The Russian welcoming party will wait at the foot of the boarding stairs, so you can stand at the top and wave at the crowd until the band finishes playing if you like."

Richard Leonard smiled, warmed by the thought of the coming welcome. Nevertheless, he continued nervously turning the pages of his arrival speech like a quarterback searching the playbook for a last-minute inspiration.

"You're sure, Thomas, that there won't be any surprises in Sokolov's speech?" the president queried the secretary of state.

"As certain as I am of anything concerning the Russians, Mr. President. He's an old man, even by the standards of the Soviet leadership. And they've been slowly downgrading his responsibilities over the last few years. Essentially he's been reduced to ceremonial functions. We've even had a report from a deep-penetrating agent that he might be dropped from the Politburo."

"Well, you'd better be right!" Richard Leonard grumbled. "The last thing I want to hear is some kind of bombshell from a ceremonial president."

Thomas Stratton smiled at his fighter's nervousness and nodded his agreement.

"I understand how you feel, Mr. President," the secretary of state replied sympathetically.

338

"You know, Thomas, you've made this arrival speech of mine pretty bland," the president continued in a quarrelsome tone. "I think perhaps I should take the gloves off and rough them up a little. Just to remind them of who they're up against!"

A cold shudder flashed through Thomas Stratton, but his outward demeanor did not reveal it. Would Richard Leonard's lust for battle permaturely disclose the trap they intended to spring?

"You could do that, Mr. President," the secretary of state responded evenly. "But don't you think that there will be more shock effect if you save all your surprises for the opening session with Sherkov?"

The trainer knew his fighter well, and Richard Leonard responded as Thomas Stratton thought he would.

"Yeah, hit him with the Sunday punch out of the blue—when he's least expecting it. Yeah, why give him any warning."

The initial hand-shaking and anthem-playing over, Aleksandr Sokolov, the aging president of the Soviet Union, stepped forward to the microphones and slowly began to read a prepared speech. He paused at the end of each long phrase or sentence, and his translator repeated the thought in English.

"It brings to me the greatest pleasure, Mr. President, to welcome you to the Union of Soviet Socialist Republics. You have come here to Moscow, at the invitation of General Secretary Sherkov, for discussions at the highest level in the cause of world peace. As you are well aware, Mr. President, lasting world peace can only be the fruit of general and complete disarmament, a step that representatives of the Soviet Union have consistently and repeatedly advocated in world forums."

Thomas Stratton beamed cherubically as old Sokolov laboriously read his speech. Richard Leonard's expression, however, slowly but surely turned to stone.

Who does that old fart think he is, the president fumed to himself. *Telling me that I came here because that bastard Sherkov invited me. And lecturing me on the path to world peace, the man who's going to go down in history as the greatest fighter for peace.*

339

Thomas Stratton anxiously monitored the president's expression with furtive sidewise glances, and, as the speech continued, the grim set of Richard Leonard's jaw intensified. Unaware of his guest's rising ire, Aleksandr Sokolov continued to read the words the Politburo had prepared for him.

"I bring to you also, Mr. President, the greetings of the great people of the Soviet Republics, people who have withstood the worst ravages war can bring and have emerged victorious, people who yearn for a world at peace and free from exploitation. I know, Mr. President, that the great American people share these dreams of a world free from weapons of mass destruction in which all peoples can pursue their legitimate desires and ambitions. The eyes of the world are on this summit meeting, Mr. President. If the United States will join the Soviet Union in rejecting the use of weapons of mass destruction and advocating general and complete disarmament, this conference of the leaders of the globe's two superpowers truly will have advanced the cause of world peace."

Aleksandr Sokolov stepped back a pace from the microphones, and, on cue, the Soviet dignitaries on the platform began to clap vigorously. Thomas Stratton joined them perfunctorily, but Richard Leonard remained grim-faced, his hands at his sides. As the crowd of lesser officials below the dais took up the applause, the secretary of state nudged the president discreetly. The latter glared back for an instant and then began to clap halfheartedly.

As Sokolov retreated to his place in the uniformly attired line of senior Soviet leaders at the rear of the platform, Thomas Stratton leaned toward Robert Leonard and whispered last-minute advice to his fighter.

"Save your Sunday punch for Sherkov, Mr. President."

Richard Leonard scowled back at the secretary of state, but his expression instantly turned to a smile when Sam Ryan indicated that he should step forward to the microphones. Ryan and the translator followed and took up positions on either side of the president, a respectful half-step behind. Richard Leonard swept his gaze majestically across the scene, surveying the crowd with a broad smile. Finally, much to Thomas Stratton's relief, the president withdrew the prepared speech from his pocket and, when the preliminary applause had terminated, began to speak in a firm voice.

"Thank you, Mr. President, for your generous welcome to the Soviet Union."

Richard Leonard hesitated, unsure if he should continue or pause for the interpreter. Fortunately, the latter detected his cue and began the prepared translation.

"*Spasebo, gospodin* (Mr. President). . . ."

When Jack Stewart had finished delivering the first sentence in Russian, the president began again, and from then on, they remained in reasonable synchronism.

"I have come here to the Soviet Union as the culmination of my efforts to achieve world peace through stable international order. As I said a year ago at the United Nations, the three prerequisites to world peace are free peoples, stable governments, and an end to the arms race. I come to this summit conference with the fervent hope that we, the leaders of the two great superpowers, can agree to a lessening of tension and subversion throughout the world and to significant reductions in both conventional and nuclear armaments. I can assure you, Mr. President, that the prayers of the American people are with us as we begin this historic enterprise. If we put aside slogans and parochial interests and join hands in the search for lasting international order, history will long remember this summit conference as the turning point away from armed confrontation toward stable and lasting world peace."

Thomas Stratton had been smiling broadly as the president delivered the words he had written. Now he vigorously led the applause as Richard Leonard beamed with self-satisfaction and again royally surveyed the crowd.

Throughout the welcoming ceremony, Jason Star stood anonymously in the cluster of American officials behind the president and the secretary of state. He strained continually for psi perceptions, closing his eyes briefly from time to time to aid his concentrations. Despite this intense effort, the man with psi received no clearly understandable signals from the stone-faced line of Soviet leaders. The cold fear of impotence began to spread

341

over Jason as he desperately tried to capture the fleeting Russian thoughts that had been darting in and out of his consciousness.

. . . day glorious . . . speeches ceremonial . . . great triumph . . . only now . . . president puppet . . . unaware plan Sherkov . . . American . . . Stratton . . . strings . . . first time seen . . .

Jason Star shook his head in bewilderment as he frantically tried to arrange the jumble of words and phrases into meaningful thoughts. He soon despaired of this hopeless task and contented himself with attempting to memorize the sequence:

. . . day glorious . . . speeches ceremonial . . . great triumph . . . president puppet . . .

No, Jason thought and stopped himself. *Something came before . . . great triumph . . . only now . . . president puppet . . . unaware plan Sherkov . . .*

30

The President's Bombshell

The opening day of the summit conference began with the reserved formality that one would expect from a Soviet government still mightily concerned with its image. At precisely nine-thirty, a line of black Zhil limousines pulled up in front of the grand old National Hotel, where the president and the secretary of state were staying. Chauffeurs alighted and stood almost at attention while uniformed police and KGB and Secret Service agents in plainclothes scurried everywhere.

The president viewed the hectic scene through the ornate windows of his room and, on seeing a crowd developing in Gorkovo Ulitsa below, decided to open the French doors and step out onto the balcony to acknowledge the attention. Secret Service agents hustled to precede him and used their walkie-talkies to notify associates in the street below of the president's intentions.

Richard Leonard reveled in the frantic activity his merest whim could generate, and stepped out onto the balcony to find agents peering frantically up and down lest ethereal assassins be lurking in the nooks and crannies of the prerevolutionary facade. The president beamed broadly at the people assembled below and raised his arms as if bestowing a papal blessing. The crowd responded with a riffle of applause and began to spill into the street. They were hastily restrained by uniformed policemen who clasped hands and marched slowly into the spectators. The crowd was swept back onto the sidewalk like flotsam thrown up the beach by a breaking wave. When the human swell of policemen retreated, the street, like the beach, was left smooth and clean behind.

The president continued smiling, marveling at the efficiency of Soviet crowd control and mentally contrasting it with the chaos that usually existed during his own campaign travels. *Why,* he thought rhetorically, *are the American people so reluctant to accept the most elementary and sensible measures for controlling their activities in the presence of their leader?*

"Mr. President," said the voice of Thomas Stratton behind him. "It's almost quarter of ten. You had better leave now if you don't want to keep Sherkov waiting."

Richard Leonard turned to face his secretary of state and scowled with annoyance.

"I'm meeting with the Russian people right now, Thomas. And that dictator, Sherkov, can damn well wait!"

Again all smiles, the president returned to the edge of the balcony and waved again to the crowd. Thomas Stratton retreated inside the room and conferred hastily with one of his aides. They would notify the Russians that the president was reading some last-minute messages from Washington and would not arrive at the Kremlin until ten-thirty. Although one could walk from the hotel to the Council of Ministers Building in the Kremlin in less than fifteen minutes, the trip by official motorcade across Red Square past the Lenin Mausoleum and through the Spassky Tower gate would undoubtedly take longer.

At a little before eleven o'clock, the American delegation filed somberly into the summit conference room behind Richard Leonard. Their Russian counterparts were already in place, standing behind the chairs they were assigned to occupy.

The president of the United States strode to the end of the long table and extended his hand to the general secretary of the Communist Party of the Union of Soviet Socialist Republics.

"It is a pleasure for me to be here, Mr. General Secretary. I believe that we can accomplish a great deal in the cause of world peace at this meeting."

At his shoulder, the president's translator repeated the greeting in Russian.

The Soviet leaders arrayed down the table smiled in unison like the friendly-appearing troop of bears in the old Moscow circus. Vasily Vasilyevich Sherkov returned Richard Leonard's greeting in Russian, and then clasped the president's hand in one of his and grasped his shoulder with the other.

A spurt of adrenalin coursed through Richard Leonard's veins, and he squeezed the massive Russian hand with all the strength he could muster, intent on avoiding defeat at this first impromptu round of summit confrontation.

Vasily Sherkov's grip also tightened for a moment, but then relaxed as his face broke into a broad smile. Sherkov spoke again in Russian, and his translator quickly conveyed the sentiment.

"Russians believe that a man's handshake is a measure of his character. If the saying is true, you and I should have no difficulty."

Richard Leonard bravely returned the smile, but his heart was still pounding. Much to his relief, Sherkov motioned expansively for all to be seated.

Jason Star was struck by how much the summit conference room resembled the pictures he had been shown in Washington. A long, massive table covered with a green felt cloth dominated the room. The Russian and American delegations sat on opposite sides of the table with their leaders at its head and lesser officials arranged in descending order toward the foot. The man with psi had been instructed to stay constantly at Thomas Stratton's side when they were in public to make plausible his seating among the leaders at the conference table, far above the station justified by David Brentwood's official position at the State Department.

Jason studied the men on the Soviet side of the table intently. Next to Vasily Sherkov was the translator, a thin man by the name of Volenchek, whose sad expression belied his consummate skill. Volenchek had a reputation for being able to translate unerringly, not only the thoughts his principal had expressed but the tone and emotion with which they had been delivered. Next to Volenchek was Vladimir Gersky, the Soviet foreign minister. Gersky would be a fine target for Jason's concentration. *So this is the man that Ambassador Basov thinks is a fool,* Jason thought, *along with Thomas Stratton,* he remembered with amusement.

Alongside Vladimir Gersky was a man whom Jason had seen before close up only in photographs—Georgi Bondarenko. A much-decorated artillery colonel during World War II, Bondarenko had risen slowly but surely through the Soviet hierarchy to the position of premier. He was widely believed to represent the more concervative members of the Politburo who viewed with skepticism Vasily Sherkov's pursuit of detente with the West. Jason decided to concentrate on Bondarenko when and if Sherkov made any conciliatory statements. Any psi impressions of dissension within the Soviet hierarchy would be of inestimable value to the president and the secretary of state in planning their strategy.

Because Georgi Bondarenko was seated directly across from Jason Star, his was the closest Russian brain to the electrochemical circuits in Jason's cerebrum that detected psi signals. Slightly farther away were the brains of Vladimir Gersky and Ivan Basov, who flanked the Soviet premier. Still more distant, separated from Gersky by the translator, was the most important brain in the room to the man with psi, that of Vasily Vasilyevich Sherkov, the undisputed leader of the Soviet Union.

Jason considered what tactics he might employ to bring his own brain closer to Sherkov's. He could certainly move toward Thomas Stratton in the posture of a dutiful and concerned aide, but that would bring him only slightly closer to Vasily Sherkov. Somewhat better would be to lean diagonally forward on the table toward the Soviet leader. While this posture might conceivably pass as that of an overzealous junior official intent on understanding Sherkov's every phrase, it would almost certainly attract undesirable attention to David Brentwood. In the end, Jason decided to sit demurely in his place until he determined whether psi signals were few and far between or many in a mad jumble.

When the delegations had made themselves comfortable and the minor functionaries had left the room, Vasily Sherkov ceremonially opened a leather-covered notebook that had been placed before him. In preliminary negotiations, the Russian and American staffs had agreed that the meeting would begin with each leader making an opening statement. The subject matter and the duration were, of course, left to the discretion of the principals. As the host, the general secretary would speak first.

Sherkov appeared to read the first page of his prepared statement, turned to the second page and scanned it briefly, and then silently shut the notebook. He waited with a beneficent look until all eyes were focused on him and then began extemporaneously. The Russian leader spoke in rambling sentences; his translator scribbled frantically. At length the general secretary paused for breath and a sip of mineral water, and, much to Jason's surprise, Volenchek began the translation without hesitation.

"It brings to me great pleasure to welcome you to Moscow, Mr. President, for this historic summit conference between the leaders of the two most powerful nations the world has ever known. The military strength that each of our countries possesses exceeds that of all the armies history has ever recorded. With my own eyes, I have seen the destruction that total war can bring. The valiant Red Army, aided by the indomitable Russian people, defeated the advancing Fascist hordes at the very gates of this city, only a quarter of a century ago."

Vasily Sherkov nodded his agreement as Volenchek spoke, and, when the translator had finished, the general secretary continued his off-the-cuff introduction.

"*Ya i ostal'nye* (I and the others) . . .*"

As before, Volenchek wrote on his pad madly, but soon he was speaking again as if the text had been prepared in advance.

"I and the others whose solemn duty it is to lead the Soviet Union today will never forget the sacrifices made by the great Russian people to defeat the Hitler armies. Never again will we allow another nation to amass such military superiority that the heartland of Mother Russia is threatened."

Jason Star stared intently at Vasily Sherkov, galvanized as much by the Soviet leader's words as by his own intense desire to receive psi signals. Jason's concentration was only slightly distracted when the translator began again.

"You, Mr. President, and even the great American people, may find Russian concern about the security of our vast and mighty country difficult to understand. Not since your own revolution, more than two hundred years ago, have the people of the United States faced a threat to their homes and families. Your men have died in war, but always in foreign lands and often in the service of imperialism. In sharp contrast, the great Red Army has always fought on the soil of Mother Russia in defense of the glorious ideals on the October Revolution!"

Volenchek delivered the translation with the fervor of a fundamentalist preacher urging his sinful parishioners to renounce the pleasures of the devil and be born again. He appeared genuinely drained after each burst of speaking and immediately returned to frantic scribbling when Vasily Sherkov resumed his diatribe. But, when his next turn to speak came, Volenchek again metamorphosed into the Russian equivalent of Billy Graham.

"The Soviet Union finds itself today encircled by heavily armed hostile powers. The villianous Germans and the rest of the NATO clique to the west and the devious Chinese revisionists to the south. And over all of this hangs the deadly umbrella of the thousands of American nuclear weapons that are indiscriminately deployed around the world. This is the background, Mr. President, against which we meet here today in a solemn attempt to further the cause of world peace through a start along the road to general and complete disarmament."

While Volenchek was speaking, the general secretary opened the leather notebook before him and began turning the pages, apparently trying to find the appropriate place in his prepared text. Thomas Stratton looked at Vasily Sherkov impassively while trying to assess Richard Leonard's reactions out of the corner of his eye. The president's face also betrayed no emotion, the result of his long experience as a poker player. Nevertheless, the secretary of state judged that his chief's ire was rising, and he hoped that the president could contain his anger until Sherkov's rambling monologue was completed.

Vasily Sherkov apparently found his place in the opening statement he had prepared in consultation with the Politburo, and, when the translator had finished, the general secretary resumed in a less emotional tone.

Volenchek's face mirrored his principal's change in mood and when he began speaking again, it was with the cold, clipped voice of a professional diplomat.

"The challenge before us today, Mr. President, is to take significant first steps toward the ultimate goal of general and complete disarmament. The Soviet Union has long advocated such measures, both in world forums such as the United Nations and in numerous bilateral discussions between the representatives of our countries. But, in the past, the forces of reaction and imperialism in the world have paid only lip service to our sincere desires for peace. The Soviet Union still finds itself encircled by hostile armies, and the United States remains the chief perpetrator of this threat. Your troops and tanks and planes are deployed in dozens of supposedly sovereign nations around the world for the sole purpose of threatening the security of the great Union of Soviet Socialist Republics. And, most dangerous of all, thousands of American nuclear weapons not only are stockpiled within your own borders but recklessly are scattered around the globe, often in the hands of fascist dictators, threatening the security of peace-loving peoples everywhere."

Thomas Stratton could see Richard Leonard gritting his teeth. *Only a little longer, Mr. President,* the secretary of state said to himself. *Hold your aces a little longer. Let the sucker raise his bet, and the pot will be all the sweeter when you finally rake it in.*

Richard Leonard glared at Vasily Sherkov with steely eyes through narrowed lids as the Soviet leader continued his prepared diatribe.

When his turn next came, Volenchek's tone changed again, this time to one of scarcely concealed hostility.

"Therefore, Mr. President, the central question that confronts us today is whether or not the United States and the forces of imperialism and reaction it leads are willing to discuss and subsequently to agree to comprehensive and balanced reductions in armed forces and weapons of all kinds and, most particularly, to lessening and eventual elimination of the American nuclear weapon threat that is spread around the globe. If you have come here to Moscow, Mr. President, sincerely ready to discuss these issues and to make agreements concerning them, you will find us, the leaders of the great Soviet Union, ready to engage in fruitful negotiation. If, on the other hand, through serious misjudgment of the will of the people of the Soviet Republics, you have come here seeking some unilateral advantage that will temporarily maintain the position of the forces of imperialism and reaction against the inevitable tide of

Marxism-Leninism, you will find us intransigent in our commitment to the security of the Soviet Union and steadfast in our struggle to free the enslaved peoples of the world."

Vasily Sherkov impassively nodded his massive head up and down as Volenchek spoke. When the translator had finished, the general secretary closed the leather-covered notebook with an air of finality and looked coldly at the president with the defiant expression of a man who has raised the limit and has the cards to back his bet.

The tension in the room was electric. The stares of all the senior officials slowly shifted from Vasily Sherkov to Richard Leonard, and at the foot of the table some American aides, unable to stand the tension, reached compulsively for glasses of mineral water.

The president relished the attention galvanized on him. Richard Leonard gave neither a hint of his reaction to Vasily Sherkov's challenge nor any indication that he, himself, was ready to speak.

More than a minute passed in silence before the Soviet foreign minister leaned across the table and spoke to the American secretary of state in English.

"The general secretary has concluded his opening remarks. Does the president wish to make a statement at this time?"

Thomas Stratton was pleased. The Russian side had blinked first. Stratton looked at Gersky quizzically as if his inquiry had no meaning.

Richard Leonard watched the exchange with satisfaction, but still he showed no outward sign of interest. The president allowed the silence to continue for more than another minute, all the time staring directly at Vasily Sherkov. Finally, Richard Leonard reached inside his suit coat and withdrew a folded set of notes on yellow legal paper. Ceremonially, the president unfolded the sheets and consulted them intently—still without speaking.

As the tension built, Jason Star concentrated solely on Vasily Sherkov. A jumbled torrent of Russian words cascaded through his brain. They came and went so fleetingly that Jason could not be certain which were psi signals and which his own thoughts.

. . . speak . . . hate . . . president . . . challenge . . . no . . . Gersky . . . tension . . . Leonard . . . Russia . . . speak . . . trap . . .

The spell finally was broken as Richard Leonard began speaking slowly and clearly in an almost Shakespearean voice.

"I have come to this summit conference for the express purpose of challenging the leaders of the Soviet Union to replace their endless words with concrete agreements and actions to achieve general and complete disarmament."

The president paused to allow Jack Stewart to translate his opening salvo, but continued to look directly at Vasily Sherkov. The Soviet leader returned the stare without sign of emotion as Stewart spoke.

Vladimir Gersky, however, revealed his evident surprise by moving forward in his chair as if to pay more careful attention. Jason sensed Gersky's anxiety and leaned forward also, toward the Soviet foreign minister. The Russian words came in a torrent again, but this time Jason had little doubt that they were psi signals and Gersky was the source.

. . . trap . . . Stratton trap . . . objective . . . Sherkov . . . angry . . . Basov . . . evil . . . Stratton . . .

When Colonel Stewart finished his translation, the president again remained silent for a moment allowing the tension to reach a new plateau. But when he sensed that the general secretary was about to respond, Richard Leonard began to speak again, in a theatrical tone.

"I come to this summit meeting with the firm conviction that every Soviet and American weapon, soldier, base, and alliance is a proper subject for negotiation."

Richard Leonard paused momentarily, surveyed the wide-eyed delegations with an icy stare, and then continued in a half shout.

"Lest there be any misunderstanding, I repeat! The United States stands ready to negotiate here and now, at this summit conference, the reduction or elimination of every kind of American and Russian weapon! Tanks are negotiable and should be reduced or eliminated! Planes are negotiable and should be reduced or eliminated! Ships are negotiable and should be reduced or eliminated! And, most important of all, nuclear weapons are negotiable and should be reduced or eliminated!"

The president paused again for Jack Stewart's translation, but the shocked faces of the Soviet leaders revealed that they had understood the English well enough. Richard Leonard eyed Vasily Sherkov with the slightest hint of a grin, like the man who has checked and then raised in a no-limit, winner-take-all game.

Emulating Volenchek, his Soviet counterpart, Jack Stewart did his best to convey the firm conviction and evangelical fervor of the president's delivery.

Vasily Sherkov sat back in his chair as the translation proceeded, and his face gradually turned to stone. Vladimir Gersky turned to eye his chief, but, on seeing Sherkov's expression, hastily faced forward again and stared intently at Thomas Stratton.

Caught up in the tension, Jason Star unconsciously leaned forward toward the Soviet side of the table, straining to clarify the jumble of psi signals that flashed through his brain.

... Leonard ... bastard ... bluff ... fool ... Sherkov ... destroy ... Stratton ... plan ... attack ... leave ... bastard ... shock ...

The lesser members of both delegations stared in disbelief at the leaders at the head of the table. The heads of state of the two most powerful nations on earth glared hostilely at each other like a pair of giant sumo wrestlers, each eyeing his opponent for the instant of inattention that would allow a lightning grab and a winning throw.

Finally, Vasily Sherkov made the slightest move as if preparing to push back his chair and rise from the table. Richard Leonard detected his oponent's twitch, sensed its meaning, and began speaking again before the general secretary could make his move.

"The American delegation is prepared to begin substantive negotiations concerning the reduction or elimination of all types of weapons immediately after these opening statements are completed. If the Soviet Union is genuinely interested in general and complete disarmament, I urge you and your delegation, Mr. General Secretary, to join us in hammering out specific steps to achieve this goal!"

Richard Leonard paused theatrically for translation and then removed two folded sheets of paper with a flourish, from his suit coat. The president ceremonially flattened the sheets on the table, and then dramatically placed one of them in front of Vasily Sherkov and began to read from the other.

Issues for Summit Negotiation

1. Demilitarization of Europe and the Mediterranean
2. Freedom of movement between Eastern
     and Western Europe
3. Arms embargo of the Middle East and Africa
4. Total ban on nuclear testing
5. Destruction of land-based missiles
6. Destruction of missile submarines
7. Destruction of strategic bombers
8. Phased reduction of standing armies
9. . . . .
10. . . . .

The president completed his reading in a triumphant voice and then sat back with hands folded, assessing the Soviet reaction. Jack Stewart began the translation, but Vasily Sherkov suddenly stood and glared across the table at Richard Leonard.

The giant conference room instantly fell silent and, after a moment of projecting the most intense hatred, the general secretary abruptly turned and strode away. The Soviet delegation hastily stood also and, amid some confusion, dutifully filed out following Foreign Minister Gersky.

When the Russian leaders had left the room, Richard Leonard smiled broadly and motioned to the American delegation to relax. He took a glass of mineral water and held it high in a mock toast. Several lesser officials at the far end of the table returned the president's salute, and a feeling of triumph spread through the Americans.

In sharp contrast, the faces of the remaining Soviet functionaries betrayed bewilderment verging on panic. Most of them also scurried from the scene, but a few chunky KGB security men stood grim-faced at the doors and in the corners of the room.

The president leaned toward his secretary of state and prepared to whisper a confidence. But, before he could speak, Thomas Stratton raised a finger silently to his lips and then pointed discreetly under the table. Richard Leonard nodded his understanding and began to scribble a note on the yellow legal pad before him. Thomas Stratton mentally despaired of communicating to his chief in time that the room probably was equipped with cameras as well as microphones.

The president finished his note with a flourish and handed it triumphantly to his secretary of state. Thomas Stratton held the yellow sheet close to his chest and tried to read the words without exposing them to view.

> We've got Sherkov on the run!
> I told you he's all bluff!
> I'll bet that Jason confirms it!

The sight of the name Jason scrawled in the president's handwriting sent a cold chill coursing through Thomas Stratton. He folded the sheet in half, and then in half again and again, and finally inserted it into the inside pocket of his vest. Seeing that the president again was about to speak, Stratton rose and addressed his chief innocuously in a stage whisper.

"Excellent statement, Mr. President. You have certainly set the direction for these negotiations."

The president looked up at his secretary of state with a quizzical expression, but at last realized that Stratton was speaking for Soviet consumption.

"Thank you, Thomas," Richard Leonard finally responded, in the uncertain tone of a forgetful actor who has at last understood the prompter's mouthings. "As you know, I always try to say what is on my mind."

The two men looked at each other foolishly for several moments, each hoping the other would ad-lib a clever line, and Thomas Stratton was secretly relieved when Ivan Basov reentered the room. The ambassador approached the president and the secretary of state and addressed Richard Leonard in a conciliatory tone.

"Please accept my most humble apologies, Mr. President. The general secretary has been called away unexpectedly on a matter of the highest importance to the Soviet Union. He has asked me to suggest to you that the meeting be adjourned until the dinner he is giving in your honor this evening."

Richard Leonard smiled benignly at the obvious lie and nodded his acquiescence.

"Certainly, Mr. Ambassador. We couldn't have Mr. Sherkov neglecting important matters, could we?"

Ivan Basov nodded his head dolefully.

"May I escort you to your car, Mr. President?"

Richard Leonard again smiled broadly and continued his sham politeness.

"Why, thank you, Mr. Ambassador. That's kind of you. This place is so large that I might have gotten lost."

Ivan Basov nodded solemnly again and then turned on his heel to lead the way.

The president surveyed his entourage at the table and grinned broadly, savoring his victory. Richard Leonard gave the classic thumbs-up sign and then rose and motioned for his aides to follow.

From the corners of the room, the stone-faced KGB men stared at the aftermath of their supreme leader's rout on his home ground in silent disbelief.

31

"I Will Crush Him"

Phyllis Jackson peered down at the prostrate form of Jason Star. The man with psi was lying on a small operating table in the center of the debriefing room in the vault in the subbasement of the American embassy. Paul Berman consulted oscilloscope traces of electrical signals from Jason's heart and brain and then nodded affirmatively, indicating that his patient was properly stabilized in a pentothal trance.

"Can you hear me, Jason?" Phyllis Jackson inquired.

The voice seemed far away, and the man with psi struggled to identify his circumstances.

"Is that you, Phyllis? Am I safe now? They were chasing me."

"You're safe with us in the embassy, Jason. No one was chasing you. You must have been dreaming."

The supine figure smiled weakly.

"Thank you, Phyllis. That makes me feel better."

Dr. Jackson picked up a clipboard, consulted the top sheet briefly, and then again leaned over the man with psi.

"Let's start at the very beginning of the summit meeting, Jason. What were the first psi signals you received?"

The groggy head on the table shook slowly from side to side.

"Not sure, Phyllis. Everything such a jumble. Russian words flying through the air."

"Just relax, Jason," Phyllis Jackson continued soothingly. "We have plenty of time. Think back to the beginning of the meeting. You all filed into the room behind the president. And he and Sherkov shook hands. And then you all sat down. Did you get any psi signals up to that point?"

Jason Star looked up at her imploringly, like a child desirous of pleasing its mother, but his mind was blank. The first waves of panic had begun to break over him when Jason was suddenly reprieved by the image of Sherkov and Leonard locked in a wrestler's handshake. Instantly his mind returned to the ornate conference room in the Council of Ministers Building, and the psi signals he had received began to appear from the shadows like reluctant actors in a play. Jason's mouth opened and he slowly began to speak.

" . . . weak . . . Leonard weak . . . strong . . . crush him."

"Very good, Jason," Phyllis responded cheerfully. "You've remembered very clearly. Please repeat the words again."

"Leonard weak . . . strong . . . I am strong . . . I crush him."

"Excellent, Jason. Now, what came next?"

Jason Star's eyes rolled as if he were searching for another image to refresh his memory. Phyllis Jackson waited another moment and then tried to prompt him again.

"You all sat down and General Secretary Sherkov began to speak. Did you get any psi signals while he was speaking?"

Jason nodded his head slightly up and down without lifting it from the pillow and then began to speak hesitantly.

". . . Stalingrad . . . many die . . . never again . . . Red Army . . . almost defeated . . . Sherkov strong . . . never again."

Bob Green slipped into the debriefing room, tapped Jack Mason on the shoulder, and began to speak to his boss in a whisper.

"Stratton is calling you from upstairs on the secure phone. He must want to know how the debriefing is going."

Jack silently nodded his understanding and then slipped from the room with Bob following. They made their way to Jack's tiny office, and he picked up the black handset of the secure telephone.

"Mason speaking."

"Please hold for the secretary of state, Professor Mason," a male secretary's voice responded.

Jack nodded his agreement but did not answer. After about a half a minute, a familiar voice boomed in his ear.

"Well, Professor? How is Jason doing?"

"They've just started the debriefing, Mr. Secretary," Jack replied. "So far, it's going pretty well. Jason seems to have received quite a few psi signals from Sherkov."

"Excellent, Professor. Truly excellent! What did he find out?"

"I didn't take any notes," Jack demurred, "but I'll try to reconstruct what he said for you the best I can remember."

"Good. You do that," Thomas Stratton persisted. "Tell me what Jason said."

"Well, at the very beginning of the meeting, when they all filed into the room behind you and the president, and the president and Sherkov shook hands—"

"Yes, Professor, yes!" Thomas Stratton broke in with exasperation. "I was there! What was Sherkov thinking?"

"Jason got a signal something like this," Jack responded hesitantly. "Leonard is weak. I am strong. I will crush him."

"Mmm, are you sure those were the words?"

"Not absolutely certain, Mr. Secretary. But that was the gist of it."

"All right, Professor," Thomas Stratton concluded. "Thank you. I want to see a transcript of the debriefing as soon as possible. We've got to get ready for the state dinner this evening."

"Yes, Mr. Secretary. It's two o'clock now, and we're shooting to have a transcript ready for review in the greenhouse by four."

"I'll be down at three-thirty. And you have that transcript ready!"

Thomas Stratton hung up the secure telephone abruptly, and a loud rushing noise blasted in Jack's ear. He instinctively jerked the receiver away from his head and slammed it down with annoyance.

"Damn that bastard, Stratton! He always hangs up the secure when you least expect it and gives you a big blast in the ear."

Bob Green nodded his understanding and grinned broadly.

"He figures that no one would dare do it to him, especially if he does it first!"

It was three-fifteen, and the secretaries still had not finished typing the transcript. Jack Mason eyed his watch nervously and was about to bug them for the third or fourth time, when Bob Green appeared at the door to his office and motioned for him to follow.

"We'd better get down to the greenhouse before Stratton does. That way we can b.s. with him while they finish the typing."

Jack nodded his agreement with Bob's ploy and followed him down the hall. When they reached the entrance to the greenhouse, they found a guard posted at the outer door.

"Let me see who you've got on the list for the meeting at fifteen-thirty," Bob said, taking the guard's clipboard. He read the list out loud for Jack's convenience.

"Mason, Green, Star, Jackson, Andromov, Stratton. Is there anyone else you want, Jack?"

"No, that list sounds okay to me," Jack responded. "We want to keep the group as small as possible."

Bob handed the clipboard back to the guard and then instructed him with uncharacteristic seriousness.

"You be certain that only the people whose names are on this list are allowed inside."

"Absolutely, sir," the guard responded emphatically. "Those are my orders."

"And be sure that they all are wearing their badges," Bob admonished. "Even Secretary Stratton!"

"Yes, sir," the guard replied, almost coming to attention. "I'll make sure that the secretary of state has his badge."

"And be sure that no one brings anything into the greenhouse with him," Bob continued. "No briefcases or papers or envelopes or anything like that."

"Yes, sir, Mr. Green," the guard nodded. "You can count on me to enforce the rules."

At last, Bob Green allowed himself to smile. "I knew I could. Now, if you'll please let us into the greenhouse?"

"Just as soon as I verify it with the main desk," the guard said, and then he pushed the button below a speaker grill on the wall.

"Main guard desk? This is Bratkowski at the greenhouse. Request permission to admit Professor Mason and Mr. Green."

"Permission granted," said a garbled voice from the loudspeaker.

The guard manipulated the buttons in the cipher-lock box on the wall next to the speaker, and his counterpart at the main

359

desk did likewise. The solenoid buzzed and the locking bolt was withdrawn, allowing them to open the outer door to the greenhouse.

Once inside, Bob and Jack encountered a second guard with an identical list of names.

"How's it going, Wes," Bob greeted him. "Are you all ready for the meeting?"

"Right, Mr. Green. I'm all set. I've got the list of names, and I won't let them bring anything in with them."

"That's the ticket," Bob responded, punching the guard on the arm goodnaturedly. "And if Secretary Stratton gives you a hard time, just tell him politely that those are the rules."

The guard nodded solemnly, but Bob and Jack smiled at each other, knowing full well that Thomas Stratton could and would change the rules if he wanted to.

"Well, I guess we're the first ones here," Jack said surveying the empty plexiglass enclosure. "How about letting us in?"

"Right, Professor Mason," the guard responded. "Just as soon as I verify it."

After conferring with another wall-mounted loudspeaker, the guard mounted the plexiglass stairs to the greenhouse and inserted a large plastic key that hung on a chain around his neck into the plastic lock on the greenhouse door. He looked like a twentieth-century version of a medieval warder, and Bob and Jack chuckled as he jiggled the key attempting to get it to turn in the lock. At last, the intricate plastic surfaces mated properly and, with a triumphant smile, the guard rotated the key and the plastic locking bolts withdrew. He pulled on the plastic handle and the plastic door swung slowly open, surprisingly massive in view of its transparent construction.

Bob and Jack mounted the plexiglass stairs and moved to the far end of the transparent conference table. Jack peered down at his feet as he walked, amused by the sensation that at any moment a shoe or a leg might sink silently through the almost invisible plastic, leaving him hopelessly mired.

The guard closed the door behind them, and they were instantly enveloped in silence. The only sound was the strange tapping of their shoes on the plastic floor. They reached the far end of the chamber and sat down in the last two chairs, facing each other across the plastic conference table. As Jack relaxed and placed his elbows on the almost invisible surface, he again had the sensation that the ephemeral plastic supports might suddenly give way, allowing him to crash ignominiously to the floor of the room, some three feet below.

"Place gives you a strange feeling, doesn't it?" Bob said, with a smile. "The thing that amazes me is how well the double plastic wall attenuates sound."

Jack nodded, noticing for the first time that he could not hear the background music that was playing in the outer room. The only sound that reached his ears was the gentle whir of the plastic fans that carried air to and from the chamber through a set of plastic ducts that twisted and turned grotesquely in space to ensure that sounds attempting to escape from the greenhouse would surely lose their way.

The eerie solitude was interrupted by a scraping noise, which a turn of his head revealed to Jack was the key being jiggled in the lock by the guard. The plexiglass door again swung open, and the sound of Muzak wafted in, followed by Phyllis Jackson and Jason Star. Jack rose to greet them, subconsciously thankful for the company.

"How's our star, Jason?"

The man with psi smiled genuinely at the old joke; he too needed relief from the tension.

"Do you have the transcript, Phyllis?" Jack continued anxiously.

Phyllis Jackson shook her head in the negative and sat down next to Jack, while Jason took the seat across from her, next to Bob.

"They're still typing it," Phyllis elaborated. "Yuri is waiting for it, and he'll bring it in as soon as it's done. Until then, Jason will just have to amuse us with his sober recollections."

The three men smiled broadly. Phyllis Jackson was not usually given to humor; she also must have been feeling the pressure of their situation.

"Thanks, Phyllis!" Jason rejoined goodnaturedly. "It's nice to know that your friends prefer you drugged to sober."

This time, Phyllis participated in the general laughter, but, after a moment, the man with psi continued more seriously.

361

"There's something I'd like to tell the three of you before Stratton arrives."

The others turned toward him, their smiles suddenly gone.

"I don't want to sound melodramatic," Jason said, beginning his confidence, "and I know that I'm under a lot of stress. But today in the summit conference room I had the most frightening sense of foreboding. Not a psi signal. No Russian words or anything like that. I just felt surrounded by some evil power that was intent on destroying me. On destroying all of us."

His three friends and coconspirators looked at the man with psi anxiously, uncertain as to how to respond. Finally, Jack Mason began to nod his head slowly up and down.

"I know what you mean, Jason. I've felt it myself, ever since I got to Moscow. Even here in the embassy. Like I was surrounded by an invisible evil force. Something I could sense and fear, but not comprehend."

The others shook their heads in a mixture of understanding and agreement, and a long, uncomfortable silence followed. At last, Phyllis Jackson spoke quietly.

"I don't want to sound like a psychoanalyst. And I'm certainly not dismissing your fears, Jason. We're doing a very dangerous thing. There's no doubt about it."

Phyllis paused for a moment to assess their reactions, and the three men smiled weakly.

"But, on the other hand, we have to understand that fears of the kind we all are experiencing are not unusual in stressful situations. In fact," she continued with a small smile, "the thing that would really concern me would be if we weren't afraid. That would be a real sign of emotional disorder."

The three patients looked a little more cheerful and nodded their thanks for her reassurance. And then the four friends sat silently for a while in their plastic womb, each contemplating their own personal fears and uncertainties.

Their period of Zenlike self-examination was suddenly ended when Jack caught sight of Thomas Stratton entering the outer room. Stratton was gesturing animatedly to the guard, who evidently was refusing to admit him to the greenhouse until he had surrendered a manila envelope. The four people seated at the plexiglass table watched the pantomime with growing

362

amusement until a standoff had been reached. The secretary of state clutched the envelope to his chest, and the guard did likewise with the plastic key. Finally, Thomas Stratton began waving to the occupants of the transparent chamber for assistance.

"Do you want to go, or shall I?" Bob Green said, with a smile.

"You're the security man," Jack responded.

Bob rose from the table and motioned to the guard to unlock the greenhouse door. When it finally swung open, the irate voice of Thomas Stratton immediately broke the silence.

"Green! What the hell do you think you're up to? This is my embassy, and I make the rules around here!"

"Yes, sir, Mr. Secretary," Bob responded, "you certainly do. And you approved the rule that Mr. Lyons is trying to enforce. It says that no one may bring anything into the greenhouse without written approval and inspection and marking of the item. And I've told the guards that—"

"I assure you, Mr. Green," Thomas Stratton injected sarcastically, "that the rule does not apply to the secretary of state!"

"Yes, sir, Mr. Secretary," Green said dutifully. "I'm sorry you were inconvenienced. Won't you join us?"

Thomas Stratton pushed past Bob Green and strode purposefully to the head of the conference table, his heavy footsteps shaking the plastic structure. He took the chair reserved for him at the head of the table and ceremonially deposited the manila envelope—the immediate fasces of his authority. The others waited with drawn breath for the tirade they expected, but, when the secretary of state began to speak, all trace of rancor had disappeared from his voice.

"Well, now, Jason, Professor Mason tells me that you received some very interesting signals from Comrade Sherkov."

"We'll have the transcript here in a moment, Mr. Secretary," Jack offered, greatly relieved. "Yuri Andromov, the native Russian that Jason practices with, will bring it in as soon as they finish typing it."

"Fine, Professor, fine," Thomas Stratton responded with a hint of exasperation. "But, in the meantime, I'd like to get Jason's first-hand impressions. What's your evaluation of Sherkov so far, Jason?"

Jason Star looked at the secretary of state thoughtfully, wondering whether or not to reveal the overwhelming feeling of foreboding that he had experienced at the opening session of the summit conference. In the end, he decided to introduce the idea gradually.

"Sherkov seems to be a tough old man, Mr. Secretary. Apparently his war experiences made a lasting impression on his character."

Thomas Stratton nodded his agreement.

"That's right. Sherkov's been through a lot. First the war, and then his rise to political power under Stalin. Several times, he almost was shunted aside by the younger ideologists. They thought him too reactionary and insufficiently inspired by revolutionary zeal. But, in the end, it is them who have been forgotten, and he who has become the general secretary."

The four students nodded appreciatively at the professor's explanation, and Thomas Stratton again turned to the man with psi.

"Go on, Jason. What specific impressions did you get?"

"Well, Mr. Secretary, I think that Sherkov is quite belligerent. I mean, look at the way he shook hands with President Leonard. Like a blitzing linebacker grabbing a faltering quarterback."

The man with psi abruptly fell silent, suddenly realizing how unflattering his assessment was to the president of the United States. But Thomas Stratton smiled wryly and urged him to continue.

"Yes, and what psi signals did you receive while they were shaking hands?"

Jason thought for a moment trying to remember the final wording in the transcript.

"Leonard is weak. I am strong. I will crush him."

"You got all that? Those complete sentences?"

"Well, not at the time," Jason replied honestly. "While I was there at the meeting, all I consciously perceived were the basic words. 'Leonard weak . . . strong . . . crush him.'"

"So where did those complete sentences come from?" Thomas Stratton said, with rising anger. "Did someone make them up?"

"No sir, Mr. Secretary," Jack interjected, coming to Jason's assistance. "When we debriefed Jason under the influence of sodium pentothal, he was able to remember the case endings on the Russian words he perceived. So we were able to piece together the sentences that Sherkov was thinking."

Thomas Stratton frowned again, unconvinced by Jack's explanation. Fortunately, the tense confrontation was ended when Bob Green pointed at Yuri Andromov, who was standing outside the greenhouse.

"Here's Mr. Andromov with the transcript now, Mr. Secretary," Jack continued with obvious relief. "We should stop our conversation while the door to the greenhouse is open."

Bob Green rose, met Yuri Andromov at the door, and took the transcript from him. Sensing a tense situation, Yuri retreated outside, and Bob handed the stapled sheaf of typewritten sheets to Jack, who passed it on to the secretary of state.

"Here, Mr. Secretary, read it for yourself."

Thomas Stratton took the document and began scanning it silently. From time to time, he frowned quizzically and then appeared to reread the offending phrase.

The secretary of state continued to the last page without speaking and then inserted the transcript into the controversial manila envelope. Having thus taken control of the treasure for which he had come, Thomas Stratton abruptly stood at his place at the end of the table and addressed the group.

"Thank you all for your efforts. And particularly you, Jason. The president and I place the utmost importance on what you are doing."

With that, the secretary of state strode to the door of the plexiglass enclosure and waited with obvious impatience for the guard to release him. Jack rose and followed Thomas Stratton, and Bob Green motioned to the guard to open the door. The trio filed down the plastic staircase, and, at a further signal from Bob, the guard opened the outer door to the hallway.

As he was about to leave the area entirely, Thomas Stratton turned abruptly and offered his hand to Jack.

"Forgive me for being so abrupt, Professor, but I have to leave now to prepare the president for this evening."

William Randolph Lowell, Jr. was pleased. The president of the United States soon would arrive to use his study in his embassy for an important conference with the secretary of state. And perhaps he would be asked to join them in assessing the impact of the president's startling proposals and the subsequent Soviet walkout. Lowell was musing idly about what he might say if asked for his reactions, when a formally attired butler approached.

"Mr. Ambassador? The president has left his hotel and will be arriving at the embassy shortly."

"Fine, Stevens, thank you," Randolph Lowell responded, in a tone that bespoke a lifetime of instructing servants. "Please ask Mrs. Lowell to meet me in the reception hall immediately. And be sure that the library is ready. Have some cognac out, and be sure it's Courvoisier. The president fancies it because it's the brandy of Napoleon. And the Cuban cigars. There's no embargo when it comes to the president. And be certain that the champagne is chilled. Dom Perignon, 1959. I want to give the president the best after the show he put on today."

Richard Hart Leonard was triumphant. He stood before the French windows of Randolph Lowell's study and gestured expansively with his glass of champagne.

"Well, Randy, what did you think of the bomb I dropped on Sherkov?"

"It was certainly dramatic," Randolph Lowell offered, a bit unsure of the appropriate response. "I suspect that the Russians were a little taken aback by the breadth of the agenda you proposed."

And so was I, the American ambassador thought to himself. *Not at all what I had expected from all those secure telephone conversations with Stratton. But that's what you get with a president who thinks he's Napoleon and a secretary of state whose idol is Metternich.*

"I really surprised you, Lowell, didn't I?" Richard Leonard continued with an aggressive grin. "You thought the old pres was coming over here to rubber stamp all that diplomatic bullshit that you and Gersky have been piling on each other. That's the trouble with you diplomatic types. You're so concerned with appearances that you forget to stick the knife in!"

Thomas Stratton was enjoying Randolph Lowell's discomfort. Ever since their undergraduate days at Harvard, a sometimes not too friendly rivalry had existed between them. Lowell, the Boston Brahmin, had had everything too easy, Stratton thought. The mansion in Prides Crossing, the private tutors, the summer and winter trips to Europe, while he, Stratton, had had to work for everything. All those hours in the library and the sleepless nights of typing and—

"Well, Thomas, do you think it's time we let Randy in on our secret?" Richard Leonard continued in a friendlier tone. "After all, I hear you've filled his wine cellar up with a computer!"

"Well, Mr. President," the secretary of state responded without a hint of emotion in his voice, "Randy knows that there's an extremely sensitive project being carried out in the basement. And that he should give it his full support and cooperation."

Thomas Stratton hesitated for just a moment and then continued.

"And perhaps you're right that Randy should know the whole story. I'll discuss it with him later, if you think I should."

The president caught the secretary of state's interdiction of further veiled discussion of Project Psi, and Thomas Stratton continued in a different vane.

"But, Mr. President, right now you deserve a toast for your magnificent performance."

The secretary of state raised his glass, and Randolph Lowell did likewise.

"To Richard Leonard!" Thomas Stratton intoned.

"To the president of the century!"

That bastard Stratton, Randolph Lowell thought. *He's gotten out of telling me the secret.* But Lowell dutifully repeated the toast.

"To the president of the century!"

And then the ambassador added his own embellishment.

"To the first president to really stand up for America's rights abroad since Theodore Roosevelt!"

Thomas Stratton frowned at Randolph Lowell's hyperbolic attempt at flattery, but Richard Leonard beamed.

"So you think I've got some of old Teddy's spunk, do ya? Well you're right! And I'll tell you something else. I'm gonna hang a few of those big Russian heads on my trophy-room wall! Like that bastard Sherkov, with all that shit about how he fought at Stalingrad or Leningrad, or wherever the hell it was. You'd think he was the only world leader who was ever in the army. Why, I was in the navy for a while myself. Did you know that, Lowell?"

"Oh, yes, Mr. President," Randolph Lowell responded enthusiastically. "Your naval service during World War Two is well known. Why—"

"Mr. President," Thomas Stratton interjected, "don't you think we'd better get down to planning for this evening? You'll have to be leaving to get ready for the state dinner shortly."

"Yeah, I suppose you're right, Thomas," the president agreed with a frown. "But what's there to prepare for? It's Sherkov who had better be preparing! I've really got him on the run!"

"Well, Mr. President," the secretary of state continued matter-of-factly, "I thought that if Randolph would leave us for a while, you might be interested in an analysis of Russian reactions to your statement this morning, prepared by one of my senior aides, David Brentwood. I believe that you may have met him on the flight over."

Thomas Stratton smiled benignly at the president, and, after a moment's hesitation, the latter grinned like a child who knows a secret and turned to the hapless ambassador.

"Well, Randy, I think Thomas is right. There are some things that he and I have to discuss in private. Thank you for letting us use your study. And for the champagne!"

The president raised his glass in a salute to the ambassador, and the latter returned the gesture as he prepared to leave the room.

"You're more than welcome, of course, Mr. President," Randolph Lowell offered, with a note of disappointment in his voice. "I'll see that you're not disturbed. Shall I send in another bottle of champagne?"

"Yeah, why don't you," the president agreed willingly. He raised his glass again, smiled at the bubbling liquid, and drank it down.

"This is pretty good stuff! Knowing you, Randy, it's probably French, or something."

Randolph Lowell smiled again and, at last, left the room. When the heavy library door had closed securely behind him, Thomas Stratton retrieved the manila envelope from where he had left it on the grand piano and ceremonially removed the stapled sheaf of papers.

"Jason received a remarkable set of psi signals, Mr. President. Truly remarkable! The transcript of his pentothal debriefing runs to more than twenty pages. Let me read some of the highlights to you."

Richard Leonard nodded his approval, and Thomas Stratton sat down in a nearby wing chair and began scanning the first page. As he found tempting morsels, he sampled them aloud for the president:

'Impressions received at the beginning of the meeting . . . while the president and the general secretary were shaking hands. . . . *Weak . . . Leonard weak . . . Leonard is weak . . . strong . . . I am strong . . . I will crush him.*"

"Weak! What the fuck does he mean, weak!" the president broke in angrily. "I squeezed his hand just as hard as he squeezed mine. Harder!"

Richard Leonard's face reddened, and he shook his finger at Thomas Stratton.

"So he's going to crush me, is he? We'll see who gets crushed! I'll grind that bastard right into the ground! When I get through with him—"

"Think what an advantage you have, Mr. President," the secretary of state responded unemotionally. "You know about his feelings, while he can only speculate about yours. Why, it's like having the other team's game plan before the Super Bowl."

"Yeah, you're right, Thomas," Richard Leonard agreed, eagerly grasping the analogy. "We know what plays that bastard's going to call, and he doesn't even suspect. But when he tries some razzle-dazzle, we'll bust his ass!"

369

Thomas Stratton was pleased at having diverted the president's anger and continued scanning the transcript for words or phrases worthy of his chief's attention.

"Here's their initial reaction to your challenge, Mr. President: 'Thoughts, believed to be Gersky's, received after the president began his opening statement. *"trap . . . Stratton set trap . . . objective? . . . Sherkov is angry . . . Basov is evil . . . Stratton is evil."'*"

Richard Leonard frowned at his secretary of state without speaking. *Damn insulting,* he thought. *Gersky attributing the whole idea to Stratton. Doesn't think I have the brains, I suppose. I'll show that—*

"Very interesting, Mr. President," Thomas Stratton continued, understanding the president's sudden silence. "And very complex. Gersky thinks we've set a trap, but he doesn't know the objective. And he knows that Sherkov is angry—which was obvious—and he suspects Basov, too."

Poor old Basov, thought Thomas Stratton, almost sympathetically. *He's spent so much time in the West that his bosses suspect him.*

The secretary of state continued to reflect on the fate of the old Bolshevik, but the president responded enthusiastically to the sign of dissension.

"So we've got them fighting among themselves already! Those damn commies don't even trust each other!

"And here, Mr. President," said the secretary of state continuing his reading, "are the thoughts that Jason received after you proposed that every kind of weapon be reduced or eliminated."

The president stopped his pacing in mid-stride, and Thomas Stratton read the fateful words matter-of-factly.

" '*Leonard is a bastard . . . he is bluffing . . . he thinks he can fool Sherkov . . . I will destroy him . . . Stratton made plan . . . should I attack or leave . . . that bastard Stratton.*' "

"I really shocked them, didn't I, Thomas?" the president interjected, smiling triumphantly. "Like a helmet in the chest at full speed! Flat on their backs, gasping for breath!"

"You certainly did, Mr. President," the secretary of state agreed. Thomas Stratton paused for a moment and then subtly changed the subject.

"Perhaps we should begin planning our strategy for this evening, Mr. President. I recommend that you and I continue to repeat the points you made in the opening statement essentially verbatim."

The president frowned, but Thomas Stratton continued professorially.

"I believe that this strategy has three advantages. First, it should convince them that you are serious and not just employing an opening gambit. Second, it should enhance the shock value of your statement this morning by driving home the main points. And, third, it won't give away any new information that might help them plan for the next negotiating session tomorrow."

The secretary of state gazed benignly at the president, pleased with his own analysis of the situation, and waited for his pupil to respond.

"Yeah, Thomas, that sounds okay to me," Richard Leonard grunted in reply. "You and I will keep the pressure on, and everyone else will play dumb, which won't be hard for most of them."

"Yes, Mr. President," the secretary of state responded with feigned dutifulness. "I will issue instructions that all of our aides are simply to say that you are absolutely serious about the proposal to reduce or eliminate all weapons. Beyond that, they should say nothing."

Coming to the topic of greatest importance, Thomas Stratton rose and continued with a touch of theater in his voice.

"And now to the man with psi. I think that Jason should play a key role this evening. I recommend that we tell him to follow me everywhere he can. Discreetly, of course. And I, in turn, will stay close to you. Hopefully, Jason will receive some psi signals about what the Russians are planning to say at the negotiating session tomorrow."

The president nodded distractedly, but his thoughts were elsewhere. Richard Leonard was silent for a while, and then he addressed the secretary of state with utmost seriousness.

"You know, Thomas, we are in the middle of a very dangerous maneuver. Like Patton breaking through the German lines and not waiting for reinforcements. As long as surprise is on our side, we'll have them on the run. But, if they somehow find out what we're up to, we're a long way from home with damn little protection. And I can't very well call in the marines."

Thomas Stratton solemnly nodded his agreement.

32

Who Is This David Brentwood?

Vasily Vasilyevich Sherkov, the supreme leader of the Soviet Union, sat stone-faced behind his massive desk glaring at the two men standing before him. When the last retreating aide had closed the door, Sherkov's anger exploded.

"Well! What do the heads of the world's greatest intelligence apparatus have to say? Of course, you know exactly what Leonard and Stratton are planning! Perhaps you did not think it was important enough to bring to my attention! But I have time! Plenty of time! So tell me! What are they scheming?"

The objects of the general secretary's rage were an incongruous pair. General Sergei Ivanovich Pipin, a much-decorated hero of World War II, was in full uniform and stood stiffly at attention. His short, muscular frame and steely-blue eyes were motionless in the face of Sherkov's anger. In marked contrast, the tall, mysterious Andrei Nikolayevich Vardo, the head of the infamous Committee for State Security, the KGB, shifted his weight from one foot to the other and furtively scanned the room as if searching for the best means of escape. Neither man answered the shouted question, and Vasily Sherkov continued his outraged monologue.

"Tell me, Tovarishch Vardo, what are the Americans doing? Is the president serious? Or is he bluffing?"

Vasily Sherkov stared intently at Andrei Vardo, who twisted and turned in front of the desk like the victim at the end of the hangman's rope.

Finally Vardo spoke apologetically.

"Unfortunately, Tovarishch General Secretary, we really are not sure. Our agents in Washington gave us no indication—"

"No indication!" Sherkov roared. "What kind of spies do you have? School children?"

Andrei Vardo shifted his weight again and then pleaded for time.

"I have Grechko gathering together all available information, Tovarishch Sherkov. I will have a full report ready for you after the state dinner this evening."

Vasily Sherkov frowned and continued the interrogation.

"What about our agents in the American embassy? What do they say? And the listening devices in the walls? And the movies that you took at the first negotiating session this morning? What have you gotten from them? And what about—"

"Please, Tovarishch General Secretary. Give us a few hours. Until after the dinner this evening. I will bring you a full report, personally."

"You had better, Andrei Nikolayevich!" Vasily Sherkov admonished, pointing his giant finger. "You had better!

"And now, Sergei Ivanovich, what do you have to say? What news from your attachés? Stationed around the world at great expense to the Soviet Union. What priceless clues have they given you to this crazy American proposal?"

General Pipin, the head of Soviet military intelligence, remained at attention. He looked directly at the party chief and spoke in a firm, but respectful, voice.

"At this time, I can report no specific information concerning the American proposal, Tovarishch General Secretary. I have sent an encrypted message to the embassy in Washington instructing them to order all agents to give this matter their highest priority attention. I will receive a report from the embassy this evening and will bring it directly to you."

"Hear me! Both of you!" Vasily Sherkov exploded again, pounding his massive desk with a hamlike fist. "Either you find out what Leonard and Stratton are scheming, or I will replace you with men who will! I do not care what you have to do, but I want an answer! Do you understand me?"

Viktor Leonidovich Grechko sat in the back of a darkened room full of his best intelligence analysts watching the movies that had been taken by hidden cameras at the first session of the summit meeting. Wide-angle lenses had recorded the scene in the entire conference room from several directions, while additional cameras with telephoto lenses provided close-ups of each of the principal Americans: the president, his translator, the secretary of state, Stratton's little-known aide, David Brentwood, and the military man in mufti, General Sam Ryan. In addition to the movies, tape recordings had been made using sensitive microphones located under the table in front of each of the key Americans.

Thus far, looking at the movies and listening to the tapes had yielded nothing. Viktor Grechko peered intently at the screen as the close-up Richard Leonard was shown for the second time. When the film reached the point where the president was about to begin delivering his opening statement, Grechko leaned forward, summoning all of the experience of his years in espionage to divine the president's purpose. Richard Leonard looked like a confident cardplayer about to lay down a winning hand. Evidently the speech he was about to make was part of a carefully orchestrated plot and not the chance result of whim or pique.

The Americans undoubtedly counted on old Vasily Vasilyevich to give his usual rambling introduction, Grechko thought ruefully. *And our great general secretary dutifully obliged them.* Viktor Leonidovich continued to stare at the screen, and slowly his detective's mind began to formulate a crucial question: *Who on the American side was aware of the president's plan? Stratton, surely,* Grechko thought, *but who else?*

Viktor Grechko ordered the film stopped, and then asked to have the wide-angle scenes replayed. From studying them, he soon became convinced that the lower-level members of the American delegation were as surprised by the president's sweeping proposal as their Soviet counterparts. This discovery made, Grechko switched again to viewing the close-ups. Leonard first; and then his translator, an air-force colonel by the name of Jack Stewart. *What about Stewart,* thought Viktor Leonidovich. *Did Stewart know? I would not think so. Not necessary. Tell as few as possible. But, let us look at Stewart again, just to be sure.*

The film was rewound and shown again, and Viktor Grechko was convinced. No, Stewart clearly was as surprised as all the rest, Grechko decided. Look at those eyes staring at the president in disbelief. And wondering if he should translate what is being said, or somehow try to leave some of it out. No, Stewart was not in on the plot, Grechko concluded. That much was certain.

Thus satisfied with his first small step toward unravelling the enigma, Viktor Grechko's methodical mind turned to the next American down the line at the conference table. *Now, who's next,* Grechko thought. *Thomas Stratton, of course. Stratton surely knew. But, let us be sure. Let us look at Stratton once again.*

The lights in the room came on as reels of film were changed, but Viktor Grechko continued to stare at the blank screen hoping for an inspiration. The room went dark again, and the Machiavellian face of Thomas Stratton suddenly filled the screen.

Look at that grin, Grechko thought. *That evil smirk of the Svengali behind the president. Look at him. He is savoring every moment. Listening to poor old Sherkov calling for help, like a man struggling in quicksand who does not realize that his apparent rescuer intends to push him down. A truly brilliant and evil man, that Thomas Stratton. And a worthy opponent. I wonder how long he has been scheming to bring this day about?*

Viktor Grechko continued musing as the close-up film of Thomas Stratton played, and eventually Grechko's gaze was drawn to the little-known aide at the secretary of state's side. *What about this fellow, Brentwood?* Viktor Leonidovich thought. *Did he know what was coming? I doubt it. But, let us be sure. Let us look at Brentwood.*

The film was changed again, and soon the face of Jason Star filled the screen. David Brentwood appeared to be staring intently in the direction of Vasily Sherkov, but his face revealed no hint of the surprise to come. Does he know? Or does he not know? The answer was not apparent to Viktor Grechko, and he looked at the man with psi with a perplexed expression.

Who is this David Brentwood? Viktor Leonidovich suddenly asked himself. Until recently, he was an obscure State Department employee, and now he is at the right hand of Thomas Stratton at a summit conference. It does not fit. Stratton is so cautious. Why a new, untried aide? Could Stratton have known him from the past? An old college friend or faculty colleague? No, Brentwood is too young. A new man sitting beside the secretary of state in Moscow. It just does not make any sense. Unless he is here for a purpose. For a purpose! But what purpose?

Viktor Grechko leaned forward again, concentrating all his faculties on David Brentwood. The voice of Vasily Sherkov rose in fervor, and David Brentwood stared intently in the direction of the speaker. Brentwood's eyes were half-closed, like an avid concertgoer straining to extract the essence of a performance. *The essence,* thought Grechko. *Brentwood is straining as if to discover the essence of Sherkov's remarks.*

What essence? Victor Leonidovich mused wryly. If Brentwood only knew how little essence there was. Just an old soldier reminiscing about the Great War. And lamenting how times have changed. And wanting to star in one last summit conference before he is put out to pasture. The Politburo should have retired him long ago. But they are all as old as he is. So if he goes, sooner or later, they will all be gone, too.

Vasily Sherkov had stopped speaking, and on the screen David Brentwood leaned forward on the conference table, eyes still half-closed. Viktor Grechko's thoughts returned to the problem at hand as Vladimir Gersky's voice asked if the president intended to make an opening statement.

When Richard Leonard finally began to speak, David Brentwood's face clearly revealed that he had no advanced knowledge of the president's sweeping proposal. Brentwood seemed as startled as all the others, and he momentarily turned toward the president. But, to Grechko's surprise, Brentwood almost immediately turned back toward the Soviet side of the table. Thus intrigued, Viktor Leonidovich visualized the seating arrangement and rapidly concluded that Brentwood was staring at Sherkov.

Viktor Grechko was perplexed. The president of the United States had just delivered a seemingly crazy proposal at a summit conference, and this unknown aide, David Brentwood, who was as surprised as everyone else, was staring at Sherkov instead of at Leonard? As if his purpose was to analyze Sherkov's reaction.

That is it! Victor Grechko thought excitedly. *Brentwood is some kind of psychologist they brought along to analyze Sherkov's reactions.*

"That is enough of the movies, Tovarishch Talko," Viktor Grechko's bearlike voice announced summarily from the back of the room. "Let us have some light."

Everyone in the room turned toward Grechko. The master spy had discovered a clue, and his aides eagerly awaited their instructions.

"The mysterious David Brentwood is the key to the American plan," Viktor Leonidovich announced. He waited for the full impact of his words to be felt and then continued emphatically.

"I want to know all about him. What is his real name? And his real background? Is he a psychologist? Or perhaps even a parapsychologist? And this evening, at the dinner, I want our best agents on him. Use Natalya! If he is not what the Americans call gay, Natalya will get him. She even gets a rise out of me. But, alas, I am too old to follow through."

33

Natalya

The state dinner was a truly grand affair. Chandeliers blazed in the high-ceilinged St. George's Hall of the Grand Kremlin Palace. Everywhere the chests of Russian men, whether or not in uniform, proudly displayed a collection of medals. The greatest of them all, the Order of Lenin, distinguished its wearers as members of the politico-military elite. The Soviet women, predominantly dowdy White Russians, were decked out in satin ball gowns reminiscent of the senior prom in post-World-War-II America. Tail-coated waiters moved among the dignitaries dispensing tulip-shaped glasses of bubbling champagne and crystal shots of one-hundred-proof vodka.

Along the walls, dazzling displays of hors d'oeuvres tempted the most jaded international traveler. Liter-sized silver bowls of beluga caviar were gracefully displayed on snowy mounds of shaved ice. And there were eggs of all descriptions to accompany the caviar—crumbled, sliced, stuffed, pickled and painted—all arranged in fanciful patterns. But the *pièces de résistance* were beautifully decorated whole Volga-River salmon. These masterpieces of culinary artistry appeared freshly caught and still alive, but were revealed by probing with a fork to be cooked and cold and fully boned.

Jason Star stood behind Thomas Stratton as the latter conversed jovially with Vladimir Gersky. The foreign minister appeared intent on exploring the genesis of the American president's sweeping disarmament proposal, while the secretary of state continually diverted the conversation to the excellent vintage of the champagne, the delicate flavor of the caviar, or the elegant good looks of the women. Jason caught himself listening to the conversation with thinly concealed amusement, rather than focusing on his task of receiving psi impressions. Forcing himself back to reality, the man with psi closed his eyes for a moment and concentrated on the voice of Vladimir Gersky.

"So, Thomas, the United States finally has a president who is willing to take your nuclear weapons out of Europe. That is something we have wanted for a long time."

"The president is quite serious, Vladimir," the secretary of state responded in a firm but diplomatic tone. "He is ready to sit down with the general secretary and to agree to the reduction or elimination of all types of weapons."

Thomas Stratton looked at his counterpart with feigned sincerity for a moment, and then smiled and changed the subject.

"But, that is a subject for tomorrow. Tonight, we must enjoy this magnificent display of Russian hospitality. I'm certainly glad to see that ideological zeal hasn't dampened your appreciation for the finer things in life, Vladimir. Why, if I didn't know better, I'd expect to hear trumpets announcing the tsar's arrival momentarily."

Vladimir Gersky smiled and tried a different approach.

"Thomas, I would like you to meet Comrade Ludmila Tarashkova. Comrade Tarashkova is the minister of culture and was responsible for the selection of the fine musicians you will hear after the banquet."

Gersky stepped aside and a tall woman with jet-black hair came forward and extended her hand to Thomas Stratton. With a twinkle in his eye, the secretary of state clicked his heels audibly, bowed slightly from the waist, and raised her fingers to his lips.

"Tsarina! I am truly honored to meet you."

Gersky grimaced, but Tarashkova appeared the master of the situation.

"Your wit and charm have not been overrepresented, Mr. Secretary," she responded in only slightly accented English. "I am sure that in the last century you would have been well received by royalty the world around."

Thomas Stratton rose to the bait of a challenge from a mind equal to his own, but Jason Star sensed a strong psi impression of hostility. *Could it be,* he thought, *that this Comrade Tarashkova is not what she appears to be?*

"Tell me, Madame Tarashkova," the secretary of state continued, exuding charm, "what musical *divertissements* you have planned for us this evening. Nothing modern, dissonant, or counterrevolutionary, I trust."

The intellectual fencing between Stratton and Tarashkova was interrupted by a flourish of trumpets at the entrance to the hall, and, when the crowd grew silent, a tail-coated official announced loudly, first in Russian and then in English:

"Ladies and gentlemen, the general secretary of the Communist Party of the Union of Socialist Republics!"

And then a moment later:

"The president of the United States of America!"

Richard Hart Leonard and Vasily Vasilyevich Sherkov appeared at the entrance to the hall, and all eyes turned toward them. Sherkov, playing the part of the amiable host, alternately pointed the way and hugged the shoulders of his guest. Leonard, too, appeared in good spirits, but mildly surprised by the size and grandeur of the affair.

Vladimir Gersky and Thomas Stratton moved to the center of the room to join their principals, and the president seemed relieved when he spotted the secretary of state. Richard Leonard smiled broadly, gestured in Stratton's direction, and greeted him loudly.

"Well, Thomas, I see that you're already enjoying the general secretary's hospitality."

"Good evening, Mr. President," the secretary of state responded formally. "Good evening, Mr. General Secretary. As the president has said, your hospitality is truly magnificent."

Vasily Sherkov beamed with satisfaction and spread his arms to the crowd like one of the dancing bears at the old Moscow circus. Senior Russians raised their glasses, and their juniors and the Americans followed suit.

"*Na zdorov'e* (To your health) *Tovarishch Sherkov!*"

"To the General Secretary!"

The shouted toasts rang through the hall, first in Russian and then in English.

Vasily Sherkov seemed genuinely appreciative of the adulation. Like the dancing bear at the circus, he turned several circles, raising and lowering his outstretched arms, and smiling and nodding his acknowledgment.

Thomas Stratton nudged the president, and Richard Leonard raised his glass and proclaimed loudly:

"To General Secretary Sherkov!"

At the president's toast, the senior Russians signaled for quiet, and, after another prod from Stratton, Richard Leonard added:

"To this historic summit conference!"

Vasily Sherkov again grinned bearlike at the president and then raised his own glass.

"To the president of the United States!" he said in Russian, and then repeated it in English.

"To the president of the United States!" echoed through the hall in both languages.

It was Richard Leonard's turn to acknowledge the tributes. The president raised his arms above his head like a triumphant fighter and smiled broadly at the dazzling crowd of dignitaries. His childhood dream of social acceptance was being fulfilled on a grand scale.

When the throng finally moved into the banquet hall, protocol left David Brentwood seated with relatively junior Soviet and American diplomats far from the brain of Vasily Sherkov.

His dismay at the seating arrangement was dispelled almost immediately, when a beautiful, blonde woman came and stood at the place beside him. Jason smiled and bowed slightly, feigning ignorance of Russian. The woman extended her hand and introduced herself in perfect English as Daphne Singer of the Institute for the USA. Jason took her hand and smiled more broadly, his eyes drawn to the tops of her ample breasts revealed in the vee of a low-cut gown.

"It's a pleasure to meet you, Madame Singer," he offered tentatively. "I'm David Brentwood of the State Department."

At the front of the banquet hall, Vasily Sherkov and Richard Leonard took their seats followed by the others at the head table. Jason Star held Daphne Singer's chair and then sat down himself.

"It must be very stimulating working for the State Department, Mr. Brentwood," the beautiful Russian said, continuing their conversation. "Visiting foreign countries and meeting interesting people."

Jason's mind raced through the cover story of David Brentwood's career at the State Department, but his eyes were fixed on the startling good looks of Daphne Singer.

"Well, I, er, am just an economic analyst," he answered hesitantly. "Not very exciting. At least, until now."

The waiters brought an appetizer of cold smoked fish accompanied by a too-sweet Crimean white wine, but Jason found his attention drawn to the gorgeous woman beside him. The fragrance of her perfume invaded his nostrils and distracted his brain. He found himself consuming the wine with sexually aroused abandon and ignoring his hopeless task of seeking psi signals from the distant minds of the Soviet leaders.

Natalya leaned toward her victim, thrusting her principal assets forward, and smiled coyly.

"It must be exciting traveling with the secretary of state, Mr. Brentwood."

Jason turned toward her and grinned foolishly, his mind bemused by the subtly drugged wine. He no longer could distract his eyes from her bosom and responded with some confusion.

"Well, ah, I don't usually travel with the secretary of state. I mean, not everywhere. This is, er, sort of a special occasion."

Natalya leaned even closer to Jason, her breasts almost brushing his chest, and continued confidentially.

"You're being modest, David. Why, I have heard that the secretary of state has the greatest regard for your advice."

Abruptly, Jason was jolted partially to his senses by a firm hand on his shoulder and an authoritative male voice in his ear.

"Mr. Brentwood! We have an urgent message from Washington for you. The ambassador wants you to go to the embassy and to read it immediately! I have a car outside."

Jason turned toward the voice and was startled to see a marine major in full-dress uniform. A sudden chill swept through the man with psi at the thought that this stern-appearing officer might have witnessed his momentary indiscretion with his beautiful dinner-table companion. Jason stared blankly at the major, who waited a moment and then spoke again firmly.

"Please come with me, Mr. Brentwood! The car is waiting!"

Jason attempted to rise from his chair, but found that his legs were rubbery and failed to respond. The officer grasped him under the arm and raised him upright with the sure strength of a combat-ready marine.

"Come this way, sir!"

Jason stumbled from the table supported by the officer like a dazed football player being helped from the field. He stole a glance back at the table, but Daphne Singer had turned to the other gentleman beside her and was engaged in animated conversation.

After what seemed to Jason like an endless journey through the marble corridors of the Grand Kremlin Palace and across the cobblestone courtyard outside, the major helped him into the rear of an embassy car and closed the door behind them. Jason sank back in the seat, and his head rolled loosely from side to side, finally coming to rest in the vee between the seat back and the side of the car.

"You're safe now, Mr. Brentwood," the major announced as the car began to move. "We'll have you back at the embassy in no time and have a doctor take a look at you."

Thomas Stratton and Jack Mason sat alone at the transparent conference table in the greenhouse. The secretary of state finished reading the document before him and then began to speak grimly.

"This is a very serious incident, Professor. The Russians put one of their best agents on Jason and drugged him at a state dinner. Even the KGB doesn't do things like that without good cause. They must suspect something."

Jack nodded solemnly and then tried to sound a positive note.

"Well, at least this report of Jason's pentothal debriefing says that woman didn't get anything out of him."

The secretary of state replied gravely.

"I hope so, Professor. I sincerely hope so."

34

"I Will Authorize Anything!"

Viktor Leonidovich Grechko and Andrei Vardo sat at a massive conference table at one end of Vardo's ornate office. The head of the KGB was nervous, and he spoke rapidly.

"Tell me, quickly, what you have found, Viktor Leonidovich. Vasily Vasilyevich is after me, and I will have to go to him within the hour."

Viktor Grechko puffed on his pipe and began like a great detective describing the trail that led him to the culprit.

"We were looking at the movies of this morning's session, and one of the Americans came to my attention. A man called David Brentwood. Although that probably is not his real name."

"Come, come, Tovarishch," Andrei Vardo interjected. "Out with it! I do not have much time."

After another puff of smoke, Viktor Grechko continued, still without excitement in his voice.

"In the close-up movies, this David Brentwood kept staring at Tovarishch Sherkov, as if he were trying to read the general secretary's mind or something."

"Read his mind! Nonsense, Viktor Leonidovich! You have been spending too much time with those people in your parapsychology laboratory."

"No, no, Tovarishch Vardo," Viktor Grechko responded good-naturedly. "I do not mean actually reading his mind. But perhaps Brentwood is a psychologist or something, brought along by the Americans to analyze the reactions of our leaders or to attempt to influence their behavior at the negotiating table."

"And you expect me to tell Vasily Vasilyevich that!" Vardo responded with exasperation.

"Wait, Tovarishch, there is more," Grechko continued, exhaling a cloud of smoke. "I had a complete dossier brought together on this David Brentwood, and some interesting things came to light. He studied languages in university, spent a few years as a junior officer in the air force, and then dropped out of sight. Probably became an analyst or a translator for the CIA. And we know that he is fluent in Russian, despite the fact that he told Natalya this evening that he did not speak a word."

"Natalya!" Andrei Vardo responded, with a lascivious smile. "You must really think this Brentwood is important if you used Natalya on him."

"The Americans think Brentwood is important, too," Viktor Grechko continued, "because they sent in the marines to rescue him from Natalya at dinner."

Andrei Vardo's eyes opened wide with surprise, but Viktor Grechko looked at his chief impassively, letting his curiosity build. When Vardo appeared as though he would lunge across the table and squeeze the remainder of the story from its teller's throat, Grechko continued.

"The Americans must have been keeping an eye on Brentwood at the banquet and seen Natalya working on him. They had a marine major practically carry him from the table and take him to the embassy."

The head of the KGB leaned across the table, his nervousness gone and his attention aroused.

"So this Brentwood may be a clue to what the Americans are scheming. What else have you found, Viktor Leonidovich?"

Now confident of his boss's attention, Viktor Grechko puffed additional clouds of smoke.

"About a year ago, Brentwood began to show up in photographs of people coming and going from a chemical research facility near Washington that we have been watching."

"Chemical research?" Vardo repeated with a frown. "What would he be doing there? Unless—do you think that the Americans are employing a poison? Or a truth serum? Or—"

"We do not know yet, Tovarishch," Viktor Grechko responded. "But I think that we are getting close to the truth. And there are some things that I would like you to authorize us to do."

"Of course, of course," Andrei Vardo answered, his nervousness returning. "When have I ever denied any of your requests?"

Viktor Grechko grinned broadly.

"Well, there was that time, two American administrations ago, when we had that woman in Washington who thought that she could—"

Andre Vardo smiled, too.

"All right, Viktor Leonidovich. You are right. I have not always let you do everything you have wanted to do. But, in the present situation, I can assure you, the way Vasily Vasilyevich is after me, that I will authorize anything!"

"All right, Tovarishch," Victor Grechko responded with a twinkle in his eye, "let us take the easy things first. I have already ordered additional cameras to be focused on David Brentwood during the negotiating session tomorrow. And, with your authorization, I would like to install air filters and samplers in the conference room in case the Americans are using some kind of poison gas."

Andrei Vardo nodded his approval, and, after exhaling another cloud of smoke, Viktor Grechko continued.

"We would like to install additional electronic sensors near all the principal Americans, Brentwood included. Microphones under the table, temperature and blood pressure sensors in the chairs, and that sort of thing."

"Fine, Tovarishch, fine," Vardo injected impatiently. "But what are the difficult requests? What do you really want to do?"

Viktor Grechko sucked on his pipe dolefully.

"Well, Tovarishch, I am beginning to conclude that the only way we are going to find out fast enough what the Americans are up to is to question Mr. Brentwood. And *not* at a state dinner."

Andrei Vardo nodded solemnly.

"I think you are right, Viktor Leonidovich. If we do not get an answer tomorrow or the next day, and the Americans continue to embarrass Vasily Vasilyevich, you and I and Pipin and a lot of others could be headed for an unexpected holiday east of the Urals."

The two master spies looked at each other silently for a moment in tacit admission of the precariousness of their own situation. At length, Viktor Grechko puffed another cloud of smoke, and Andrei Vardo posed the ultimate question.

"All right, Viktor Leonidovich, out with it. What kind of invitation do you plan to send our friend David Brentwood?"

35

"I Have Killed Better Men Than You!"

The second negotiating session of the summit meeting was held, as was the first, in the ornate conference room on the second floor of the Council of Ministers Building, within the walls of the Kremlin fortress. Despite their walkout of the previous day, or perhaps because of it, the Soviet delegates had greeted their American counterparts with warm smiles and hearty handshakes, and the two sides now sat facing each other across the long conference table.

Vasily Vasilyevich Sherkov rose from his seat at the head of his country's delegation as would the chairman of a giant corporation about to begin a meeting of an overly large board of directors. Sherkov was dressed in a dark blue, double-breasted suit reminiscent of the style popular in America before World War II. His barrel chest was adorned with a row of four medals, apparently intended as fasces of his courage and authority. The general secretary's gaze slowly inspected the Russian and American negotiators, arranged from the greatest at the head of the table to the least at the foot, some twenty meters distant.

The mammoth conference table was draped in green felt like a giant billiard surface, and in front of each participant lay an identical yellow legal pad and several pens and pencils. Down the center of the table, circular silver trays displayed a variety of bottles of mineral water and numerous glasses.

Vasily Sherkov observed the now silent delegations with a beneficent smile for more than a minute. Finally, Sherkov opened a leather folder before him on the table, glanced briefly at its contents, and then began to speak in a deep, firm voice, directing his remarks toward President Richard Leonard.

When the general secretary finally paused for breath, Volenchek, his frenetic translator, began earnestly.

389

"We, the representatives of the two most powerful nations on earth, the Union of Soviet Socialist Republics and the United States of America, are engaged in this Moscow summit conference on disarmament during a crucial period in the history of civilization. The time has come for a president of the United States to summon the courage to throw off the chains of the capitalist warmongers, who for too long have dictated the policies of his country, and to join with the free socialist peoples of the world in traveling the road to peace through general and complete disarmament."

Vasily Sherkov surveyed the delegations with the self-satisfied smile of a fundamentalist preacher who has eloquently expounded the revealed truth. Several of the lesser Russian negotiators nodded their agreement, like new outside directors seeking favor with an omnipotent chairman of the board. Sherkov's smile finally alighted on a seething Richard Leonard, who sat grim-faced across from the Russian leader. Satisfied that his initial thrust had drawn blood, Vasily Sherkov continued aggressively.

"Gospodin President, . . ."

And, when his turn came again, Volenchek delivered his translation in the bombastic tone of the general secretary's original Russian.

"Mr. President, as a first step along the path to peace through general and complete disarmament, I propose that we negotiate the terms and schedule for the removal of all soldiers of the United States from Western Europe. The garrisoning of the vast number of American fighting men on foreign soil, far from home and close to the Soviet Union, is an anachronistic remnant of World War Two conquests that no longer can be tolerated by the free peoples of Europe."

Who the fuck does that pompous bastard think he is, Richard Leonard fumed to himself. *Lecturing me about troops in Europe. Why, those goddamned Russians have troops in Poland and Czechoslovakia and Hungary and . . .*

The president's adrenaline started to flow and his heart began to pound. His face reddened and his neck began to thicken. Richard Leonard could barely control his anger and was about to leap to his feet and upbraid the Russian leader, when Thomas

Stratton leaned over and, putting his hand on the president's shoulders, whispered softly in his ear.

"Steady, Mr. President. Stick with the game plan. He's just bluffing."

Richard Leonard grimly nodded acknowledgment of his coach's exhortations and then relaxed somewhat in his chair.

Thomas Stratton removed his hand from the president's shoulder and smiled benignly at Sherkov and Gersky. The foreign minister had been watching the president and the secretary of state intently, but the general secretary had begun to speak again, like a minister in the pulpit feigning obliviousness of fidgeting in the front pew. Vasily Sherkov's oration reached a crescendo, and he dramatically relinquished the floor to his translator.

Richard Leonard still had difficulty controlling his rage as Volenchek brought the passion of his principal's Russian to the English translation.

". . . and so, Mr. President, in view of your statement yesterday that all American soldiers and weapons are suitable subjects for these negotiations, I would like to hear your proposals for removing American troops and nuclear bombs from Europe!"

Vasily Sherkov grinned at the delegations with the self-satisfaction of a chief executive who has turned a dissident stockholder's proposal back on its perpetrator. The Russians nodded their support enthusiastically, but the Americans frowned or did their best to remain expressionless. After receiving the silent approbation of his countrymen for more than a minute, Sherkov ceremonially closed the leather folder and took his seat.

The giant conference room was transfixed, and the massive delegations were mute. What would be the American response to this Russian counterattack?

Another minute passed in silence before Vladimir Gersky leaned across the table toward Thomas Stratton and inquired quite audibly in English:

"Does the president wish to make a statement at this time, Thomas?"

"Most assuredly, Vladimir. Most assuredly!" Stratton responded sarcastically.

The secretary of state waited a moment more and then stood at his place and glared at the Russian delegation like a tyrannical conductor demanding the attention of every eye in the orchestra before signaling to the soloist to begin. When convinced that the appropriate tension had developed, Thomas Stratton turned to Richard Leonard and announced solemnly:

"Mr. President."

Richard Leonard rose from his chair to his full six-foot-two-inch height, squared his shoulders, and surveyed the Soviet side of the table with the steely-eyed glare of a commanding general about to dress down a poorly performing staff. The president was impeccably dressed in a dark brown, pin-striped suit with matching paisley tie, and his wavy, silver-gray hair was meticulously groomed.

Richard Leonard looked like a cross between Billy Graham and Dale Carnegie about to convince a roomful of sinning salesmen that religion and gumption could change their lives and save the world. The president glanced at the first of a pack of white note cards in his hands and then began to speak loudly and firmly.

"As I stated yesterday at the opening session of this historic summit conference, the United States is prepared to embark on unprecedented disarmament negotiations with the objective of reducing or eliminating every type of Russian and American weapon. Troops are negotiable, tanks are negotiable, ships are negotiable, planes are negotiable, and most important of all, nuclear weapons are negotiable! Every type of weapon is negotiable and should be reduced or eliminated!"

Richard Leonard paused with a glow of evangelical satisfaction, and Jack Stewart began translating the president's opening salvo into Russian. As Stewart spoke, Richard Leonard rocked up and down on the balls of his feet, like a coach in the midst of a half-time pep talk, and surveyed the Soviet delegation for signs of inspired conversion.

The Russians were clearly less surprised by the president's sweeping proposal than they had been at the opening session, and they seemed intent on projecting the appearance of studied indifference.

This lack of visible audience response goaded the president, and, when Jack Stewart had finished, Richard Leonard rose to the challenge like a preacher whose congregation has yet to shake off the torpor induced by the previous night's indiscretions.

"The eyes of freedom-loving people everywhere are focused on this summit conference. We, whose privilege it is to represent our great countries, have an unique historical responsibility and a rare personal opportunity to serve the cause of world peace. If we seize this opportunity and accept the awesome responsibility, we will be remembered forever in the pages of history. As our Lord Jesus Christ said, almost two thousand years ago, 'Blessed are the peacemakers'!"

Richard Leonard again rocked up and down, allowing time for his words to be translated and their impact to be felt.

The senior Russians maintained a stony silence, but at the far end of the table, junior members of the Soviet delegation revealed, by quizzical expressions, their incredulity at the president's religious fervor.

Convinced that the heathen congregation had begun to receive his message of salvation, Richard Leonard began again in an emotion-tinged voice and with his forefinger upraised.

"If, because of stubborn adherence to outmoded social ideologies, we fail to grasp the unique opportunity offered us, history may well record that we, at this summit conference, through failure to agree on major reductions and eliminations of weapons, plunged the world into the final escalating spiral of the arms race that led to Armageddon!"

Richard Leonard radiated the evangelical zeal of the true believer, as Jack Stewart attempted to convey the president's fundamentalist conviction in Russian.

By now, the incongruous sermon was beginning to have a visible effect on the senior Soviet leaders. Even Vasily Sherkov and Vladimir Gersky could no longer conceal their bewilderment, and Georgi Bondarenko, the aging premier, shook his head in disbelief.

But, convinced that the audience was now in his hand, Richard Leonard began to deliver his ultimate challenge.

393

"General Secretary Sherkov has suggested in his opening remarks this morning that we discuss the removal of foreign troops and weapons from Europe. I suspect that he raised this issue with the expectation that I would shrink from the implicit challenge."

The president rocked forward again, raised his forefinger high, and continued emotionally.

"But, no! I accept the challenge of God and history, and dismiss the negotiating ploys of the Soviet delegation! I propose here and now, before God and the eyes of the world, that every Soviet and American soldier and weapon be removed from Europe!"

Richard Leonard surveyed the room triumphantly as his blast was translated and then continued aggressively.

"But, let the Soviet leadership harbor no illusions that the United States' withdrawal will be unilateral! Soviet troops and weapons must be withdrawn too! Withdrawn from East Germany! Withdrawn from Poland! Withdrawn from Czechoslovakia! Withdrawn from Hungary! Withdrawn from Romania! And withdrawn from Bulgaria!"

The president again paused for translation, although it was evident from the faces of the Russian leaders that none was necessary. When he began speaking again, Richard Leonard glared directly at Vasily Sherkov and shook his finger for emphasis.

"And so, Mr. Sherkov, if you possess the hero's courage that you are so fond of boasting of, I challenge you here and now to accept in principle the withdrawal of all Soviet and American troops and weapons from all of Europe. All of Europe!"

Vasily Sherkov stood abruptly and glared back across the table at the president. Richard Leonard tried to continue his speech, but Sherkov's face reddened, and he began shaking his fist at the president and shouting in Russian.

Stratton and Gersky rose almost simultaneously, and each moved to restrain his principal, like a pair of managers attempting to prevent a premature skirmish at the weighing-in ceremony.

The dutiful Volenchek began to translate Sherkov's epithets, but he was abruptly silenced by the foreign minister.

"You cowardly bastard! I have killed better men than you! You dare insult me and the great Soviet—"

Pandemonium gripped the conference room.

Knots of senior officials formed around Sherkov and Leonard, who continued to yell at each other, each in his own language. Stratton and Gersky stepped between the red-faced leaders and eased them back from the conference table. Finally, the shouting subsided as the heads of the two most powerful nations on earth realized that no one was listening. And, after a hurried conference with Stratton, Gersky summarily announced in both languages that the session was adjourned.

36

A Frightening Revelation

Jason Star lay on the operating table in the center of the debriefing room in the vault in the subbasement of the American embassy. Around the man with psi was clustered a group of white-coated figures led by Dr. Phyllis Jackson. Phyllis looked down at the supine form of her friend and coconspirator and calmly began to question him.

"Can you hear me, Jason?"

The man with psi was reassured by the pleasant face he knew so well and nodded his head on the pillow.

"Yes, Phyllis, . . . hear you fine."

"All right, Jason," she continued, "let's get started. What was the first psi signal you received?"

Jason Star's drugged mind flashed back to the Council of Ministers Building in the Kremlin. He was following Thomas Stratton who was following President Richard Leonard down a long marble corridor. They entered the ornate summit conference room and took their seats at the head of the table. Vasily Sherkov rose and surveyed the Soviet and American delegations, and Jason leaned forward on the cool felt covering the table and concentrated his attention on the general secretary. Jason's trained mind was purposely blank, like a dry sponge awaiting the first drops of psi communication. And they came suddenly with remarkable clarity.

"*. . . Brentwood . . . Who is David Brentwood? . . .*"

Cold fear gripped Jason Star. His eyes opened wide, and he stared at Vasily Sherkov in stunned disbelief. But the general secretary smiled benignly, his gaze circulating around the room, seemingly ignoring David Brentwood.

"Jason! What is it? Are you all right?"

Phyllis Jackson's alarmed voice snapped Jason Star's thoughts back to the present and he found himself tightly gripping the cushions beneath him as terror tightened his stomach. He stared wide-eyed at the pretty face above him, but did not answer.

"Paul! How are his signs?" Dr. Jackson anxiously queried the anesthesiologist.

"Pulse is one sixty, pressure one hundred over fifty," Dr. Berman replied. "Something terrified him."

"Jason! It's Phyllis! You're all right. You're at the embassy. What scared you?"

The shaken man with psi looked blankly up at the concerned face of his friend and began hesitantly.

"It, it was Sherkov, Phyllis."

"Sherkov?" she repeated incredulously. "How could Sherkov scare you, Jason?"

"Thinking, he was thinking, about *me*," the prostrate figure answered weakly, "about *David Brentwood*."

It was Phyllis Jackson's turn to feel the sudden chill and tense gut of fear. Her slender body shuddered involuntarily, and she stared down at her friend and patient in shocked disbelief.

"Sherkov was thinking about David Brentwood?" she finally managed.

The head on the table nodded slowly and silently in the affirmative.

Phyllis Jackson's eyes widened, and she suddenly was speechless. The frightening revelation spread through the room like an icy blast, and the cluster of figures attending the man with psi was abruptly silent. After several anxious moments of suspended animation, Phyllis Jackson partially regained her composure and tried to resume the questioning.

"What was he thinking, Jason? Exactly what was he thinking?"

Thomas Stratton sat at the end of the transparent conference table in the greenhouse flanked by Jack Mason and Phyllis Jackson. The secretary of state had just finished reading the transcript of Jason Star's pentothal debriefing. He placed the document on the table between them and addressed Phyllis.

"Tell me, Dr. Jackson, what the chances are that all of this is a figment of Jason's imagination?"

Phyllis nodded her understanding of Thomas Stratton's question and began her answer quietly.

"That possibility occurred to me too, Mr. Secretary, while I still was debriefing Jason. So I went back several times, over all the impressions and psi signals he said he received. You'll see in the transcript that—"

"Yes, Doctor," Thomas Stratton interrupted, "I understand that you were very thorough. But, what I am asking you is whether it still could be possible that Jason's mind played a trick on him? And a terrible joke on us in the bargain!"

Phyllis and Jack smiled weakly at the secretary of state's attempt at humor and, after a moment's hesitation, Phyllis again tried to answer his question.

"Well, Mr. Secretary, the best I can tell you is I don't think so. Jason reported too many specific psi signals for it all to be a bad dream. 'Who is David Brentwood?' 'Why did Stratton bring him?' 'What is Brentwood doing?' "

"I understand, Dr. Jackson," Thomas Stratton persisted. "But isn't it at least remotely possible that Jason's mind invented all those Russian thoughts, as a result of the stress he's been under?"

Phyllis Jackson was silent, her mind debating between the honest professional answer and the emotional one as Jason's friend and protector. Finally, she responded with a note of sadness.

"It's possible, Mr. Secretary. Not likely, but possible. With all the stress he's been subjected to, Jason would have to be superhuman not to show some signs of paranoia."

Thomas Stratton sat back in his chair, apparently satisfied at having wrung this concession from her. The three conspirators sat in silence for a moment, and then the secretary of state turned his probing to Jack.

"Well, Professor, where does this leave us? Your star psionaut either has been discovered or has come down with a bad case of the nerves!"

Stratton seemed to relish stating the gravity of the situation, while subtly shifting the blame to others. He sat smugly, with hands folded, awaiting Jack's response.

The color had drained from Jack Mason's face, and he began his answer defensively.

"Well, Mr. Secretary, I don't, ah, think that we should necessarily jump to either of those conclusions. It may just be—"

"So you think *I've* jumped to conclusions, do you, Professor!" the secretary of state interjected antagonistically. "Perhaps you suggest that we bury our heads in the sand and pretend that nothing has happened?"

Thomas Stratton's tone revealed his growing anger, and Jack's reaction was to raise his own voice in reply.

"I'm not suggesting that at all! What I *am* saying is that you shouldn't write Jason off so quickly. He's got a fantastic talent! The most amazing ability—"

"Don't shout at me about your wounded monster, Professor Frankenstein," Thomas Stratton exclaimed, leaping to his feet. "He's frail and mortal, like all the rest of us. And right now he's *hors de combat!* And we have to figure out what to do next!"

Richard Leonard paced the giant Kerman rug in Randolph Lowell's study and gestured at Thomas Stratton with his brandy snifter.

"So our mind reader's got a headache! That's what we get for trusting a bunch of goddamned intellectuals! The enemy puts a little pressure on and they turn chicken!"

Thomas Stratton sat in one of the ornate chairs arranged around the massive wooden table that dominated the center of the room. He warmed his snifter between the palms of his hands and inhaled the heady aroma that issued from it. The secretary of state watched the president pacing and gesturing and listened to his disjointed ranting like a patient mother waiting for her child's tantrum to dissipate.

"He's like a quarterback who can't take getting sacked!" Richard Leonard continued vehemently. "They look flashy in college, but they never stick in the pros! Those two-eighty blitzers blind-side 'em a few dozen times, and they develop all kinds of imaginary illnesses. And once they turn chicken, they never come back!"

The president stopped striding, scowled at the secretary of state, and shook his upraised forefinger.

"You mark my words, Thomas! Your man with psi is through! He's turned chicken! And from now on, all he'll be thinking about is his own skin!"

Thomas Stratton stared impassively at the president for a long moment, inhaled deeply from his snifter, and then sadly nodded his agreement.

37

The KGB Hit-Man

Jason Star and Phyllis Jackson were talking quietly in her tiny office in the vault in the embassy basement. Phyllis sat behind her desk in a white doctor's coat, her hands folded, listening to the man with psi. Jason fidgeted continually, alternately sitting in a small, straight-backed chair or pacing the miniscule space between the desk and the door.

"Do you think I'm losing my mind, Phyllis?" he enquired nervously. "Imagining that the Russians are after David Brentwood?"

Phyllis Jackson shook her head slowly from side to side.

"No, Jason, I don't think that you imagined those psi signals. Evidently the Russians are curious about who David Brentwood is and what the purpose—"

"*Curious!*" Jason injected agitatedly. "It's more than curiosity when someone at that table was thinking, 'We will crush David Brentwood, whoever he is.' "

The man with psi got up again and began to pace in small circles, constantly encountering the walls and the furniture. Phyllis Jackson looked at him sympathetically and nodded her understanding.

"You've got a perfectly legitimate reason to be concerned, Jason. But you've also got a job to do. The president is counting on you. And the secretary of state. And all the rest of us."

"Yeah, you're right, Phyllis," Jason responded, brightening considerably. "I've got to put those thoughts out of my mind. And to start getting ready for the next negotiating session. If there *is* one!"

Phyllis smiled to encourage Jason's change of mood and answered lightly.

"After the way Leonard and Sherkov went after each other this morning, they may decide to settle it in a boxing ring."

Jason smiled too as he visualized the two aging world leaders stumbling around a ring, shouting epithets, each hesitant to strike the first blow for fear of retaliation.

"Thanks, Phyllis," he said genuinely. "You've really cheered me up quite a bit. I guess I've just let the whole thing get to me. And being cooped up down here in this tomb doesn't help."

Phyllis kept smiling, nodding her agreement, and Jason continued.

"Do you think that you could intercede with Bob and Jack to get me a little fresh air? They can send the marines along if they want to! You know, tell them that my psychological health demands it. Or that it will help me—"

Phyllis grinned broadly and reached for the telephone. She dialed Bob Green's extension and was greeted by a cheerful:

"Green speaking."

"Hello, Bob. This is Phyllis. And I'm sitting here talking with Jason."

"Hi, Phyllis. How's your star patient? Feeling better, I hope."

"That's right, Bob," Phyllis replied. "Jason has just been telling me that he's feeling quite a bit better. But he'd really like to get out in the daylight. And get a little fresh air. Do you think that—"

"Yeah, Phyllis, I know how he feels," Bob injected, trying to deflect the request he knew was coming. "We all get that way, locked up down here in this dungeon. But after that confrontation this morning between Leonard and Sherkov, and what with those signals Jason thinks he received, I really believe that it would be better if we kept him out of circulation."

Phyllis frowned and continued earnestly.

"Well, Bob, as Jason's physician, I have to recommend strongly that you let him go outside for a little while. It will help him to get mentally prepared for the next negotiating session."

"Okay, Dr. Jackson," Bob conceded good-naturedly. "I know when I'm outranked. I'll take him for a walk around the block myself. I could use the fresh air, too. Tell him to come down to my office when he's ready."

Jason Star and Bob Green emerged from the American embassy into the late afternoon sunlight. Although it was the middle of May, a cool breeze greeted them, and they buttoned up their trench coats. Jason smiled broadly and made a show of swinging his arms and breathing deeply. As they left the embassy gate, the two friends turned down Chaikovskovo Ulitsa toward Kalinina Prospekt, intending to follow it to the river Moskva. A pair of athletic-looking CIA bodyguards followed them discreetly, some thirty yards behind.

But across the street, behind the oblivious strollers, a rear window was rolled down in one of several similar black cars that had been waiting patiently at the curb. The muzzle of a high-powered rifle emerged into the twilight and the marksman steadied himself awkwardly between the windowsill and the back of the seat. He peered into the low-power telescopic sight and brought the cross hairs to the center of Jason Star's back. The KGB hit-man smoothly squeezed the trigger and the strange weapon responded with a pop and the hiss of a puff of compressed gas that propelled a hollow gelatin dart on its deadly flight.

Jason felt a sharp pain below his left shoulder blade as if he had been stabbed in the back with an ice pick. His arms flew wide as his back muscles contracted and he was catapulted forward by the dart's impact. Jason's mouth opened involuntarily, and he uttered a grotesque cry, but the fast-acting drug already was speeding to his brain.

The man with psi gasped weakly again and stumbled a few more steps before his legs went rubbery, and he collapsed to the pavement. Bob Green rushed to Jason and crouched over him, his heart pounding. The two bodyguards began to run frantically, but, before they could reach the stricken pair, another black car raced down the street, jumped the curb, and struck them from behind. One sailed through the air, arms akimbo like a department-store mannequin, while the other was crushed beneath the wheels of the speeding vehicle.

Following Viktor Grechko's carefully planned choreography, the plainclothesed KGB agents who always surrounded the embassy flocked to the scene of the accident. Bob Green rose to a karate position to protect his fallen friend, but quickly was restrained by strong arms from behind. He struggled frantically until a sharp blow to the neck instantly rendered him unconscious.

On cue, an ambulance roared down Chaikovskovo Ulitsa and screeched to a halt opposite the milling crowd. Uniformed attendants burst from the rear door with a stretcher, and Jason Star was quickly loaded in and whisked away.

Thomas Stratton sat grim-faced at the head of the plexiglass conference table in the greenhouse. To his right, Jimmy Calderone, the CIA station chief, was rapidly scanning a pile of documents. To his left, Jack Mason slouched in silence with a dazed expression, his thoughts jumping randomly back and forth among the fragmentary reports he had received.

Could it be, Jack thought, *after all these years of preparation, that the man with psi was gone. Killed or kidnapped in broad daylight. Could it be that the stories he had heard about the Soviet secret police were true? Tales of people disappearing from their homes or offices and never being seen again.*

"Well, Jimmy," Thomas Stratton said impatiently, "what have you got?"

"The story is still a little confused, Mr. Secretary," Calderone responded in a monotone, "but I think I've got the basic facts. Star and Green left the embassy at about 1620 to take a walk. Dr. Jackson had recommended that it would be good for Star. At Green's request, I sent two of my men, Callahan and Robinson, along to watch them. Apparently Star and Green started to walk toward Kalinina Prospekt on this side of Chaikovskovo, and Callahan and Robinson followed some distance behind."

The secretary of state nodded solemnly and Jimmy Calderone continued his damage assessment.

"The next report I've got came from a clerk who was entering the embassy at about 1625. He saw a car race down the street and go up onto the sidewalk. It hit two men, probably Callahan and Robinson. Our witness thinks the driver did it on purpose, because the car didn't weave or anything. It just headed straight for the men on the sidewalk. And after hitting them, it swerved sharply back into the street and sped away. Not like a drunk or—"

"But Jason!" Jack broke in impulsively. "What happened to Jason?"

"Well, Professor, we're not certain," the CIA man responded with little emotion. "But we don't think he was hit by the car. At about 1630, an attaché on the fourth floor looked out the window and saw a group of people gathering below. They looked like KGB types, so he paid attention. Most of them were around a man lying on the sidewalk some distance down the street. But two smaller groups were right below his window. One group was around a body that was up against the embassy fence, and a few more of them were standing over another body on the sidewalk.

"The KGB men didn't seem to be making any effort to help the victims. They were just standing over them. The attaché ran to the phone and called the marine guard station in the lobby. By the time he got back to the window, the man farther down the street was being loaded into an ambulance. I described Star to him, and he thinks it probably was Jason."

Thomas Stratton shook his head gravely.

"What story did Lowell get from Gersky?"

"Gersky didn't return the ambassador's call, Mr. Secretary. He had a low-level assistant call back instead. I've got the translation here of what the guy said. Would you like to hear the gist of it?"

The secretary of state nodded in the affirmative, and Jimmy Calderone opened the appropriate document.

" 'Moscow police reported to the foreign ministry that four Americans were struck and injured on Chaikovskovo Ulitsa this afternoon by a car driven by a drunk.' They've apparently been taken to a hospital," Calderone continued, "but the guy who called didn't know which one."

"Thank you, Jimmy," Thomas Stratton said somberly. "Do you have anything else?"

"That's about it for the facts, Mr. Secretary. But if you want my opinion, I think that my men were run down on purpose and that Star and Green have been kidnapped!"

PART VI
THE BRINK OF WAR

38

"I'm the President!"

The president and the secretary of state were closeted in Randolph Lowell's study, and, unlike previous occasions, the ambassador had been invited to participate in their deliberations. Richard Leonard was furious.

"What the fuck kind of country is this, Lowell! Don't they have laws! Killing and kidnapping people in front of the American embassy in broad daylight!"

Randolph Lowell blanched at the president's foul language, but Thomas Stratton's benign expression signaled that the wisest course was to wait impassively for the tantrum to subside.

"Randolph has filed a strong protest with the foreign ministry, Mr. President," the secretary of state offered somberly. "Along with a request for more information on the condition of the four men."

"Protest! Protest! What the fuck good does it do to protest when you're dealing with animals!" Richard Leonard's face reddened, and his voice rose to a shout. "I should call in a few SAC bombers and then maybe those Russian bastards would get the message!"

Thomas Stratton visualized with ironic amusement the ludicrous Armageddon in which a ranting president called down upon his own head the hydrogen bombs of a squadron of SAC Valkyries circling over Moscow.

Even Richard Leonard seemed to sense the futility of his threat, and he abruptly became more reasonable.

"Well, Thomas, what do you recommend we do?"

"First of all, Mr. President," the secretary of state began pedantically, "I recommend that you go ahead with the private discussion with Sherkov tomorrow morning. If you cancel the

409

meeting, it certainly will draw attention to the special concern we have for David Brentwood."

"Why should I meet with that bastard Sherkov!" Richard Leonard responded angrily. "After the way he shouted at me this morning, I've got half a mind to just pack up and go home. And then maybe put SAC on alert and scare the shit out of him!"

For the first time, the secretary of state appeared genuinely concerned.

"But, Mr. President. What of your place in history? What of your reputation as the most skilled summit negotiator the world has ever known?"

The two men stared at each other in anxious silence for a moment. Thomas Stratton knew that a crucial ego battle was raging within Richard Leonard. Should he succumb to his natural instincts for violent action or continue to be guided by the Machiavellian grand schemes of his secretary of state?

Thomas Stratton strained to prevent his face from revealing his anxiety, lest the slightest sign of weakness convince the president to abandon his advice and rely on his own animal instincts. Finally, Richard Leonard broke the silence and began to speak in an unusually collegial tone.

"We've got a lot invested in this, don't we, Thomas? We've come a long way on the world scene together. You with your clever schemes and me with my tough talk. And now we're facing the biggest challenge of our careers. To defeat the Russians in a decisive summit conference. And show the world that we're the men to lead it to a decade of peace and stability. I guess we owe it to the world to continue, don't we, Thomas."

Jason Star was slowly regaining consciousness, but his eyes were blinded by an intense battery of lights. As his mind struggled to regain reality, he vaguely perceived the ominous shadows of a circle of giants above him. For anxious moments, the terrifying image came and went and, with each disappearance, Jason hoped with all his strength that the nightmare was over.

At last, however, Jason's brain cleared sufficiently that it could no longer deny the reality of his circumstances. He was lying on what felt like an operating-room table surrounded by a group of grim-visaged people, some in white medical coats and others in dark street clothes. The alternation of white and black images above him heightened Jason's terror as he frantically searched the faces for one he recognized. Finding none, he cried out weakly, like a desperate baby whose mother's face is missing from the sea of heads above its crib.

"Phyllis? Are you there?"

The stony faces glared down as before, seeming to mock his plaintive cry, but finally a deep voice answered from behind his head, where Jason could not see the speaker.

"Who is Phyllis, Mr. Brentwood?" the voice boomed gutturally. "And, more important, who are you?"

Jason's eyes involuntarily rolled upward in a vain attempt to glimpse the source of the voice behind him, but the glare of the lights was blinding, and leather straps restrained his body. Jason's eyes closed tightly again, and terror gripped him.

Where was he? Who were these men? Were they Russians? They must be Russians. What would they do to him?

"Come now, Mr. Brentwood," Viktor Grechko continued the interrogation in heavily accented English. "We do not have much time and you have so much to tell us. Will you do it voluntarily, or must we drug you?"

Jason's mouth and eyes opened wide simultaneously. He was blinded again instantly, and he uttered a shrill, gasping cry.

"What is your real name, Mr. Brentwood?" Viktor Grechko persisted. "Tell us your real name."

"My, my name, is David Brentwood." Jason responded in a ghostly whisper.

A pair of strong hands seized Jason's head from behind and shook it violently from side to side as if intending to wrench it from his restrained torso.

"I am losing my patience, Mr. Brentwood!" Viktor Grechko shouted. "Tell us your real name!"

The man with psi tightened against the leather straps in a vain attempt to rise from the table, and Viktor Grechko nodded to one of the white-coated attendants.

A sharp pain shot through Jason's left arm, and a cool fluid entered a vein and raced to his brain.

General Sam Ryan rose from his chair and spoke to the assembled group solemnly.

411

"Gentlemen, please rise for the president."

Richard Leonard strode into the secure conference room on the sixth floor of the American embassy and took his place at the head of the table. To his left was Thomas Stratton, and, next to him, Randolph Lowell. To the right were Sam Ryan, Jimmy Calderone, and Jack Mason. The president stood surveying the group until the marine guard had closed the door and then he spoke firmly.

"Be seated, gentlemen,"

When they had complied with his request, Richard Leonard sat down himself and turned to the secretary of state.

"Well, Thomas, I hear that you have more bad news."

"Yes, Mr. President," Stratton responded somberly. "Gersky called me about a half hour ago and said that Brentwood and Green are being held on charges of espionage. And that Callahan and Robinson are dead."

"Dead!" Richard Leonard shouted. "So those commie bastards have killed a pair of freedom-loving American citizens! You mark my words! I am not going to let them get away with it!"

"Well said, Mr. President," Sam Ryan chimed in enthusiastically. And the others dutifully nodded their agreement.

"And they're holding Brentwood and Green on charges of espionage? How the fuck can they do that?" Richard Leonard continued heatedly.

"They probably made them talk, Mr. President," Jimmy Calderone offered matter-of-factly. "I think we had better assume that by now the Russians know all about Project Psi."

The room fell silent. Everyone stared at the CIA station chief.

Thomas Stratton was the first to recover from the shock. He attempted to speak calmly, but his voice revealed his agitation.

"That is certainly a possibility, Jimmy. However, you will have to admit that it is also possible that the Russians got nothing out of Green and Star and are simply holding them in the hope that we will tip our hand."

The secretary of state's clever denial of the likely situation greatly reduced the anxiety at the table. Jack nodded his agreement with Stratton's suggestion, and the president encouraged him to continue.

412

"Suppose that you're right, Thomas. What should we do next?"

"I have given that considerable thought, Mr. President," Thomas Stratton said with relief. He waited for the president's attention to be firmly focused on him and then continued dramatically.

"I now believe, Mr. President, that you should leave Moscow immediately!"

The secretary of state paused for the impact of his words to be felt, but continued before the president could interrupt.

"There are *two* principal reasons for this recommendation, Mr. President. First, if the situation deteriorates further, you would be in a position to take whatever action was necessary. Second, your leaving will give me additional leverage in continued negotiations with the Russians. If they want you to come back, they will have to make concessions."

Thomas Stratton folded his hands and looked at the president, like a knowing statue of Buddha. Richard Leonard stared back impassively, but slowly his eyes narrowed, and finally he spoke with a touch of sarcasm.

"So you think that *I* should cut and run, do you, Thomas. And leave *you* in charge of things!"

It was the president's turn to wait for the impact of his words to sink in. The superior smile slowly disappeared from Thomas Stratton's face. The others at the table looked at the two men with rapt attention.

"You think I'm not up to the situation, don't you, Thomas," the president continued emotionally. "Too stupid and irrational to cope with it. Well, I'll tell you something, Thomas! I'm sick of your clever ideas and fancy schemes. Sick of being manipulated like a ventriloquist's dummy! So I think it's about time you understood who's the president. I'm the president! Do you understand me, Thomas! I'm the president!

Richard Leonard glared triumphantly at Thomas Stratton. The secretary of state sank back in his chair, the color rapidly draining from his face. The president continued to glare with growing confidence, and the deposed puppet master was finally forced to respond weakly.

"Yes, Mr. President. What do you want us to do?"

Surveying the small group at the table, Richard Leonard beamed triumphantly, as the leader of men he had always wanted to be. He basked in their new, silent respect for more than a minute, and then addressed Sam Ryan authoritatively.

"Sam, I want you to order a full nuclear alert! Cancel all military leaves. Get as many bombers into the air as possible. And as many submarines to sea. And be sure that the reporters know what we're doing!"

"Yes sir, Mr. President!" the general responded enthusiastically. "Immediately, Mr. President!"

Sam Ryan's chest swelled with patriotic zeal. He rose from his place at the table and eagerly requested the president's permission to command the preparation for Armageddon.

"Shall I go and do it now, Mr. President?"

"Immediately, Sam! Immediately!" Richard Leonard responded, his voice revealing the pride he felt in his newly exercised authority. And, as the general left the room, the president turned to instruct his secretary of state.

"Now for you, Thomas! I want you to deliver the following ultimatum to Gersky. If Star and Green and the bodies of the two other men are not back in this embassy by noon tomorrow, the Soviet Union will face the direst consequences from American strategic nuclear forces!"

The president smiled happily at the secretary of state, but the latter stared back in white-faced disbelief.

"Did you get that, Thomas?" Richard Leonard persisted. "Perhaps you had better write it down!"

39

The Confession

In the scant twelve hours since Richard Leonard had ordered the nuclear alert, the American embassy on Chaikovskovo Ulitsa had taken on the frantic chaos of a fort under siege. The president and the secretary of state had taken up residence, and Randolph Lowell's study had become the oval office of a tiny foreign enclave deep in hostile territory. Everywhere, messengers hurried through the halls delivering folders of top-secret documents.

Sam Ryan had converted the sixth-floor secure conference area into a twenty-four situation room. From this transplanted piece of the Pentagon, he issued orders in the president's name, which, if carried to completion, would result in his own vaporization. Oblivious of the ultimate insanity of his suicidal position, the general bustled authoritatively, commanding a small corps of colonels and sergeants who enthusiastically planned their own destruction.

Richard Leonard and Thomas Stratton were alone in the commander in chief's newly constituted office. The president was seated behind Randolph Lowell's massive mahogany desk. The Secretary of state stood dutifully before him.

"I have just spoken with Gersky again, Mr. President," Thomas Stratton began somberly. "He still refuses to return Brentwood and Green. And, what is more ominous, he says that they will be displayed to the world at a televised news conference to be held tomorrow morning."

The secretary of state paused for a moment, certain of the president's reaction to the remainder of his report.

"Finally, Mr. President, I must tell you that Gersky suggests that you leave the Soviet Union this afternoon."

Richard Leonard rose from his chair, his face reddening with rage.

"Who the fuck does he think he is, telling *me* to leave the Soviet Union! All he is is a goddamned flunky to Sherkov! I'll leave the Soviet Union when I'm goddamned good and ready! And not a minute sooner!"

Thomas Stratton disingenuously nodded his agreement while mentally searching for a way to convince the president to accept the inevitable.

"You may wish to consider holding a news conference of your own, Mr. President."

Richard Leonard's expression gradually changed from anger to canny appreciation. He slowly nodded his approval of the suggestion, and Thomas Stratton continued matter-of-factly.

"It will be important to let the world know who is responsible for the breakdown of this historic summit conference."

The president nodded more vigorously and picked up on the theme.

"You're right, Thomas. The world has to know what a cowardly faker that bastard Sherkov is! How all that stuff he keeps mumbling about the tragedy of war and Soviet casualties and all that other crap is just a load of horseshit to cover up his real plans to take over the world! And now that I've called his bluff, he's wrecked the summit conference! And torpedoed the chances for world peace."

Richard Leonard's rage was slowly changing to righteous indignation. He sat back in his chair and wagged his forefinger at the secretary of state.

"It's important for the pages of history to accurately record who was in favor of stable international order and lasting world peace. I came here to Moscow and made the most sweeping disarmament proposal history has ever recorded! And that bastard Sherkov turned it down!"

Thomas Stratton nodded enthusiastically and continued his oblique approach to the real issue.

"Shall I request that all three networks make an hour of prime time available to you this evening, Mr. President?"

The president stared at the secretary of state for a moment as the true import of the question sank in.

Thomas Stratton held his breath, scrutinizing Richard Leonard's expression for a clue to his likely response. Finally, after agonizing seconds, the president smiled and wagged his finger assertively.

"You do that, Thomas. Immediately! And tell Sam to get *Air Force One* ready as soon as possible. I'm wasting my time here with these lying Russians!"

Vasily Vasilyevich Sherkov sat behind a massive podium in front of a giant, red, hammer-and-sickle flag of the Soviet Union. Sherkov drank from a glass of mineral water as television technicians made final preparations for his speech. In an adjacent studio, a battery of linguists nervously awaited their task of translating his words into a dozen foreign languages. After a final whispered conference with Sherkov, the director signaled the control room, and the monitor speakers blared with the strains of the Soviet national anthem. Vasily Sherkov's chest swelled with pride, and his posture stiffened involuntarily, as memories of a thirty-year military career flashed through his brain.

When the patriotic music had ended, a solemn voice intoned in Russian:

"Fellow comrades, you are about to hear the general secretary of the Communist Party of the Union of Soviet Socialist Republics."

Vasily Sherkov opened the notebook before him and began to speak in a firm voice. Separated from each other and the general secretary by soundproof walls, the chorus of translators began their recitation of American duplicity. The English version was delivered in the clipped tones of an Oxford *poputchik* (ass-kisser).

"Peace-loving people throughout the world undoubtedly shared the high expectations of the brave people of the Soviet Union that the Moscow summit conference would bring to reality their most cherished hope, the achievement of general and complete disarmament. In the months leading up to this historic meeting and in the past week of summit negotiations, the leaders of the Soviet Union have striven with all the resources they possess to achieve this most important objective. Tragically for

417

the world, however, the American side has not shared our tireless efforts and unceasing desires for peace. Rather, the leaders of the United States have come here to Moscow in the guise of peace and friendship to perpetrate the most dastardly act of perfidy in the annals of international diplomacy."

On the television monitors, Vasily Sherkov beamed with self-righteous satisfaction and reached for a glass of mineral water, allowing the translators an opportunity to catch up. Having quenched his thirst, the general secretary resumed the condemnation with increased vigor, and even the flat-voiced British translator revealed a hint of emotion.

"The president of the United States today has been forced to leave the Soviet Union in total disgrace, with his tail between his legs like a cur of uncertain ancestry. This cowardly flight from the conference table and the spotlight of world attention was necessitated by our discovery of his attempt to perpetrate the most treacherous crime in the history of meetings of heads of state."

Vasily Sherkov paused momentarily, allowing the tension to build, and then continued in a half-shout, pounding his fist on the table. And finally the English translator echoed his principal's emotion.

'He has tried to poison the Soviet delegation at the conference table!"

Jason Star and Bob Green slouched on tall stools like a pair of dunces in the corner of a one-room schoolhouse. Bright lights blazed down on them, and uniformed guards with menacing AK-47 machine guns stood on either side.

Viktor Grechko sat behind a table opposite his captives watching the conclusion of Vasily Sherkov's emotional introduction on a monitor screen suspended from the ceiling. A tiny earphone brought Sherkov's voice to Grechko's left ear, while a television technician whispered last-minute instructions into his right.

A warm feeling of professional pride swelled through Viktor Grechko. Pride in a job well done, and a rare opportunity for public recognition. Grechko looked impassively at the pitiful Americans on the stools, mere pawns on the deadly chessboard of international power politics. He felt no emotion toward them, not the hatred of a driven pursuer who has finally captured his ancient foe, and not the twinge of empathy of a philosophical victor who understands that but for the twists and turns of fate, the roles of winner and loser might well be interchanged. Rather, Grechko regarded them like inanimate objects, pieces of evidence to be displayed before the court of international opinion in proving the case of American perfidy at the summit conference.

Vasily Sherkov's voice blared in Viktor Grechko's ear with a final denunciation of Richard Leonard and a compliment to the master spy for discovering the president's villainy.

". . . and now the dastardly deeds of the American president will be revealed to the world by his own agents. You will hear them confess of their own free will to the heinous crimes they have committed against the Soviet Union and the cause of world peace. They were brought to the bar of Soviet justice and the scrutiny of world opinion by the tireless and heroic efforts of Tovarishch Viktor Leonidovich Grechko. And now, Tovarishch Grechko will lead these pitiful agents of American imperialism in public confession of their crimes!"

Vasily Sherkov folded his hands and smiled triumphantly from the monitor like a satisfied bear that had just completed its dinner. As his own face appeared on the screen, a technician pointed at Viktor Grechko. He began to speak firmly, and, again, the battery of translators echoed the message to the waiting world.

"Fellow peace-loving peoples around the globe. It is my solemn duty to bring to you the public confession of two American agents who were brought to the Soviet Union by the president of the United States to perpetrate a dastardly crime against the honorable leaders of the Soviet Union and the noble cause of world peace. You will hear in their own words the story of their villainous deeds and the details of the sinister instructions they received from President Richard Leonard, his Machiavellian secretary of state, Thomas Stratton, and the evil Central Intelligence Agency."

Viktor Grechko paused for a moment at the direction of a voice from the earphone, and then continued dramatically.

419

"You now will hear the confession of a man who called himself David Brentwood. A man who came to the Soviet Union disguised as an advisor to the American secretary of state, Thomas Stratton."

The image on the monitor screen switched to Jason Star, and the camera zoomed in. The man with psi appeared to be in a daze, staring blankly at the floor in front of the camera. Viktor Grechko's voice boomed across the television studio accusatorially, and Jason's head snapped back and his eyes opened wide in response.

"Tell us who you really are, Mr. Brentwood!" Victor Grechko said loudly and firmly in English.

"My name is Colonel Elwood Thorpe," Jason Star began in a monotone. "Serial number zero five zero nine four two seven one."

Viktor Grechko nodded approvingly, like a teacher of the handicapped encouraging a stumbling pupil.

"Tell us who you work for, Colonel Thorpe."

Jason's head fell to his chest and rolled listlessly from side to side.

"Tell us, Colonel Thorpe!" Viktor Grechko shouted. "Who do you work for?"

Jason's head snapped back again, and he stared at the camera with dilated pupils.

"I, I work for the Central Intelligence Agency."

Grechko nodded again and closed in for the kill.

"What do you do for the CIA, Colonel Thorpe?"

"I am an agent, a spy," Jason droned in a monotone.

"And what did you come to the Soviet Union to do, Colonel Thorpe?" Victor Grechko said triumphantly.

"I came, I came, to ad— to administer—a secret, poison, gas, to the Soviet leaders. To weaken, their minds, at, the, negotiating table."

420

40
Shifting the Blame

A makeup man crouched in front of Richard Leonard, administering last-minute color to his cheeks. Lights and cameras filled the Oval Office amid a tangle of cables crisscrossing the carpet. The president sat behind his massive desk and swiveled his high-backed chair to face the man with the kit of cosmetics. Thomas Stratton stood at the president's side and stooped to whisper in his ear.

"This has to be the finest speech of your career, Mr. President. Your place in history is at stake. The world must know that the Russians, and not we, are responsible for the collapse of the summit conference."

Richard Leonard nodded his agreement with the self-serving advice as the makeup man daubed frantically at his five-o'clock shadow.

"Five minutes to air time! Five minutes!" echoed through the room.

Technicians began to retreat behind the cameras, and the makeup man delivered a final swipe at the president's jaw. Richard Leonard swiveled to face the cameras, and Thomas Stratton laid a firm hand on his shoulder.

"Good luck, Mr. President. I know you'll make a fine speech."

"One minute, Mr. President!" the director shouted. "One minute, Mr. Secretary!"

Thomas Stratton retired from the field of view, and Richard Leonard folded his hands and looked at the cameras solemnly.

"When the red lights come on, you're live, Mr. President!" the director coached.

Richard Leonard summoned a confident smile for a prime-time viewing audience conservatively estimated by the networks at eighty million. The collapse of the summit conference and the fear of war with Russia promised a maximum number of viewers for this, his most fateful television appearance.

Red lights flashed on, and the president began in a confident tone.

"Ladies and gentlemen across the United States and throughout the world. It is my solemn duty to report to you this evening on the series of dastardly acts by the ruthless Communist leaders of the Soviet Union that have torpedoed the Moscow disarmament conference, shattered the hopes for peace of freedom-loving people everywhere, and led the world to the brink of nuclear war."

Richard Leonard paused to allow the frightening import of his words to be absorbed by the television audience and then continued in a statesmanlike voice.

"As you know, I left the United States ten days ago, full of the high hopes of the American people for dramatic reductions in all types of troops and weapons and for the achievement of a new era of peace through stable world order."

The president again paused for effect, and then continued dramatically, his forefinger upraised.

"Unfortunately, I must report to you tonight that the Soviet leaders did not share our hopes and desires for peace. Instead, they hatched a bizarre plan involving the murder and kidnapping of *American citizens!*"

Richard Leonard eyed himself in a monitor screen behind the cameras and then began again with the righteous fervor of a fundamentalist preacher.

"As I speak to you this evening, two brave, young Americans lie cold and dead in Moscow! Victims of a brutal attack in broad daylight by the infamous Soviet secret police. These fine, loyal Americans had committed no crime. They were innocently walking on the street in Moscow, in front of the United States' embassy, when a KGB agent deliberately drove his car onto the sidewalk at high speed and ran them down!"

The president paused for a moment and then continued in simulated rage, pounding his fist on the desk and shouting at the cameras.

"The Russians have murdered two young Americans! And I do not intend to let them get away with it! And I know that you, the courageous American people, will close ranks behind your president and support whatever actions he is forced to take to punish the Russians for this heinous crime!"

Richard Leonard folded his hands and stared grimly at the camera, allowing time for the massive, prime-time audience to be jolted to attention by his emotional call to arms. Then he began again slowly and firmly.

"In addition to the vicious murders I just have described, the Russians are holding two other Americans prisoners, against all principles of international law. These two State Department employees were abducted in broad daylight in the same incident in which the other two Americans were killed. The Russians have apparently subjected these loyal employees of the United States government to torture and brainwashing. In the most blatant violation of international conventions on the treatment of prisoners, these American citizens were displayed on Russian television in a state of drugged torpor and were interrogated by a well-known master agent of the Soviet secret police."

The president stared, looking sincerely at the cameras to reinforce his protestation of the Americans' innocence and their inhumane treatment at the hands of the monstrous Russians.

"Finally, it is my duty to inform you, the brave American people, of the steps I have taken as your President to force the Soviet Union to release the two State Department employees and return the bodies of the dead Americans. I have ordered the Strategic Air Command placed on alert. SAC bombers will be in the air twenty-four hours a day carrying live nuclear weapons. In addition, I have ordered all available Polaris and Poseidon nuclear missile submarines to sea. Furthermore, I have . . ."

A week had passed since the president placed American strategic nuclear forces on alert, and the Soviets replied with an alert of their own. After several days of mounting tension, the Russians announced without fanfare that the bodies of two CIA agents killed by a drunken driver on a Moscow street had been flown to Helsinki and turned over to representatives of the United Nations.

The United States continued to demand the release of Brentwood and Green, but the Soviet Union steadfastly refused, asserting that they were spies and would be placed on trial. To bolster this contention, the Russians distributed video tapes of David Brentwood's interrogation by Viktor Grechko with dubbed translations into numerous foreign languages.

On the fifth day of the American alert, the press began to question openly the wisdom of the president's actions. The *New York Times* reported that a B-52 bomber carrying hydrogen bombs had made an emergency landing at the municipal airport in Bangor, Maine, and asked in an editorial whether Richard Leonard might be contriving to cause a nuclear incident in order to draw attention away from the failure of his trip to Moscow. The next day, the *Washington Post* carried a story that Brentwood and Green had worked at the Exotic Chemicals Research Facility of the American Chemical Company. The story concluded with the speculation that there might be a grain of truth to the Soviet accusation that they were engaged in some sort of chemical warfare at the summit conference.

On the seventh day, without public announcement, the president ordered the strategic forces to stand down. When the White House press office was questioned, it offered a terse "no comment" and referred reporters to the Pentagon. There, a public relations officer made everything perfectly clear by maintaining that:

"The armed forces of the United States remain in a continued state of readiness adequate to counter any foreseen strategic threat from any potential adversary."

The crisis was over.

41

Evacuation

The Project Psi vault in the subbasement of the American embassy in Moscow was in chaos. CIA security men, aided by marines from the embassy's guard detachment, were frantically trying to destroy all evidence of the project's clandestine activities. Mounds of classified documents were being fed to groaning paper shredders producing voluminous plastic bags of confetti to be fed to the embassy's incinerator.

In the computer room, Paul Rosenfeld and Ken Anderson stared in disbelief as muscular marines, armed with sledge hammers and fire axes, pounded and chopped at sensitive electronic equipment until it was reduced to a jumble of twisted metal and shattered circuit boards. The marines loaded the grotesque debris into diplomatic pouches to be flown out of the Soviet Union as a final precaution.

The greenhouse had been disassembled and its plastic panels were being cut into neat one-foot squares by screaming circular saws in preparation for a final journey to the incinerator. Jack Mason watched the destruction catatonically. His deadened mind distractedly envisioned amused Russians pointing at the clouds of black smoke that undoubtedly were billowing from the chimney at the rear of the embassy. Jack's thoughts finally were jolted back to reality by a firm hand on his shoulder and an authoritative male voice in his ear.

"It's time to go, Professor Mason. Your car is waiting."

Jack turned and nodded to the marine major who had appeared at his side, and the defeated creator of the man with psi shuffled from the room without a word. As the pair walked slowly down the corridor toward the exit from the vault, the major continued.

"I will remain with you until you are safely on the plane. We don't expect any trouble, but it's better to be safe than sorry."

The trip to the airport was uneventful, and Jack found it strangely relaxing after the discouraging experience of seeing Project Psi pounded to bits before his eyes. He stared disconsolately out of the window of the embassy car at the telltale signs of Moscow's final bursting emergence from spring. Colorful flowers in intricate geometric arrangements bedecked the squares, and vivid green leaves silhouetted against a clear blue sky crowned the tall trees that lined the route. Bustling crowds of people flooded the wide Leningradsky Prospekt, anxious for the sights and sounds and smells of summer.

When they reached Sherementevo International Airport, the major escorted Jack to the departure area reserved for official visitors, where they joined a line of diplomats waiting to have their credentials checked by a seemingly disinterested uniformed bureaucrat.

As they waited in the queue, Jack's thoughts flashed back over the dizzying events of the past month.

His arrival in Moscow, and then Jason's. The frantic preparations in the embassy basement. The exhilaration when Jason had reported the first psi signals from Vasily Sherkov's brain. And then the panic when Jason was abducted.

Jack's disconsolate recapitulation was interrupted by a tug at his sleeve and a hesitant voice speaking in broken English.

"Professor Mason? Are you not Professor Mason?"

Jack turned and saw a small, disheveled Russian man carrying a bulging briefcase. Jack stared blankly, and the Russian continued his halting explanation.

"I Professor Ivan Smirnitsky. Of Institute for Research of Neurophysiology. I come America ago seven years to see your laboratory."

Jack's mind raced back to the days before Project Psi. To the time when he was a little-known professor at MIT studying the neurological structure of the eye and brain of the chimpanzee. Jack could not place the deminutive Russian, but vaguely thought that he might have been a member of a group that had

426

come to his laboratory during the Fourth International Neurophysiology Conference that was held in Boston in the spring of 1965. Jack was trying vainly to visualize the faces of some of the people in the visiting group, when the Russian professor began again.

"Make new paper . . . neural signal processing . . . optic tectum cat."

The small man bent down and rummaged through the large leather briefcase. At length, he straightened up with a pleased twinkle in his eye and handed a few stapled sheets of paper to Jack.

"Found it. Here copy paper, Professor Mason. It bring to me great honor. You read."

Jack smiled weakly, extended his hand, and took the sheaf of paper. He raised it to eye level and began to study the Russian intently for cognates he recognized. Jack still was struggling to decipher the title, when shouts in Russian jolted his attention back to reality.

A dozen burly KGB agents materialized from the crowd and surrounded the two professors. The leader of the band of thugs snatched the paper from Jack and held it aloft triumphantly, as if for the benefit of hidden cameras.

The marine major struggled to reach Jack's side, but was quickly subdued by a troika of goons and hustled away. Jack stared with ever-widening eyes at the massive Russian holding the paper. A sudden chill swept through him, and his heart began to pound frantically. Jack turned and attempted to run, but he was instantly restrained by strong hands and forceably turned to face his captor.

The Russian waved the paper accusatorially and shouted at Jack in English.

"What has this man given you, Professor Mason! It appears to be military information! You are both under arrest as spies!"

42

A New Life

Jack Mason sat huddled on the floor in one corner of his tiny, cold, damp cell. A single, bright, naked bulb hung from the ceiling above his reach. The light burned continuously, making it impossible for Jack to judge the passage of time in his windowless solitary confinement. Periodically, he thought in the evening, a small panel near the bottom of the door slid open and a burly hand placed on the floor a tin cup of water and a crust of bread.

The cell reeked from the stench of a pail in the far corner that Jack was forced to use as a toilet and which had not been emptied since his captivity began. His body ached from sleeping on the hard stone floor, and his mind was beginning to wander from lack of sleep and nourishment. Jack had attempted without success to converse with the jailors who brought the food, first with polite requests for the day of the month or emptying of the bucket, and lately with shouted insults in the desperate hope of prevoking a response. Despite Jack's protests, the hairy arm that delivered his meager rations would silently withdraw, and the panel in the door again would slide tightly closed.

At the beginning of his captivity, Jack had attempted to maintain his physical vigor by jogging in place. But, as time wore on, he had lost weight and strength and, finally, the will to exercise. Jack now spent most of his time huddled on the floor in the corner farthest from the sickening pail, with his head down on his chest to avoid the glare of the ever-present light. He occasionally thought of suicide, but the lack of an obvious instrument and his weakening physical condition fortunately precluded action. His sleep, such as it was, occurred in short and fitful bursts, often punctuated by nightmare reenactments of his arrest and imprisonment. Jack was sure that he was slowly losing his mind and, worse still, the will to survive.

One day, after he had lost all hope, Jack was shaken to consciousness from a rare moment of peaceful sleep. Strong hands seized him violently and then jerked him to his feet by his arms. A pair of guards had entered the cell while he dozed and were now half-carrying and half-dragging him through the open door. Jack tried to walk but found his legs rubbery from lack of use. But for the support of his captors, he would have staggered and collapsed to the floor.

The warders took him down a long corridor lined with cells similar to his own and then up several flights of stairs. The first were the damp stone steps of a dungeon, but the later ones were tiled as the incongruous trio emerged into the above-ground portion of the building. Finally, after traversing another long passageway, the guards unlocked the door to a small, barren room and deposited Jack on a straight wooden chair drawn up to a table. When they released his arms, Jack slumped forward onto the table, his heart pounding in anticipation of the fate to befall him.

At length, Viktor Grechko entered the room and spoke to Jack in heavily-accented English.

"How are you, Professor Mason?"

Jack's brain was shocked by the sound of a human voice, and he rolled his head on the table to glimpse the speaker. Viktor Grechko grasped him gently by the shoulders and raised him to a sitting position in the chair.

"How would you like to take a little ride in the country, Professor?" the master spy asked without a hint of rancor.

Viktor Grechko's car raced through the countryside east of Moscow. Grechko and his prisoner sat in the back seat, a guard and the driver in front. After several hours of high-speed driving, they stopped at a small inn at a crossroads, and Jack was given real food for the first time in a month. He ate ravenously, like a stray dog, and soon his formerly empty stomach began to ache from unaccustomed fullness.

The three burly Russians and the pitifully thin American consumed their food in silence. But, when the meal had ended,

Viktor Grechko ordered a round of vodka and raised his glass in a toast.

"*Na vashe zdorov'e* (to your health)!" Grechko intoned, and then he added in guttural English:

"To your new life, Professor Mason!"

Jack looked blankly at his KGB master, straining to comprehend the remark. But his dulled mind only could repeat the words without perceiving their meaning. Finally, at Grechko's insistence, Jack downed the vodka and felt its searing warmth descend his gullet and enter his stomach. The alcohol burned his throat and dazed his brain, and Jack sat wide-eyed at the table staring at his Russian companions.

After the midday stop, the car raced on for several hours more, finally arriving at dusk at a military installation. The driver conversed with the sentries at the gate, and the car shortly was waved to the interior. They drove on for several kilometers, passing isolated buildings surrounded by high security fences topped with menacing barbed wire. Jack stared through the window of the car with growing apprehension, fearful that he was about to be deposited in a camp of the dreadful Gulag Archipelago.

At length, the car pulled up at the gate to one of the compounds, and further conversation with guards secured their admittance. Once inside the fence, the driver parked in front of the nearest building, and Viktor Grechko motioned to Jack to get out. The structure was low and sprawling, like a military hospital, and Grechko led the way to the main entrance.

Once inside, they immediately encountered additional armed guards, to whom Grechko displayed an elaborate set of credentials contained in a folding leather wallet he had withdrawn from an inside breast pocket. The guards motioned to the party to proceed, and Viktor Grechko led the way into a long hall. They walked its entire length past numerous work areas that appeared to Jack to contain various kinds of mechanical and electrical equipment. At the end of the corridor, they reached yet another guard station and Grechko again displayed his credentials.

Much to Jack's surprise, his guard and the driver proceeded no farther, but Grechko beckoned to Jack to follow him. This time, they were admitted to what seemed to Jack to be a security vault, and Viktor Grechko led the way down an interior hall. He stopped at a door secured by a cipher lock and pushed the appropriate sequence of buttons. The bolt retracted with a loud buzz, and Grechko motioned to Jack to enter.

Jack suddenly was filled with fear as he grasped the handle of the mysterious door and his weakened muscles strained to pull it open.

The interior of the room was brightly lit, and Jack's attention was immediately drawn to a pair of technicians working on something mounted in the far wall.

It unmistakably was a crude version of the *two-person chair.*

Jack let out an astonished gasp, and Viktor Grechko spoke with quiet satisfaction.

"How do you like it, Professor? It still is crude, but you will have a lot of time to improve it."